TELL ME WHY

STELLA CAMERON

TELL ME WHY

WHEELER
PUBLISHING, INC.
ROCKLAND, MA

★ AN AMERICAN COMPANY ★

Published in Large Print by arrangement with Kensington Publishing
Corp., in the United States and Canada.

Wheeler Large Print Book Series.

Set in 16 pt Plantin.

Library of Congress Cataloging-in-Publication Data

Cameron, Stella.
   Tell me why / Stella Cameron.
      p. (large print) cm.(Wheeler large print book series)
   ISBN 1-58724-117-X (hardcover)
   1. Women musicians—Fiction. 2. Divorced women—Fiction. 3. Jazz
musicians—Fiction. 4. Seattle (Wash.)—Fiction. 5. Pianists—Fiction.
6. Large type books. I. Title. II. Series

[PS3553.A4345 T45   2001b]
813'.54—dc21
                                                        2001046587
                                                            CIP

For Claire

*It is good to have an end
to journey towards,
but it is the journey
that matters in the end.*

—Ursula Le Guin

One

Students emerged through the doors of the Pacific Northwest Ballet School. Carolee Burns's heart thudded sickeningly. She was sweating. This was the second time she'd watched from a corner of the building before escaping into the shadow of courtyard walls at the nearby Intiman Theater. Thc theater was one of a cluster of tall white buildings in the Seattle Center complex. She stood against a wall where she had a clear view of the steps from the ballet school to the sidewalk on Mercer Street.

And Carolee was ready to run.

The first time she had given in to her longings and waited here had been dangerous. Today, the risks had to be cranked up even higher.

She'd had to come again, but she also had to keep an eye on the cars that swept along Mercer Street and drew in to pick up angular, black-garbed dancers who moved with studied grace. The man who must not see her would arrive soon. He would be driving a silver Porsche, and if he should spot her, he could destroy the one hope she clung to.

Playgoers marched purposefully past on their way to one of Intiman's early evening performances. Their chatter and jostle helped Carolee feel safer, less visible. From behind her, in the center of the theater courtyard, came the rushing sound of water cascading from a fountain. Noisy traffic on one-way Mercer flowed steadily eastward toward I-5.

There was only one face she wanted to see, Faith's face as she came through those doors carrying her bag and with a cardigan tied around the waist of her leotard.

In groups of ones and twos and threes, the students dawdled into the sunlight. Talking, laughing, angling their heads. The girls with tight chignons. The boys with long hair brushing their shoulders or drawn back into tails at their napes.

Carolee studied the arriving cars again. Kip was bound to arrive soon and then Faith would probably come out just in time to run directly to the car and jump in. There would be no chance to watch her for a few precious minutes while she waited for her father.

A door at the top of the steps opened again and there she was. Carolee curled her fingers against the rough wall. To hold herself up? Oh, no; to stop herself from dashing recklessly to the girl. Unlike most of her peers, Faith made no attempt to tame her hair into an accepted style—not that she could. An explosion of tight, sandy-colored curls sprang from a center part and reached her shoulders. From where Carolee stood, she couldn't see her

2

daughter's gray eyes clearly, but she didn't have to. They were large and surrounded with thick, reddish lashes. Carolee had always been able to look into those eyes and see her child's gentleness and intensity. At not yet twelve, Faith already had her causes, her beliefs, her principles, and she was too young to consider that there could ever be more than one side to an argument.

A smile only made Carolee's throat tighten even more. She held the neck of her denim shirt and strained to make out every detail of the child she had all but lost.

Faith was still short for her age but she'd grown a little, and lost most of her little girl softness. A rounded tummy had given way to a waist, and her legs, clad in tights, showed signs of becoming shapely. The child was turning into an adolescent.

Carolee blinked rapidly. It was all happening in chunks and mostly while she couldn't be with Faith. Visitations were allowed on one weekend a month, four weeks in summer, and two weeks every other Christmas. How could a mother live with that? And no matter what had been said about her, or what the court chose to believe, surely she had already shown that she would give up anything to change the way things were. Kip said she must be patient, but when she asked if that meant he would relent in time, allow her to share Faith's life fully again, he didn't answer unless it was to say it was too soon to discuss such things.

She could see Faith's pointed chin—and

imagine the dimples beside her pretty mouth when she smiled.

One of their favorite things used to be story time. Carolee would climb into Faith's bed and they'd snuggle down close, giggling. And the stories took weeks to unfold. So many times Carolee would hear her daughter's breathing grow even and deep and she'd pause then, waiting, only to hear Faith say, "Don't stop, Mom. What happens next?" And when Faith did finally fall asleep, Carolee didn't leave immediately. Instead she indulged the wonder of holding her child's warm, relaxed body close and drifting sleepily with her.

Faith stood with her toes overhanging the top step to the street. And she looked in the direction from which Kip would come.

Carolee pressed her forehead to the wall and welcomed the pressure of the cool rough surface. For an instant she dropped her hands. Drawn to the child, she took a step into the open. Why wasn't she allowed to talk to her at times like this? Why couldn't she go and wrap her arms around her? Why had she been ordered to stay away from her own child except when she was on a sanctioned visit, or if Kip should decide to allow an extra meeting. Children needed their mothers as well as their fathers. A girl changing from a child into a woman probably needed her mother more. Sure, she'd made mistakes, been careless, taken too much for granted, but most of the things that had been said about her weren't true, not really. Too bad she hadn't been able to make anyone who counted listen to her.

She could make sure Kip's car wasn't in sight yet and run to Faith. Just hold her for an instant and say how much she loved and missed her. Carolee crossed her arms and rocked, feeling Faith pressed against her, the beat of her heart, her warm breath on her own skin.

Faith wouldn't tell Kip... No, it wasn't fair to involve a child in her mother's lies.

Without intending to, she took several steps. Faith's eyes were clearer to her now. Thirty seconds at the most and they could be face-to-face. Even a few seconds, passing, smiling, a quick kiss and a hug, would be something Carolee could use to soften the helpless days and nights.

She didn't notice the Porsche until Faith jogged down toward the sidewalk. Then it was too late. Kip was out of the car, taking Faith's bag and tossing it behind the passenger seat before the girl climbed in.

Then he looked up.

Carolee didn't move. The crowd was thicker and streamed past her, but she felt naked, revealed. A tall man, Kip looked straight in her direction. His hair, the color of Faith's but straight and crewcut rather than curly, made his handsome face look even more appealing. A tight white T-shirt and jeans only added to an impression of youth, not that thirty-three was very old. They'd known each other since they'd been kids. How could all the love have turned into indifference?

Ducking into the courtyard in front of the Intiman Theater was the best way to escape. It wasn't until Carolee hurried through the iron gates that she remembered there wasn't another way in or out. Last time she'd been certain Kip had no idea she was there and had waited a few minutes before leaving. This time Carolee's only option was to stay where she was and hope he hadn't noticed her.

Willing herself not to look over her shoulder, she went to a nearby wall and pressed herself into the red-leafed ivy that grew thickly there. And she waited. If he had seen her, he would come and threaten her. He liked to frighten her with the official right that was on his side.

Engines thrummed on Mercer but she couldn't make out the distinctive sound of the Porsche drawing away. He must have seen her and now he was talking to Faith, telling her he'd be right back, before tracking Carolee down to punish her. He could try to stop Faith's summer visit. No, please no—there were only two more weeks before Carolee and Faith were due to be together at Carolee's place.

Nausea attacked her, made her muscles tremble and threatened to make her pass out. She breathed through her mouth and looked at her watch. Cars weren't supposed to do more than load and unload in the spot Kip was using. He must have been there for five minutes. She looked sideways, searched the faces coming from the street, and edged out of the gates again. If he was going to find her, he was going to find her. She couldn't stand the terror tearing at her stomach.

The Porsche was gone.

Uncontrollable shaking overtook Carolee. Laughter bubbled from her chest. He hadn't seen her after all. She stopped laughing. Neither had she gotten any closer to Faith than the last time and the void hurt even more.

She couldn't go on, not like this, and she couldn't give up. Whatever it took, she was going to fight for her daughter.

A hand settled on her shoulder and she jumped so violently her teeth slammed together and pain shot through her head. Gasping she turned, expecting to see Kip scowling at her.

She was confronted by a beautifully dressed middle-aged woman. Carolee knew a cream Armani suit when she saw one, and matching Weitzman pumps. Between a short skirt and the elegant shoes, well-shaped legs were encased in sheer ivory hose. The purse was Chanel. Frosted hair curved to the jaw and sported the required beige velvet headband.

The woman was peering at Carolee. "Are you all right? I couldn't help noticing that you seem distressed."

"I'm fine," Carolee said, desperate to slip away and drive back to the Eastside and her home in Juanita. "Crowds make me a bit nervous, that's all."

Not to be deterred, the good Samaritan moved even closer. "Something upset you, didn't it? Something you saw. If you're in danger, you ought to get help."

7

A smile cost Carolee dearly. "You have quite an imagination. I'm not in danger. I already told you I don't do well in crowds."

"You aren't going to the play?"

"No." She satisfied the woman's curiosity without realizing quickly enough that there was no reason to do so. "Excuse me, please."

The woman stared baldly at her and said, "I thought I knew you. Now I'm sure I do— even though you look a bit different. You're that Carolee Burns."

*T*wo

*T*hat Carolee Burns.
    Even after several hours the words continued to sting, the words and the judgmental stare on the woman's face. What did she know? What did any of them know?

Running lights on an anonymous small craft traveled along Carolee's small corner of Lake Washington. From her perch on the dock that poked into the water from her property, she heard laughter above the muted sound of the engine.

It was one of those nights when water slipped silently around the pilings beneath her. A chill hung out in the lining of a warm breeze. A sliver of the downtown Seattle lights shimmered in the distance.

Each breath felt soft, as if it hardly moved her body, and stillness grew deeper. Like a lull before a storm? Maybe. Or perhaps she was growing numb, too numb to hurt anymore.

She'd taken a year, more than a year since the divorce, to beat down some of the shock that had stopped her from taking action. Still she'd done nothing definite to fight her ex-husband for the right to spend at least equal time with Faith. But in the beginning she'd panicked, and afterward Kip had made it clear that if she attempted to ignore any part of the court's ruling, she'd run the risk of not seeing Faith at all.

No tears came. She'd cried them all, but her eyes stung and her throat burned, and the too familiar shaky sensation weakened her legs. Kip had insisted he wasn't punishing her, just doing what was best for Faith, and for himself. Carolee had, he said, followed her own star and neglected her family in the process. She had abandoned them, caused Faith to become insecure, and undermined his own promising career as a painter. And the court agreed.

And she hadn't been able to argue convincingly enough because, on the surface, Kip's accusations could be considered true.

That Carolee Burns.

The media that had loved Carolee the wildly successful jazz pianist had been quick to grasp the sensational divorce buzz, to make the sordid wrangling between Kip and Carolee Burns even more sordid, and babble the story

9

from talk show to tabloid and every paper and magazine in the land—and elsewhere. And people like the Armani woman had rubbed their hands and salivated as they'd watched a celebrity disintegrate.

"Carolee?" Her father's raspy voice only beat the man's heavy footsteps by an instant. His boots thumped on the dock and she felt vibration in the old wood slats.

"Hi, Sam." She raised a hand high in greeting without turning around.

When he reached her, he puffed a bit but, despite arthritis, lowered himself beside her. "Missed you at soup," he said. *Soup* was Sam's code word for supper. "Outdid myself tonight, too. Butternut squash with rosemary and garlic, and fresh cream on top. And a piece of Copper River salmon so good I needed a bib for the drool."

"Sam."

"Waited as long as I could for you."

"I didn't say I'd come," she reminded him

"Didn't say you wouldn't, either. Keeping your options open. Don't blame you."

"Poor Sam." She looked sideways at him. The moon turned the sky silver-gray and outlined her father's thick white hair, and his stooped back. She drew in a breath and said, "You're a patient man to put up with me. Are you still glad you didn't tell me I'm too old to run back home?"

"It's your home," Sam Davis pointed out. "Your mother left it to you, not me, I'm just the caretaker when you aren't here."

There was no bitterness in his words. Lake Home had been in Ella Davis's family for eighty years and she'd always intended for Carolee to inherit the property. After Ella's death, Sam's wish to live in a cabin hidden from the main house by a slim stand of trees had pleased Carolee and been convenient for both of them. "You love it here," she told him. "Mom would be pleased to know we're together."

"Things are changing, aren't they?" Sam said.

He had an irritating habit of sensing important shifts in Carolee's moods almost before she'd accepted them herself.

"You've decided something. Is that it?" he continued.

"Don't push," she told him, and regretted it. "I'm sorry. You're waiting too, and you want to be back in Faith's life the way it used to be. Oh, Sam, how can this still be happening?" She wouldn't tell him what she'd done earlier in the day. He'd only worry.

His long, indrawn breath was very clear and meant he was trying to practice being calm—not a natural state for Sam Davis. "Only two weeks till Faith comes."

Carolee rubbed her face. Lights across the water blurred. "The first time she'll have been with us for more than a weekend in fourteen months. Maybe she doesn't want to come. She's so quiet around me now. I don't know what she's thinking. They said I wasn't fit to be with—"

"No," Sam said, his tone harsh. "They didn't say you weren't fit. They said her father had always been there for her and it only made sense for him to be the primary caregiver."

"Yes." She wouldn't argue. And she wouldn't remind him of the other things that had been said, the accusations that had been repeated for all the world to hear.

Sam patted her shoulder and said, "I thought I'd rent that pony she loves. The one from the stable in Woodinville. Plenty of trails for her to ride on around here."

"I don't want her riding alone," Carolee said at once, and sucked in her bottom lip. She'd never been a relaxed mother.

"Fine," Sam said easily. "I'll see what I can find for you and you can ride together."

She opened her mouth to remind him she didn't ride, but stopped herself. If necessary she'd learn.

"None of this should be going on," Sam said abruptly, surprising Carolee. He wasn't an introspective man and usually offered blunt questions and solutions rather than speculations. "I should have stopped you from marrying that bastard."

"You couldn't have," she told him quietly, and without reminding him that he'd been taking one of his sabbaticals from his wife and two daughters at the time. "Anyway, if I hadn't married Kip, there wouldn't be a Faith. I don't even want to think about that."

Another boat, this one with white lights along its rigging, slipped through the darkness.

"He had to be planning the whole thing for years," Sam said.

"That's ridiculous."

Sam snorted. "For a long time, then." He scooped pebbles from the top of an upturned barrel and let them plop, one by one, into the water. "You don't come up with a story like that overnight—or all the stuff he had documented."

Hairs on her spine prickled. "Let's drop it, please."

"I reckon it's time we looked into Kip Burns's past—and his present."

"There was never any question about Kip, you know that." Something had set Sam off. "I couldn't even argue about what he said. He told the truth—about everything but the way I felt and what I thought and believed. He guessed at those things and he was dead wrong, but the facts were the facts. I took him for granted until he couldn't stand it anymore." The other didn't help, the recollections of longing to cut down on her schedule because she wanted to be with her husband and to care for their child as the mother she'd been born to be. And she couldn't know why Kip had insisted she continue, insisted on a series of occasions when she'd told him she didn't want to be away so often.

Sam slapped a hand on the surface of the dock. Carolee jumped. "I can't swallow it anymore, girl. I kept my mouth shut because I knew that's what you wanted. But you gave in too easy. And he counted on you doing that. He knows you so well. He knows you're too gentle for your own good."

"I'm not as gentle anymore." She meant it. "All I needed was enough time to come to grips with reality. I think I figured Kip was just trying to shake me up. I know I did. After the divorce I kept expecting him to call me up and say it was a joke. But it was too late for that."

Sam got to his feet. "If he wanted you home and playing the obedient little wife, he should have suggested it. Did he ever suggest it?"

"You've never asked me questions like this before," Carolee said.

"I'm asking them now. Did he ever say he didn't like having a famous wife who kept him in clover? Did he? Did he beg you to chuck it all in and be with him? For richer, for poorer, and all that bunk?"

"Leave it." Kip had said he was thinking of her, making decisions for her so that she didn't have the torment of turning her back on her music.

"Did he?" Sam asked again.

"No, he didn't, but I have never denied that my career was really important to me, either."

"He never wanted you to give it up." Sam spoke more loudly. "It's your money that gave him the life he wanted—still does."

She shook her head, trying to close it all out. "I hate talking about this. And you don't know anything about what Kip might have been feeling, or what he went through before he did what he did." She didn't know either. "Maybe I really didn't give him the attention he deserved."

14

"Do you still love him?"

Carolee sat quite still.

"Do you?"

"He's Faith's father."

Sam rested a hand on Carolee's head and she felt him staring down at her. He kept on staring until she looked back at him. "I know he's Faith's father," he said. "That wasn't what I asked you."

"We've got a history. You know that. We've known each other since high school. We did everything together. I was so proud of his painting and he was proud of my music."

"You were proud of his painting. You were the one who said you'd help him do what he had to do and your career could come later."

It grew colder. Wraiths of dark cloud obscured the moon for seconds at a time, pulling a dark wash over land and water. Hearing Sam voice the facts of her life with Kip aloud only made it harder to sort out what she really felt and what she ought to do about it.

"When you started to get offers from all over, Kip was quick enough to insist you should take 'em while he painted at home. Dammit, Carolee, it didn't take long before you could make sure he had everything. No one could have had more advantages than Kip Burns. What other no-name painter wouldn't have killed for the studios he had in New York and Los Angeles—and then in Seattle? And what has he really done with all that?"

"You're not being fair. I traveled a lot and

15

kept the kind of hours that didn't fit with a child's schedule or needs often enough. Kip always had to think about Faith first."

Sam said, "And you didn't think about her? You were able to pretend you didn't have a kid at all? Funny I don't remember it that way. Come to that, did I imagine the nanny and the household staff?"

"I'm going in," she said. "Thanks for caring so much. About Faith—and about me. But trust me to do what should be done, please."

Sam offered her a hand and she let him haul her up. "So far you haven't done anything, girl," he said. "The longer I watch you let this happen to you, the more I want to take Kip Burns by the throat."

"Don't talk like that." She walked past him and started up the steep, narrow path toward the stone house where lights glowed from every ground-floor window facing the lake.

"Okay, okay," Sam said, thumping along behind her. The dirt path had been beaten by years of passing feet rather than design. "Different topic. You need to get back in the harness."

Carolee leaned into the incline and marched faster.

"What are you proving by staying away from what you do best? You need to play. People want to hear you play. Shouldn't mean you're cut off from Faith. You gotta look at the whole picture, long term."

She started to run, her breath coming in short bursts. He didn't understand, but then, she'd never told him. All but giving up her career had been the most difficult thing she'd ever done—other than living without her daughter. "I'm still playing." She panted.

"Once a week in a spaghetti joint in Kirkland." Sam was gasping and had to shout louder as he fell behind. "You play and they don't even quit yakking and pushing noodles in their faces."

He was laboring and Carolee took pity on him and his arthritic knees and questionable heart. She stopped and waited for him. "You are an ornery old man," she told him, shaking her head. "You take mean pills."

"Because I love my daughter and granddaughter?"

"No. Because you're deliberately trying to goad me. You think if you make me mad enough, I'll... I don't know what you think I'll do."

"Get on with living again," he said, reaching her. "I want you to get it that you don't have to sit here waiting for that moron to do you some favors. It's not going to happen. You've got to make things happen. That doesn't mean you have to quit being who you are."

Arguing wouldn't help a thing. "I'm going to play for those noodle pushers again in a couple of days. Maybe I'll go commune with the keys before I fall into bed."

"You should call Leo Getz and tell him you're ready to take on some engagements again."

It was enough that her manager had called

that very day and made the same suggestion. True, he'd backed off the instant she'd told him it wasn't going to happen—and he'd promised not to mention the issue again. "Leave it, Sam."

"Let him know you'll be available after Faith's visit."

"I don't want to think about Faith's visit being over. I'll cook dinner tomorrow if you want to come. Night."

"You're trying to shut me up."

"I've always said I had a smart father. Want me to drive you to the cabin?"

"I'm not that old," Sam said. "The walk's good for me."

He took off and didn't look back. She knew he got angry only because he loved her, and because he was almost as frustrated as she was. Slowly, she covered the rest of the distance to the wisteria-draped porch that stretched the width of the house. She climbed steps that creaked, reminding her that there were repairs that were long overdue. Sam would drive in some nails if she reminded him.

For a moment she considered sitting on the porch swing but thought better of it. Even if the piano didn't call to her, being alone in a swing meant for two only made her lonelier.

The screen door squealed when Carolee opened it and she smiled. She really had better get some work done around here.

She let the door go but the sweetness from boxes of night-scented stock followed her inside.

Carolee's upright piano stood near square paned windows in the big room that had been divided into living room, dining room, and kitchen before she decided to have walls taken down. She pulled off her nylon windbreaker and hung it on one of a row of brass hooks screwed into golden cedar paneling. Overhead, exposed beams glowed the same color. The old house had been polished to a patina by the years. During the renovation, a new staircase had been built near the longest wall in the sitting area. The steps, with their uniquely carved balusters, rose to a door that led to the bedrooms.

The textures and colors in the house used to soothe her, but they didn't have the power to comfort, or make her feel safe tonight.

With the light on inside, there was nothing to see through the windows. Carolee sat at the keyboard and glanced at the mirror-blackness that sometimes made her feel vulnerable and watched.

She wouldn't attempt to go near Faith again before her visit. It was almost unbelievable that she'd risked jeopardizing their time together twice.

Music, the way she naturally made whatever she wanted of it, pleased her as it always did, but even as she closed her eyes and leaned over her hands, she felt tears prickle, those tears she kept telling herself she couldn't and wouldn't cry.

Faith would be a good pianist—if Kip made sure she kept up her lessons. Not that Carolee was the product of a lot of formal training. She couldn't remember when she'd first started climbing on her mother's piano bench and pretending, very seriously according to Ella Davis, that she was making important music. She'd had lessons, plenty of them, but she'd simply become the musician people had clamored to hear.

Faith had shown similar talent.

She could call Kip's penthouse condo in Seattle's Bell Town. Faith might pick up. The number at Lake Home was blocked so no one could know if she made a call. And she wouldn't say anything to Faith, just listen to her voice until she hung up. One word, *"hello,"* would be enough. Or it would be better than nothing.

What if Kip answered, which he was likely to do?

Then she'd hang up on him.

She stopped playing. The piece she was composing, supposedly a humorous number about a woman putting up with a man spoiling her, wasn't amusing Carolee.

From where she sat, she could reach the old-fashioned black phone that stood on a table behind the softly cushioned plaid sofa. She lifted the receiver and began to dial, hesitating after each number.

There weren't any sounds here that would give her away. But why not be straightforward and ask how Faith was? Who could take exception to that?

The receiver rattled when she dropped it back again. This was no good.

Faith was quiet when she came for weekend visits. Kip dropped her off on the third Friday evening of each month. He had never accepted Carolee's offer to stay for dinner and tended to come back for their daughter at least a few hours early on Sunday. On those occasions the warning in his expression was implicit; unless she wanted trouble, she wouldn't complain.

Quickly, not allowing herself to think, she snatched up the phone and finished dialing this time.

"Hello," Kip said.

Carolee struggled against the desire to hang up again. After a deep breath she said, "Hi, Kip. It's Carolee."

Silence.

"I'll come clean. I've been sitting here thinking about Faith and wondering how she is. What about her piano lessons? Are they going well?"

"We decided she had too many activities. She'll probably take them up again later but for now she's concentrating on other things."

His flat voice chilled her. She wanted to rage at him, to tell him she knew he'd been the one to decide the piano lessons should be the thing to go, but she swallowed and stayed quiet until she was calmer. "These children today," she said, forcing a laugh. "Things have changed from the days of playing with the kids next door and maybe going to the pool to swim now and then."

"Was that all you called for?"

She squeezed her eyes shut. How could he

have come to hate her so much? If she'd hurt him, it had been by accident. "I guess so, unless Faith is up. I'd like to ask what she's hoping to do when she's here next month."

"She's not up."

"Oh, no, I suppose she wouldn't be." Through the threatening tears, her worn black and white piano keys wavered and ran together. "Well, I won't keep you. Good—"

"I saw you this afternoon."

Her heart stopped. Her heart and her breath. The only thing that stirred within her was blood that pounded in her ears.

"Did you hear me?"

"Yes," she said quietly. She could deny it, but what would be the point?

"You were told how important it is for Faith to know what to expect. She must know what the routine is. She doesn't need to have you following her around."

There was nothing to say.

"If I hadn't been in a loading zone, I'd have found a way to get to you without frightening Faith."

"Yes."

"You were always a sneak in your way. You'd do anything to get what you wanted and you still would."

Carolee covered her mouth. Any moment now and he'd tell her she wasn't getting Faith for a month. She'd fight it, but she didn't know if she'd win.

"Are you listening to me?"

"Yes."

"Good. The reason I'm not going to report what you did is because I believe Faith needs to spend time with you. I don't want to stop her from being with you on the occasions that were agreed on."

"Thank you," she whispered.

"I'm not doing it for you," Kip said. "I'm doing it because I want my daughter to believe her mother isn't a total loser after all. She needs that for her self-esteem."

Damn him. Bending forward, Carolee rested her forehead on top of the piano.

"Don't do anything to change my mind," Kip said, and hung up.

Three

"Ladies and gentlemen," Brandy Snopes said, tossing back her luxurious auburn hair and wetting carmine lips. "I give you— Carolee Burns!"

Applause broke out and Carolee entered from Brandy's office at Bistro Brandy on Kirkland's Lake Street. The full skirt of her black silk dress flipped about her calves. Her bare shoulders and the décolletage at the neck of the backless halter top were luminously pale.

Wearing a stretchy strapless dress of turquoise sequins, Brandy kissed and hugged Carolee, then backed away, clapping as she went.

Max Wolfe sat at a small round table to the right of the baby grand piano. To the right and with one table closer to, but not blocking, the makeshift space where Carolee performed.

He knew that she and Brandy were old friends—that they'd known each other since grade school. Max and Brandy had met more recently—four years ago when they'd had a brief fling and been lucky enough to realize they weren't meant for each other but that they liked the friendship.

It was Brandy who let Max know each time Carolee was going to play at the bistro. He didn't like feeling disappointed that this would be her last night here for more than a month.

When she sat down, the black dress swirled around slim ankles and drew attention to high, very sexy sandals.

She played, and Max sipped a glass of red wine. He didn't know the names of her pieces, but every one of them turned him on. A feeling that he wouldn't be anywhere else but watching her rattled him. Max Wolfe, the man no woman had managed to tame, had a bad case. Even though he'd been smitten by someone whose complicated life was public knowledge, including the fact that she wasn't interested in a new man, he wasn't finding a way to switch off his feelings. He lowered his eyes. If his history was repeating, the challenge she presented could add to her appeal.

He wasn't looking for a way to stop the feelings.

She looked at him.

Max smiled, just a little, and rolled the bowl of his glass between his hands.

Carolee seemed to keep looking at him but he couldn't be sure she actually saw him. When she played, her whole body moved. She wasn't thin and he liked that. He also liked the way she wore her thick, dark hair rolled away from her face and caught loosely at the back of her head. Her face was heart-shaped, her chin pointed. There was nothing typical about her. She'd been described as interesting but not conventionally good-looking. Max had spent more than one solitary evening enjoying visions of her, and wishing he could figure out how to spend a lot more time looking at her unconventional face.

"You again, huh?"

Max jumped and glanced up at a white-haired guy who was probably seventy, even if his light eyes could pierce a man.

"Have we met, sir?" Politeness to older males had been an obsession Max's father passed on.

"No," the man said. "I'm Sam. You expecting company?"

Max shook his head no, and Sam promptly commandeered the second chair at the table.

"What d'you think of this place?" Sam asked. "Hokey, huh? Faux Italian."

Max smiled and glanced around at rough-plastered terra cotta walls and silk grapevines draped along pink beams. "I don't know," he said. Bunches of purple plastic grapes dripped from the vines. "Have you been to Italy?"

"Nah. Why would I go somewhere foreign when I live in the best country in the world?"

"I went there a couple of times," Max said. "I liked it. Beautiful country. Nice people. This place isn't so far off some of the ones I ate in there."

Sam snorted. "I guess that puts me in my place. Did you have dinner yet?"

"Nope."

"You gonna eat?"

"No," Max said. "Just stopping in for a drink. Can I buy you one? Or are you hungry? Don't let me put you off."

"Just coffee," the man said. "I'm not hungry and I abused the other privilege a long time ago. Now I don't need it."

Max signaled a waiter and ordered coffee.

"I saw you here before," Sam said. "Several times. You must be a real music lover." His sharp eyes skewered Max again.

"Depends on the music. I like this. I heard her play in New York once. She's got a supper club there. Or she did."

"Still does." The guy cleared his throat. "At least, that's what I'm told."

"Nice place. Burns Near Broadway. Good food. But I've got to confess I went for her, not the food. She's phenomenal. I don't guess she gets to New York much now."

Sam shrugged and cleared his throat. "You live around here?"

"Uh-huh. A condo. Here in Kirkland."

"I wish these bozos would quit talking and eating," Sam said of diners at the bistro.

Max didn't point out that Sam hadn't stopped talking since he sat down. "They do quiet down while she plays," he pointed out. "They know they're in on something special. I keep expecting the word to spread so much it'll be impossible to get in here, but this is mostly regulars and Brandy doesn't advertise."

"Carolee wouldn't come if things got out of hand."

Max noted Sam's confidence when he made statements about Carolee Burns, but made no comment.

She ran her fingers over the keys, and those who continued to eat did so discreetly. Sam's coffee was delivered but he ignored it. He bent forward over a bright yellow tablecloth, his eyes fixed on the pianist, and Max frowned. For Sam to have seen him here before meant the other man had also been present.

"What do you think of her?" Sam leaned close and whispered. "She's something, huh?"

"Yes, something." Her fingers skimmed across the keyboard and she sang in a husky voice, a slow, husky voice. Her eyelids closed and he could see her eyes moving beneath. "Gutsy, too. I like that."

"I know who you are, y'know," Sam said. "I bet everyone here does. Must be hard to hide when you're bigger than anyone else around."

"It might be if I was trying to hide." Max didn't want to talk about himself. "She shouldn't be shut away in this backwater. She's a woman who needs to be free and that

27

doesn't make her a bad wife—ex-wife—or mother. She got a bum rap."

The unwavering attention that comment brought him wasn't too comfortable. "You ever been married?" Sam asked.

"No."

"Are you involved?"

"No." Max raised his eyebrows.

"I know, I know," Sam said. "Nosy old bastard, aren't I? Just wondered. What d'you do now you can't play football anymore?"

The waiter put a basket of warm bread on the table and Max tore off a piece. He made a diversion of gathering crumbs into a small pile. "I own a software company," he said finally. "And I help out with high school football for The Lakes. I'm kind of a visiting motivator who gives pointers."

"Must have been a helluva shock. The accident. Trapped under a pickup like that. Then watching your best buddy get your job had to hurt."

"I'm a grown-up. I got over it." More or less. "And Rob Mead is still the best friend a man could have. He couldn't help what happened to me." Max didn't want to talk about this anymore. Avoiding comments on what people liked to call his "tragedy" could keep him at home for long periods.

"Do you like kids?"

Startled, Max looked at him quizzically. He thought for a moment. "Yes, I guess I do. I don't think I'd have wanted to get involved with a high school team if I didn't."

"Ever think about having your own?"

"My own?" Max was having difficulty listening to Carolee Burns and understanding Sam's oblique questions.

"Your own kids."

He gave that some thought, too. "With the right woman, sure." Carolee was looking in his direction again and he smiled, making sure his expression was open and friendly. She smiled back but he still didn't think she was really aware of him.

"She's a charmer," Sam said. "Never saw a woman with so much to offer who had so little confidence in herself."

"Maybe you're right, but I like her just the way she is."

"You do, huh?"

"Well..." Max drank more wine and followed it with a bite of bread. "Well, I don't know her, do I? But I think I'd like her a lot if I did."

Sam sipped at his coffee and grimaced. "Swill," he said. "This stuff never saw a coffee bean. Do you ride?"

"I'm sorry?" Max set his glass down on top of the wet circle that had already formed on the cloth.

"Horses," Sam said. "I'm getting a couple out at my place for when my granddaughter visits. I'm too old to keep up with exercising 'em."

"I grew up riding on my folks' farm. And if that's an invitation, thank you. I might take you up on the offer one of these days."

"That's good." The man's broad grin disconcerted Max.

"Do you know what this piece she's playing is called?" Max asked to change the subject.

Sam considered, then said, " 'I Know You in the Dark.' Strange she never wrote any words."

"Do you know if she wrote the music?"

"Sure, she wrote it. When she was married to that moron, the guy she was supposed to have taken advantage of. I ask you, does she look like she could take advantage of anyone?"

Good old Sam knew a great deal about Carolee Burns and Max intended to find out why. "She looks intense to me, intense but gentle."

"And she's beautiful if you like a face that's all eyes."

Max grinned. "She is beautiful."

"You must be pretty well fixed," Sam said offhandedly. "All that money from playing in the pros, and now your own software company."

"I can pay my bills."

The piece of music Carolee played didn't need any words. Just knowing the title conjured images of heat and damp skin that caused Max to ache in places where he enjoyed the sensation. She was really sexy, he hadn't noticed just how sexy before. Now and again she ran her tongue over her full lower lip and she kept her eyes closed almost all the time she played, only to open them with a vaguely startled expression, as if she was surprised to discover she wasn't alone.

He could watch her and imagine she was playing for him, telling him she'd know him in the dark.

She didn't know it, but they had things in common. The losses were different, but they had both lost. First her marriage had failed and her child had been all but taken from her. Then she'd chosen to walk away from a dynamic career. She could go back to the career. He didn't have that choice. He'd been a wide receiver with the Broncos. Speed and his teammates' confidence in his reliability went with the job. After the accident he'd brought himself back to excellent physical shape, but the metal plates in his legs meant he wouldn't play again. Carolee obviously wasn't sure exactly what she wanted for the rest of her life. Neither was he.

He'd just like to talk to her—alone. She might turn out to be vapid, but he didn't think so, and he couldn't shake the feeling that they'd have plenty to say to each other.

Sam didn't talk anymore, and soon the only sounds in the restaurant came from the piano and from Carolee singing. Her mood changed with the mood of each piece, but Max couldn't get that one melody out of his head. "I Know You in the Dark." He wanted to know her in the dark, and in the sunlight or the rain.

He'd been alone too long. It was time he found a new lady.

Max looked at a clock on the wall. Carolee had been playing almost forty-five minutes. A crowd hovered inside the front doors, straining to get a better look at her. He saw her nervous expression when she turned her head and saw them.

"Uh-oh," Sam said, pushing back his chair. "She's about had enough. Time to get her out of here."

Bodyguard, maybe? Or her driver more likely. Max pushed back from the table, too. He'd follow at a distance but make sure they got away safely.

The moment she finished the number she was playing, Carolee rose from the bench to bow and smile in all directions. The applause would be loud even in a much larger room. She walked toward Sam, caught Max's eye, and veered away toward Brandy's office.

A man reached for her arm as she passed. She sidestepped him, but without appearing angry.

"Parking lot at the back," Sam muttered. "She's not usually this edgy. I'd better get her out through the kitchens."

"I'll make sure no one bothers her," Max said, doing what came naturally and using his height and muscular weight to wall off a path from the office to the kitchens. "Tell her she'll be fine and walk her out. These folks think she's great, that's all."

Sam opened the office door and said something Max couldn't hear. Grinning and waving, Carolee came out, offered Max a grateful wink, and hurried into the kitchens.

Just that quickly she was gone.

And just that quickly Max was left with a wonderful picture of her winking one definitely green eye.

Italian music came from overhead speakers.

Chatter and laughter meant everyone was having a good time and that they hadn't noticed any awkwardness on Carolee's part.

"Hey, Max," Brandy said, placing her tall, shapely body in front of him. "She's great. You've got good taste."

"I like listening to her. Thanks for giving me a call and letting me know she'd be here."

Brandy ran her hands up and down his sides and puckered her lips at him. "I was watching you. You look lonely to me, Max. And frustrated, maybe? How about getting together later—for old times' sake. No expectations, just good company."

He really did like her. "Not tonight, kid. I'm beat. Can I have a rain check?"

"You bet." She pressed her elbows to her sides, showing off awe-inspiring cleavage. "Just one little kiss, though?"

He dropped a kiss on her brow, but when she caught his head in both of her hands, he gave up and pressed his lips to hers. Fortunately he'd had enough practice to manage sliding contact. "That was nice," he said honestly. "We'll get together soon."

"Oh, yes we will," she said. "Now run along."

He did as he was bid and didn't get a single comment from the staff when he exited via the kitchens as Carolee and Sam had.

The lot behind the bistro was small, badly lighted, and smelled dank. Sudden shrieks from cats of the night startled him, but Max's luck was holding. He made out Carolee leaning against the side of a one-ton Dodge pickup. The hood was propped up and he could hear Sam's voice spitting a venomous tirade from the depths of the engine compartment.

Max hadn't expected to feel shy if he was ever more or less alone with Carolee, but he did. Still he pushed himself to amble toward the Dodge and call, "Hi, Sam. It's Max. You having some trouble?"

Sam's head emerged and he wiped his brow on his sleeve. "Nothing but trouble. Never has been."

"It's been perfectly fine for fourteen years," Carolee said. "It's tired and neglected is all. Time you traded it in."

"No way." Sam used a wrench like a baton. He made a growling sound and said, "Carolee Burns, meet Max Wolfe. You youngsters are to blame for all this planned obsolescence. If something breaks down, you want to throw it away and buy new. If I didn't have a bit of arthritis, I could keep this thing going until we get home. It starts, but it's touchy. If you could drive it, girl—"

"But I can't drive a stick shift. We both know that. I'll take some lessons."

"That's not going to help us now."

Max tossed around the possibilities before saying, "I could drive you in my car, then come back and get you in the morning so you could deal with the Dodge."

"I'm not leaving my truck here," Sam said, all sharpness. "You might not get it, but there are a lot of young whippersnappers just dying to get their hands on something like this. If they couldn't steal it, they'd strip it. I'd better get help."

"I could drive it for you," Max said and shook his head slightly. What was he thinking of, getting involved here?

Carolee spoke to him at last. "Then you'd be marooned without wheels."

"He could drive your car back," Sam said quickly. "We'd come into Kirkland for it in the morning. Max lives up the street here in a condo."

"I see." Clearly she didn't see, but she wasn't sure how to argue what Sam seemed so sure of.

"You two could drive out in my car while I drive this," Max said. "That would solve everything."

"What do you drive?" Sam asked.

"A Cadillac," he said and laughed uncomfortably. "One of the drawbacks of having mostly metal legs is that it's more comfortable to stretch them out."

"We're not driving your Cadillac," Sam said. "No way. Might do something to it. No, if you'd be kind enough to drive us back, you can use Carolee's wheels for tonight."

Max wanted to ask how Sam intended to get anywhere tomorrow if he didn't have a vehicle. He kept his mouth shut instead. The time always came to give in gracefully.

Carolee went to the driver's side of the truck and Max handed her up. Promptly she slid to the middle of the bench seat and angled her legs to the passenger side of the cab. Sam got in beside her and slammed his door.

Max took a cleansing breath through his nose and climbed behind the wheel. "Here we go," he said and turned the key in the ignition. The engine turned over immediately and smoothly, but he treated the gas and clutch gently just in case.

"I'll bring you home," Carolee said. "Then you'll be put out as little as possible."

He shouldn't be so pleased at the idea of spending more time with her—alone.

Beside him, close enough for their arms to touch, Carolee sat quite still. He wore a gray silk shirt and darker gray pants. It was impossible to ignore the warm feel of her when he turned the wheel. Each time he shifted, his hand brushed her thigh. When he glanced down, he saw that her skirts were hiked above her knees. The sight of her long, well-shaped legs tightened his belly.

"You and Sam seem to know each other," she said to him. "Do you fish?"

Questions, questions. "Not often."

"Play golf?"

"Occasionally."

"We met watching you," Sam said, evidently unnerved by the third degree. "He's Max Wolfe the pro-football player."

"Ex-football player. Don't forget to give me directions."

"Turn left on Central Avenue," Carolee said promptly. "Then take a right on Market Street."

Kirkland was crowded. Cruising cars jammed the narrow streets. Groups on the sidewalks hollered responses to blaring horns. Some danced to music blasting from clubs, and from vehicles with rolled-down windows. Warm weather had brought out halter tops and shorts. In-line skaters dodged among walkers, skateboarders, cyclists, and runners.

Sam's truck didn't have air-conditioning. "Don't need it around here," he'd said and Max had been glad it was Carolee who responded, "You're the only one who thinks so." But to-night Max enjoyed feeling the town's energy, and smelling flowers in overflowing hanging baskets. He liked Kirkland a lot.

"Son of a...will you look at this place?" Sam said. "Damn carnival. They think they own the roads. Look at that. No signal. Geez, move it, will ya? Honk, Max. We should be halfway to Juanita by now."

Carolee's sudden laugh made Max grin and look sideways at her. She gave him a conspiratorial smile that wrinkled her nose and Max felt almost as if she'd put her arms around him. Intimate, that's how her smile felt.

Four

As instructed, Max turned right on Market Street. They traveled a long way in silence and he felt any hint of intimacy slip away, replaced by strained awareness. Even Sam had run out of things to say.

The drive to what he'd discovered was actually Carolee Burns's place took about thirty-five minutes. When the headlights of the Dodge flashed against a faded sign that announced LAKE HOME, and he headed onto a steep, rutted driveway lined with trees to the south, Max was still trying to think of a way to ask the relationship between Carolee and Sam. He was also struggling with a sense of unreality that this woman was sitting beside him.

"Straight down past the trees," Sam said. "Carolee's house is there. I can walk to my place."

"Drop Sam first," Carolee said. "He thinks he's Superman. He isn't. Take a left here and skirt the trees."

"Straight ahead," Sam said. "I'm not dead yet."

Max chose what seemed like the safest course and went straight ahead. He felt Carolee shrug.

A lot of lights shone from inside a two-story stone house with a steeply sloped roof. When Max pulled toward the side of the building, he could see the faint glitter of the black Lake Washington ahead. From what he could tell, the property had to be big, a couple of acres at least.

"I'll take off, then," Sam said, scarcely waiting for the Dodge to come to a full stop before throwing the door open. He went immediately to the driver's side and said, "I hope you will come over. Give me your number and I'll call."

Max released his seat belt and reached into a back pocket for his wallet. He handed Sam a card. "Sure you don't want a ride home?"

Sam's response was a shake of the head and a rapid departure behind a detached carport and out of view. The man's behavior was curious. He almost seemed obsessed with making sure Max became a friend. It could be some sort of infatuation with major league sports figures, but Max hadn't been one of those for three years and Sam had asked personal questions to which he'd already have answers if he really followed the game.

"I'm embarrassed you've been put to so much trouble," Carolee told him. She slid to the open passenger door and jumped out. "I need to go in and get my keys. The car's over there."

He had no right to be disappointed because she didn't invite him in. He was a stranger.

He *was* disappointed.

She took off her sandals and ran, barefoot, toward a porch that faced the lake. His reaction to her flying skirts, the pale gleam of her skin, and the rapid flash of the soles of her feet unnerved him. He was seeing her in a way he didn't remember seeing any women. Even the simplest detail made his palms sweat.

He got out of the truck and shut the door. The car she'd pointed out, an older model Mercedes convertible, was parked in one side of the carport. The other side was stacked to the roof with firewood—some recently enough split to load the air with the scent of pitch.

"If this old thing decides to play up, I'll die with embarrassment." She came silently up behind him and went to open the passenger door. "Hop in."

When she laughed, he stopped with one foot inside the car. "What?"

"I should have said squeeze in. Are all football players as big as you?"

"Most of them are bigger." He felt aggrieved. He might be big by some people's standards but there was no fat on him and he'd been one of the fastest receivers in the game. "Try fitting a line backer in this." He got in and couldn't keep the frown in place.

"I didn't mean to be rude," Carolee said, quickly joining him. "I don't know much about sports. But you don't play anymore, isn't that what you said?"

How easy it was for a stranger to say that. "Not football. Except for helping out with The Lakes team."

"You help The Lakes?" She turned the key in the ignition and gave him a freshly interested look at the same time. "That's a nice thing to do."

"I do it for me as well as the kids. How's your daughter?" Damn, but he was a clumsy idiot. "Forgive me. I didn't mean to blurt that out like that. I was thinking about the team. Your daughter must be about that age."

The car jerked. "She isn't twelve yet. She's fine."

"I'm really sorry I—"

"Don't be. So you know all about me. A lot of people do." In the light from the dash, her profile was unyielding. The corner of her mouth drew down.

He remembered that she was married when she was seventeen and the girl was born when Carolee was eighteen. She was thirty—three years younger than Max.

Concentration was important here. "I heard you play in New York once. At your supper club."

She nodded.

"Look, I just want to say I think you got a lousy deal. A lot of us thought it all sounded like a setup."

"It wasn't a setup. I was guilty as charged and now I'm paying for it. Let's drop the subject."

"Sure." He looked out the side window and wished he could take back the last five minutes of conversation.

"You and Sam mentioned metal plates in your legs." She was driving slowly but Max had the feeling it was more because she was pre-

41

occupied than out of any desire to spend more time with him. "Is that why you aren't a professional athlete anymore? You don't even limp."

"I'm not malingering, if that's what you mean." He rushed on before she could respond. "I had an accident and couldn't come back far enough to be useful again. They put me on injured reserve, and when my contract ran out the following year, I was finished. It tore me up at the time but I'm over it now. That's one of the rules of being a grown-up—you learn to quit griping over the past."

She pushed at her hair with the back of a hand. "Where's your car parked?"

"At my place. If you'd drop me there, I'd be grateful."

"I'm the one who's grateful. You went out of your way for complete strangers."

"Yeah. It's really a drag being with you, but I'm a martyr."

That got him another sideways look, and a slow smile. "You're a nice guy. Thanks."

"Sam's very protective of you. Has he been with you long?"

She chuckled and put on her left turn signal. "Just about all my life—except when he decided he was bored and needed a break." She turned from Market up a side street. The car moved smoothly, its engine very quiet.

Max wrestled to find the right response. He settled on, "What does that mean? Has he always worked for your family?"

"Oh dear." Her laughter made his skin tingle.

"Sam's my father. He's been a good one in his way, too. Loving. But he had this thing, this need to drop out of my mother's and our lives for a few weeks or months now and then. I've got a half-sister from Sam's first marriage. He doesn't go far from Lake Home anymore, though."

"Your mother must be a saint."

"She wasn't a saint at all. She was very human. She's dead. Lake Home was in her family for years and she left it to me. Sam loves it there. He lives on the property and looks after it—more or less. There, now you know my life's history."

He didn't know the stuff he really wanted to know, like the real facts about her divorce and why she'd scaled back her career to almost nothing, and why she'd returned here to Washington State. He also didn't know if she was ready to date again. That was the most important question of all.

Another turn and they were on the street where he lived.

He wanted to date her. He wanted to do a whole lot more than date her but he didn't think she was a woman who would be easily talked into getting to know a stranger intimately—even if he had driven her home.

"Here," he said when they had reached his condo building. "Come in and have a drink." He wanted to pound his head on the dashboard. Couldn't he have come up with a more original invitation?

"Thank you, no. I'd better get back. Sam will be waiting for me."

"How far away does he live from your house?"

"Only half a mile, but his heart isn't great and he's got arthritis badly."

He let that hang there. She was a smart woman, she'd know he was thinking that Sam had gone to wherever he lived and wouldn't be waiting for her.

"Why do you suppose he wanted me to drive home with the two of you?"

She looked straight ahead at a couple walking arm in arm and weaving back and forth on the sidewalk. "I don't know what you mean."

"Sure you do. He joined me at the bistro and asked all kinds of questions. Now I think of it, they were the kind of questions a father might ask a man who was dating his daughter."

She settled against the back of the seat and crossed her arms. "You aren't dating his daughter. His daughter doesn't date." The hand closest to him made a fist and the knuckles glowed.

"He figured I'd follow through the kitchen to make sure the two of you were okay."

"I need to go home."

"Of course. But that Dodge is fine. You know that, don't you?"

In a small voice she said, "Yes, I know it. And I'm sorry for your trouble."

"Don't be. I've loved every minute, except for the way I can't control my careless mouth. I've spent a lot of time alone so I'm probably socially out of practice. Will you forgive me?"

"I don't know why you care."

"I do care, that's all."

"Then I forgive you. Good night."

He was being dismissed. "I'd like to have you to dinner. I'm not a bad cook."

"That wouldn't be a good idea."

He wasn't about to give up. "Why?"

"For reasons I don't want to discuss. I'm glad I met you, though. Be happy."

"Can't. Not unless you come to dinner." He was rusty, but his man–woman skills could be brushed up quickly enough.

"You're not being fair. You think you know a lot about me but you've only got the public facts. I can't risk being involved—or even friendly—with another man."

"A man other than your ex-husband? You're divorced, remember. Time to start living again."

"Please let me go."

Max heard her distress and it shocked him. Shocked him and made him feel like a heel. "Of course. I didn't mean to push you." He got out but bent to lean through the window. "You're spectacular. I just wanted to tell you that. And I don't give up what I want without a fight."

"If you're saying you want me, forget it. I'm not available." Carolee steered away from the curb.

With his hands sunk deep in his pockets, Max watched her go. The excitement he felt was familiar. It hit him on the rare occasions when he smelled a chase he intended, and expected, to win. "I'm going to make you want me as much as I want you," he said quietly but aloud. "You're going to know me so well in the dark."

Five

A country and western album started over again. It had started over many times that afternoon. Stretched out on Carolee's porch swing, her head pillowed on one of its arms and her jiggling feet overhanging the other arm, Ivy Lester's eyelids drooped. A transplanted Tennessee girl, and owner of the music album, Ivy lived to line dance.

She let one hand trail to the ground. "I'm way too comfortable, Carolee. I don't think I could get myself out of this swing if Antonio Banderas asked me."

Carolee said, "Oh, sure—especially if he was asking you to dance," and laughed. Sitting in a wicker chaise with her knees drawn up, she rested her palms on the warm skin of her thighs and said, "You're good for me. I can't remember the last time I sat outside and did nothing for an afternoon, or wore shorts."

"I'm irresistible," Ivy said, shading her blue eyes. "So they all tell me. All I have to do is make a suggestion and there's a rush to do my bidding. Seriously, though, you've got to start doing things for yourself. If you're not practicing, you're—"

"I'm playing anyway because I have to, just like I have to breathe. Or I'm working on this place—which I love. There's a lot to do here." She couldn't bring herself to say that what she enjoyed most was pretending her days were ordinary and that Faith would walk through the door at any moment, bursting to talk about what she'd been doing.

Ivy was wide awake again and frowning. "What does Linda say?"

"Linda? Why would you bring her up now?"

"Because she's your sister and I gather she's very happily divorced."

Four years separated Carolee from Linda, with Linda being the older sibling and Sam's daughter by a first marriage. The two girls had been inseparable—if very competitive as very young children—and would have continued to be friends if something Carolee wouldn't think about hadn't come between them. After that, they became wary strangers in the same house. In the three years since Linda's divorce, their relationship had grown even more distant with Linda making it clear that she was having a good time and didn't want Sam's or Carolee's opinions.

"I still don't see the connection," Carolee told Ivy. "We care for each other in a way, but we grew up to be very different."

Ivy snorted and pushed curly blond hair away from her forehead. "Don't tell me you haven't even discussed your situation."

47

"There's no way Linda would be a help to me now."

"But you've talked?"

"You don't give up," Carolee said. "Yes, we've talked. Many times. She can't stop talking about it and she doesn't see my situation the way I do. She thinks I should make the best of what's happened and move on."

Ivy righted herself to sit up in the swing. She hauled her full white skirts above her knees and swung her shapely legs. She had a figure men stared at, and an open, all-American face that drew both men and women to her. Right now Ivy's frown was ferocious. She wagged a finger at Carolee. "You have a beautiful spirit, but you can be maddenin'. Linda's right, and it isn't as easy for me to say that as you think it is. Bill and I were your friends—yours and Kip's friends—as couples. We're still your friends and we're still Kip's friends. We want both of you to be happy. But your marriage is over. There's never going to be a replay. You're too young to back out of your life."

"I'm not *backing out* of my life. And I can't back away from Faith. I won't. I'm never going to understand exactly why Kip did what he did. I had no inkling it was coming. Why didn't he want to at least warn me how he was feeling?" She waved both hands. "That was rhetorical. You don't have an answer either. Kip went for my throat. He was disappointed and desperate and I've got to keep trying to forgive him. I think I'll be able to do it once I get joint custody of Faith."

"You think he's ever goin' to give you that?"

"I don't know if he'll give it willingly," Carolee said. "But if he won't, then it'll have to be unwillingly. And I *will* find a way. I haven't told this to another soul, but I sometimes wonder if he really wanted a divorce. He could have gotten in too deep and been embarrassed to pull back. If so, I guess there's a possible solution there."

"You're not serious." Ivy's soft voice turned surprisingly harsh. "I swear, Carolee, if you make a fool of yourself by trying to get that man back, why, I'll...I'll never speak to you again."

Carolee couldn't help laughing. "Fess up, Ivy, there isn't anything that could stop you from talking."

Ivy huffed. "I mean it. It's time for you to find yourself a hunk of a man who'll show you what it means to live again—you know what I mean—*live.*"

"Without Faith, life wouldn't be worth a thing," Carolee said and she wasn't laughing anymore.

Ivy slid forward and hopped to her feet. "I'm startin' to glow. I'll go get us some lemonade."

Carolee watched her leave. Through everything, Ivy and Bill had been good to her, but they didn't seem to understand what made her tick. Maybe if they'd been there on the afternoon she thought of as the end of life before her world changed shape, they'd see why she wasn't ready to "move on," or to find a man who would show her what it was like to *"live."*

The tour of Europe had been a triumph. With only a week to go before Christmas, she'd dashed to New York aching to be swept into Kip's arms and to draw Faith into a family hug. She'd let herself into the beautiful apartment overlooking Central Park and called out her two favorite names.

"Kip, Faith, I'm home!"

She pushed open the front door and staggered inside with her roll-aboard bag, and the huge stuffed bear she'd bought for Faith at Harrod's in London clamped under an arm. A familiar green and gold carrier from the same magical emporium contained a stack of CDs by British groups Faith and her friends screamed over, British teen magazines, candy, and a small pair of gold "H" earrings.

For Kip she had a set of keys to the silver Porsche Twin Turbo he'd admired but insisted he didn't need. The wonderful outrageousness of the gift made her shiver. She intended to tell him she was giving him a Christmas present a week early.

"Kip! Faith! Where are you?"

She slipped off her coat and draped it over her case. "Come out, come out wherever you are," she cried, laughing. The apartment had already been professionally decorated for the season and the scent of fresh evergreen garlands was heavy.

When she hurried to the living room, her heels echoed on marble tiles. Gold ornaments glittered on a ceiling-high Christmas tree, but the room was empty. So was the dining room, the den, the media room, the huge cozy kitchen, and all three bedrooms. She should, she realized, have thought to go to Kip's studio first. Sometimes Faith took books in there and read while Kip painted.

There was no canvas on the easel and no sign of her family. When was the last time she'd actually seen Kip paint anyway?

That didn't matter. Every artist had slumps.

She hurried back to the foyer and carried her gifts into the den, then returned to take her coat and bag to the bedroom.

On the circular gilt table in the middle of the foyer, beneath a sparkling Austrian crystal chandelier, stood a brilliant poinsettia. Beside the plant's brass pot was a single, official-looking envelope she'd been too preoccupied to notice before. It bore Carolee's name. She picked it up and examined the return address. "Perkins, Savich, Lazlo and Green, Attorneys at Law."

They weren't the lawyers she and Kip used. Her stomach clenched. Was someone trying to sue her? It wouldn't be the first time, and even though she couldn't think of a thing that would give anyone cause to attempt legal action, she felt unsteady.

She turned the envelope over and over and, finally, all but ripped it open in her haste to be rid of the terror.

Folded sheets of dense legalese with bullets and underlined subheadings. The journey back into the den took a long time, or felt as if it did. Carolee made that journey with the sensation that although her legs were heavy, her feet were bouncing off the floor in slow motion. She heard rushing noises like water driven past her ears by a harsh wind. Sounds, wrenched and raw, surprised her—they came from deep inside her body.

There was a terrible mistake. Kip wasn't divorcing her.

How could this Ronald Green have made such a mistake?

She stumbled over the edge of the den rug, but managed not to fall. Rather than sit in her usual spot on the couch, she went to Kip's leather chair. With the envelope and papers on her lap, she settled her hands on the flared arms. Kip did that, flattened his hands on the smooth, soft leather and rubbed.

He knew she was due home about now—why wasn't he here? And Faith?

Faith. No, Kip wouldn't do something like this to Faith. He loved his daughter and wanted more children just as much as Carolee, had suffered as much as she had over their failure to conceive again.

Her hands were icy.

There was nowhere to go, no one to talk to. The last thing she must do was mention this mistake to anyone. Her mother told her when she was quite young, that troubles kept to yourself were the troubles least likely to hang around.

She heard the front door open, and Faith's high voice punctuated by Kip's deeper tones, and scrambled to her feet. Quickly, she pushed the letter out of sight behind a cushion.

"Mom," Faith called. "Mom, where'd you go?"

She'd seen the suitcase and coat. "In the den," Carolee said as loudly as she could. "Hi, honey."

Faith dashed into the room, her cheeks glowing from the icy air outside. She jumped and threw her arms around Carolee's neck. "Dad thinks I'm not getting outside enough so he made me go for a walk. I didn't mind, though. I love being in the snow with all the pretty lights on."

Carolee held Faith several inches off the ground. And she looked past her head at Kip. She smiled. He didn't. He crossed his arms and looked at the floor. She wanted to tell him she loved him, that although she loved what she did, she loved him and Faith so much more and in the end it was all for them. And she wanted him to smile at her and show her with his eyes that he wanted them to be alone.

"That's enough, Faith," he said. "You're too heavy for your mother."

"I've got something for you," Carolee said, giving the girl another hug and bending gently until her feet were on the rug again. "Close your eyes."

Obediently, if giggling as she did so, Faith squeezed her eyes shut while Carolee turned her around and pointed her in the direction of the Harrod's bear and bag. "Now you can look."

Faith let out a shriek and pounced. At four months short of eleven, she was an endearing muddle of little girl and pre-teen. "He's so cute," she said, then spotted the bag and looked inquiringly at her mother.

"That's yours, too."

"Oh, wow. Oh totally cool." The CDs and magazines were the cause of the rapture. "Can I ask Melody over to listen—"

"Not tonight," Kip said rapidly. "Your mother's only just back from her long trip."

Faith's freckled cheeks flushed. "Oh, right."

"Why don't you go to your room and listen. Your mother and I could use some time alone. Okay?"

"Yes, please." Faith was all smiles again. With full arms she left the room. She hadn't noticed the gold earrings.

In moments Faith's door slammed.

Carolee took a step toward Kip.

He turned away.

"Kip—"

"You read the letter?"

Her breath came in short bursts. "You know about it?"

He looked at her then, his eyebrows raised. "Of course I know about it. Why do you think it was sent to you if I didn't arrange it?"

She blinked and blinked but still saw him through a stinging haze. "I don't understand." Her voice broke and she could do nothing to disguise her distress.

"It would be best if you went straight to a hotel. I'm going to tell Faith that Leo came and you had to leave again."

"We don't lie to her." Her heart hammered. "What is it, Kip? What's happened?"

His expression was different, new, something she'd never seen before. Not angry...indifferent. "You took your eye off the ball one time too many. You didn't notice when I started to break.

54

But you did that to me, Carolee. You took advantage of me and you were looking somewhere else when I finally realized it."

"No." She went to him but the light in his eyes changed and she did see anger now. Rather than touch him, she wrapped her arms around her ribs. "That's not true. If it had been, why didn't you say something? Why did you tell me not to cut back when I wanted to—several times?"

"I knew you didn't mean it when you said you wanted more time with Faith and me."

"I did mean it. Why did you send me off on this last tour as if you couldn't bear for us to be parted?"

Kip's sneer sickened her. "You're so tied up in yourself, you don't see what's happening to anyone else." He sounded venomous. "You looked at a man who couldn't take what you were doing to him anymore and thought he was dreading sleeping alone. I've slept alone too often for that. Maybe if you hadn't been gone more often than you were with me, we'd have had more children."

Carolee opened her mouth, but couldn't speak for the tears that flowed freely and closed her throat.

"That's something else you thought was only painful for you. Wrong again. But maybe it wasn't so painful. After all, another pregnancy would have cramped your style, wouldn't it?"

She could only shake her head.

"You got everything you wanted. I got nothing but Faith, and she's all that matters to me now. Hearing people applaud and call out your name

is what you live for. Great. Now you won't have to pretend you care what happens to us. You won't have to factor us into your schedule at all. I've got to make sure Faith doesn't start to think there's something lacking in her that takes you away so much. If we go our separate ways, she'll think the problem was only between you and me and that's what I want."

He turned and strode from the room, then returned carrying her coat. With mock gallantry, he held it open for her. When she didn't make a move to put it on, he stood aside and flipped it like a matador's cape.

"No," she said, finding a faint voice. "I'm the one who pays for this apartment. I don't have to go anywhere."

His low laugh horrified her. "That's right, sweetheart, you're the one who brings in the big bucks. Nice of you to remind me. Maybe once you're not around I'll be able to concentrate on the talent I wasted while I was Mr. Carolee Burns, house-husband. Stay. You're right—you pay the bills. I'll leave, but I'll have to take Faith with me. You can't stop that. I'm the one who's always around for her. She'd be confused if I left her behind like you do."

"It's not true. None of it. You're twisting everything." She grabbed his arm and hung on. "Let's stop this right now. Please. Oh, please let me hold you. Hold me. Say we can make things work again."

"Don't touch me." Kip gritted his bared teeth and pushed her hard.

Carolee attempted to clutch his sleeve and save

herself, but he was too strong. Staggering back-
ward, she flung out her arms—and slammed into
a wall. She slid to the floor and held her hands
up to her husband. "Please, Kip. I love you so
much."

"Don't beg." He threw the coat at her. "I
hate sniveling, begging females."

In the breathless heat of late afternoon, with
bushes of fragrant sweet peas vying with the
pungent aroma of scorched and brittle grass,
Carolee didn't notice Ivy had returned from
the kitchen until she felt an arm slide around
her shoulders. With her forehead resting on
Carolee's temple, Ivy wiped away her friend's
unknowingly shed tears.

"I guess you missed me," Ivy said. She
groaned and added, "That wasn't funny but
it's the best I've got."

Carolee tried to laugh but succeeded only
in choking. Ivy produced a glass of cold
lemonade and pressed it into her hands.

"What are you going to do?" Ivy asked.

The lemonade cooled Carolee's throat.
"I'm going to find a way to turn the clock back."

"Oh, honey, you know you can't."

She fished a piece of ice from her glass and
rubbed it on the sides of her neck. "I've got
to. It isn't as if Kip met someone else—he'd
just had enough of being taken advantage of,
and of having everything revolve around what
I was doing. Or so he managed to convince
everyone. I have to be patient—not rush any-

thing—but I can do it, I know I can. Even if I do know Kip's enjoying having the upper hand while I pay the piper—literally." She groaned at Ivy. "Sorry. I shouldn't talk like that. It puts you in the middle."

"Forget it." Ivy sat on the edge of the chaise. She raised her own lemonade glass to her mouth and paused. "Ooh, wow, who's *that?*"

The direction of Ivy's fascinated stare was obvious. Coming from his cabin, Sam emerged from the trees with Max Wolfe at his side.

Carolee felt even hotter and hoped she hadn't turned red. "A friend of Sam's," she said offhandedly. "I think they met recently." Darn Sam anyway. She hadn't seen Max again after the disturbing time she'd spent with him more than a week earlier, but he could very well be right about her father trying to make a connection between them. He had called her twice, and been charming, talking about general matters on both occasions. But he'd also repeated the invitation to dinner.

"They don't make a very likely pair," Ivy commented. "I didn't think Sam made new friends."

"You mean you didn't think he had friends at all."

Ivy hadn't taken her eyes away from Max. "I didn't say that, but they don't match. Who is he?"

"I don't know," Carolee said. She couldn't bear telling lies but neither could she stand the prospect of Ivy grilling her about Max.

Ivy took her lemonade to the swing, sat down, and finger-combed her hair.

"You're primping for a man who isn't your husband," Carolee said, but not very seriously. Ivy was a flirt.

"You know what they say about being on a diet," she murmured, evidently keeping her voice low because the object of her interest was strolling in their direction. "Doesn't mean you can't look at the menu."

"*Ivy.*"

Max walked slowly to allow for Sam's arthritic gait. The question was, had Sam invited Max out here, or had Max invited himself? The latter didn't seem likely, but he had made it clear that he was interested in Carolee. And Sam hadn't missed an opportunity to mention the man and how much he liked him.

"He's gorgeous," Ivy murmured. "Is he married?"

"What?" Carolee lowered her voice. "Why would you ask a question like that? I don't know. But you're married, that's all that should matter to you."

"You aren't." Ivy's smug grin meant she was satisfied with having shocked Carolee, and she had shocked her. "Look at that face, those eyes. There's a lot going on inside that beautiful man. And the body. Whew, all that lean, mean power. If I didn't know better, I'd think I was having a hot flash."

"Don't say another word," Carolee warned. "The man's a stranger and I'm not looking for company."

"Afternoon, girls," Sam said. "Just been talking to Max about when those horses get here."

Ivy made an interested sound, but Carolee said nothing. Sam was determined he would follow his plan to bring in the pony for Faith and another horse for Carolee. There were stalls in the barn from when a previous generation of her mother's family used to ride.

The two men arrived at the porch and climbed the steps to stand between Carolee and Ivy.

"Max Wolfe," Sam said. "Meet Ivy Lester. She's an old friend of Carolee's."

Ivy dimpled and looked up at Max from beneath thick lashes. "How d'you do?"

"Fine, thank you." Max shook Ivy's proffered hand. "And I think you're fine, too. Hot day." He gave a smile that shouldn't be wasted on Ivy, who took such memorable events as her due.

"It surely is," Ivy said and gave a perfect example of what it meant for a woman to flutter. She pressed her arms to her sides, touched the side of her neck, and never took her eyes from Max's.

Carolee scowled at Sam. He tipped his baseball cap farther to the back of his head and pulled up two chairs. He sat down but Max indicated he'd rather stand.

Silhouetted against an almost unbearably blue sky, he was every bit as impressive as Ivy suggested.

"Let me get the two of you some lemonade," Ivy said, sliding out of the swing.

Max Wolfe's eyes were dark brown and steady. He showed no sign of having heard Ivy's offer. "Good to see you, Carolee," he said.

She nodded and knew Ivy's legendary curiosity would be on alert.

From Max's unwavering attention, only an unobservant person would fail to notice he behaved as if he and Carolee were the only people present.

Carolee tried not to return his gaze but failed.

He stood with his sneakered feet braced apart and his thumbs hooked into the pockets of his jeans. He was certainly a big man but still there was a lean impression about him. From what she'd seen of him on their first meeting, she'd thought his hair was mid-brown. In fact, it was lighter, sun-bleached in places and cut to brush back. His nose must have been broken at least once but the effect pleased her, and while he didn't have a film-star-quality face, she found it easy to look at.

"Thank you for driving me home that night," he said.

The silence went on too long and Ivy, who hadn't mentioned the lemonade again, would already be drawing conclusions Carolee hated to think about.

Sam, ever the helper, said, "You drove her home first. That would all have been a mess if you hadn't stepped in."

"It was my pleasure," Max said and smiled at Carolee. She smiled and his attention took a rapid trip to her feet and back, but not without the slightest pause at the level of her bare thighs.

She hooked another piece of ice from her glass and applied it first to her temples, then to the sides of her neck again.

"You're getting your blouse wet," Max said, producing a white handkerchief from his back pocket and giving it to her.

Carolee peered down to see drizzles of water slipping into her cleavage. In spots, her white cotton shirt had turned transparent and stuck to her breasts above her bra. She used the handkerchief to do some modest dabbing, and wished she could disappear.

She looked at Max. He watched what she was doing.

Ivy cleared her throat and Carolee saw her friend's lips part.

Carolee didn't dare meet her father's eyes.

"You've got it," Max said and accepted the return of his damp handkerchief. "Except for this." Holding her left shoulder, he made a slow, single downward sweep toward the vee of her collar. He smiled at her again. "The sun will dry out the rest. I'm going to come back on Sunday and exercise the horses for Sam. I hope you'll have time to come to my place afterward—for that dinner I promised you."

Six

"They're coming," Sam said at the other end of the phone line. "Did you decide if you're going out to meet 'em? I say you go out there. Be out there smiling for Faith. Make her real welcome."

Carolee went to hang up, but remembered she hadn't answered Sam. "They aren't due for hours. How do you know they're coming now?"

"I was putting up a new birdhouse. I could see the road."

"Not without binoculars." Nothing mattered but making sure she did everything perfectly from the moment Faith arrived. "Unless you can still shimmy up a tall tree. You were on the roof, weren't you? That's it. Climbing on the roof like a daredevil kid. Did you call Max and tell him not to come tomorrow?"

"No—just forget about that, will ya? And what the Sam Hill does it matter how I saw 'em? Get out there or it'll be too late." Sam was the first to hang up.

Kip had brought Faith early. Carolee glanced around the lower floor. Everything was ready and she'd prepared Faith's room days ago.

The kitchen smelled of freshly baked apple pie, well laced with cinnamon. That was a good homey smell and apple was Faith's favorite. Carolee walked jerkily onto the porch and down the steps. She heard the engine of the

Porsche moments before she saw the car surge along the gravel track from the road.

She waved, and smiled, and couldn't understand why she felt like crying at the same time.

Kip swung his car to face up the drive, and came to a stop.

Up the drive so he could get away quickly.

The driver's door opened and he got out. From behind his seat he pulled a big plastic bag. Faith's sandy curls came into view on the passenger side.

"Hi," Carolee said, waving again. "What a day. The weather must have known how special it ought to be."

Kip turned to her. He held his bottom lip between his teeth and looked unhappy. Silently, he unloaded a duffel bag, a suitcase, and a cardboard box. He didn't want to be parted from Faith for a month, that was it. How would he feel if he only got to see her as much as Carolee did? There was no point in making comparisons between their situations.

Her heart thumped. She placed a hand on her ribs and felt the beat. Faith slammed the car door and went to her father. She clung to his arm but Kip murmured something and she let go. He gave her the box and carried the rest of her luggage himself.

It will be okay. "Hi, you two." She knew she sounded artificially cheerful. "Kip, say you'll stay and have hot apple pie with Faith and me."

"Not this time," he said as if he'd already anticipated an invitation and rehearsed his refusal. To Faith he said, "Don't forget to watch what you eat. We don't want to waste all of Mrs. Jolly's efforts."

Faith nodded. Mrs. Jolly was the housekeeper Kip had hired since making Seattle a permanent home. Surely he couldn't be talking about having Faith on some sort of diet. This wasn't the time to ask.

"Let me take that," Carolee said, relieving Faith of the surprisingly heavy box. Impulsively, she set it down on the gravel and hugged Faith. She buried her face in soft curls. "You smell wonderful. I'm so excited you're here. I told your Gramps he has to wait before he tries to get you to himself. My turn first. He'll be pacing though. He can hardly wait to see you."

Faith's hands rested at Carolee's waist. "I miss Gramps, too," she said.

"I'll take all this to Faith's room," Kip called and Carolee looked up to see him open the screen door.

"We'd better go in," she said. "Do I get a kiss first?"

Her daughter's gray eyes looked into hers. Faith returned Carolee's hug and accepted a kiss. Then she spun away and ran after her father.

He had brought Faith and would leave her for four weeks. This was a happy day and the first of many more...before they returned to the abbreviated visits on one weekend a month.

Carolee picked up the box and went back

into the house in time to see Kip run downstairs and meet Faith at the bottom.

"You've made this place really nice," he said.

"Thanks." Although Lake Home had once been as familiar to Kip as it was to Carolee, in the months since she'd moved there from New York to be close to Faith, he hadn't entered the house until today. He preferred to honk the car horn, drop Faith, and drive away.

He started a circuit of the kitchen. "It was a great idea to get rid of all the little rooms down here. And bathrooms off both bedrooms are a natural. There was always plenty of space up there."

She got the familiar warm and happy feeling his little compliments used to bring. "I think the new bathrooms are my favorites."

He smiled at her, the old conspiratorial smile. "You always were a bathroom junky."

Their eyes met. She didn't recall his smiling at her since she'd left on that last tour. He seemed to try to see inside her. She smiled back. They had so much good, shared past. In time, if they were open to the idea, perhaps they could forget the wretched things that had been said during the divorce, and be friends again.

"Daddy?"

Kip turned his attention to Faith and the moment was over.

"Daddy, I forgot to close the door to my room. Would you tell Mrs. Jolly the cleaners don't need to go in there while I'm gone?"

"If I remember. It's not a big deal, kiddo."

Carolee stopped herself from saying, *"It is if Faith thinks it is."* She didn't have the right to question the way Kip brought up their daughter.

"I'd better hit the road," he said. He kissed Faith and she hung on his neck. "Don't forget your mother has her own life to live. You're a big girl now. It's time you stood on your own feet. You mustn't be a nuisance while you're here." Kip straightened, breaking her hold.

"She couldn't be a nuisance," Carolee said. She didn't care if Kip did object to her comment.

Faith probably hadn't heard the reassurance anyway. She followed her father out onto the porch. Carolee joined them.

Kip said, "Bye," and headed for the Porsche. Every move he made was familiar. He flexed his shoulders and put his hand into the pocket where he kept his keys. He wouldn't take them out until he reached the car.

Faith went to one end of the porch, to the railing, and leaned out. "Bye, Daddy. Love you."

The key to the Porsche was in Kip's hand and the lock released with a sharp click.

Faith's tone rose. "Bye, Daddy."

Kip slid behind the wheel and started the engine. He drove away without ever looking back.

Damn you. Carolee put her hands on Faith's shoulders. It would be so easy to say nothing and let her child come to negative conclusions about her father's behavior, and it would be so wrong. "Your Dad didn't want you to see how sad he is. He was probably afraid he'd cry if he didn't leave quickly."

"He brought me way early." Faith's voice was steady, too steady. She turned around and said, "Is it okay if I get settled in my room?" Her eyes were downcast, her mouth set in a straight line.

Carolee nodded. "Of course. Then we could go over and see your Gramps." She'd barely said the word when she saw her father approaching. "Hey, there he is. I should have known he wouldn't be able to stay away." In truth she was glad to see him. Kip had managed to leave a sour note behind and she didn't think it was an accident. Sam's gruff love for Faith would lighten things up.

"Hey, girlie," he hollered, speeding up his stiff walk. "About time you were here. Whatever your Mom says about me, don't you believe it."

Faith smiled, then grinned, and the dimples near the corners of her mouth appeared. She ran from the porch and across the track and the rough grass to meet her grandfather.

Once again Carolee's throat clogged. When Faith reached him, Sam caught her up and swung her around without so much as a stumble. Their laughter traveled on the warm breeze. When Faith's feet were on the grass again, Sam put his head close to hers and they hugged.

So simple and so right. There was room in a child's life for as much love as a family could give, all members of a family.

Finally the two-person reunion faced Carolee and came her way, the old man's gnarled hand wrapped around the girl's soft, much smaller one.

"Hey, hey, hey," Sam said when they drew close. He raised his face and sniffed. "Nah, can't be. Could be, though. What's your favorite pie, girlie? Give you a hint. It's my favorite, too."

Faith said, "Apple?" as if she hadn't already known. The two of them played similar games each time Faith came.

"Grab that pie and follow us," Sam told Carolee. "We've got business that won't wait."

"What?" Faith said. "Tell me what?"

"Nope. It'll be a better surprise when we get there. You gonna get that pie, daughter?"

Carolee threw up her hands and hurried to bring one of two pies from the kitchen. Sam and Faith were already on their way to the cabin. Carolee followed as fast as was safe for the well-being of the juicy pie.

The walk through tall pines, firs and cedars interspersed with alder, birch, and the occasional strapping oak, was short, but she loved what she and Linda used to call, "the forest," and the entire property her mother had left her. She wished her mom could be there today. Although Ella Davis had met Kip, and registered her disapproval of so early a marriage, she hadn't lived to see Faith. It was from Carolee's mother that Faith got her profusion of curls. Until the day she died, Mom had worn her hair in much the same style Faith wore now, only Mom's corkscrew ringlets had turned to soft gray with white streaks, particularly at the hairline.

A picture, more an impression, came fleetingly to Carolee. Firelight in a dark room. A man and woman on a couch—laughing, and not knowing she was there. She had heard the laughter in her mind many times and never allowed herself to concentrate on what it meant.

Sam and Faith broke free of the trees and Carolee was close behind them. Framed by firs, the mix-and-don't-match cabin that was Sam's home stood on a rise in the middle of a soft green field. The original building had been one room down, and a loft with an open balcony upstairs. At that time there hadn't even been indoor plumbing. Pieces had been built on, in part by Sam, who wasn't a builder. And he believed in "using stuff up." Horizontal siding covered the oldest parts of the small building. A bathroom added on one side had been made of logs split in half, stripped, and treated. Pushed out from the other side was a larger addition, this of vertical bits and pieces of lumber, and with a tin roof. Sam insisted he liked hearing the rain up there, even though cedar shingles coated with fir needles and moss covered the other roofs.

Warm it might be, but a stream of wood smoke curled from the rock-covered chimney.

Faith skipped now. She had always been in love with Sam's homey cabin.

Taking Carolee by surprise, grandfather

and granddaughter veered away from the cabin and went left, in the direction of the old barn with its ramshackle paddock at the back. Carolee halted for a moment and frowned. That Sam was a manipulator. He knew Faith was an animal lover. He intended to make big points by showing her the horses he'd moved in the previous day while Carolee was out shopping. So far she'd refused to go see them—and she'd begged Sam to send them back because she was worried about her own ability to keep Faith safe on horseback. Sam had the gall to point out that Max Wolfe would be along to help out, and had absolutely rejected any suggestion that he should not encourage Max to visit Lake Home again.

She entered the open door to the cabin and stopped in her tracks. Along the sagging, brown tweed couch Sam would not give up sat a row of well-used stuffed animals. They'd been Carolee's and Linda's when they were girls. Sam had kept them hidden away until Faith was a baby, when he'd set about making sure she fell for them. At one end of the couch was a folded woolen blanket, rose colored with bleach spots and a threadbare satin binding. Sam bought the blanket when Faith was born, then kept it with him so she would associate it with her Gramps.

The fire in the woodstove crackled cozily and didn't overheat the room, where the couch and several overstuffed chairs made for a comfortable sitting room at one side, while an oak table and four mismatched chairs filled up a smaller space to the right. A door on the same wall as the woodstove led to the bathroom. Dutch doors on the rightmost wall stood open to show off the shiny little kitchen in which Sam took pride. Stairs rose from the very center of the room to the loft above where colorful quilts were draped over the balcony railings. The old cabin had come a long way.

Aware of deliberately giving Sam and Faith more time together, Carolee set off again without hurrying. She wasn't going to allow Sam to press either her or Faith into the saddle today. He'd say they were both in jeans and sneakers and could manage perfectly well. Carolee wouldn't consider allowing Faith to ride without a helmet and appropriate gear.

The doors to the barn were on runners and had been slid wide. From inside came the clear nickering of horses.

There was the awful issue of Max, who was supposed to come tomorrow, ostensibly to exercise the animals. Carolee paused, listening to Faith's excited voice and wondering how to convince Sam to stop the man from visiting. Ivy had called at least once a day since the debacle when Carolee had pretended she didn't know Max, only to have him make it more than clear that they had met before. Ivy was incredibly impressed with him and had already decided he was Carolee's great hope for the future. Ivy's suggestions annoyed Carolee and made her nervous.

"He's beautiful." Faith's voice was raised. "Look at his color. He's all sandy, like me."

"Nice little pony. Good personality, too. But watch out for his teeth when you give him treats. Name's Star on account of the little white burst between his eyes. You'll have to help me look after these critters. Can't do it all myself."

Carolee strolled into the barn. She smelled wood chips and oats, hard earth and a lifetime or so of dust packed into every cranny. Hay and bags of feed were stacked almost to the roof. Two wooden bins, one holding carrots, one apples, stood beside a bench, and Sam had cut some apples and carrots into chunks and put them on a metal plate. Faith held the palm of a hand under Star's nose to offer him some pieces of apple. The pony drew back his lips and snuffled up the goodies in a quite gentlemanly fashion. One moist brown eye was fixed on Faith.

It was then that Carolee noticed not one, but two more horses, one of them very large, very black, and quite fierce-looking.

"You can't judge a horse by its exterior," Sam said. Evidently he'd been watching her. "This is a big, impressive guy but he's very manageable. His owners are away and they're glad he's getting out of the boarding stables for a few weeks. And this little lady"—he scratched between the ears of a chestnut mare—"well, she's a love. She's for you and I think you'll get along great. But Max'll be here tomorrow to get you both going."

The black was for Max...

73

Carolee narrowed her eyes and shook her head, doing her best to shoot a negative reaction at Sam without telegraphing concern to Faith.

"Who's Max?" Faith said, and Carolee almost groaned aloud.

"Good friend of mine," Sam said easily. "And a good man. He used to be a pro-football player but he got injured. Now he works with a high school football team and has a software company in Seattle. He lives in Kirkland so he's almost a neighbor."

"Oh." Faith's attention returned to the horses. "I guess he'll ride the big horse. That one would scare me. Can we ride today, Mom?"

Later she'd have a talk with Sam about this interference—it was backfiring. "Not today, sweetie. I thought we'd take it easy. Spend some time with your Gramps so he can eat all of our pie, then get you properly settled."

"And I'm inviting you to soup. Good stuff tonight."

She didn't like to disappoint him but she must make him understand that she needed the next hours to be alone with Faith. "Could we come to dinner tomorrow instead? Or are you busy?"

His smile puzzled her, but he said, "Tomorrow's fine, right, Faith?"

"Yes, fine. D'you still make gooseberry fool?"

"You can just bet I do," Sam said, obviously pleased that one of his dishes was a hit with Faith. "And you shall have it soon. I do have

74

to take you up to my place now so you can visit Taffy. She's one old cat, but she's still enjoying life. That means she sleeps most of the time—when she's not eating. She'll be offended if you don't pay your respects."

"Yes, please," Faith said and left the barn with a longing backward gaze.

Carolee gave the animals a last, apprehensive stare, and followed.

Taffy liked to sleep on her back with all four legs splayed. She was Taffy because she had coffee-colored fur randomly striped and swirled with white and brown. She weighed twenty pounds, and in her current position, her stomach overflowed the sides of her down-filled bed.

"How about some of that pie before you go?" Sam said.

Carolee shook her head. "I think we'd better get back." She wanted to talk with Faith. "I've got another pie over there, so you enjoy this one. I baked it for you anyway."

Sam patted her arm. There was understanding in his eyes. Faith was on her knees beside Taffy, who purred loudly while her tummy was rubbed.

"Well," Sam said, "there is one other small matter to attend to before the two of you take off. I couldn't have my favorite girl come for her special visit and not have a thing to give her."

Carolee frowned at him. She'd been very clear in the warning that it wasn't wise to overdo gifts.

Expectation shone in Faith's expression. She picked up her old pink blanket and a stuffed polar bear and hugged them.

"Sit right down there," Sam said, indicating the couch.

Faith sat among the animals she'd played with all her life and looked just as Carolee hoped she would look while she was here—happy and comfortable.

Sam climbed the stairs slowly, and by the time he returned, Carolee's imagination had dreamed up some scary possibilities for a gift he might have decided was just the thing. A scratching sound from inside the box he carried didn't comfort her.

She sat in the chair closest to the couch and warned herself that she must be sensible about whatever came.

"Close your eyes," Sam told Faith in a whisper. "No peeking."

Faith did as she was told and sat with her hands folded in her lap.

Gently, Sam lowered the box onto her knees but kept a hand on top to steady it. "Okay, now you can open it."

Faith paled beneath her freckles. Excitement had a way of making her do that. She started to shake the box but Sam said, "Uh-uh. Not a good idea. Open it up."

Gingerly Faith parted the flaps and peered inside. "Oh...oh, Gramps. Oh, Gramps."

"That all you've got to say?" His smile was huge and his eyes glittered. "Aren't you going to let the rest of us see?"

Faith stood up and put the rocking box on the couch. She made crooning noises and delved inside with both hands. And out she pulled a black dog. All coltish legs and wagging tail, his tongue had enormous range. On the small side for the length of those legs, his coat glistened like that of a wet seal in sunlight and his body wiggled all over.

Even as Carolee enjoyed the picture made by the child and the dog, her mind raced in search of how she would deal with this latest poor choice made by her well-meaning father. Then she met his eyes again and read a message there. He was warning her not to do or say anything to spoil what Faith was feeling. And he was right. But there would be hard times ahead because of this.

"He's crated," Sam said. "Know what that means?"

Faith shook her head and pressed her face into the dog's coat.

"I've got it upstairs. They told me it's the best way to make sure a dog's happy and everyone likes having him around. You put him in there when you go out and you're not taking him. This fella's housebroken, but you can keep a dog in there at night till it's properly trained. They feel safe, like no one can get at them. This one's already used to his. Good for the car on long trips, too. He's about eight months but he hasn't had a steady home before. Got him from the pound. That's where I got Taffy. They get good critters there."

"That's terrific," Carolee said. "I think we should leave him here tonight and get started with him tomorrow."

"Please, Mom," Faith said at once. "He's mine now and we need to be together. See, he likes me."

The dog still stood on the couch, but he leaned on Faith and looked up into her face.

"Let's put this on," Sam told Faith, and snapped a red leather leash to the dog's collar. "Keep a good hold on him. He's stronger than he looks."

"What's his name?" Carolee asked.

"That's for Faith to decide. First she'll have to get a feel for him. Take him outside while I get the crate."

Carolee didn't go outside with Faith. Instead she waited for Sam to return with a blue plastic crate and said, "Sam, that wasn't smart. They live in a penthouse apartment in Seattle. What are they supposed to do with an energetic dog, or any dog when there's usually nobody at home?"

"Except the housekeeper and all those other people who look after the place." Sam showed no sign of feeling chastised. "This isn't heavy. Make sure the door's closed right when the dog's inside. I'll let the two of you walk back without me. It'd be easy for me to hang around all the time but I know better than that."

"Thanks. But you aren't off the hook. You've got plans for Max Wolfe, haven't you—other than having him ride those horses and help Faith?"

Sam rubbed the back of his neck. "Time you learned not to second-guess everyone. You sure as hell don't like it if I pry."

"You pry anyway. Answer the question, please."

"Okay, I'll be honest. I think it's time you were around people your own age."

"I'll be right out, Faith," Carolee called. She lowered her voice, "People? Or men? Don't say anything else. I know the answer and it won't work. If you were really thinking, you'd figure out I can't afford to be seen around another man. Especially now—with Faith here. How would that look?"

"Darn it, you're a free woman and—"

"Faith's been out there too long." She picked up the awkward crate. "Bye, Sam."

He didn't answer, but when she glanced back just before she and Faith entered the trees, her father stood in the doorway to the cabin.

Seven

Most days Max had breakfast at Nellie and Fritz Archer's diner in downtown Kirkland. On Sundays, he usually made it brunch, and came in late enough to avoid the after-early-services rush, but on this Sunday he'd arrived before eight. Sleep deprived, unshaven, and on the hunt for serious caffeine, he'd commandeered a booth by the windows.

Fritz spent most of his time in the kitchen dreaming up "specials," some of which were special enough never to make another appearance on the menu. He was a small man with dark, wiry hair brushed back into a helmet that looked like a toupee but wasn't. Max assumed Nellie—who ruled over the dining room—must have commented on his early arrival and on his morose countenance, because Fritz had left the kitchen to his three wise-cracking daughters and joined him.

"You want something to eat now?" Nellie asked Max, hovering, her hands on skinny hips. "How about eggs Benedict?"

"This isn't the place to come for eggs Benedict," he said. "Mostly because you don't make them."

"We'd make them for you." What Nellie lacked to the south, she more than made up for to the north. Good thing since she needed solid support for her many strands of tiny clicking Niihau shells.

"Eggs Benedict's sissy food," Fritz said. "Get the man a steak. Don't he look like a steak man to you? Steak and eggs. Hash browns. Tell Donita he wants 'em brown but not black. Side of fruit—just to pretend he's being healthy. Toast. He don't want no juice—"

"Hey," Max interrupted. "You know I never eat that stuff for breakfast."

" 'Cept on Sundays—when you make a religion of being late—you ain't never in here

80

long enough for breakfast at breakfast time, that's why. Hi, Billy," Fritz shouted to the latest of a scatter of customers. "Sit down wherever you want. It'll be right out. Nellie, get the man his coffee."

In turn, Nellie motioned to a waitress and said, "Coffee for Billy when he perches."

"Put in Max's order," Fritz told his blond wife. "Can't you see he needs serious food?"

Nellie patted Max's shoulder and said, "Coming right up," before she made for the kitchen.

"I guess it wouldn't do any good to repeat that I don't eat big meals in the morning."

"No." Fritz had brought his own mug of coffee with him. "You and me have known each other for a piece. I ain't seen you look this down in a long time. I got a good ear. You want to talk? I'll listen."

Max didn't want to tell a kindhearted man to back off. He eyed the green decor. Avocado green plastic-covered benches in booths where an artful scatter of coins was embedded in a thick, clear coating over Formica table tops—also green. "I like your place," he said, and meant it. "There aren't enough family-owned businesses left. All these chains and franchises lose something. Heart, I guess." A faint pall of bacon-scented steam wafting from the kitchen pass-through was nose-wrinkling good.

Fritz sucked noisily on his coffee and wrapped his worn hands around the mug.

"I came here the first morning after I moved

into my condo. It felt right and it's felt right ever since. Are you ever going to retire?"

Fritz shrugged. "Nah. What else would I do—die? All I know is cooking. Nellie and me, we're a team. And the daughters. Too bad they all married such tight-asses. Not a sense of humor between 'em. Pencil pushers."

"One of those pencil pushers is my company attorney, and he's a very talented guy. And from what I know, you've got two other sons-in-law—"

"Yeah, yeah. I got brilliant sons-in-law. If they're so brilliant why don't one of them want to take over a good business like this one day? Tell me that."

Max managed to say, "You've got a point," without laughing. Fritz would never understand why any man wouldn't want to run a diner and work twenty out of every twenty-four hours. Max could see the sad side of a man who had built a solid little business but who thought that because he had no sons, he had no one to pass it on to. It probably wouldn't be a good idea to suggest that the daughters obviously loved the place and would do a good job running it. Fritz was an old-fashioned man.

"You know Sam Davis?" Fritz asked.

Max hesitated with his mug halfway to his mouth. "Why would you ask me that?"

"He mentioned you is all." Fritz's eyebrows went up, and so did his shoulders. "Comes in a lot of afternoons. Has for years. Last time he was here your name came up."

"Uh-huh." Eggs weren't the only things cooking around the diner. "Why would my name come up?"

"Can't remember. Just something in passing."

Fritz and Sam had talked about Max, and right about now Fritz was wishing he hadn't allowed his curiosity to take him on a fishing trip this morning.

The bell over the door rang again.

"The place is getting busier," Max said. No point in having the man keep on squirming. "Thanks for the company, but you don't have to babysit me. I'm okay, Fritz."

"Max Wolfe." Brandy Snopes arrived at his table and leaned down to kiss him. "What are you doing in here so early on a Sunday? God, you look awful."

Fritz slid from the bench, taking his coffee with him. "I'll check on that steak," he said and Max noted that the man's thin cheeks flushed.

"Did you hear what I said?" Brandy took Fritz's seat. "You look like hell."

"Thanks. I heard you the first time."

"Don't get snippy with me. What's wrong? Tell me right now."

Brandy's curly auburn hair was gathered into a band at her crown and didn't look as if it had been brushed. It definitely hadn't been brushed. Red pillow creases lined one cheek. She wore mascara but no lipstick or other makeup, and her gray sweatsuit looked as if it had been pulled out of a laundry hamper.

"What are you doing here so early on

Sunday, Brandy? After the big Saturday night bash? You're the one who sleeps till Sunday afternoon because she needs to recover."

"Sometimes I wake up early and I've got too much energy going to loaf around." She yawned, and glared when Max snickered.

"Nellie called you," he said bluntly. "She told you I didn't look so hot."

"Whatever."

Whatever was Brandy's catchall word when she didn't know how to get out of a corner. He was getting an unnerving picture of her hob-nobbing about him with Fritz and Sam Davis. This was a small area. It made sense that everyone knew everyone—especially the long-timers.

"You haven't been to my place since Carolee played the last time."

"Haven't I?" Max frowned. Of course she was right but he couldn't tell her he didn't want to be at her place if Carolee wasn't there.

"You know you haven't." Brandy ordered orange juice and a piece of dry wheat toast from the waitress, who brought Max a platter of food so huge, it could feed four—at least. "Oh, I see. That mass of food explains everything. You're a hungry boy."

"I'm not hungry. This is your friends' prescription for dealing with an unshaven face. I didn't get a choice. But it looks good."

She sat sideways on the bench, leaned against a narrow strip of wall beside the window, and pulled up her knees. "Have you seen her since that night?"

Max cut a piece of steak, put it in his mouth, and chewed. A guy couldn't be expected to chew meat and talk at the same time.

"You have." She made patterns on the sweating outside of a water glass. "Some men lie so well. You don't."

He swallowed. "Who's lying?"

"Maybe not lying, just avoiding. She's not available."

"Why? She isn't married anymore."

Brandy caught an ice cube between her teeth and moved it around in her mouth. "There's a lot I don't know. Carolee's a private person. But she's got a heavy load and the last thing she'd be interested in is another man. Anyway, you're not her type." The ice made a squarish bump inside her cheek. "I do know something awful happened when she was a kid and she's never gotten over it completely. Don't ask me what it was. All I know is it was something to do with her mother. Best stay out of her life."

Max buttered a piece of toast. Another flawless day was tuning up outside. He took a bite of bread and watched people pass on the sidewalk. Despite the hour, shorts and sleeveless tank tops were already in evidence. Fritz and Nellie's Irish terrier stretched his red body out in the sun and ignored those who stooped to stroke him.

"Max?"

"I'm thinking," he told Brandy without looking at her. "Why do so many people think they've got the right to tell someone what to do? What they can and can't do, and why? Maybe it would be better for some if they spent less time gossiping about others."

"Well, *excuse* me. I know when I've been told off. I'm a friend and I care about you is all."

His coffee wasn't hot but he drank some of it anyway. "Why aren't I Carolee's type?" Damn, he hadn't wanted to show he was that interested.

"Because you aren't. Her ex is her type. Artsy. Oh, he's very good-looking and built, but he's a *painter.*"

"And I'm a businessman. So what?"

"You're an ex–wide receiver. You look like a wide receiver. You're an athlete. You still coach football."

He looked at his plate. "I mentor high school football players. Don't get me wrong, I enjoy it. Most of all I enjoy the kids. But it's a very different kind of ball."

She reached across the table and placed a hand on his. "You're great. I've told you that from the night we met. You were an angry man then. Maybe you're still angry. The difference is you've stopped showing it, or allowing it to mess up your life."

"Yeah. Thanks. Why wouldn't a woman who used to love a painter..." He shook his head and attacked the hash browns. His tongue wasn't usually this loose.

"Why wouldn't she be able to love a businessman instead?" Brandy didn't quite manage to sound detached.

"That isn't what I was going to say. I meant,

why can't a person be attracted to more than one type? The answer doesn't matter."

Juice and toast were set before Brandy, who immediately stuck a knife in Max's butter and loaded up. "Have you seen her?"

He really didn't lie well. "I drove her and Sam back to their place after that show. Sam was having trouble keeping the truck running."

"That was nice of you." Brandy did sarcasm very well.

"They thought so. I'm a nice guy."

"And after that?"

"You don't give up." But Brandy was a good sport. He knew she would have liked them to continue as an item, but she hadn't let their difference of opinion on the subject get in the way of a friendship.

She turned her face toward him and finished the piece of toast. Rather than use a napkin, she sucked melted butter from her fingers. She was unconsciously earthy, voluptuous.

"Did I tell you Rob Mead's coming out for a few days next week?"

Her spine straightened, but she held on to the nonchalant tone when she said, "Really? Nice guy. Tough thing the way you two got dragged into such an impossible position."

"We're great friends. Always will be. What happened wasn't Rob's fault. He just happened to be the obvious choice to take over my spot on the team."

She didn't look convinced and studied her fingernails closely.

"When are you going to make some lucky guy happy, Brandy?"

Rolling her eyes, she drank the rest of his cool coffee. "With the exception of you, I've only had boring affairs, thank you."

"If that was a compliment, thanks. I was talking about marriage."

She held up both forefingers in a cross and said, "Watch your mouth. If the affairs were boring, how do you think a marriage would be?"

"Okay, Ms. Cynic. I'll just sit back and watch till some guy sweeps you away." Since he'd first introduced Rob Mead to Brandy, he'd wondered if they might get together. Rob had certainly shown more than casual interest. "Sorry, but I'm going to have to love you and leave you now." He signaled to the waitress.

"Have you met Faith yet?" Brandy asked.

He was perplexed and shook his head.

"Faith Burns. Carolee's daughter."

The child, Carolee's child, didn't seem real to him. "No, why would I?"

"You could have." Innocence didn't suit Brandy's face. "If you saw them yesterday. Faith's here for her summer visit. She arrived yesterday. Carolee hasn't talked about anything else for weeks."

Max squinted against the light and bought time to think.

"This is the first long visit since the divorce. It's four weeks," Brandy said. "The divorce was more than a year ago. Whenever they're not together, Carolee's in a kind of mourning for that child."

"Never having been a parent, I'm not an expert on things like that."

Brandy put her feet on the floor and sat upright. "You don't have to be a parent to understand how it would feel to have someone you love a lot taken away."

He didn't say he wasn't sure he'd ever loved anyone that much. Maybe he had, but he just didn't realize it because he'd grown up on a barely surviving farm where his mother had been too busy to show much affection, and his father didn't know how—unless it was through brooding silence.

Max smiled at Brandy. "You're really something. I should tell you that frequently. Thanks for dragging yourself out of bed on my account."

"Any time." She grinned. "Of course, it would be easier if you just joined me."

"You know how to tempt a man." He slid out of the booth and this time he was the one to offer a kiss. She accepted it with enthusiasm and Max walked out into the sunlight.

Sam hadn't said the child was coming to Lake Home this weekend. He'd been insistent about Max working with the horses, that's all. And Max was still daring to hope Carolee would have dinner with him afterward. Obviously that wouldn't happen if her little girl was with her.

He bought a newspaper from a vending machine and stood at a curb waiting for the lights to change.

Sam did have an agenda and it wasn't hidden. He liked Max and had decided he'd

89

be good for his daughter. Max had a vivid rec-
ollection of water running down Carolee's
pale throat and disappearing between her
breasts. She'd been embarrassed to have him
see how her damp blouse turned transparent
and stuck to her skin.

The fleeting contact with her skin was a
memory that didn't help him feel peaceful.

He crossed the street. This fixation he'd
developed wasn't going to accomplish a thing.
She hadn't made a single move in his direction. Not that he could imagine her making
a move in any man's direction. She was the
reserved kind of woman who would need digging out of her shell.

Forcing himself on women wasn't his thing.

His condo on Central Avenue was in sight.
Several floors up, the flowers in planters on
his terrace pushed their many-colored heads
through the railings. A family could live there.
The place was big.

Another light changed and he crossed again.
Brandy had told him, more than once, that he
only wanted what he couldn't have. He'd
better take notice and do something about
that—and apply it to what he really felt for Carolee.

She wouldn't want him around her place at
all today. When he got home, he'd call and reassure her he wouldn't intrude.

Eight

Faith and her new sidekick played at the edge of the lake. The bonding had been instant and already the leash was discarded. The previous night, their first night together, Faith had told Carolee how tired she was, and gone upstairs without dinner. The dog had gone with her, and later, when Carolee peeked into the bedroom, the dog was curled at Faith's feet on the bed.

So much for crates. But there had been no accidents and the two young ones looked as if they'd been together all their lives. Kip wouldn't be pleased, but that problem would have to wait.

Faith threw a stick into the water. Without hesitation, the dog swam after it and carried it back with the assurance of any lake dog.

Carolee sat on the crumbling wooden bench she needed to replace and watched. She'd been disappointed that Faith hadn't wanted to talk the night before. In her own bed she'd remained awake for a long time while she worried about making sure her child was happy. If Faith told Kip she didn't like being away from him for a month at a time, what would happen? Faith wouldn't do that. She was a preteen with a preteen's muddled thoughts and feelings, and the situation was still new. Any girl in Faith's position would be confused.

Sam was expecting them to help with the horses. She sighed but couldn't feel angry. He was having a great time being Faith's on-duty Gramps for more than a day and a couple of nights and he'd held out the white flag by agreeing to let Max Wolfe know Faith wouldn't be able to start riding until all of her gear was ready.

The dog rushed to Carolee and shook himself, spraying her with water. As if he knew he'd been a nuisance, he pressed his stick against her shins. The peace offering made wet black lines on her jeans.

Faith arrived and said, "Come here, Digger." The dog looked uncertain, but went to lean against her. Faith avoided looking at Carolee and the awkwardness was so obvious, it hurt.

"Digger?" Carolee said. "Cute name. I knew you'd come up with something good."

"It suits him," Faith said shortly. To protect her nose from the sun, she wore a coating of yellow zinc almost the same color as her tank top and shorts. "We said we'd help Gramps with the horses after lunch. Lunch was a long time ago. I can hardly wait till I start riding."

Carolee wished she felt excited. And she wished Faith didn't sound snippy each time they were together. She got up and clapped her hands at Digger, who ran back and forth between the two of them, madly happy. "Nothing I like better than mucking out horses on a Sunday afternoon—a *warm* Sunday afternoon."

"I don't need you to help," Faith said, and Carolee came close to telling the girl she was out of line.

With Digger scampering around her feet, Faith went ahead of Carolee up the sloping trail from the lake. She turned around and walked backward. "Will we be able to take the row-boat out?" she asked. Her legs were strong and the muscles in her thighs flexed with each step. Sunlight shone through her hair, lighted spots of red that definitely clashed with the yellow nose.

"Of course we can take the boat out." She'd have to make sure Faith wore a life vest. "Gramps uses it and it's kept in good shape."

"I like going out in Dad's boat, but there are always other people there."

Carolee digested the information. "I didn't know your father had a boat." Faith would probably enjoy Kip's boat more if just the two of them were along.

"He got it last winter. It's good for parties when he has art people in from New York and stuff. He calls it a floating gallery 'cause there's paintings everywhere and they're for sale."

"You never mentioned it before."

"Didn't I?"

"You'd better turn around before you trip backward," Carolee said. "Or wear out your legs."

Faith did turn, and Carolee was grateful not to be observed too closely. Kip had bought a boat big enough for parties? She hadn't even known he liked being on the water. He'd never been in the rowboat here at Lake Home.

What did that kind of thing cost? "How big is your Dad's boat?" She shouldn't be grilling Faith.

"I don't know. Ask him. He doesn't like me to talk about our personal stuff but I forgot."

Once more Carolee felt as if she'd been slapped. Her own child was pushing her away.

But the boat was a surprise. Perhaps Kip was finally selling some of his paintings and making a lot of money.

Once at the top of the path, Faith and Digger raced away from the house and toward the trees. Faith kept the wildly energetic dog running after sticks, which he often took out of sight before returning with an empty mouth.

The house was beautiful in the sun. Windows reflected bursts of light, and stone facings turned almost white. Bees swarmed over the elegant lavender-colored blossoms on the wisteria that draped the porch. This could be a happy place, a perfect place for a family to live a simple life. That was all Carolee wanted, a simple family life. No, not quite true. She did still want, and would always want, her music. And she'd like people to believe she was a good mother, and to stop being critical of her. She was a single mother who wanted to provide for her child and to be with her. Depriving Kip of their daughter wasn't her aim, but he was using her and no mother could stand that.

By the time she emerged from the other

side of the path through the woods, Faith and her lissome companion were gamboling toward the barn. Carolee frowned when she saw Star, the blond pony, trotting around the paddock at the back of the barn. Posts sagged at points in that paddock, and cross-members had fallen away.

Sam came from inside the barn carrying a bucket. He'd traded his baseball cap for a favorite straw Stetson. He walked with more difficulty than Carolee ever remembered seeing. The pang of worry she felt expanded her lungs uncomfortably. She must go easy on him, humor him. And he must not overdo just because he wanted so desperately to show Faith a good time.

A flash of movement caught her eye. The big black came over the rise where Sam's cabin stood. There was no doubt, even at a distance, that it was Max Wolfe who rode him.

Anger replaced panic, but not for long. Carolee felt so nervous she wanted to grab Faith and flee. Sam hadn't kept his word. She stood and watched the rider approach. His seat was relaxed and he handled the animal with confidence. Max liked being on horseback.

Carolee knew the moment when he saw her. He cocked his head to one side and looked in her direction from beneath the wide brim of a black hat. He waved. And Carolee waved back. He drew closer, and the pleasure in his smile at seeing her was so genuine, she smiled too.

He made a wonderful, masculine picture on

the horse, and when he drew up beside her and bent to pat the animal, the faint gleam of sweat on Max's neck and on the hair that showed at the open neck of his denim shirt only added to the all-man impression. Even his scuffed, brown boots appealed to her.

And she was slipping back into sophomoric daydreaming. He was just a man and most men looked good in a Stetson, with a film of healthy sweat on their bodies and a big, powerful horse between their thighs.

Max had particularly fine thighs...

"Afternoon, Carolee," he said. "I haven't had this much fun in a long time. I'm grateful to Sam for letting me come and work with the horses."

He had a low, pleasant voice and a kind of boyish charm. He could probably turn on that charm at a moment's notice. No doubt he had bands of women ready to fall at his feet.

Well, Carolee Burns didn't fall at men's feet, and she wasn't the type who appealed to men's more base instincts. In other words, Max was just being nice because he liked Sam.

"I'll follow you over," she said. "That's Faith up ahead. My daughter. The dog is called Digger. Sam gave him to her last night. Now all I have to do is figure out what to do when they have to return to a condo in Seattle."

"What's the big deal? Dogs do just fine in condos."

"I'm sure they do." She let the topic drop.

Max slipped from the horse's back and

offered Carolee a hand. "You ride him in. I'll walk with you."

Her stomach made a roll. "No, thank you. He's just getting used to you. We wouldn't want to confuse him."

"Confuse him?" From the way Max rolled in his lips, Carolee figured he was trying not to laugh. "This fella's used to lots of different riders. Come on, up with you."

Her choices were to scare herself half to death, or feel foolish. She decided being scared was the lesser of the evils. She looked at the reins Max held, then at the animal's back above the level of her head. There wasn't time for more decision making about how she would climb into the saddle. Max's hands closed around her waist and he hoisted her up before handing over the reins.

This was how she got herself into trouble, by not speaking up and admitting she was afraid of some things. She couldn't reach the stirrups and she was too far off the ground. The horse wouldn't respond to a thing she tried to make it do. Carolee sat there, unable to decide what she was supposed to do next. She glanced down into Max's upturned face, at his nice teeth shown off in one of those spontaneous smiles of his.

Suddenly, he frowned and appeared about to say something. He cleared his throat instead, took hold of the animal's bridle and started to lead him. Like she was a child. She must look as terrified as she felt.

"I don't think I've ever been on a horse

this big," she said, hoping to rescue her image a little. "In fact, I haven't ridden at all in years."

"No," he said, noncommittal. "What did you do to your pants?" He rubbed her jeans where they covered her shins and brought up fingers smeared with black grease.

Carolee stared at his hand, but continued to feel his touch on her leg.

He held his fingers to his nose and sniffed. "Tar, maybe?"

Immediately she bent to rub at first one shin, then the other, succeeding only in making a mess of her own hands, and unsettling her seat on the horse.

"Whoa, boy," she said, moving more firmly into the saddle. She remembered Digger. "Faith's dog did it. Just a stick he brought out of the water."

"The horse's name is Guy. You're never going to get that mess off those jeans."

She shrugged. "I guess not." How did two people who should have something interesting to say to each other manage to sound so dull?

"You look good on horseback," Max said. "All you need is practice and you'll do great. You move very well."

Carolee blushed. So much for complaining to herself about dull comments. "I thought you looked sexy riding in." Aghast, she managed to pull the horse to a stop. "That is *not* what I meant to say. Everything has a sexual angle these days, so we just slide right into using inappropriate terms."

"You mean I didn't look sexy?" Max asked, his face completely straight. "Hell, how do you think that makes me feel? One minute I'm a sexy stud. The next I'm nothing."

"I didn't say anything about you being a stud," she told him. "Only that you looked sexy on the horse. But I meant..." Carolee Burns had always had a gift for getting herself into verbal disasters. Some had been too expensive.

"What did you mean?" He inclined his head to look at her and a devilish glint was in those dark eyes.

She couldn't answer. Her face felt fiery and she perspired inside her blue T-shirt.

Max started walking again and Guy moved with him. "Forgive me, Carolee. I have a nasty habit of baiting people sometimes. I don't want to do that to you. I do want you to be at least a little interested in me."

"Hush," she said. "Faith might hear. As for Sam, he's in deep trouble for setting the two of us up like this."

"He's not in trouble with me."

She chuckled and said, "You don't give up."

"You've got a wonderful father. He lives for you and your daughter. He called me up earlier and told me he didn't really want to take any time away from the two of you, but he needed help with the horses. He's asked me to give your girl some lessons. He thought you'd rather keep things informal for Faith. I've never given lessons before but I guess I ride

99

well enough to help her. And I'm glad to do it. I don't have a busy private life."

"Are you always so honest about yourself?"

He scrunched up his eyes. "No one ever asked me that before, but yeah, I guess I am. What's the point of lying?"

Sam and Faith came toward them and Digger rushed at Max. The animal planted his paws on Max's belly and panted.

He gave the dog the rough love he wanted, and reached to shake Faith's hand. She blushed. "I'm Max," he told her. "A friend of Sam's. He talks about you all the time."

"Don't go givin' all my secrets away," Sam said. He slid a sideways stare at Carolee. "Max here worked on that old paddock. Fixed it up real good."

"It'll do for now," Max said. "It needs a lot more work."

Without asking her if she wanted help, he held her waist once more and eased her from the saddle to the ground. He seemed to know her legs were shaky and kept holding on to her. She rested her hands on his biceps and felt how solid they were.

Enough, you idiot. "You're very kind. Did Sam tell you we don't have Faith's helmet yet?"

"He did. But he said it'll be along in a few days. Maybe we'll try to get in a couple of evening sessions. Would you like that, Faith?"

"She'd love it," Sam said before Faith could say a word. "Let's get these critters into the barn and go up to the cabin for a cold drink."

He took off in the direction of the paddock, and the pony. Max led Guy into the barn. Digger ran after him and Faith was close behind. Carolee followed more slowly. She must not be weakened by her loneliness and insecurity. Max might be a very nice man, but he was also convenient, and she was vulnerable. The facts didn't add up to an encouraging picture, and they certainly didn't add up to a reason for her to consider getting involved with him.

Inside the barn, Max put the black into a stall. The chestnut was already peacefully chomping on straw and showing no particular interest in what went on around her.

An unexpected flurry of wings made Faith duck. "Barn swallows," Max said over his shoulder.

Carolee managed not to say, "I know." The nest was tucked into a rafter joist. She signaled to Faith and pointed silently to the female's visible head. Her bossy mate flitted about her, showing off his red-brown throat and cinnamon underparts. "They come back every year."

The pony trotted into the barn beside Sam, who followed Max's lead with Guy and gave the smaller animal a quick rubdown.

Twenty minutes later they were back at Sam's cabin. Max excused himself and went into the bathroom, from which sounds of the shower soon came. Faith was still entertaining Digger outside.

Carolee pulled Sam into the kitchen. "You told me you'd call him and say Faith couldn't—"

"Couldn't ride until she has all the gear she needs. He knows that."

"You know I wanted you to uninvite him. You fudged just enough about the whole business to pretend you'd done what you promised."

Sam turned up his palms. "You never used to be so selfish," he said, and opened the oven to check the contents of a casserole dish. "So I bent things a bit. I needed the help. He's handy. Grew up on a farm and knows all about mending fences and dealing with horses. You didn't even ask how the stalls got mucked out."

She breathed deeply. "I'm sorry. I forgot about them. I didn't notice they'd been cleaned."

"Even though you and Faith were expectin' to do it? Max did it for you. If you don't at least give it a chance—"

"There's nothing to give a chance to. Please, don't do this."

"Just don't shut out the possibility," Sam said. "That's all I'm asking you. No pressure. He's smart, he's got a sense of humor, he's not my type, but I've got it on good authority he's real good-looking. Couldn't find a better built man and he's nice with kids and animals. And he's established in a business that's going places. *And* he's got money."

"When did you become a matchmaker?"

He caught one of her hands between his. "When I saw my daughter alone and lonely, that's when. When she'd been worked over by a man who never deserved her."

"Thanks for caring," she said. "I'm not looking for a man, and if I were, I wouldn't bc worrying about how good-looking he was, or how much money he had. Neither are necessary."

"Why? Wouldn't it be nice to have a fella who didn't wait for you to bring home the bacon? You don't worry about a man havin' money because you're used to keeping some bloodsucking son of a gun. It shouldn't be that way."

The shower stopped running. Carolee whispered, "That's sexist talk. If people love each other, what does it matter if the woman makes more money than the man?"

"Doesn't work for a man to live off a woman. Doesn't look good, not that Kip Burns seemed to mind. Still doesn't mind taking your money. Selling any paintings, is he?"

Carolee felt an unexpected spark of defensiveness on Kip's behalf. "As a matter of fact, I think he is. Faith says he has a lot to do with people from the art world now."

The sound of the bathroom door opening was a blessed interruption to Carolee. She went back to the living room in time to see Max emerge from the steam.

He'd changed into a clean chambray shirt and jeans, and carried his dirty clothes in a bag. His feet were bare and his wet hair slicked back.

Carolee's insides made a series of vaguely familiar bumps and turns. She was actually reacting to him like a girl developing a crush. Or should that be like a woman who wanted a man. The timing couldn't be worse—not that it would ever be good.

He carried a wet washcloth. "This is mine," he told Sam. "But it's old, so it doesn't matter." He'd sprinkled something carbolic-smelling on the cloth and went to work cleaning the tar from Carolee's fingers. Clamping her wrists between a thumb and forefinger, he held both of her hands in one of his and she remembered he was a man who used to catch footballs and run with them while men built like meat lockers tried to make him drop them. He scrubbed the gooey mess, and Carolee's legs became shaky. He bent over her and concentrated, and she failed to stop herself from taking him in at close range, and liking what she saw.

There was shower water in his eyelashes. Where he hadn't completely gotten himself dry, damp spots bled out on his shirt.

Carolee looked up and met her father's eyes. He didn't grin, or give her an "I told you so" look. Sam seemed a little sad and a lot serious.

"Got it," Max said. "No more playing in the dirt unless you want to get whupped."

"Thank you."

Nine

Max put his bare feet up on a green tapestry ottoman and sank back among a row of worn stuffed animals. He guessed leaving would be the politest thing to do. But he didn't want to leave. In fact, he liked where he was just fine, right down to the lumpy, homey toys at his back. He lowered his eyes to half-mast and let his breathing deepen.

"Do you take anything in your coffee?" Carolee asked, carrying a tray in from the kitchen. Only Faith had decided she'd rather have lemonade than something hot.

"Just black, thanks," he said. "Am I in the way?"

Carolee put the tray on the dining room table and cast him a very direct stare. For a moment he thought she'd be blunt enough to tell him she'd like him to leave, but she shook her head, unsmiling, and said, "I just made this coffee because you said you wanted it. You'd better not take off without drinking any."

"No, ma'am," he said, moving to get up.

"Stay where you are. I'll bring it to you. I've got to make up for not having to muck out the horses." With her father in the kitchen where he couldn't see her face, she widened her eyes at Max. "Of course, I'm putting on a good front, but I'm not happy about you taking over one of my favorite jobs."

She brought him a mug of coffee that smelled

strong, and offered him homemade oatmeal raisin cookies. He accepted the coffee and took three cookies. "My stomach's forgotten lunch," he said, by way of apologizing for being a pig. Faith was with her grandfather so Max dropped his voice and said, "You're prickly. You try not to be, but I don't think you can help it. I'm not a threat to you, Carolee."

"I didn't think you were."

"I was going to say you seem afraid of me, but changed my mind."

Her green eyes snapped. "I'm not afraid of you."

"Now I'm changing my mind back. I think you are. Why would that be?"

She shook back her very dark hair. Her coloring was vivid, almost so bright it made a man want to squint. "Why are you trying to goad me, Max?"

He'd taken a bite of cookie and shook his head while he swallowed. "No such thing, ma'am. But it isn't easy to figure you out. You're obviously gentle and reserved—most of the time—but you've got a thorny side you show around me. I'm just trying to decide why that is."

Tar on her jeans didn't take a thing away from her swept-clean appearance. A short blue T-shirt fitted loosely. As he'd already been aware, she was nicely, but comfortably, made. More rounded than bony. Max liked that. He kept on giving her a questioning stare.

"Okay." She bent her head forward. "You've made it clear that you want to—well—know me. I can't get to know any man at the moment. I just can't, but if I could, I'd probably like to know you. There. That's as honest as I can be, so could we let it go?"

He didn't dare let it go too completely, not when he'd just seen the first and only chink in her armor. He felt ridiculously optimistic.

A thunder of footfalls and Digger leaped over the arm of the couch to land on top of Max, who barely stopped his coffee from slopping. He held his remaining cookie between his teeth and rubbed the dog hard, enjoying his obvious bliss. Max removed the cookie from his mouth. "Carolee? I still get the feeling I frighten you."

"You don't have that power," she told him. "Sure, I've got some awkward things to deal with, but that doesn't make me afraid. Of you or anyone else."

Digger flopped, all four legs spread eagle, on top of Max, and rested his head where his wet nose poked beneath Max's chin. "Nice dog. Just my type. Okay, you're not afraid of me, or anyone else. But you are scared of something and I want to help you out. I don't like the idea of you being unhappy. In fact, just thinking about it makes me an angry man."

He thought she seemed suddenly alarmed. "Forget it," she said. "I'm not your concern and there's nothing wrong with me anyway."

"Whooee, that's a lot of denial on a single breath."

She walked away and he didn't figure he'd made any points after all. Sam finished banging around in the fragrantly scented kitchen and carried in his own coffee. Faith came with lemonade and Carolee returned to pour herself a mug of coffee.

At first they sat and drank in silence. The wind had picked up and the branches of a little spruce tapped the windowpanes. Through the open door, dust eddies were visible curling along patches of hard-packed ground. This was something Max had never been part of, a family unit that gathered quietly and felt comfortable together. His own parents hadn't been talkers for any reason. There hadn't been gatherings, or even casual day-to-day get-togethers where they felt companionable.

Sam swallowed his coffee in a few gulps and put the mug on the tray. "We'd better have that chat, girlie," he said to Faith, and the two of them went outside.

Max studied Carolee's reaction. Her edginess showed. She hadn't expected this development, and yet again, it made her nervous. She was one easily rattled woman.

He set his mug aside and wrapped his arms around Digger, who started to snore gently. "This one's still a baby. All energy, then completely pooped."

"He's a perfect dog for a place like this," Carolee said.

"But you don't think he'll be so perfect in a condo? That's where Faith lives when she's with her father?"

She nodded once.

"Maybe it would be best to keep him here. Then he'll be waiting whenever she visits."

She moved to the couch beside him and stroked the dog gently. "I thought of that, but I know how kids are. Faith's never going to settle for one weekend a month with him."

He hadn't known any details of the custody rights. "One weekend a month doesn't seem like much."

"It's *nothing.*" Her vehemence changed her. The gentleness was gone, replaced by agitation. "It's so hard..." She turned her face from him, but he could see how her chest rose and fell with each impassioned breath.

The most natural thing would be to touch her. The most natural, and the biggest mistake. Waiting, letting her talk if she wanted to was the only safe way, though she wouldn't say much now, not with Faith likely to come in at any moment.

"You don't have any children?" Carolee asked, catching him off-guard.

"No."

"Did you ever think you'd like to?"

His turn for interrogation has arrived. He guessed that was fair. "I never thought much about it at all—not till recently. I guess I'd like kids."

"Because it's the thing to do when you reach a certain age?"

With his arms still around Digger, he pressed his lips together and thought. "I don't think that's it. We all change. I used to be a bit of a wild boy. Stuff happened and I grew up fast. I don't walk around longing for kids, but it would be nice."

"Never been married?"

He almost laughed at the hesitant way she asked the question. "You were taught it's rude to ask personal questions, weren't you? It's not if that's where the conversation takes you. I've never been married." Would she ask him if he wanted to be? He wasn't sure he'd know how to answer.

"My husband and I were married when I was seventeen. I felt I went from being a kid to being a wife and then a mother, and that was fine with me. I didn't want anything else." She looked away again. "Except to play and sing—and bring people pleasure."

Faith came through the door with Sam. In a different way, the girl would grow into as stunning a woman as her mother. Her gray eyes were completely clear and honest.

"Hey, Sam," Carolee said, much too enthusiastically. "I forgot to get your stamp of approval on Digger's name. It was Faith's own idea. Cute, huh?"

Sam grimaced. "You sure you think so?"

"Gramps." Faith frowned at him.

"I do think so," Carolee said. "It's Australian for 'buddy' and I think that was very clever of Faith."

Max hid a smile. Sam and Faith's expressions were priceless.

Sam said, *"Australian* for buddy?"

"Sure." Carolee sounded miffed. "You know. Like mate, only, digger."

Faith scuffed her tennis shoes on the wooden floor.

"Digger means digger, daughter," Sam said. "Don't tell me you haven't noticed this mutt digs up everything in sight, and buries everything in sight. Faith here must have been doing a great job of replanting your flowers."

Carolee looked blank but Sam and Faith sniggered. All of his decisions weren't smart, Max decided, but he knew when to be quiet.

"You'd have got it soon enough," said magnanimous Sam. "Faith and I are going to walk him over to your place and put him in his crate for the evening."

"Why?" Carolee asked.

Sam avoided eye contact and said, "Faith and me are going out for dinner and a movie. It's our date night. Dinner's ready for you two anytime you want it."

The dog was too comfortable to disturb so Max didn't move. He did wrinkle his brow and wait with interest for Carolee's response.

Her lips parted and stayed that way. She didn't say a word.

"It's okay for me to go, isn't it, Mom?"

Carolee started and looked at her daughter's hopeful face. "Of course it's okay. You and Gramps need time together."

The time seemed right for Max to add, "Why put this one in his crate. Leave him here. He's a sociable guy."

"You sure?" Sam said. A dull flush darkened his tanned face.

"If Carolee is."

She said, "Yes," but there was no missing her uncertainty, and it wasn't about being left with the dog.

Faith smiled at Max and the feeling she gave him wasn't anything he'd expected. That smile was accepting—or he thought it was. She actually seemed to like him.

"Off we go then," Sam said. "There's a stick-to-your-ribs stew in the casserole. It's done, and good and hot. Rolls. Salad and a cheesecake. Couple of bottles of red wine on the counter."

Sam and Faith left the cabin and Max soon heard the sound of the truck engine. The vehicle bumped and ground its way toward the road.

He rested his chin on top of Digger's head and fought to quell the laughter that threatened.

Carolee moved to a chair and sat there, her arms crossed, a hand over her mouth.

Digger made a chomping sound and whined a little in his sleep.

Faded black and white photographs were arranged along the mantel. Max could make out people in dated clothing but little else.

The smell from the kitchen made his mouth water.

Shifting, Carolee crossed her legs and fussed with her hair.

Max lost his battle with laughter. A deliberate cough killed the first chuckle but then it was all over; he laughed and the sound grew louder. And his shoulders quaked. He slapped the one thigh not covered by Digger, who opened his eyes and blinked.

"What's so funny?" Carolee asked.

He shook his head. There wasn't enough breath to talk.

She pursed her lips but the corners of her mouth quivered.

"Your dad," Max managed to say at last. "He's one subtle guy, isn't he?"

Carolee gave up and her laughter joined his. An abandoned laugh that scaled higher, the more out of control she became. Tears squeezed from the corners of her eyes and she wiped them away.

"Must have been great when you were in high school. Did he choose your dates?"

She shook her head and curled over as if her stomach hurt. "No. Then all he did was try to stop me from dating at all—which probably helped drive me into an early marriage. This is a new phase, but I do think he's picked you. If you're wise, you'll start running as fast as you can."

It wouldn't be tough to blow this. "I like what I smell in the kitchen. If you don't mind, I'll eat before I run away."

"By all means." She fell against the back of her chair and continued to convulse. He thought he was seeing the edge of hysteria. She'd been too uptight for too long.

Setting Digger down, he gathered the coffee tray and carried it into the kitchen. Place settings for two had been laid out. These he took back to the dining table and carefully arranged.

The dog had wiggled close to a soft pet bed behind the couch where an oversized brown, caramel, and white cat lay on its back. Digger poked his nose into the cat's considerable tummy and Max waited for the fight. No fight came. The cat purred like a mower in need of oil and encouraged Digger by tapping his head with a curled foot.

"Let me set the table," Carolee said.

Max told her, "I like doing it," when he didn't care one way or the other. "Can you see the animals?"

She knelt on the couch and looked over the back. "That's Taffy. She's a user and the dog's enjoying being used. Let me deal with the table, Max."

He waved her back into her chair. "My turn. You stay where you are. Sam's left everything ready."

The beef in the oven stew fell apart as he served it. Browned potatoes, carrots, onions, and corn sizzled in a rich gravy. Max heaped two plates, found green salads already served, and was glad Sam had opened the wine to let it breathe.

With Digger staring up into his face, Max enjoyed every mouthful and could have eaten more. Carolee's halfhearted attempt to eat anything at all dampened his appetite.

They agreed they weren't ready for cheesecake, but each drank two glasses of a decent enough pinot noir.

Another long quiet settled on them while they finished their second glasses but Max decided it wasn't so uncomfortable.

Without discussion, the table was cleared and the dishwasher loaded. Digger got some leftover pieces of beef that sent him tearing around and around the cabin.

Everything was cleaned up. They both said they didn't want more coffee. Back in the sitting room they stood a few feet apart, each with their hands in their pockets.

Digger tired of racing about and flopped down on Max's feet. He wouldn't, he decided, mind having a dog like this one.

He shifted his weight.

Carolee coughed into a fist.

Hell, he never had difficulty coming up with something to say. "It's turning into a nice evening." Oh, real smooth.

"Yes."

"Look at the water. It's pink." The sun had gone behind the mountains but continued to color the clouds and the lake.

She looked over her shoulder and said, "Yes."

O-kay. He had choices. Sit down. Go home. Come up with something that just might help them to relax with each other.

"Are you warm enough?" It had to be around seventy still...

"Yes, thank you."

Now for something original. "How about a walk along the lake?" He held his breath. Why should he blame himself for old lines? He hadn't learned any new ones.

She said, "C'mon, Digger. Time for a walk," and left Max searching around for his boots.

Ten

A man, a woman, and a dog. Skirting a band of trees on their way to walk by a lake. What could be more ordinary?

A man and a woman who belonged together would be more ordinary.

"This is a good piece of land," Max said, and shied a stick high in the air for Digger. "Not many parcels this size still in one piece around here."

"I love it. It was in my mother's family for a long time. She knew how I felt about the place, so she left it to me."

"How did Sam feel about that? And your sister?"

"Linda is Sam's by his first marriage, remember." She thought briefly of her parents' unusual relationship. "He felt fine. Sam took a long time to grow up and when he did, he was lucky he still had a family waiting. He's grateful for that. When I was growing up he was off doing his thing more often than he was with Mom, Linda and me. I'm glad he's here now."

"The kind of guy who probably shouldn't have married at all," Max said. He stopped to watch Digger, who was rooting through grass at the base of an alder. "You've got to admit that's a clever canine. I'm not surprised you didn't notice he digs. Chooses soft earth in long grass or weeds. Bye-bye stick and not much evidence if you aren't looking for it."

"Well, at least I gave all of you a laugh." The conversation was light but Carolee wasn't relaxing. He was right about men, though. Some of them should never marry. He might not realize it, but he was probably talking about himself.

They reached a spot where the big, mowed field around Sam's place dropped off toward the lake. Carolee stood beside Max and looked out over the water. At moments like these, she never felt like talking. He seemed either to understand that, or to react the same way.

Although there was still plenty of dusky light, a double-decked charter boat already had strands of party lights switched on. Probably making for the Marina in Kirkland, passengers crowded the rails of the wallowing craft to stare at the mostly unspoiled shores.

A parade of arguing geese broke the peace. They strutted their stuff through the bubble-edged shallows, picking fights as they went.

Max drew in a deep breath. When she looked up at him, his mouth was set, but softened by the natural upward tilt at the corners. His hands were on his hips and the stiff breeze whipped at his hair.

This was not ordinary. It was not appropriate when she knew he was interested in her yet she had nothing to offer him.

Without asking, he caught her hand in his and led the way down the dry and crumbling earth on the bank.

Once she faltered and he steadied her, looked back, but hesitated for not more than a second. She'd automatically tightened her grip on him. His hand was large and warm, and steady. In that second he smiled slightly, crinkled his eyes.

Had there ever been times when she felt aware of Kip in quite this way? As if every pore in her skin were open to him. In a sexual way, yes, but more because he made it clear that she owned his whole attention and he wanted it that way?

Max had her attention, also. She reacted to him with a weightlessness in the pit of her stomach, with the awkward way she took each step. She didn't want him to let go of her hand.

"Alone and lonely," Sam had said of her. Loneliness could distort dangerously.

"Your house is even prettier from here," Max said, looking upward from the shore and to the left. "The sun sets on your windows, too. I couldn't see the flower garden from the porch. It's great. What wild colors."

Digger passed them in pursuit of the geese, who took flight, their wings battering the air. The disappointed dog waded into the lake.

"That garden's really old," Carolee said. "I just add to it and keep it happy. I knew I had to come back here. I knew this was where I'd find some peace." As much peace as she

118

could possibly hope for while she was all but separated from Faith.

"Come here from where?"

"New York." She didn't usually discuss any of this, but he made it too easy. "For the first months after...after the divorce I stayed in the New York apartment and commuted here for my visits with Faith. I cut down my schedule but kept working. At least when I was performing, I could forget. But Faith and I were spending our time together in a hotel in Seattle and nothing was normal. Sam was living in the cabin, but Lake Home had been closed up for some time. It came to me that although it would never be enough, at least if I was here all the time, I'd know Faith was near and we'd have our visits in a place she loves."

"Where did you and your ex-husband meet?"

He always carefully exaggerated the "ex." "At school here. This is where Mom and Linda and I lived—and Sam when he paid a visit. Kip and I also had a place in Los Angeles but it was sold. He got the proceeds from that, and moved to the Seattle condo. He always loved the light there. The studio is wonderful."

Max said, "That's nice." He still held her hand. Carolee looked pointedly at their joined fingers. He raised his eyebrows, bent over, and gave her knuckles a light kiss before releasing her.

She shouldn't be comparing him to Kip, but Kip wouldn't have made a disarming gesture like that.

People were different. It wasn't fair to look for parallels.

Max put a hand at her waist and ushered her slightly in front of him. The light was weakening faster. Across the water, and with part of the 520 bridge in the foreground, Seattle was tuning up for another night. The tops of its elegant skyscrapers were visible and they glittered.

The dog lolloped from the water and ran ahead to flop down and wait. He chewed on some hapless object he'd found.

"Are you getting used to the arrangement with your ex-husband? About Faith, I mean."

"*No.*" She crossed her arms and stared toward Seattle. "*No.* How could you even think I might? I never will. I'm not going to. I'm going to fight him for her. I keep hoping he'll make it easy and say we should share custody. Sometimes he hangs out a sort of carrot and makes me think that's what he's going to do, but it's just a game he plays."

Carolee saw Max's boots before she registered that he'd come to stand immediately in front of her. "Hey, it's okay," he said. "Sorry I said the wrong thing. You've got a right to be upset."

"Upset is too weak for what I feel. I've been all but robbed of my daughter and I'm not going to put up with it forever." She met his eyes. "I've already been punished for my carelessness—taken advantage of because I was dumb enough not to see what was coming— but I'm going to fight back. I've got to do it for Faith, for me, and for every other woman who gets manipulated by a man who figures out how to get the system behind him."

"Not all men—"

"I didn't say *all* men would do something like that," she said, too fast, and sighed. "Sorry."

He made a move as if to touch her face, but drew back. "Have you taken any steps?"

It always came down to this question. "No. I've got to be very careful."

"Want to explain that?"

"Not really."

"Okay."

"But I will explain. When it happened, I was too shocked to fight. I gave in on everything. I agreed that every accusation made was true. Kip had proof of the role he'd played in Faith's life, and how much less time I'd spent with her. It didn't matter that he encouraged me to keep building my career, or that I thought he accepted everything."

Max frowned. His gaze was steady but clearly a reply didn't come easily.

Gulls screamed and swept inland. "The weather's going to change," she said, glad of the diversion. "You always know it will when the seagulls do that."

He made a noncommittal sound.

Streaks of red and pink in the violet sky made a potential lie of her weather forecast.

"So your ex-husband didn't really like you having a career?"

She went from him to the edge of the lake where shiny pebbles showed through glassy ripples. "I didn't know he hated it till he said he was divorcing me."

"But he never discouraged you before that?"

"He said he was proud of me and that he wanted me to have my chance. We should take advantage of the opportunity we'd been handed—that's what he told me. The money would set us up. He soon had his studios—he's a painter—and he told me he wanted to be with Faith. I guess the whole thing grew old but he didn't want to upset me by saying so."

"Until he threw the works at you?"

"I'd suggested I should stop performing," she said softly into the breeze that stole into her throat. "As soon as I moved here to live, I did stop. Except for occasional appearances. I haven't toured since I got home—it was the Christmas before last—and he told me what he was doing."

"You're talking about the occasional appearances at Brandy's?"

"Yes. And I do a monthly show at my supper club in New York. If I'm going to keep it, and I want to, I've got to have a presence there. I'm not going this month because of Faith being here."

"But nothing could make Kip change his mind?" Max asked.

She closed her burning eyes. "He said it was too late. I'd emasculated him, that's how he felt. And he'd put his own career on hold for so long he was afraid he'd lost the will and the talent. He'd waited and waited, hoping I'd make up my own mind to come home to him and

Faith. I'd made enough money, he said. There were people willing to say I was a party girl. They said I was *fast* when I was away. What a lie. I'm a loner. Always have been. But loners don't have witnesses."

Tense lines tightened Max's face. He stooped to gather several pebbles and Carolee figured he was buying time to think.

"Want to sit down?" he asked. "There's a bench a bit farther on."

Carolee straightened her back and blinked away the budding tears. She put on a smile and looked at him. "I know that bench well. It belongs to me and it's falling apart." Attempting lightheartedness, she looked him over critically and took pleasure in his bemused expression. "We'll give it a try, but it may take one look at you and give up."

She took off at a smart clip and heard his faint chuckle behind her. Funny how one learned to stuff down feelings, or at least to put on a good front.

Digger beat her to the bench and danced there as if he knew it was her destination.

Carolee didn't sit down, but stood aside, waiting for Max to catch up. "You don't have to be polite," he said. "Take a pew. Get a load off. Whatever."

"You've got to be kidding. After you. If it holds you, I'll think about risking it."

Max gave the bench a once-over and sat down with confidence. He rested an ankle on the opposite knee and crossed his arms. And he squinted up at Carolee.

Men had wanted her—many men. Show business and sex went together. She'd ignored every advance, never wanting anyone but Kip. He'd decided he didn't want her anymore, but her feelings for him hadn't died a fast death. She couldn't be certain there wasn't still something left of her love for him.

"What is it?" Max asked.

"Nothing." Careful to keep some distance between them, she sat down. But this was not nothing. Max Wolfe had reached a part of her she'd begun to ignore. A part that wanted to sleep in the arms of a man she was crazy about, and who was crazy about her, and to wake up in those same arms. She glanced sideways at Max. His sleeves were rolled back over strong forearms, tanned and sprinkled with bronzed hairs. His long, broad hands fascinated her. A brief sensation that he'd touched her set off a fire beneath her skin.

The dog gave up waiting for attention and curled on his side, chomping a rock between his back teeth.

Max leaned forward and rested his elbows on his knees. "Tell me to go and I will."

Who could blame him for growing tired of the long silences? "I know I'm awkward to be with," she said. "For someone who's spent so much time performing and being in front of people, I don't have great social skills."

"Don't change."

She leaned back and pushed her fingers into her hair. "I don't know what to say to that."

"It was a compliment. You've got every reason to be arrogant but you're the opposite."

"Don't go." She lowered her gaze, knowing she'd made a move he could construe as encouraging. She wasn't sorry.

Dusk deepened a notch. Like multiplying dust motes, a mesh of gray drew over the lake, the sky, and fuzzed the headlands. The temperature lowered, but not enough to be uncomfortable.

Max looked backward at her. "I think you just asked me to stay. Or am I dreaming?"

She locked her fingers together behind her head. "I'm not the kind to gripe about being lonely, but it's nice to have company."

"You're alone a lot?"

"It works out that way. Sam likes his own space and so do I."

"In other words, you don't really need people."

She could say, "No," and make things easy on herself. Or would that be so easy?

"I never thought much about having friends," Max said. "Not till I had the accident and I learned how quickly you can be forgotten. I'm not complaining about that, just making a comment."

Carolee looked briefly into his eyes. In this light, they were completely opaque. "I don't know much about football. Nothing, really. But you were famous, weren't you? Sam said you played for the Broncos."

He sat up and rested his arms along the back

of the bench, which meant one of his arms stretched behind Carolee. "Mm. I had a lot of luck. Yeah, I was famous. I got used to it—but you know all about that feeling. Then I was nobody—or I thought I was—and that's what I had to get over. I had to go inside myself and figure out that with or without football, I was someone."

"Sam told me a truck fell on you."

He laughed shortly. "A pickup. One minute I was changing a tire, the next my legs were trapped and I'd never play pro-ball again. The pickup was on an incline. It slipped off the jack and slid downhill onto me. That's it. Short story. Except I'm lucky that truck didn't come farther and faster—and that my legs have done so well.

"But sports took me off the farm and into college. Football gave me the future I never expected to have.

"I was mad as hell at the world for far too long. Then I wised up and figured out it's okay to feel badly, but the reasons have to be right. I'd made a bundle, enough to allow me to go into the kind of business I'd always dreamed of. True I hadn't wanted it quite so soon, but we don't get to call all the shots. And now I stay close to the game by working with kids."

"But you got over what you lost really quickly? You didn't keep on feeling you'd lost everything?"

His fingers settled on the back of her neck.

So small and innocent a move shouldn't have the kind of reaction it had on Carolee. She didn't want to move away, but she was terrified to stay where she was. Shortness of breath gripped her but she held absolutely still.

"I told you I was mad at the world for a bit. But it was for the shallowest reasons. When you come from nothing and suddenly people know who you are—when they point you out and kids gape at you—you actually begin to think you *are* someone. Women fawn on you." He shrugged. "Hey, that sounds shallow, but I'm only a man. Afterward there was all the pity and the whispering, and looking quickly away. That was what I really hated. Pity."

"I don't blame you." She spoke so quietly she wouldn't have been surprised if she were the only one to hear. "People didn't pity me. They judged me and decided I was a bad mother who didn't deserve to have her child. I'm still recognized and the stares embarrass me. I'm the woman who used my husband while I lived the high life. And I caused him to put his own plans on hold because he had to be both mother and father to our child."

Max rubbed his fingers lightly up and down her neck but she got the impression he was unaware of what he did.

"Your ex-husband couldn't paint just the same? Wasn't there any help with looking after Faith?"

"Of course there was. We had a nanny when she was little, and after that there was always a housekeeper and other household staff. There still is." She hadn't intended to add that information.

Max said nothing else on the subject.

"What was your major?" Carolee said.

He wound a lock of her hair through his fingers. "Computer science. I was recruited onto the football team out of high school and I didn't even know I was choosing a hot field. It sounded good, so I said I'd do it. Dumb luck."

"You have a software company?"

"We're in the security business. What we produce protects large corporations, big e-tailers and so forth from break-ins—that's break-ins that can disrupt their businesses big-time. It's complicated, but damned exciting."

It meant little or nothing to Carolee but she was interested. "Your offices are in Seattle."

"In Pioneer Square. If you're interested, I'll show you around sometime. Just be prepared for a motley crew of geniuses who are hooked on foosball."

With the fingers spread wide, his hand came to rest on her back.

Carolee said, "It's getting chilly."

"Want to go in?"

"Not really, but I'd better. Would you like some coffee?"

"I'd love some coffee." He sounded as if he really meant every word.

She got up and he was instantly at her side. "Come on, Digger," she told the dog, who yawned and stretched and got to his feet like a newborn foal. The rock continued to churn in his mouth.

"Hold my arm," Max said. "Maybe we can help each other get up there in one piece."

As soon as she slid a hand around his elbow, he clamped it to his side and they started up the path. He said, "Funny how we can make up stupid reasons for things. I want to feel your hand against me. Neither of us is likely to fall down if we don't have support." He laughed, awkwardly, Carolee thought.

"This may be the hardest thing I've ever done," he told her. "I know I've got to tread lightly with you, be careful, avoid frightening you off. What I'd like to do is hold you, Carolee."

The thud of her heart echoed in her ears. "You're a nice man. I think you're real. I haven't met many real people. But this is a time when I've got to make sure not a finger can be pointed at me."

"Because you're going to make a legal move with Faith?"

"I'm going to make some moves. If it's possible, I'd like to keep the legal system out of it. Faith's already been through too much. But if I have to go to court again, I will."

They walked slowly. The angle at which he held her arm meant her hip brushed his thigh with each step.

"You're single. You should be free to have a male friend if you want to."

"That's what Sam says." She halted and pulled her hand free. "I'm just scared, Max. Kip could say it's not good for Faith to see that I can forget him and find someone else. He could point out that I'm proving I can move on—from both him and Faith."

"What are you supposed to do—mourn the loss of him forever." A new, tougher note entered Max's voice. "Is he celibate?"

"I don't *know*. It isn't my business."

"But what you do is his business?"

She thought for a moment. The wind was definitely growing colder and clouds had drawn over the moon, blotted out the gunmetal glow it had cast. "It isn't his business, but it was already decided that he's the good one and I'm the bad one. I don't like it and I'm not bad, but I don't trust the system enough to take chances."

"Come here, Carolee."

She was only feet from him.

"Please. It's chilly. Why shouldn't we keep each other warm?"

"Because I want it too much," she blurted out. "I try not to lie. I'd like you to hold me. I'm tired of trying to figure everything out alone."

He captured her wrists and brought her close. "I'm going to fish and ask if any man would do, or if it's me in particular you'd like to hold you?"

"You are fishing."

His movements were subtle, the slow bending to bring his mouth close to her ear. "I like you a lot," he said. She felt his breath on her hair.

"I like you, too." Impetuousness and honesty had taken their toll on her before.

So lightly she might have imagined it, his lips brushed her cheek and he embraced her.

130

Swaying, they stayed there, pressed together, Carolee aware of every part of him. She grew hot again, hot and turned on. Max stroked her from neck to waist and back. His hands were steady. He stroked her again and this time he cupped her bottom and eased her to her toes.

Carolee slipped her arms around his neck and pushed her hands into his hair. Her face was tilted up to his. The glint of his eyes, the whiteness of his teeth—the scent of the soap he'd used in the shower—his presence touched her in deeper places than his hands could ever reach.

Her breasts pressed against his chest and she felt what she hadn't felt in far too long: totally aware of her body.

Max placed his mouth on her cheek again, but made no move to do more.

"Hold me tighter," she whispered, and her voice broke.

He slipped his hands under the back of her sweater and pressed her closer, rubbed the skin at her spine, then over her ribs, and finally, settled his fingers just beneath the waistband of her jeans.

Carolee returned the caressing hug. The sides of his neck where she could push his collar away were smooth, and she settled her mouth there—and felt his steady hands grow shaky. She made space enough between them for her to stroke his chest, and heard his rapid intake of breath.

She wished he would touch her breasts, but he didn't.

When he spoke at last, he sounded hoarse. "I should get you up to your place."

"Yes, of course."

When she made to step away from him, he held her tightly enough to wind her. "May I kiss you first?"

How could she refuse? She didn't want to refuse. Instead, with her hands hooked over his shoulders, she brought her mouth to his. When she touched him, it was with closed lips, but immediately she parted them. He kissed her back, first with restraint, but very quickly with abandon, and she had to cling to his shirt to stop herself from overbalancing.

The seeking and taking turned wild. They sought out every angle, every surface. Carolee reached and reached, and he met her every time. Gradually they calmed and rocked their mouths together, ran gentle tongues along sharp teeth, and leaned into a sweetly intimate embrace that was the only way to keep them from falling to the sandy grass and tearing off each other's clothes.

"This is what I've thought of since the first time I saw you," Max told her. "Don't worry, we'll go slowly and carefully."

His reassurance reminded her that this could be dangerous, but she wasn't ready to deny herself the pleasure of being with him.

"Will it be okay if I ride with Faith, or would you rather I didn't?"

And so he tossed the ball into her court again. This was one more way of saying, *Do we go on, or do we stop?* "As you already saw with

Guy, I hardly ride at all, and Sam isn't up to much of it anymore. I just don't want to send Faith off to riding lessons when we have so little time together. So I guess it's you by default." She smiled wryly. "Thank you."

"The pleasure is mine." He sounded funny.

Eleven

"Play for me." A better man would have seen her home and left. He couldn't pretend to be other than he was—reckless, and doing his damndest to get into her life.

Carolee brought coffee to him where he stood beside the piano. "There is Sambuca, and I think a little Drambuie if you'd like some."

He sipped the coffee. "Can't imagine wanting anything but this, thanks. You make great coffee." The thought of her playing just for him brought a rush, but she didn't make a move toward the piano bench.

"Faith's interested in computers," she said, hovering in the middle of the room. "If I brought her down to see your offices, that would be a right-out-in-the-open thing. Probably no one would know anyway, but just in case it did get back to Kip, he couldn't say I was doing something behind his back."

Max took too large a mouthful of the very hot coffee and could barely swallow.

Carolee's face turned pink and she said, "I've made you uncomfortable. That's awful. I shouldn't have made such a suggestion."

"I'm not uncomfortable," he could finally say. "I'm choking. Drank too fast. Absolutely, bring Faith. She'll fit right in. Most of the people who work for me are like very bright children. Tell her she'll have to learn to play foosball and eat hamburgers at the same time—and listen to heavy rock on a headset so she can't hear if someone wants her."

Carolee laughed. "Sounds mad. But you don't have to do it, really."

He put down his coffee and held her hands, and didn't miss the way she took a step away from him. Pushing her too fast could bring an end to the start they'd made. "I want you and Faith to come. Okay? When would be a good day?"

She took her hands from his, but touched his shoulder briefly as she passed him. "I'll call you."

"I'll make sure you have the number—all of my numbers."

By the time he turned around, she was seated at the piano and staring at the keys.

He was afraid to move or say a word for fear of changing her mind about playing.

Notes flew in fitful rushes. She curled over the keyboard, experimenting with a melody he didn't at first recognize. Over and over again, she raced the fingers of one hand back and forth, bending her head, turning her face from him to listen closely with her right ear.

When she lifted her head again, she gave him an almost impish smile.

Max got a chair from the kitchen and stationed himself as close to her as he dared.

Not so long ago he'd have laughed at the idea, but this was real intimacy. Her body moved to the rhythm she made. Her lips parted and she tipped her head back. It didn't matter that she wore jeans and a T-shirt rather than a gown, she and the piano were the same instrument, only the piano couldn't make it without her magic.

"Recognize this?" she asked.

He scrunched up his face and tried to look as if he was lost in intelligent thought.

"You don't!" She shook her head, smiling all the time, and paused, both hands raised. "Hint. King Henry the Eighth."

"Why would you play beautiful music about him?"

She sang—when she wasn't giggling. "Got it now?"

He got it that he wanted to stop the world right here and now. "Oh," he snapped his fingers. " 'Greensleeves.' *'Greensleeves'?* Henry the Eighth?"

"He wrote it."

"Nah."

"Yeah." Her eyes glittered. "Methinks the man was deeply in love."

" 'Greensleeves' was his delight," Max said. "Too bad he had so many delights."

"Some people are like that. Madly in love again and again, and again."

All signs of humor fled her face. What, he wondered, was that about. Carolee became immersed in her music. She slipped away from the room and from him. And she looked so sad.

As suddenly as she'd started playing, she stopped and put her hands in her lap.

Anything he said could be so wrong.

There were tears in her eyes.

That did it. He got up and put a finger beneath her chin until she looked at him. "Sorry," she said. "I don't know why I'm weepy."

He was sure she did know but the last thing she needed from him was prompting. "You're uncertain about the things that matter most to you. That can get overwhelming."

"I've got to put some things behind me and make a plan. I'm wasting too much time."

Max kissed her forehead. "You're going to do it." He'd give a great deal to know about all the things she had to put behind her. From the suggestion Brandy had made about Carolee's mother, she might not be referring only to what had happened to her marriage.

When he raised his face to look at her, she'd closed her eyes. She looked wounded and adrift. Max knelt beside the bench and took her into his arms. Carolee didn't attempt to embrace him, but neither did she pull away. Her head came to rest on his shoulder. He stroked her hair and swept it away from her neck.

She was needy. If that was the only reason

136

she was turning to him, Max wasn't sure how he felt about it.

"Why do I feel comfortable with you?" she asked.

Why, oh why? If he was very lucky, she might be vulnerable enough for him to find a way into her world, deep into her world. "Maybe it's because I want you to be comfortable with me so badly. I've exercised psychic power over you."

She kissed his neck, as she had on the way back from the lake, and he didn't give a damn if she only wanted him because she was needy. Give him time and he'd find a way to make her want him regardless.

"Carolee," he whispered, and when she leaned back to see him, he pressed his lips very softly to hers. He eased up and sat beside her on the piano bench. The kiss was the dangerous kind, the beginning kind that had places to go.

The heel of her hand pressing into his belly didn't help his self-control. He tipped her backward over one arm and nuzzled her throat—and opened his mouth on the soft rise of her breast above her bra. Max had a great imagination, great enough not to forget that the T-shirt was the only thing between his lips and her warm flesh.

Footsteps on the porch broke through his concentration and he straightened. Carolee moved farther along the bench and he returned to the chair. She looked mussed and sexy, and guilty.

The screen door flapped open and Faith came

in with Sam at her heels. Faith didn't look directly at either Carolee or Max but went to huddle beside Digger and gather him onto her lap.

"Good time?" Max asked.

"The best," Sam said loudly.

Carolee met Max's eyes. Sam's cheer was overdone.

"How about you two? How was that stew of mine?"

"Fabulous," Carolee said. "Digger took us for a walk afterward. He's pining because the geese wouldn't play."

Sam guffawed. "Hear that, Faith? You've got a feisty one there."

Max caught the way Carolee glanced at her father. The depth of love he saw there moved him, but there was another element and it wasn't happy. Either she was worried about Sam or they had unfinished business. Surely she'd let go of his wandering past by now. There was no changing it.

"I'd best be on my way," Max said. "Work in the morning. Your mom says you're interested in computers, Faith. I run a business that deals with some specialized software. Would you like to visit and take a look around?"

She nodded.

"Great. These are my numbers." He fished his wallet from his back pocket, took out a card, and put it on top of the piano. "Have your mom bring you downtown. You can see the offices and I'll take the two of you out to lunch. Do we have a date?"

That earned him another nod from Faith, but Carolee said, "We'd really like that."

"Good. On second thought, leave it all up to me. I'll call and fix things up."

Sam was edging to the door. "Better get some shut-eye. Gotta be in top form for this grand-daughter of mine. Night, all."

There was a chorus of good nights and Sam walked out into the darkness. He invariably drove past the upper limits of the wooded land to park near the barn, then walked between the cabin and the house.

"Okay, I'm out of here, too," Max said. His hat was at Sam's but he'd get it later. "Take care of yourselves. Make sure you lock up, Carolee." Of course he shouldn't fuss over her, but he couldn't help it.

"Night, Max," Carolee said, and she looked at him in a way that left no doubt she was fighting her own battle with feelings.

"Bye," Faith said, getting up. She gave him a mechanical smile, but at least it was something and he waved at her before going outside.

His car was parked up by the road and he set off, walking uphill. Not looking back was too hard and he gave in several times. The lights in Carolee's house spilled out in gold puddles on the surrounding flower beds and pathways.

If she didn't want a reason to be with him, she wouldn't have dreamed one up.

Disengagement could be achieved simply. He didn't have to call her, or agree to anything

139

Sam asked of him. And if he saw Carolee, he could walk the other way, or just pass her by, say "Hi," and keep on walking.

Some hope. He wasn't into rescuing people. Dealing with his own phantoms was enough. But he kept getting the sensation that if he had to say goodbye to Carolee Burns, he'd regret it forever. Just maybe, they could each be what the other needed.

Oh, yeah.

Twelve

"You and Gramps had a good time?" Faith remained on the floor with Digger's head in her lap. "It was okay."

"What does that mean?" Carolee would not have Faith behaving like a spoiled brat.

"It means I had an okay time with Gramps. I can't tell you something that wasn't true, can I?"

Leave it alone. "No, you can't. What did you have for dinner?"

Faith's eyes slid away. "Shrimp kebabs."

"Yum. One of my favorites."

"I know. Gramps ordered for me and said I'd like them because you do."

Disappointment came close to overwhelming Carolee. Faith was being deliberately difficult. "I've got some of your favorite ice cream.

Caramel and praline swirl. Why don't we have some? We'll work it off tomorrow." She winked.

"I used to like it," Faith told her. "That was when I was younger. I don't eat it now."

Carolee recalled Kip's instruction to Faith that she watch what she ate and not waste Mrs. Jolly's efforts. Hesitantly, she asked, "You aren't trying to diet, are you? You don't need to and it isn't a good idea at your age."

Faith bowed over Digger, but not before Carolee saw the glisten of tears.

"Okay, all the more for me." How dare Kip do something to give their daughter a bad self-image. "Is there anything you feel like doing? We could play a game of Scrabble. You used to love Scrabble."

"It's okay, but not tonight." Faith scrambled up. "Is it okay if I call Daddy?"

Carolee's stomach twisted. She felt sick. This was the first time she'd ever seen Faith turn so truculent—or struggle with feelings that were too much for her. "Of course you can, honey. He'll be so pleased to hear from you. I think he tries not to call when you're here so he won't interrupt anything we're doing." Which was mostly nothing.

Faith went to the black phone and dialed the number, sighing from time to time to show she considered the old-fashioned instrument a drag.

After a long interval during which Faith pressed the handset to her ear, she said, "Hi, Daddy. Are you there?" and waited before adding, "Okay. It's Faith. I wanted to talk to you. I'll call back tomorrow night if Mom says it's okay."

She hung up and her downcast expression made Carolee want to weep.

"Sometimes he doesn't answer," Faith says. "If he has company, he ignores the phone. Or he could be out."

Carolee had an urgent desire to know who came to Kip's place as "company." What was the matter with her? She never used to consider such things.

"I'll go up to bed," Faith said. "Out you go, Digger. Be quick." She opened the door for the dog and stood just outside while she waited for him to scuffle around and, finally, return with dusty paws and a bleached bone in his mouth.

Carolee wiped off the dust.

Slapping her thigh to summon Digger, Faith went wordlessly upstairs.

The phone rang and Carolee snatched it up, "Hello?"

She expected to hear Kip's voice, but it was her sister, Linda, calling from Chicago. "Hi," she said. "The prodigal sister here."

Rolling her eyes, Carolee sat down and prepared to listen to Linda's latest stories about her exciting and supposedly dangerous existence, followed by an uncomfortable stream of advice for "Mouse," as Linda called Carolee.

"You there?" Linda said.

"I am."

"What's going on?"

"I'm at Lake Home. Faith's here for her summer visit. Sam's good and enjoying being a full-time gramps. He's brought in some horses for us to ride."

Linda yawned loudly. "Ivy called. She said there might be a fabulous new man on your horizon."

Carolee turned cold. "She's off her head. You should have seen the way she behaved. This guy who's a friend of Sam's was over. He happens to be in his thirties and good-looking. Used to be a pro-football player. The Broncos. When Ivy finished drooling—which was probably after he'd left, she rambled on about what a good pair Max and I would make. Forget it. It's a myth."

"Too bad." Linda's affected drawl was almost natural now. She had a husky, attractive voice. "I met this financier. What a hunk. And, Carolee, the man has so much money, he tosses it at everyone." She giggled. "Including me. He sends gifts all the time. He wants me to marry him, of course, but I'm not getting tied down to another man. Maybe I'll live with him."

Carolee didn't feel like encouraging Linda's favorite subject; her conquests. "Do you ever see Ted?" She admired Linda's ex-husband.

A long sigh gusted from the phone. "Only when he wears me down and makes me feel guilty enough to have lunch with him. Which is about every week. I tell him to forget me and find someone else. You'd think after two years he'd have got the message, but no. You know how Ted is, he hates change."

"He loves you," Carolee said. "But that's your business."

"I'm bored." Linda was an Olympic-class whiner. "Please say I can come out for just a few days. Maybe four. I could leave Chicago on Wednesday and come back on Saturday. Albert's having a party for me on Saturday night. I think he's going to try to trick me into saying I'll marry him. Making an announcement in front of a lot of people because he thinks I won't have the guts to say it's not true is just his style."

"Faith's—"

"I know Faith's there. Don't you think I'd like to see her, too? I promise I'll be really good. I wouldn't hog her, but at least we could have the odd meal together and ride, maybe, not that I enjoy that much. The rest of the time I'd be with Dad."

Carolee looked toward the upper floor. She wasn't even sure she could keep on trying to like the girl she'd grown up with, not when Linda was responsible for the blow Carolee had never managed to put behind her. It had happened when Sam had done one of his disappearing acts. She would not allow herself to think about the shadowy images Linda had painted of Carolee's mother.

"You still there?" Linda asked.

"Yes. Okay. Would you mind staying at Sam's? I don't want to be crammed in here, not now."

A long pause invited her to feel guilty and reverse the request. Carolee kept quiet.

"Okay," Linda said. "If that's the way you want it. See you Wednesday."

She hung up before Carolee could suggest she wait and come next week.

Leaving a single light on in the kitchen, she climbed the stairs, suddenly weary, and went to Faith's room. She knocked on the door and said, "Faith? It's Mom. Okay if I come in?"

There was rustling from inside the room and Faith called, "If you want to."

The snug room was paneled in cedar, like the rest of the house. Blue chintz balloon shades were lowered in puffs over the windows, and matching cushions covered a windowseat. Bookcases on either side of the bathroom door were filled with books Carolee had bought for Faith. A chest of drawers with a mirror above it stood against one wall, and a tiny round table—covered with a cloth in the same chintz as the windows and windowseat—and two chairs were set beneath the sloping ceiling. Posters of animals were pinned on the ceiling. Faith had picked out each one of them only months ago and Carolee hoped she wouldn't soon hear how her daughter was too old for them.

Faith stood beside the double brass bed watching her.

"Do you still like this room?" Carolee asked, willing to risk the consequences of the question.

"It's okay."

The girl was trying to goad her, Carolee realized. What she didn't know, was why. "What's
the matter with the bed?" she said, going
closer. "What's in it?"

Faith raised her chin. "My sleeping bag.
Daddy said I could bring it if I wanted to. If
it made this feel more like home. My pillow,
too. Don't worry, the sleeping bag's been
cleaned and Mrs. Jolly sent some pillow slips
with me."

Carolee almost flinched. She made fists
inside the pockets of her jeans. She noticed
an empty garbage sack on the bedside table.
It must have been the one Kip brought—and
it had contained the sleeping bag and pillow.
Any negative reaction would be a mistake, but
her next breath was painful. "Looks like
you've made up a cozy bed."

"Yes." Faith helped Digger and his bone onto
the comforter—also of blue chintz.

Once more Carolee opted not to mention
how she felt about the dog being on the bed
without something to protect the comforter.

She sat down beside Digger and stroked his
head. Very quickly that head was on her thigh.
"Do you remember how we used to snuggle
up in bed together and I'd tell you stories?"

Faith made much of finding a clean nightie.
"I used to make up stories, remember?
They were like serials in comics. They went
on and on, and every time I thought I was at
the end, you'd beg for another installment."
*And I want to cuddle you again, Faith. You
aren't too old. I want to cuddle you and make up*

stories for you. I was your age once, I'd know what you like.

With her nightie and slippers under her arm, Faith gave Carolee one of the sliding glances she'd perfected. "I remember vaguely. That was when I was a real little kid." She went to a bookshelf and selected a book. This she set beside the bed and Carolee saw it was *Under the Greenwood Tree* by Thomas Hardy. It was part of a set intended for when Faith was older.

"You like Thomas Hardy?" Carolee said.

Faith glanced quickly at the book as if seeing it for the first time. "Yes. I'm going to take a shower now, then read before I go to sleep. Night, Mom."

A wedge of weak, yellow light cut into Carolee's room from the door she'd left slightly open.

Sleep wouldn't come.

She breathed through her mouth and blinked back tears. The pain in her throat was something she couldn't do anything about. Kids grew up and changed, but they didn't have to pull away from their parents quite so soon.

The performance in Faith's room had been just that, an act to exert her independence, her lack of need. But she did need, and Carolee felt it so sharply it hurt. She gave up on stopping the tears and they slipped, warm and wet, from the outer corners of her eyes, past her temples, and into her hair. Her cheeks were damp. How had it happened that she'd started crying again? Scooting down into the bed, she pulled the covers over her head.

Her daughter didn't mean to sadden her. Faith was unhappy and it was because she'd rather be with her father than with the mother who was becoming a stranger to her.

She mustn't smother her. With care, Faith could be won over. Carolee filled her head with the positive words, but doubt chipped away at them.

A sound, a squeak, came from the direction of Faith's room. The door opening slowly, then closing slowly, the latch clicking carefully into place.

Carolee turned onto her back and watched the slice of light against the wall. She pulled up onto her elbows and smiled. Faith was still a little girl who wanted comfort.

Soft footfalls approached, a shadow flitted through the light, and the footsteps continued on toward the stairs. Each tread creaked a little as Faith went downstairs.

Carolee sat up and hugged her knees to her chest.

Faith needed her. Not bothering with her robe, she slid from bed and pushed her feet into her slippers. Moving swiftly, she went to the top of the stairs and looked around the ground floor. There was no sign of Faith, and although the screen was shut, the front door stood open.

She couldn't allow a child to be out there alone—even if she would be angry at Carolee for following her.

Very quietly, she slipped down the stairs and crossed to the screen. Slowly, grateful Sam had finally applied some oil, she opened it and peered outside. Except for a faint glow from the kitchen window and the front door, the porch was in darkness.

A shadowy figure at one end, Faith stood hunched over the railings, her head pushed out as if to see up the driveway. Did she expect Kip to appear? Or hope he would?

Carolee felt sweat break out on her back. Her mind racing, she stepped back inside. She wanted to comfort her girl—if Faith would allow it.

She pushed the screen outward again, this time making plenty of noise, and said, *"There* you are."

Faith said, "Don't fake it, Mom. I'm not a little kid anymore. You came out and saw me, and went back in. Now you're pretending you only just noticed me. You want an excuse to be here."

"Okay, I did all that. And I do want to be here with you. I heard you come downstairs and followed to see if you were okay. I can't let you be out here on your own."

"Why?" Faith spun around. "Most of the time you don't know where I am anyway."

"Oh, Faith." Carolee fumbled her way to a chair and sat down. "Sweetheart, I want to know where you are *all* the time."

Faith sniffed. She walked slowly to the top step from the porch and sat down. She leaned against a post. "Ever since I was little, you kept on going away."

"I... Yes, my work took me away."

"You liked your work best. Daddy..."

Faith stood up and Carolee could see her stark face, and the way she slapped her hands against her sides.

"Nothing is more important to me than you are. It never was. Music is a way I express myself. You're part of me."

Faith rubbed her face. "If I was part of you, how could you leave me? You chose the music then, but it doesn't take you away all the time now. You change your mind about things."

"That's because I decided I wanted to be close to you whenever it was possible."

"Why didn't you decide that a long time ago? Why did you ever leave Daddy and me alone?"

Carolee held her throat and drew in bitter breaths. "Your dad and I had an agreement. We didn't have much money at first. Then my career started working well and we decided I should go with it while I could." This was so dangerous. If she wasn't careful, she would sound as if she was blaming Kip. "Come and sit with me on the swing."

Faith turned away. "I...can't." Choking sobs shook her.

"Sweetheart. Oh, baby." Carolee scrambled from the chair and tried to hold Faith.

She twisted away. "I get frightened. Grownups have their own things to do. I understand that. You did what you wanted and you went away."

"Faith—"

"No, you don't hear me. Neither of you hear me, not really. If Daddy hadn't been there to look after me, you wouldn't have liked me because I'd have been a problem."

"You could never be a problem. Please listen to me. We can talk about these things now because you need to. And I want to."

"Daddy couldn't do his painting because of me." The sobs subsided but Faith still took loud, shallow breaths. "He couldn't have his time. There was always me and he gave everything up."

Carolee didn't say that she'd never understood why Kip didn't paint while others were looking after Faith. She had to ask, "Did your father tell you that's how it was for him, that he minded choosing to be at home?"

"No." Faith sniffed. "But he said I've got to grow up now. You heard him."

"He didn't exactly say that."

"Sort of, he did. And he brought me early and went away as soon as he could." Faith scrubbed at her eyes. "And he didn't answer me when I said I loved him."

She would have to call Kip. The thought turned Carolee cold. She would have to ask him to reassure their daughter. "I told you I was sure he didn't want to leave you at all so he hurried. People do that when they want to get through something that makes them sad. Your dad really loves you."

"I know. But I know you do, too."

Of course. This was what she should have expected, this growing conviction of Faith's

151

that love could have limits, that her mother had been able to love her but not to give up something she seemed to love more. How could a child be blamed for thinking that?

"Daddy should be able to have his chance, just like you. I know he's ready. I can tell. One day soon... One day soon he'll go, too."

Thirteen

A purple corduroy couch, loveseat, and chair left just enough space in Brandy's office for her glass-topped desk. White wood shutters were closed over the windows, and lamps, turned on low, gave the impression that it couldn't really be early afternoon.

Despite protests, Brandy had one of Carolee's CDs playing. Carolee stretched out on the couch with her head on a pile of cushions, while Brandy took her favorite position, on the loveseat with her legs trailing over one end. The skirt of her clingy forest green dress had hiked to a barely decent level on thighs that were worth showing off.

"What time is it?" Carolee asked.

"Five minutes later," Brandy said, regarding her friend. "Faith's at the library, where she evidently likes to be. She's safe. And you're with your best friend. We're way behind on news. We *need* this time together. Relax."

"Yeah. Relax when I'm sitting on a couple of time bombs."

Brandy shifted to prop herself on one elbow. "Okay, spill it. Don't leave anything out."

"I don't want to go into it too far. Faith's an unhappy girl and she's got a reason to be. It's largely my fault—"

"Garbage."

Carolee looked at her. "Are you going to let me finish?"

Brandy made a face but pressed her lips together.

"When I had Faith, I didn't know a thing about children. I'd never even been a babysitter. For some stupid reason I didn't consider that even very young children figure out who they can and can't trust. Who's always there for them, and who isn't. That's it. I can't talk about it anymore. I've got to find a way to work things through with her—preferably before I approach Kip with a proposition for shared custody."

The wide grin on Brandy's face seemed out of place until she said, "Damn, I'm thrilled to hear you say that. You kept telling me you were going to do something, but you never had a plan."

"No. I had to decide what to do first. And I still haven't made any formal moves. I won't have Faith in court and being asked to make choices. It could come to that if lawyers are involved. Kip won't want that either and I think we can work it out together."

Brandy settled back on her cushions.

"What?" Carolee said.

"Kip. I try not to think about him because he's an idiot. I'll never believe he planned for things to go as far as they did. He wanted you to be successful and you were, but much more so than he ever dreamed of. You made him feel threatened."

"No." Carolee laced her hands beneath her head and looked at lamplight patterns on the ceiling. "He did what he wanted to do. He didn't want to be married anymore."

"He wanted to scare you and make sure he got to call all the shots. You were supposed to be shaken up enough to fall over yourself trying to make him happy. I think he finally wanted to take you out of the limelight before you found someone else more interesting than him."

"*He* divorced *me*. I begged him not to but he wouldn't listen."

"Sure." Brandy dangled her shoes from her toes and jiggled them. "Things got out of hand. But he still thinks you belong to him. The way you gave him everything he wanted must have made him believe that. He's having a good time, but he intends to put your marriage back together when he's ready. You're his big meal ticket. He'd never really let you go."

Carolee turned on her side to face Brandy. "I knew you had an imagination, but that's ridiculous and you know it."

"Maybe. I'm just glad you're ready to do something about Faith. What do you think of Max Wolfe?"

A complete and empty blank filled Carolee's head.

"You know? Max Wolfe?"

"Yes, I do. How do you know him?"

"He's a friend of mine. He found out you were playing here one time and turned up. Afterwards he asked me to let him know whenever you were coming back. He's not a sociable guy—not anymore—but he came here on the busiest nights I ever have, thanks to you."

Sometimes the world was just too small. "And Max told you he spent some time with me?"

Brandy's expression became remote. She didn't answer.

"Speak to me. You look unhappy. It's me who should be upset if a guy talks when he shouldn't."

"He didn't." Brandy grinned at her. "But I faked you out. I found out he helped you get home the last time you played here and asked if you two had seen each other again. He wasn't talking. But you have. Do you like him?"

This wasn't something they should discuss. "He's a nice man."

"A *nice* man?" Brandy laughed and her flat tummy jerked. "He's frigging fantastic. He's a dream in every way. And he sure thinks you're wonderful."

"I'm taking Faith to his offices tomorrow," Carolee blurted out. "He's going to show us around and have Faith play foosball. And we're going out to lunch with him."

Another silence fell on Brandy's side of the room.

"It doesn't mean anything. He's been out at Lake Home to visit Sam and help him with the horses he got for while Faith's there. It's a friendly thing."

"Oh, yes, a friendly thing. Men like taking little girls to lunch just to be friendly. They certainly wouldn't do something like that as an excuse to be with a little girl's mother."

Playing games didn't agree with Carolee. "Sarcasm is ugly, but you're right. Max is interested in me."

"And you're interested in him?"

"Drop it, please."

"Can't," Brandy said. "He's a good friend, used to be a *really* good friend. Is he another of your time bombs?"

Without warning, the door opened. Linda walked in and wasted no time before stooping to plant kisses on Carolee. "Hi, Mouse. This looks cozy. Hi, Brandy. How come you're neglecting your customers?"

"We only serve drinks and take-out between lunch and dinner." Brandy had closed her eyes and crossed her arms. She didn't like Linda. "How did you know we were here?"

"My father. I left Chicago at some ungodly hour so I could spend as much time as possible with Carolee. We've only got a few days."

Carolee winced. Subtle Linda was hinting she'd like Carolee to leave with her. "Sit down. I've got half an hour before I go to pick up Faith from the library."

Linda dropped her red skin purse on the floor and settled in the chair. Her red dress had a short, flippy skirt and she wore high pumps that matched the purse. Thick chestnut hair reached below her shoulders and she hadn't lost the habit of throwing it forward, shaking it back, and fluffing it with her fingers.

"You look great," Brandy told her and Carolee loved her for the generosity.

"Thanks." All of Linda's attention was on Carolee. "So tell me who this Max is? Dad said you were the one to ask."

Blood flew to Carolee's face. Sam never learned that there were things he shouldn't talk about.

Linda pointed at her and wrinkled her nose. "You never could hide what you feel. My, you do blush. He must be something. I'm looking forward to meeting him tomorrow."

"He won't be over tomorrow." Carolee wanted to disappear.

"I know that. You and Faith are going downtown to have lunch with him. Of course you'll take me, too. She can't leave me behind, can she, Brandy?"

Wisely, Brandy didn't say a thing.

"I'm glad you've finally met someone else," Linda said. "You're young and you're overdue for some great sex. I mean really great, not like whatever you had before."

"What are you saying?" Carolee sat up. "You don't have to be outrageous around me. I'm not impressed by it. You know nothing about my past sex life, and now I don't have one."

Linda looked offended.

A knock preceded the latest arrival. A man with startlingly hazel eyes and a clever, narrow face put his head into the room. Brandy's hands went to her face. There was a moment when the color left her cheeks and her eyes glistened, but only a moment before she whooped and held out her arms. "There you are at last, Rob Mead. Come here. I ought to send you away for ignoring me for so long. But I'm a weak woman. Kiss me."

He closed the door behind him and the rest of the man was as interesting as his face. Athletically built and tall, he wore a cream T-shirt that showed off his tawny skin and revealed impressive biceps. His shoulders and pecs would have turned any head.

"I've had some interesting business to finish," he said. "Now it is finished and you're the first one I wanted to see." The tone of his voice, the solemn, intense expression in his eyes, didn't suggest he was joking.

Carolee looked from his face, to Brandy's. There was much more than simple friendship, or an uncomplicated sexual attraction between them. *Rob Mead.* Carolee realized the name sounded familiar, but couldn't remember why and, after all, it wasn't unusual.

He knelt beside Brandy, settled a hand on her thigh, and gave her the kiss she'd asked for. What a kiss. Carolee was too fascinated to be embarrassed, or to stop watching. He abandoned Brandy's thigh for her bottom and half lifted her from the loveseat—which was an easy feat from the look of him.

Carolee bit down on her bottom lip and looked at Linda.

Her sister was sizing up Mr. Mead with much more than casual interest, and without amusement. The hungry look was in her brown eyes. That hunger had wrecked her marriage.

Brandy pushed on Rob Mead's shoulders and said, "Where are your manners? I've got company."

He got up at once and sat beside Carolee on the couch. "I was only following your instructions, Brandy." He had a great grin, even if he was wearing traces of Brandy's lipstick.

"You're sitting by Carolee Burns, and the lady in red is her sister from Chicago, Linda Gordon."

"Linda," he said and shook her hand before turning to Carolee. "*The* Carolee Burns? The jazz pianist?"

"Yes," she said simply.

"Is Max coming in?"

That's who he was, the Rob Mead that Sam had told her about, the one who was Max's best friend and who had inherited his place with the Broncos after Max was injured.

He'd asked *her* if Max was coming here. "I don't know," she said, taking another look at her watch. If she left now, she'd be early to pick up Faith, but she wanted to go.

"He mentioned you," Rob said.

159

Linda moved to the edge of her chair and her knees almost touched his. She watched his mouth when he spoke.

"Said he's crazy about hearing you perform. He's been into music, big time, for as long as I've known him. That's a long time."

"That's nice. Thank you for telling me."

"My pleasure. Max has had some hard knocks. You already know about that. It's good to know he's met someone who can make him sound so good."

She got up. "Forgive me, but I have to meet my daughter."

Concern darkened Brandy's eyes. "I'll call you later," she said.

Carolee nodded. "Later. Okay, Linda. The library's only a few blocks away but we'd better start walking."

"Oh, don't even mention walking. I had to go miles to the gate at O'Hare. I'll meet you back at the house." She moved to the seat Carolee had vacated. "Maybe I could talk someone into having a glass of wine with me."

The Kirkland Library was a yellow brick building on the corner of Second and State. Rain had threatened all day but in the ball field beyond the library, grade school boys played baseball. Carolee didn't listen closely enough to the address system to hear what was said. She did hear shouts and screams from the boys and their supporters.

Large, scattered raindrops started to fall, but

in front of the library a scampering group of preschoolers begged their parents for turns at sitting on a carousel horse that was part of a metal sculpture.

While she ran for the entrance, Carolee's nostrils flared at the scent of earth growing damp.

The library was busy, every computer terminal taken, and every table and chair Carolee passed, full. She hurried along an aisle between the stacks and arrived at the young adult section. Faith wasn't there. Carolee's pulse quickened before she noticed unmistakable curly hair caught up on the back of an arm chair that had been turned to face a large window. With her legs stretched out in front of her, Faith had slipped far down into the chair. If her chin weren't sunk on her chest, Carolee might have thought she was staring past the ball field toward a children's play park, and Central Avenue beyond.

Faith's eyes were half-closed, her hands were in the pockets of her shorts, and she had no books.

"Hello," Carolee said softly, and smoothed the top of her head. "Penny for those thoughts."

"Nothing," Faith said. She stood up abruptly as if just awakened. "I wasn't doing anything."

"That wasn't what I asked you, honey. You looked deep in thought." And lost, Carolee thought.

"I want to go home."

She'd expected this to happen, but she still wasn't prepared. "Could we talk about it? You aren't giving this a chance."

161

Faith moved closer to the window, walled herself off from Carolee and anyone else nearby. She muttered something and Carolee stood beside her. "I'm tired," Faith said. "I want to go to sleep. I want to be with Digger."

Relief rushed at Carolee. She needed to sit down. "You look tired. Do you feel ill?"

"No." Faith looked up into Carolee's face. "It's been days, but Daddy's never called back."

"Maybe he did but we weren't in."

"He'd have left a message. After you dropped me here, I tried to call him again." She stuck her hands in her pockets. "Mrs. Jolly says he isn't at home. He's gone away. She isn't sure when he'll come back. She said she'll let him know I called—if he checks in."

Fourteen

"We could have found our own way in," Carolee said and put an arm around Faith's shoulders. "You didn't have to meet us in the parking lot."

"Yes, I did." Max held the door open from Occidental Avenue into the building that housed his offices. "And no, you couldn't find your own way in. I wouldn't let you." He allowed the door to swing shut behind him and

162

led the way up a flight of stairs. "Pioneer Square's on everyone's list of favorite places in Seattle. I guess a lot of people don't see how tough life is for those on the street—or how tough some of them are."

The stairs were of old polished oak and carpeted in dark green. Plaster had been removed from every wall to expose brick. Carolee liked the feeling inside these old buildings. She and Faith followed Max upward. He wore a burgundy-colored chambray shirt and dark navy pants. Regardless of what he had on, she'd already decided the man made the clothes. Her own white silk blouse and soft gray skirt could be a little less snug in places. Losing a few pounds and putting in some real exercise again might be a great idea, and she'd do those things if they ever mattered enough to her.

"We've got three floors," Max said, arriving at a landing where New Age music floated from one cubicle to clash with reggae from an uncertain location. "This is mostly accounting and shipping. We'll go up to where the scary ones live."

"Scary?" Faith was immediately interested. "What kind of scary?"

"You'll see for yourself." He sent a smile toward Carolee but she didn't miss the way it became fixed, or his concerned frown. Evidently she wasn't doing a great job of hiding her feelings. She must track down Kip.

Max offered Faith his hand and she amazed Carolee by taking it without missing a beat.

163

Watching the two of them climb stairs together gave her a funny sensation. They continued to hold hands when Max took Faith through a labyrinth of corridors lined with windowless cubicles on one side, and offices with a view on the other. Here the noise was jarring. Clicking keyboards droned like the harmony beneath a melody of rising and falling voices, yells, bangs on walls, music, and what sounded like the frequent fall of cans from pop machines. Looking around at empty cans dropped on the floor, Carolee decided she'd guessed that one right.

"Watch out for electrical leads," Max said, raising his voice to be heard.

The leads and cords in question were of a variety of colors, turquoise seeming to be a favorite, and they crisscrossed and snaked around each other in remarkable confusion.

A slender, good-looking—and very young—man came from a corner office. He wore metal-rimmed glasses over dark, intelligent eyes, and a Seattle Mariners' baseball cap—back to front. "Yo, Max," he said.

"Yo, Bryan. How's it going? We gonna make it?"

That earned Max a shrug. "I sure hope so. If the feds quit messing with us, it'll save us a lot of time."

He carried on, stepping over leads as if he knew exactly where they were. Passing the open door of his office, Carolee heard easy jazz coming from a radio and she smiled.

Max said, "The reference to the feds isn't

unusual. The kind of work we do keeps them looking over our shoulders."

"Bryan seems like a nice kid."

"Nice man with a great wife and a cute kid. He's a smart cookie. That's what keeps everything buzzing, all these smart people in one place. And they've never even considered the word *can't.*"

"What do you think, Faith?" Carolee asked. "Would you like to work in a place like this?"

She looked dubious. "I haven't seen any girls here."

"There," Max said, pointing into a cubicle and at a woman's back. "And there. And there." He continued to make his point. "I'll have a job waiting for you when you're ready."

Faith laughed and Carolee grinned at Max. This was the perfect thing to do today. Something entirely different that would help divert Faith's mind from worrying about where her father was—and what he was thinking about her.

"Prepare yourself. We come to the great foosball hall."

Here the biggest sounds came from slamming rods in the foosball table. Players wore headsets for their music but that didn't stop them from voicing disgust when things didn't go their way. Carolee had never seen so many pairs of too-short black pants and white socks in one place. These guys gave the game their all. Each one had a distinctive style, from those who planted their feet and put all their body weight behind each thrust, to the jumpers who became airborne every time they rammed home a stainless steel rod. The little game men skewered along the poles reminded Carolee of macabre shish kebabs.

Max caught one female player's eye and indicated Faith. In minutes she was being taught the game and Carolee smiled at the way she accepted her own baseball cap and settled it, back to front, of course, on her head. Max went around the table to speak to the woman quietly, then to Faith.

"Now I'll take you up to where the sane people are," he told Carolee when he returned to her side, and they retraced their steps to take another flight of stairs.

"You know Nellie and Fritz Archer? The ones with the diner in—"

"Yes, of course. In Kirkland. I love the place."

"I have breakfast there most days. I've never seen you."

"I don't like early mornings—or breakfast, very much. I like to come around slowly with a cup of coffee, in my own kitchen. No radio, no TV, no noise of any kind. I do read the newspaper sometimes. I'm very difficult in the morning."

"I'll remember that," Max said, and the look he gave her wasn't innocent.

She went on as if she hadn't noticed his expression. "I don't even want anyone to talk to me. The worst thing I can think of is being around someone cheerful." She shuddered. "I *hate* people who sound so proud when they announce that they're *morning people*, as if night people like me are handicapped, or even immoral. And if those creeps grin, ooh, I feel murderous."

Max had stopped on the stairs and so had Carolee. "I guess I know how you really feel about mornings now." His eyes made a swift downward passage, all the way to her feet. "I'll have to be careful—should the need ever arise—not to get your dander up like that."

She ought to mind his innuendoes, but she didn't. She liked this man's attention too much. Carolee moved purposefully ahead and he fell in at her side. He indicated an office with the door closed. "What I was going to say was that one of Fritz and Nellie's sons-in-law works for me. Steve Acton. That's his office. He's on a conference call or I'd introduce you. He's the in-house lawyer and my right hand. My office is at the end. The lady out front with the Edith Bunker do is Mrs. Fossie. She's worked for me awhile now and I still don't have permission to use her first name, but she's absolutely the best watchdog a man could have. And she's efficient."

He slid a hand beneath her elbow. The dark green carpet on the stairs covered the entire floor as far as Mrs. Fossie's domain, where green-veined Italian marble took over.

Mrs. Fossie of the tight gray curls and springy bangs was exactly what Carolee had visualized. When Max's heels hit marble, the lady got up from her unnervingly tidy desk and all but stood at attention.

"Back, are you, Mr. Wolfe?" she said, with a trace of censure in her voice. "Bugoff has called twice." Her thin face was powdered and she wore definitely pink lipstick. Mrs. Fossie didn't approve of her boss being anywhere but in his office, that much was clear.

"That's Bugulf, Mrs. Fossie," Max said. "If I'm not here when he calls again, please tell him I'll get back to him."

Mrs. Fossie straightened her back inside a navy blue linen suit and stared pointedly at Carolee.

"This is my good friend, Carolee Burns," Max said. "She and her daughter are visiting me."

Lively blue eyes shifted from Max to Carolee, to Carolee's unadorned left hand, and back to Max. "I see," she said, and her expression gave the impression she liked the idea of his having a "good friend" visit him. Carolee liked it that he had called her that.

"Would you like coffee?" Max asked her.

She would, desperately. "Yes, please."

"I'll see to it," Mrs. Fossie said, and set off in sensible, low-heeled shoes.

"She's something else," Carolee whispered as Max showed her into a large office where once again the floors had been refinished and left uncovered except for several rugs, and the warm-colored brick walls had been exposed.

"Do you like it here?" Max asked, as if he hoped she would.

Below a beamed plaster ceiling, exposed pipes ran from one side of the room to the other. "It's

168

wonderful. You must have had a lot of work done on it."

"To achieve the new, old look?" He smiled broadly. "You're right. Everything was here. All we had to do was peel away years of junk."

The phone rang on a mahogany desk that looked antique and incredibly heavy.

Max picked up the handset. "Yes. Hi, Steve." With a hand in one pocket, he listened. "What did you tell them?" His face, the way he carried himself, his mannerisms were familiar in a way that made Carolee warm when she watched him. He was a self-assured man, and best of all, he had obviously made peace with misfortune and moved on. "You sure you need me?" he said, and listened with downcast eyes, rocking his hips from side to side a little. Occasionally she had noticed that he flexed his legs after he got up from a chair. Apart from that, there was almost no evidence of what must have been a serious accident.

"Okay." He hung up. "I've got to go see Steve. Shouldn't take long."

There was a discreet tap at the door and he said, "Come on in," admitting Mrs. Fossie carrying a tray of coffee mugs, a tall pot, and a plate of cookies.

She put the tray on a low table in front of a long, green leather couch and prepared to pour.

"Oh, please let me do that," Carolee said. "Really. I'd like to."

Wordless but smiling, Max's assistant withdrew.

169

"You know exactly how to deal with people," he said. "If you'd said something about her having better things to do, she'd have lectured you on how looking after me is part of her duties, thank you. I'll go see Steve and get back as soon as I can. Stock up on cookies and coffee."

Carolee said, "I'll do that," but watched every step he took to the door and his backward glance at her on leaving, before she approached the coffee and poured a mug. She had just received a loaded look, and liked it a lot.

Rather than sit, she strolled around the office. The complete absence of photographs intrigued her. Most people had photos of someone or something they cared about. Max didn't even have a shot of his parents, or wherever he'd come from, or even a dog. He did have a single and very large three-dimensional bronze relief of stampeding buffalo on one wall.

From the windows she could see Occidental Avenue. Below, men and women dressed for business, many talking into headsets, strode through the hodgepodge of artisans who sold their pieces in the Pioneer Square area, droves of tourists, and all the homeless drifters Max hadn't wanted her to be alone with.

To the left of his desk and beside a credenza heaped with folders, a pocket door stood open to a bathroom. She went closer and peeked inside. Simplicity reigned there. Gray stone walls and countertop, a shower and another sliding door that probably led to the toilet. Max's scent hung vaguely in the air. She hadn't really been aware of noticing it until now.

Her feelings for him shouldn't be an issue. They'd met only a few weeks ago.

She couldn't let any more time pass without making an all-out effort to find Kip. Two calls, one last night and one early that morning, had got her to the answering machine. Even the staff wasn't answering anymore. With her coffee in her hand, she walked to the couch and sat down. Her phone was in her bag. Setting the coffee down, she dialed Kip's number with a thumb and listened to ringing at the Bell Town condo. Eventually she got voice messaging—and hung up.

Bill and Ivy Lester spent a lot of time with Kip. The next number she dialed was theirs and Bill picked up at once.

"Bill—it's Carolee."

She thought he hesitated, as if surprised to hear her voice. "Ivy's not here. She's visiting her mother."

"I see. Can I talk to you? I need some help."

This time the pause was more definite. "You've been a stranger over here," he said. "I know Ivy gets to see you, but I miss you when you don't visit."

"You could always come with Ivy when she visits me," Carolee said gently. "I don't bite."

"Oh, sure," Bill said, laughing. His business was putting deals together and he had a nat- urally easy way with words. "You're single and

I'm a handsome devil. I've got to be strong for both of us."

Carolee wasn't sure she was amused, but she said, "Admirable of you. Bill, I'm trying to get ahold of Kip. Apparently he's out. Any idea where I'd find him?"

Bill cleared his throat. She wasn't imagining his unusual awkwardness.

"Are you uncomfortable talking to me?" Why pretend?

"Of course not." More overly enthusiastic laughter followed. "What a crazy suggestion. Are you okay, Carolee? Are you sure you don't need to talk to someone?"

She quelled an urge to get mad. "You mean should I see a psychiatrist because I'm trying to get a message to my ex-husband?"

"You sound anxious, that's all."

He was probably right about that. "Not at all. Faith's visiting me at the moment and I want to discuss something with her father."

"Is that why Linda was looking for him, too?"

Linda? "Linda called you?"

"Yes. I assumed you knew."

"I've been out with Faith." Why would Linda call Kip? She'd never taken the time to know him well—or ever given the impression she liked him. "She may have been trying to help me." When Linda had arrived on Carolee's doorstep before eight that morning, she hadn't said a word about anything but how much she wanted to go to Seattle with Carolee and Faith.

"I told her he's on his boat."

Carolee pushed herself to the back of the

couch. Mrs. Jolly would be aware of that. She must have been instructed to tell Faith she didn't know where he was.

"Okay." She wanted to get off the phone.

"Carolee," Bill said and there was a change in his voice, a hint of something tentative. "This isn't my place, but Kip misses you."

It took too long for her to say, "No, he doesn't. But you're nice to be so kind."

Bill sighed. "I mean it. He's in a corner and doesn't know how to get himself out, but he wants you back. Help him, Carolee. You two had something great and you can have it again."

"This discussion isn't a good idea," she told him, deeply shaken.

"Okay, we'll drop it, but I've got to say one more thing first. Getting involved with this football player is a bad idea. To those types, women are just notches on their belts. Don't risk ruining a reconciliation with Kip."

She trembled. "I don't understand what you're talking about. I just need to talk to Kip about Faith."

A long, long sigh from Bill didn't help settle Carolee's jumpy stomach. "Try his cell phone," he said.

No way would she tell Bill she didn't have Kip's cell phone number, or any number except for the condo. And she would not admit she hadn't known about the boat until Faith arrived. "Thanks. I'll do that."

"Good. He's just messing around. He said he'd be at his moorage here most of the time."

Fifteen

Max didn't try to go into his office quietly, but apparently Carolee hadn't heard him arrive. He closed the door firmly. She sat sideways on the couch with her legs drawn up on the seat and crossed at the ankles. A cell phone rested in a lax hand.

The ongoing threat from a competitor who could be trying to sabotage tracking software at key global locations was serious, but not going anyplace fast. This business he'd built was what he wanted most. Wasn't it? He had only himself to please. Nothing and no one tied him down. And if he was smart, that was the way it was going to stay.

But if this woman decided she couldn't afford to have him around, he wouldn't give up. Tomorrow he might change his mind, but today he figured he could have a relationship—a man–woman kind of relationship—and stay focused.

She said, "Games people play," quite clearly and leaned her head and shoulder on the back of the couch.

"Carolee," he said. "You okay?"

"Just dandy, thanks."

In other words, she wasn't okay. "What happened?" He made a casual approach and stood over her. "I know when I hear tears."

"There's nothing more boring to a man than listening to a woman cry—or whine." She slapped the phone against her thigh. "I don't understand why I've started crying again. I quit the habit months ago."

He chewed the inside of a cheek and thought about what she said. "Maybe you weren't allowing yourself to feel anything because it was safer. Now, for some reason, you want to feel again." And maybe he was airing his own wishful thinking.

Carolee still didn't look at him. "My problems are my own. Thank you for being so kind to Faith. She needs that. And she likes you."

"She's worth being kind to. But I'm not easily diverted. Give me a chance and find out what a good listener I am."

Carolee shook her head once. "No, thanks. I met Rob Mead yesterday. At Brandy's."

"I know. He already told me."

She turned her face up to his then. An empty look made her eyes deep and sad. "I didn't know you and Brandy were old friends."

This was one subject that was bound to show up. "Yes. She's special. She was there when I thought the bottom had fallen out of everything for good."

"You've got good taste." She wrinkled her nose. "At least where Brandy's concerned."

"I've got good taste in people, period," he said and scrambled for the right things to say here, the right moves to make—and not to make. "Lunch is being ordered in. Mrs. Fossie spoke to Faith about her favorites. Should arrive in about an hour."

Carolee stuffed the phone hastily into her purse and stood up. "I'd better check on Faith myself."

"She's having a great time. It's good for her, isn't it? I mean, I don't have kids but I was one a long time ago and I hated it that I was never allowed to just be, with no one showing up to stop me. Sorry. Not my business."

Tears, sliding down her cheeks, bewildered him. What was he supposed to say now?

"You're right," Carolee said, swiping at her face. "I'm not on very firm ground with what's been happening—with trying so hard to make her happy so she'll like being with me like she used to. I'm trying too hard."

She smoothed her skirt over her hips and checked the blouse that crisscrossed in front and tied at one side.

If he couldn't stop himself from studying each small gesture she made, and if she noticed, he'd have an even tougher job of persuasion ahead. Saying something light was the answer. "I want to know how it would feel to be kissed by you." Laughing, even at himself or covering his face, wouldn't help. He was an ass.

Carolee walked around him, never taking her eyes from his. He expected her to leave. Instead she said, "We already did that. More than once. Did you forget?"

"No," he told her. "I've done the kissing and you were kind enough not to slap me. But I want you to really kiss me. Just do it...but only if you want to."

She blew out through pursed lips and walked

on. Max followed her without getting too close.

Facing him fully, a flush rising in her cheeks, Carolee came at him abruptly enough to catch him off balance when they collided. He caught her by the waist and she reached up to put her hands behind his neck and pull his mouth to hers.

A small part of his mind told Max that this great dream could have a high price tag— like the lady's guilt and a subsequent *sayonara*.

But hell, she could kiss. *Don't think, take it and give it back.* She didn't quit. He grew hotter, and harder dammit. But she wasn't a baby—she had to know what kissing him like she wanted him for lunch and dinner would do to him.

He heard only her breathing, and his, and the faint sound of her silk blouse rubbing against his shirt, her skirt on his pants. And he felt her pressing into him.

Guys who couldn't or wouldn't get into foreplay missed out. Not that this was exactly foreplay. Max used Carolee's hair to ease her head back. Holding her still, he narrowed his gaze and looked at the excitement in her glittering eyes before he opened his mouth on her neck.

As suddenly as she'd launched herself at him, she pushed him away.

Without any fumbling, she undid and unwrapped her blouse. She was panting. The white bra she wore fastened in front and she slipped the hook undone.

Her skin was very white, her nipples large, a rosy color and erect.

This didn't happen, not to him. He couldn't take his eyes from her breasts.

"Lock the door," she said.

Max didn't argue, he just did as she asked.

"Take off your shirt."

He would regret asking this, but he had to. "Are you trying to prove something?"

"You told me what you wanted and I gave it to you. I'm not telling you what I want. You'll work it out."

The shirt took too many seconds to shed, and her help only slowed him down. They were both breathing hard, both seeking each other desperately. And he didn't need to be told she wanted him to kiss her breasts. She arched her back and he obliged. Geez, she was amazing, but she wasn't herself.

"Carolee—"

"Please don't talk."

There was no hesitation when she undid his belt and zipper. He cast around. The couch, he guessed, only he didn't want to make love to her on his office couch. He wanted much more, an occasion and a situation to remember.

Carolee didn't bother to take her blouse and bra all the way off. Holding his wrists, she walked backward until she bumped into the credenza. Files slid past her and onto the floor—and kept on sliding when she released his wrists to hike herself up and sit.

She used her feet to pull him between her thighs and worked her skirt up.

Max felt hot and cold at the same time. His skin tingled. He looked down at her bare legs, at white lace panties. "Carolee?" He'd better get his act together while he still could. "I need to get something."

She kissed his lips again, and held him scissored against her. "That's not an issue." His hands, she took to her breasts.

When Carolee reached down to push him past the panties and inside her, he had to grab her shoulders and rest his face on top of her head. She buried her mouth beneath his chin to smother a cry, and pulled herself from the credenza so that he carried her.

With strength that seemed unreal, she wrapped her legs around his waist, and took him. No, not Carolee Burns, the shy one who said she couldn't have a man around. Yet hers were the knees clamped at his sides, hers were the heels drumming his rear at each thrust.

He couldn't hold back any longer—and he didn't.

She closed her eyes and he felt her ripple around him.

There wasn't anything clever to say. Carolee kept her arms around his neck and slid to stand on the floor.

"Don't say anything," she told him. "Let's just pretend there isn't anything else but this—just for a little while. Then we'll forget it because we have to."

Sixteen

"Dad's old," Linda said. "He's not dead. Quit trying to be his mother."

"He's out riding with my daughter—who doesn't know how yet. It's okay for me to be concerned over Sam's health and whether or not he's strong enough to take care of more than himself."

Linda poured herself another cup of coffee and returned to her seat at Carolee's kitchen table.

"You know his heart isn't good. And he's got arthritis, for Pete's sake—arthritis that only gets worse." Carolee finished rinsing dishes and stacking them in the drainer. She took pastry makings from the refrigerator where they'd been chilling and moved her big mixing bowl onto the table beside Linda.

"Ms. Domesticity," Linda said, stretching out her legs and breathing in the scent of her coffee. "Dad's resilient and he used to ride a lot. He's got a lot of years left in him yet."

"I hope he does. He's been a wonderful father to both of us."

Linda put her cup down very carefully. "You never say anything, but you haven't forgotten what I told you when we were kids, have you? No one forgets something like that."

"You didn't have to tell me anything. I was there, like you. I know Sam liked his travels

180

now and again, but that doesn't mean I don't believe he's an essentially good man." She didn't want Linda to see how her hands shook, so she rested a wrist on the edge of the bowl while she measured out flour. "Mom thought the same thing. If she hadn't, she wouldn't have waited for him every time."

"So you have forgotten. Or you're pretending you have. Have you ever noticed how you call Ella Mom, and I call her Ella?"

Carolee grew still inside. She was clammy. "Mom looked after you as if she was your own mother."

"But she wasn't. How about the way you say Sam, and I say Dad?"

"Drop it. Let it go." After the complete emotional upheaval of the last few days, Carolee couldn't take anymore.

"You know Dad kept going away because he couldn't take it," Linda said. "He was only trying to stay sane when he couldn't figure out a way to change things."

"Stop it." Carolee dropped the sifter into the flour and covered her ears. "Even if you were ever right, it's history."

"I've got to speak out for the truth." Linda stood up and approached Carolee. "My father's blamed for things he wasn't guilty of and you think I'm wrong for putting things straight."

"You've rewritten history."

"I know what I know, and so do you. Don't tell me you never saw anything."

"I'm going outside," Carolee told her, hurrying toward the door. "Please don't follow me."

The morning was humid and gray, the sky pressing so low it seemed held up by the tops of tall cedars and firs. She walked slowly downhill to the lake and stayed at the edge of the water, watching small waves make scalloped edges along the pebble beach.

Sam and Faith were riding on some nearby trails and Sam, who was on the chestnut, had promised they would take things easy. Carolee got the occasional tummy flip thinking about Faith on those trails when she was still so new to riding, but she wasn't deeply concerned. Linda was right—Sam was no stranger on horseback.

Every thought she had led to Max. After they'd made love, she'd gone through the motions of having lunch in his office, and the moment she could, she'd excused herself and Faith, pleading her need to get out of Seattle before rush hour.

Max had been quiet, but he'd refused to let Carolee take Faith to the car on her own. Looking at him had been devastating. When he caught her eye, she blushed instantly. What she'd done had been amazing, but she'd wanted it just the way it was.

Twice since then he'd gone to Sam's and given Faith riding lessons. Carolee had refused to join them.

She wanted to be with him again.

This was suicidal behavior. What did a man think of a woman who demanded sex from him, then took the initiative to make sure she got it? He could have stopped it, but he wasn't a fool. Of course he'd been willing. He was a willing participant—an engrossing lover, just as she'd wanted him to be. Now she must never see him alone again and perhaps that's what she'd wanted—to finish it by making their being together impossible.

A lie. What she'd wanted was for him to touch her intimately, and to be inside her. She'd wanted to be held in just that way and to feel the power in him while he took what she offered.

Moisture hung in the air, warm moisture. There were few humid days in the Northwest. She walked farther along the beach until she was completely out of sight of the house, before cutting back uphill and through a stand of trees between her property and an unimproved lot next door.

"Keep quiet," Linda said, taking hold of Carolee's smaller hand and squeezing until the bones ground together. "Just tiptoe with me and don't do anything dumb. Don't snivel or say anything. You got it?"

"Yes," Carolee whispered.

Carolee felt the blood drain from her face. She was light-headed and sat on the rotting trunk of a fallen tree. Sooner or later she needed to face the past. Maybe she'd find out that all the shadowy memories weren't real.

Sam was away again. Carolee wished he was here because Linda didn't get mean if he was around. Linda was nine. That meant she was pretty grown up now. And it meant she expected five-year-old Carolee to do as she was told.

"When we get downstairs, you forget you've got a tongue, Mouse, or I'll wait till you're asleep and cut it out with Ella's sewing scissors."

Carolee put her free hand over her mouth and shook her head. She couldn't help crying.

"Stop it." Linda took hold of a handful of Carolee's hair and pulled it hard.

"Ow!" Carolee sniffed and gulped.

"Come on."

They trod down the stairs, pausing at each step for Linda to listen. She led the way out into the night, across the driveway, and beside the wood-shed toward the forest.

Carolee pulled against Linda and whispered, "Why are we out here? Mom's going to be so mad."

Linda put her face next to Carolee's and said, "She isn't going to know."

On they went, and crossed the field toward the old cabin that wasn't used anymore. Linda pulled Carolee along one side of the cabin to a door that led into a tiny kitchen that smelled funny.

Carolee's heart bumped so loudly she heard it. She didn't want to stay here.

Linda crouched and Carolee copied her. A few steps and they were in the single downstairs room.

A fire crackled in the fireplace.

Carolee tried to drag Linda backward but she was too strong.

Soft laughter came from a couch that faced the fire. Laughter and sounds. Linda took hold of the back of Carolee's pajama collar and pushed her lower to the ground. She pointed. In the flicker of light from flames, pieces of clothing could be seen scattered around. Linda shook her and pointed to a particular spot. A striped bathrobe lay there, one that was like Mom's, and what looked like a nightgown nearby.

A man's chuckle came from the couch, and a sound as if a woman's laugh was cut off. Those people breathed loudly and the couch creaked.

It was Mom. Mom playing with a strange man. That was wrong. Linda said Carolee didn't know anything, but she knew her mother shouldn't have taken off her clothes to be with a man on the couch. He'd taken off his clothes, too. His pants hung from a chair, and other things were on the floor.

Linda started crawling backward. She tugged Carolee's pajama top until she retreated, too. Once more they reached the outdoors and the dark night. It was cold and Carolee shivered. She shivered and began to sniffle. Linda hustled her away and through the trees again, telling her all the way home to be quiet.

They shared a room, slept together in a double bed pushed into a corner because there wasn't room for two beds. Carolee used to like it because the night frightened her sometimes, but with Linda there, she didn't have to be alone.

"Get in," Linda ordered, holding the covers up until Carolee scrambled under them, then getting in beside her. "Don't bawl. How d'you think I feel?"

"I don't understand."

"Of course you don't. Do you know where babies come from?"

Carolee wanted to put her pillow over her head. "Sort of."

185

"They come from a man and a woman taking off all their clothes and kissing and stuff."

"Oh." Carolee was fuzzy about the "and stuff," but Mom shouldn't have been with that man.

"Now you know why Dad goes away?"

Carolee moved closer to Linda and curled up beside her. "I don't know. I think he gets tired of being with us."

"He never gets tired of being with me," Linda snapped. "But there's things that make him so sad he goes away. Things Ella does."

"No."

"Yes. Ella's got friends. Men. I found out where she goes when she thinks we're asleep. It's always when Dad's gone, but he knows about it and that's why he goes away."

Carolee did pull the pillow over her head, but Linda tore it away. "Dad went away the first time after you were born. I had to think about it for a long time but then I knew. He found out Ella had been kissing other men and he knew you weren't his baby."

They'd been little kids, for goodness' sake. If Sam had indeed gone away for the first time after Carolee was born, Linda would have been about four herself and couldn't have been sure about a thing.

Mom's clothes had been on the floor.

Carolee got up and filled her lungs with damp air. Maybe the clothes hadn't belonged to her mother. Maybe some lovers had stumbled on the closed-up cabin and decided to use it.

She shoved her hands into the pockets of her

jeans and walked out from the trees. The house was close by. Something in her life had hurt Linda so deeply that she wanted to strike out at Carolee. Only an unhappy person would do that, an unhappy person who was really asking for help and understanding.

In the kitchen, Carolee found that Linda had finished making pastry and was rolling it out. Without looking up, she flapped dough over a pie dish and deftly trimmed and pinched the edges. Carolee got a bowl of chopped rhubarb and strawberries from the refrigerator, poured them in, and added sugar. Linda set a pie funnel in the middle, spread on a top crust, and brushed it with egg yolk and more sugar. She cut slits and, while Carolee held open the oven door, slid the pie inside.

"Do you want to talk about it now?" she asked, washing her hands. "You were too young to understand."

"So were you. And I don't ever want to talk about it again."

Linda gave her a measured look. "Okay. But it'll always be there." She finished stacking dirty utensils in the sink. "I should have told you this before. I tried to find Kip."

Anxious as she was, Carolee could have hugged her sister for coming out with the truth.

"I called Bill Lester and he told me Kip was on his boat. I didn't know he had one."

"Oh, yes," Carolee said offhandedly.

"I went looking for him. The thing was all open, but Kip wasn't there. That is one big hummer of a boat. A man was aboard, painting. He said Kip had gone to meet friends and wouldn't be back for a few hours. I didn't feel like waiting."

"Why did you want to see him?"

"To tell him he's bloody unfair and needs to get a life. That means he's got to stop entertaining himself by making you miserable. Faith should be with you as much as she's with him."

"You wonderful idiot." Carolee pulled her close and held on tight. "You pretend to be so tough, but you're a jelly roll."

"Watch it." Linda's voice was muffled against Carolee's cheek. "Enough with the jelly roll stuff."

"I love you for wanting to stand up for me, but I'm glad you didn't find Kip. And you mustn't try again, okay?"

Pulling her head back enough to see Carolee's face, Linda said, "Not okay. You won't start living again until you're not afraid to. You're afraid of Kip not liking it if you get involved with someone else. You think he could use it against you when you try to get more time with Faith. You worry too much about that. How was it when you went to Max's place? You haven't said a word about it and I can't be patient anymore."

"It was nice. Very good for Faith. Look, everything you just said may be right, but I can't risk that you're wrong. Promise me you'll stay away from Kip."

"Promise me you'll tell him you want your

fair share of Faith. And start seeing men again—this Max will do if you like him cnough."

"I'm not promising you anything."

Linda shrugged.

"Mind if I play the piano?" Carolee asked. She hadn't forgotten that Linda used to get annoyed if she practiced.

"I don't mind." Linda went to a chair and propped her feet on the ottoman.

Yawning, Digger appeared and loped slowly downstairs. He was waking up, and like Carolee, he liked to do it slowly.

Linda said, "Where's he been?"

"On Faith's bed. He's still a baby who needs naps."

Digger snuffled the edge of a carpet up and produced a hidden rock which he chewed on his back teeth. He settled under Linda's legs.

"He's cute," she said.

Carolee sat at the piano and set her fingers on the keys. Almost immediately, she felt lighter. She played, and the knots in her muscles went slack.

"I'm jealous of you," Linda said loudly. "Did I ever tell you that?"

Carolee smiled and shook her head. She broke into "Shimmy Like My Sister Kate," but substituted Linda's name for Kate.

Linda laughed, closed her eyes, and rocked her head in time to the music.

This was the talent Carolee had been given and she loved it. When she didn't play, even for a few hours, she was distracted by her need to get to the piano.

The phone rang and she jumped. Please don't let it be Max trying to do the right thing again, and calling to be nice.

She picked up and said, "Hello."

"Leo Getz," said the caller's rumbly voice. "Time I checked in on you again."

"Hi, Leo." In addition to being a fine and savvy manager, Leo was a dear friend and she hadn't got over feeling she'd let him down. "Where are you?"

"New York, of course."

Of course. Why would she think otherwise. Leo was a New Yorker to his blood and bones, and for him there was a black hole west of the Hudson.

"I know I said I wouldn't press you about business, but I've been fielding offers for a long time, sweetheart. You're missed and getting more missed all the time. I could fill your dance card every night for a couple of years out. You ready to roll again?"

The question caught Carolee off balance. When they'd last spoken, she'd told Leo she couldn't foresee a time when she'd perform again, at least not anywhere but at the club. He didn't know about Brandy's place and wouldn't be interested.

"Carolee?"

"Why would you ask me now? I told you I'd let you know if I ever thought I was ready to take on more gigs."

190

Linda turned in her chair. She raised her eyebrows at Carolee.

"You did. Listen kid, outside of this issue, there's business to attend to. I don't like troubling you but I should have you sign some contracts."

She stared directly into Linda's eyes. "Contracts?"

"Even if we're not going to be doing anything tomorrow or next week, there are recording contracts to be renewed."

"But I may never record again."

Leo coughed. "You'll record again, even if it's a way off, and you're still a hot property. The people who have been good to you in the past want to make sure you remain their girl. Just sign on the line and take the upfront money."

"I don't need the money," she told him.

"Maybe not now," Leo said, "but you've got expensive commitments. I know how important Faith's trust fund is to you, and what you want it to represent for her future. If you're going to keep on dealing with that, and everything else, taking advantage of what you're worth now is a good move."

Carolee turned from her sister. "I don't know," she said.

"Think about it and we'll talk again," Leo said. "Meanwhile, what I've got in mind is a tour. I'd make sure you got time to rest between engagements—and that would be when you could see Faith."

She chased her own puzzled thoughts. "I don't get it. We talked all of this through and you said you supported me. I don't want to tour. You didn't even mention it the last time you called."

"I'd support you in anything, sweetheart, but I think you may be too nervous to do what you want to do."

"Where are you getting these ideas?"

Leo whistled through his teeth. She could visualize his round face and thinning hair, and the way he rolled his tongue behind a gap between his front teeth. The tuneless whistle was his way of making time to think.

"Come clean," she told him.

"Sure. Why not? Kip called me a short while back. He's worried about you, Carolee. He thinks you may be depressed—big time—and he's flat out nervous you might do somethin' stupid. Look, I hate the guy's guts, but maybe he's not as bad as I thought."

She marched back and forth as far as the telephone cord would allow. Bill Lester's suggestion that she might need to "see someone" came back.

"Speak to me," Leo begged.

"Kip is trying to spread the word that I'm suicidal and you're buying it?"

"No, I'm not buying it. But I do think he's right when he says you need your career to give you purpose and he thinks you should tour again."

"He thinks I should tour again," she said slowly. "Kip thinks I should tour again. He doesn't care what I do, Leo. He already got half of everything I earned and bought for the two of us while we were married. He doesn't stand to get a share of anything I make from now on."

"I know it, kid. I'm still getting over you giving him the Porsche when he'd already had papers served."

If she could only go to sleep and wake up to peace and a certainty about what she should do. "I had a car. I didn't need two."

"That's not an excuse, but we'll drop it. You set up the trust so Faith's perfect dad doesn't even have to worry about her education or any other big-ticket items she wants. You also pay enough to—"

"Please stop it, Leo. We agreed not to revisit any of this." The monetary settlement and child support Kip had been awarded apparently allowed him to buy large boats, and to neglect his painting—still. "Between the club and my recording royalties, I take care of everything."

"Everything but your own needs if I know you," Leo said quietly. "I was surprised he called. In fact, I thought it was weird. Didn't he make a big deal about you going on tours? Said they'd estranged the two of you?"

She wished Linda weren't listening to all this. "He hated it that I got successful so I stopped being successful. I've tried to do whatever I could think of to change his opinion of me so I could talk him into making a new agreement about Faith."

Leo coughed and did a little more whistling through his teeth.

"Do you think he's figured out what I intend to do, so he's decided to make sure I don't look good to a judge if it comes to that? He wants to be able to say, 'She hasn't changed.' Or maybe he just doesn't want me so close geographically, and he's trying to get rid of me."

"I think you've got the truth somewhere there, but I had to check up on you, Carolee. If Kip was lying, he's good at it."

"If?" She was past being diplomatic. "He's an expert, and he's patient. He wants something and that doesn't make me feel too comfortable. There are other things going on here. I'm not talking about them now, but Kip's definitely up to something."

She talked a few more minutes with Leo and hung up with a feeling it wouldn't be too long before he checked on her again.

"Kip's a snake," Linda said. "No matter what he says to you—no matter how much honey he ladles on you—don't believe him."

Carolee looked at her curiously. "I'm scared, but I'm not sure I understand you. One minute you're trying to rake up history and make me miserable over things that can't be changed even if they were true. The next you're sounding sincere when you defend me against my ass—against my ex-husband."

Linda smoothed back her shining hair and said, "I would stand up for you through anything. You've been good to me. When everyone else turned away because they couldn't stand me anymore, you were still there." She turned her face up to the ceiling. "Anyway, I love you."

She just had to choose now, when Carolee's days were upside down and falling apart, to dump a statement like, "I love you," for the first time ever.

"And I love you," Carolee said. "If I could ever teach you to quit being blasé and outrageous, I'd probably adore you."

Linda laughed. She got up and danced—outrageously—to something Latin American which she hummed. Moving around the room, she wound her hips, stretched her hands overhead, clapped, and pushed her notable bosom to the fore.

"You've got a lot of rhythm," Carolee told her. "And you used to sing well. I bet you still do. By the way, don't get the wrong idea, but weren't you supposed to be back in Chicago already?"

"Changed my mind," Linda said and stopped moving. She pointed, a wide smile on her face.

Carolee looked over her shoulder, at the screen door, and saw Max standing there with his black Stetson tipped forward over his eyes. He had an oversized bouquet under his arm.

"That's him, isn't it?" Linda muttered. "Oh, my God, he's gorgeous."

Seventeen

From what Max could see, uptight didn't come close to describing Carolee's state of mind. She reached into a high cupboard for a crystal vase. He barely saved it from hitting her as it toppled over.

"Nice catch," her sister said. This was the Linda that Rob mentioned meeting at Brandy's. "Very nice to meet you, Max. Carolee, I'd better love you and leave you. I'm going over to Dad's. Promised him I'd get something good going for dinner."

Carolee filled the vase from the faucet. "It isn't even lunchtime."

"Dad and Faith will be out for a couple of hours yet. Dad's taking her to see some crony before he brings her back. And what I'm making for dinner will take a long time. Hope you'll join us, Max."

He smiled, but didn't accept or refuse. Carolee's sister looked nothing like her. Linda was shorter, more provocatively dressed in a tight T-shirt that didn't reach the waistband of equally tight black pants, and had sharp brown eyes rather than the soft green of Carolee's. She wore her red-brown hair below the shoulders and frequently tossed it, but she seemed nice enough, even if she did look him over like a juicy steak.

"Yes, well, I'll be on my way, then. See you later."

Carolee said, "Bye, sis," and Max gave Linda a brief wave. He was glad when she'd left.

"You didn't need to go to the trouble of bringing flowers," Carolee said. Now he was here, she wanted him to stay yet was afraid to be alone with him. Whom did she fear? Max had never seemed ominous.

"I absolutely did not have to bring you flowers, but I made a trip to Pike Place Market because they have the best cut flowers in town and nothing but the best would do for you." He smiled sheepishly. "I sound like a real operator, but it's true."

Sunflowers and orange lilies, madly purple gerbera daisies and eucalyptus, peach-colored roses and sprays of tiny ginger-colored orchids. They were special. "I'm a flower lover. I'll take good care of them. Instead of saying you shouldn't have brought me flowers, I needed to tell you I'm fine and there wasn't any need to come and check up on me."

"Okay, more truth and to hell with the consequences. I've wanted to see you—and be alone with you—since we shared the best thing that ever happened to me. But you shut me out on the phone and I figured you might tell me to get lost if I came to you. First I thought I couldn't face that, then I couldn't face not finding out."

She had nothing to say.

"Your sister said Sam and Faith will be out for a couple of hours. Please would you come for a drive? We need to talk. I don't think you'll argue about that."

Not argue? The idea of willingly getting into his car with him and being in a situation where she couldn't escape was awful. How could she know what he intended to say to her?

He put a hand on her arm but she moved away.

"Please, Carolee."

"I've got a pie in the oven." *A bona fide way out.* The realization was wonderful.

"Give your sister a call. She seemed happy to see us together. She'll check your pie."

"I can't ask her to do that."

Max knew she was making excuses. He pulled out his wallet and found the card he'd used to jot down Sam's number. Within a minute he'd dialed and Linda had agreed to take the pie out of the oven. He didn't dare look at Carolee but reached for his hat instead. "That's fixed. It's a pretty day. You can give directions, if you like. We'll go wherever you want to go."

Her hands hung at her sides and her body language screamed indecision.

"It'll look weird if we don't go after calling Linda," he said.

"You're a manipulator."

"Necessity does that to every one of us." They needed some space where they could be alone without some artificial deadline.

"Okay, have it your way." Grabbing up a purse, she marched from the house and went directly to his car.

She should have known there would have to be a conversation between them. If he were the type of man who was happy to take what a woman offered, then wait for her next move—and not care if she didn't make one—he could have stayed away permanently. Max wasn't that type. He'd feel guilty and probably wouldn't even realize that she had taken the entire initiative.

"I like you in pink," he said, opening the passenger door for her. "Brings out some pink in your skin. Suits you."

The pink in question was a pink V-neck T-shirt so old it used to be fuschia. She got into the car, dropped her purse on the floor, and stared straight ahead. Max took too long closing her door and she felt him looking down at her. Finally he shut her in and went around to take his own place.

"Any idea where we should go?" he asked.

She shook her head.

He started the engine and traveled smoothly uphill and onto the narrow road at the top. His seat was pushed far back and he drove with his legs stretched out. Carolee wondered again just how bad his injuries had been.

They took I-405 South as far as the junction with I-90, where Max headed east and through Issaquah, a quaint town that blended old and new and did it very well. Max said, "We could have lunch at Gilman Village," referring to a collection of Issaquah shops and restaurants with a reputation for old-world charm.

"I'm not hungry," she told him honestly. "But don't let me stop you."

"Snoqualmie, here we come."

Alarmed, she told him, "I can't be gone too long. Faith will get back and I've got to be there."

"If we're late, it won't be by much."

She didn't relax until she realized he'd referred to the town of Snoqualmie just a few miles away, rather than to Snoqualmie Pass, the skiing area that was much farther.

They made the drive along the highway into the mountains. Rapidly civilization felt like a memory. Douglas firs, their tops sharp against cloudless blue skies, covered hills that blended into more hills and trees, onward and ever more distant to the snow-capped peaks of the Cascades.

Max turned off onto a side road and slowed after a few miles. He parked in a lot adjoining a heavily treed park. The only amenities Carolee saw were a few picnic tables close to the road.

Before Max could get to Carolee's door, she'd jumped out of the car. He walked at a deliberately measured pace while she rushed ahead, passing up picnic tables to take a narrow trail into the trees. He wasn't managing this well, but he would manage it just the same. Being with her was unforgettable and he didn't intend to try to change that. He was going to have to learn more about her and manage to keep her at the same time.

The trail started rising, but when he turned the first bend, he was confronted by a small lake surrounded with scrub grass. Carolee crouched at the edge of the water.

Catching up and sinking to his haunches beside her, he said, "I knew this was here all the time but I didn't want to give away any hints about how beautiful it is."

She tossed one tiny rock after another into the still lake, each time waiting for circles of ripples to spread wide. "You're fibbing," she said, but there was nothing lighthearted in her voice.

"Can we talk?" Wanting but not daring to touch her made him crazy. "We have to. The sooner the better."

"I don't do that. I mean I'm not like that." She stood up and blinked as if a nonexistent wind were stinging her eyes.

Max stood, too. "What aren't you like?"

"I don't just...well, I don't screw around." She winced and gritted her teeth. "That sounds awful, but it was."

"Oh, no it wasn't." He tossed away caution and took hold of her hand. When she tried to pull away again, he held her tightly enough to make it impossible for her to evade him. "Time to get down to it. I know you don't have indiscriminate sex. You're not the promiscuous type."

She looked pained.

He had to press on. "So why me? Why then? Did I just happen to be there when the mood struck? Would any man have done?"

Damn him. "Damn you." With her free hand she slapped his face, but didn't know what to do next. Her palm burned and Max had turned his cheek aside as if inviting her to hit him again if she wanted to. He made no attempt to stop her. "Damn you, Max. You could have refused."

His laughter made her feel more embarrassed and out of control.

This was not the type of woman, Max thought, who slapped men. She was on the edge and it was up to him to bring her back to safe ground. "Okay, now it's my turn," he said and pulled her along beside him to a grassy ledge a few yards from the water.

"Let me go."

"No. I told you it's my turn."

She drove her heels into dusty dirt but he wouldn't stop until he'd plopped her down on the ledge and joined her. "I asked you to kiss me as if you really wanted to—if you wanted to," he said. "I didn't ask you for sex, you wanted it."

Carolee turned on him, pounded a fist on his thigh. "And you wanted it, too. I gave you every man's dream. I was a woman forcing herself on you."

"You couldn't have forced yourself on me if I hadn't wanted you to." Anger overtook him. "Not all men are alike."

"I'm sorry." Carolee looked at her fist on his leg and flattened her palm to stroke him instead. "I am so freaked out. I don't think all men are alike. You could just be the best man I ever met. But I can't afford to find out. You already know why."

"Your ex-husband can't use it against you if you decide to see another man."

"I didn't think he could do what he did when he divorced me. I was wrong. And now my little girl is adrift and scared. Sometimes she puts on a tough act, sometimes she even seems happy for a while. The rest of the time she's frightened and tries to hide it by going to sleep."

"A girl needs her mother," Max said, startling Carolee. "Faith's at that age when she's starting to go through all kinds of changes. You're the one who ought to help her understand and feel good about herself."

"When did you become an expert on prepubescent girls?"

"Played ball with a lot of guys who had kids. I listened to them and to their wives—and sometimes acted as a kind uncle to a youngster or two. It wouldn't be so hard to figure out for myself either, would it?"

She thought it would be very hard for some men. "I'm too much trouble." The words bypassed her mind and emerged uncensored, but they were true. "You've had your own hard times and I admire you for getting yourself all put back together. I'm a mess. I haven't recovered from an ugly, unexpected divorce and I'm about to fight to change the custody agreement for my child. Nobody in his right mind would want to be bothered with me."

"I haven't put myself back together," Max said. "Sure, I've done a fair job of getting on with things, starting a business, volunteering for something I like to do, but don't kid yourself—I'm still angry at what happened to me.

I want to be catching and running footballs. I want to hear the crowds yelling. That's all over and I hate it. Now Rob Mead's shown up again and I'm stumped. Don't know what to do about him being right under my nose. Don't know what to believe."

She looked into his face. "Why would I assume you didn't miss what you had? Why would I think I was the only one with a right to be grieving over the past?" When he looked at her the way he was looking at her now, all she could think of was wanting to kiss him again. "What do you mean about Rob Mead?"

Max's concentration wandered repeatedly. Carolee had been right, she was trouble and nobody in his right mind would mess with her. His mind hadn't felt right since the first night he'd watched her at Brandy's.

"Rob's quitting the team," he said. "He wants to put money into my business and work with me. I'm not sure I could hack that, not when he might be trying to work through some sort of guilt."

Carolee was one of those rare women who could listen without thinking about what she wanted to say next. She waited patiently for him to continue.

"He was there when the pickup slipped the jack and slid sideways onto my legs. For some reason he figures he's Superman in disguise and should have been able to lift the thing off. He can't live with being in my place on the squad. Or so he says. But he didn't cause the flat tire, or make the jack slip. I don't know how to react."

She ran her fingernails up and down the seam in his jeans, the seam on the inner thigh. "He has to do what he thinks is right, but you don't have to take him into your business unless you want to. I can tell you like him, so you'll be glad to have him in the area, just not in the next office. When I saw him with Brandy the other day, I got the impression they're trying not to be in love with each other. That's an issue that could take up all of Rob's energy. He may lose interest in you."

The seam on his jeans pressed into muscle. Pretending he neither noticed nor reacted in any way cost him considerably. "You're smart," he told her. "I've got to stay detached. Too bad there isn't any such animal as an uncomplicated human being."

"Max"—she bowed her head so he couldn't see her face—"what I did yesterday was outrageous. I put you in a difficult position."

"Awful," he said, holding the corners of his mouth down.

She looked up at him again. "Don't make fun of me. I keep seeing it all in my mind and I blush." Which was exactly what she was doing now and Max enjoyed watching. "I want you to believe me when I say I didn't have any notion of coming on to you like that."

"You didn't?" He didn't know how to deal with this other than with quips. "You mean you didn't plan to seduce me? I'm shattered."

She poked him in the belly and he liked seeing her eyes grow round when she didn't meet anything soft.

"Hey, Carolee, okay if I kiss you this time?"

"Mmmm."

The sound was more a question than an agreement but he'd use the interpretation he preferred. He spun her around and rested her head in his lap. His idea had been to slow himself down a little. Her head where it was could achieve the reverse.

"I want to look at you while I decide." Her eyes were so green.

Her throat jerked when she swallowed. "Decide?"

"Yeah. How I'm going to kiss you."

She shifted to get a clearer view of his face. Another not-so-helpful idea—unless she'd decided she wanted to repeat yesterday's experiment. He'd better not go there.

"Kissing got us into trouble," Carolee said. "I like kissing you but it's not wise."

"It's very wise." His buttocks tightened, and his belly. He tucked escaped hair behind her ears. "The ponytail suits you."

She didn't thank him for the compliment. "I want you to tell me you believe I'm not a person who goes after sex."

Her sincerity had only one effect on him—he wanted to grin.

"I'm not. Nothing like that ever happened to me before."

"I was the lucky one," he said. "I do believe you, and I think you feel something for me or it would never have happened."

Carolee wanted him to touch her, but wasn't sure she could control herself if he did. He settled a hand on her shoulder and rubbed his thumb back and forth along her collarbone. When he turned his head sideways to look at her, she knew she must not stay here like this.

Max put his arms around her, lifted her for the promised kiss. She smelled fir and pine, faintly heard skittering squirrels in tree branches and bird cries overhead. The rest was Max and his mouth moving on hers. He weakened her and she liked it too much, could come to need it too much.

Quickly, she wound her arms about his neck and returned the passion she felt in him, but when he pulled one side of her T-shirt from her jeans, she wriggled free and was grateful he didn't attempt to take her back.

When she stood, so did he, and they faced each other.

"I don't want to lose you," Max said.

"This sounds ridiculous, but we've got to pretend we didn't make love and go slowly now." She dragged the rubber band from her hair and combed it with her fingers before arranging another ponytail. "Listen. Okay, how about this? You've got your life and I've got mine. They both need attention, but we really like each other, don't we?"

"I more than like you, Carolee."

She smiled a little and felt faintly shy. "Thank you. So we'll do our things separately but we'll be friends."

Max wasn't sure he liked the sound of this.

"I mean we'll be there for each other but not

if one of us doesn't want it. There'll be no strings attached and we'll get together some-times—as friends."

"What do you mean by friends? I'm not sure I'll be able to behave as if I were one of your girlfriends."

"I don't want you as a girlfriend, Max." She stepped closer and held onto his belt. "I've already got girlfriends. I don't need more."

"But you want me to be a no-strings-attached friend. If I ask you to come to me and stay the night because I'm afraid of the dark, will you do it?"

"Not if Faith's with me. She comes first. But if I possibly can, I will."

"And you'll let me know when you need me?"

"Yes. But we both know it wouldn't work for either of us to put too many demands on the other. When one of us needs the space, for a long time maybe, it'll be no big deal."

Sure, sweetheart, I'll say whatever it takes for now. "No big deal. We'll get together when we both want to, and stay away when it seems right."

She wouldn't know how happy her "Yes" made him. That little word left just about everything open to interpretation.

Eighteen

A breeze through the open windows at Brandy's whipped the skirts of freshly laundered yellow tablecloths. Carolee sat with Faith and they both drank lemonade while they waited for Brandy and Ivy to arrive.

"How are you feeling?" Carolee asked. "You're pale."

"Don't fuss," Faith said. "I feel great."

"No need to snap, young lady. Moms are allowed to be concerned for their children."

Faith stirred her lemonade with a straw. "Why do I have to be here? I'd rather be riding with Gramps."

"You can ride later. Brandy wanted to see you. She thought it would be nice to have the four of us at lunch." She looked around. Brandy had said she'd be there when they arrived.

"Brandy's flashy."

Surprised, Carolee frowned at her. "Where did you learn to say things like that?"

"There's nothing awful about being *flashy*. I think it's very descriptive."

Eleven, and she was categorizing people—judging them. "I asked where you learned to say, or even think that."

Faith turned bright pink. "If you must know, Daddy said it because of the way she dresses."

"Brandy's theatrical," Carolee said, dropping her voice and checking around. "The clothes she wears suit her personality and they suit *her*. She's also kind and supportive and she's been a wonderful friend to me."

Faith crossed her arms. She appeared suddenly very young and vulnerable. "I'm sorry. I like the way you dress best. You only dress up when you need to. The rest of the time you're a mom."

The fact that Faith had complimented her took a while to sink in. The realization made Carolee glow inside. Now her job was to avoid overreacting and smothering the child. "You make me smile all over," Carolee said. "I'll keep right on dressing the way I do." Was the ice cracking?

"Hi, there!" Ivy Lester, wearing one of her favorite full-skirted dresses, this one light blue, hurried past other tables to reach Carolee and Faith. "I'm so dadburned late, I can't believe it. I left home in plenty of time but every errand took twice as long as it should have." She took a seat with her back to the window, beside Faith and facing Carolee.

"You've been a stranger," Carolee said.

Ivy took a long drink from her water glass, batted her lips with a napkin, and said, "Days fly. And I'm tellin' you, girl, I've been having busy weeks."

Each day that passed burned a notch into a stick only Carolee saw, and each notch brought her closer to Faith going home. It had been four days since she'd last been alone with Max. She hadn't called him, and he hadn't called her. She had seen him with Sam, and with Faith as the three of them went riding. They'd exchanged waves.

"Are you still with us?" Ivy asked Carolee. She was in a glowing mood. Her pale skin looked dewy, her lips moist, her eyes bright. "I guess you and Bill talked."

Carolee looked hard at Ivy, trying to warn her off that subject.

Ivy ran her hands from the back of her neck, over her hair to a loose, blond topknot. "He said you were lookin' for Kip?"

Carolee turned to Faith, whose eyes were downcast. "I just wanted to talk over some business with him."

"And Linda? What did she want with Kip?" Ivy used the napkin to wipe the palms of her hands. "Bill said he thought she was going over to the boat."

Ivy's persistence irritated Carolee, but short of telling Ivy to change the subject, all Carolee could do was try to divert the other woman's attention. "How's your mother?"

"Her usual ornery self, thank you. Bill said Linda sounded mad and you sounded uncomfortable. Why would you ever be uncomfortable calling Bill?"

Carolee managed a laugh. "Of course I wasn't uncomfortable. That Bill has such an imagination." Faith had shifted to the very back of her chair and clenched her hands in her lap.

"I guess Bill also flapped his mouth about his opinions. About your future." She glanced at Faith. "He shouldn't have done that. It's none of his business, and he's wrong anyway. Can you imagine the two of you... Well, it would never work, that's all."

"You and Bill worry too much about me," Carolee said when what she wanted to tell Ivy was to leave her alone when it came to really personal matters.

"Have it your own way," Ivy said. "Kip's been on his boat for the last couple of weeks, or so I'm told. If you'd left a message at the condo, he'd have gotten back to you."

"I left messages," Faith said, sounding short of breath and panicky.

Ivy raised her light brows. "Where's Brandy? Cookin' our lunch herself?"

"Her manager said she'd been called away. She'll be back shortly."

"Well," Ivy said, fanning herself with the napkin, "there's no reason not to go ahead and say what needs to be said. Right here and now. Faith's a big girl, aren't you, Faith?"

Carolee's stomach clenched. She glanced at Faith, who stared, unsmiling, at Ivy.

" 'Course you are." Ivy shifted her water glass in little circles.

Wearing her favorite turquoise and with auburn hair mussed prettily by the wind, Brandy clicked toward them in backless, high-heeled sandals. "Hello, gorgeous, gorgeous, and gorgeous. If I'd gone willingly to that meeting, I'd deserve fifty lashes. Why does every business on earth revolve around meetings, and meetings about meetings? This group can't understand why I don't want partners to help me 'put Brandy's on the map.' Why not a whole string of Brandy's Bistros? Clowns. They never once asked me what I want for my business or my future. Burley," she called to her appropriately named manager, "tell the kitchen we're ready. They know the menu. And pick out a wonderful bottle of champagne, would you? We're celebrating." She sat down and put a narrow red box on the table.

"What are we celebrating?" Faith asked quietly.

"You, sweets," Brandy said, her face as somber as the girl's. "We love you and we need to celebrate having you with us. Your mom barely lives between your visits. I never see her smile the way she does when you're here."

Carolee swallowed hard. Faith was too young for such heavy stuff.

Ivy, trying as usual to gloss over any tension, said, "How is that Max Wolfe, Carolee? I asked Linda and she wasn't talkin', which means there's something going on. I want to talk to you about that."

"Do you know what jousts were?" Brandy asked Faith.

Faith shook her head.

Brandy's freckles became more evident. Like Faith's, they did when she was angry— and her face grew paler. "I'll get you a book on them. Way back men used to fight each other on horseback with long, pointed weapons called lances. Ladies gave them their own colors to wear during the battle. Colors, as they were called, were scarves or ribbons in the colors of the lady's family house. Open this." She pushed the red box to Faith.

Inside the box were three chiffon scarves, one turquoise, one purple, and one yellow, braided loosely together and tied with gold braid at each end. Faith lifted the brilliant rope and looked inquiringly at Brandy.

"My colors." Brandy grinned. "I wanted to get you something really clever. All I could think of was you learning to ride with Max and your Gramps. Not exactly a battle, but who cares? Now I want you to wear those colors for me. You tie them around your upper arm."

Faith said, "Thank you. I like them. They're...*dashing.*"

"You've got it," Brandy said and Carolee chuckled with her.

"So you ride with Max Wolfe?" Ivy said.

Carolee pressed a knee into Ivy's leg but she showed no sign of noticing.

"He's really nice," Faith said, still running the scarves through her fingers.

"You're sad," Ivy said, her own eyes turning somber. "You miss your daddy. And you can be sure he misses you too."

Faith replaced the scarves and put the lid back on the box.

"I've thought a long time about this," Ivy said. "All the while I was with my momma, I kept worryin' about it. I know you think I'm an airhead, Carolee. If I am, I'm an airhead with a heart and soul—and a brain some-where in there, too."

"Perhaps we should get together later," Carolee suggested. "When we can stretch out and take our time."

"I might lose my nerve by then. Why do you think Kip isn't returnin' telephone calls—now of all times? It's because he's one confused man and he's suffering. He's scared, too."

Faith found tissues in her pocket and blew her nose.

"Reconciliation would be a disaster," Ivy announced.

Her words dropped through the air, leaving silence in their wake. Brandy sat, straight-backed, holding the edge of the table. Faith's concentration was on Ivy.

"Oh, you're going to make me suffer through this, aren't you?" Ivy said. "Couldn't you make it a bit easier by discussin' things with me? Faith needs both of her parents, Carolee, but not under the same roof. It would be hell."

"Kip is my ex-husband," Carolee said, her lips stiff. "And I have no interest in getting back together with him."

"Maybe not, but you want to be a big part of his life again."

"That's not true." There seemed no way out, no escape, and the damage being done had to be huge.

"Carolee," Ivy said earnestly. "Have an affair with him if you want to. Sex was good between you, wasn't it?"

Brandy said, *"Ivy,"* while Carolee took a little longer to recover from the shock of Ivy's announcement and say, "Don't you ever talk like that in front of my daughter. Never again, understand?"

Ivy shrugged, but had the grace to look self-conscious. "Maybe I did say a little too much. But I know Kip well enough to worry about him and try to help all three of you."

"What do you know?" Faith stood up and clutched her red box to her chest. "When you come over, you don't talk to me. You don't know me and you don't know Daddy. He doesn't want me anymore, that's why he's pretending he's away."

Both Carolee and Brandy stood up. "Your dad loves you to pieces," Carolee said. "And Ivy is only trying to turn something sad into something happy."

"Thank you for having me to lunch," Faith told Brandy. "My tummy isn't feeling very good. I want to go home." At that, she turned pleading eyes on Carolee.

Carolee drove back to Lake Home as quickly as she dared. As soon as the car came to a stop, Faith jumped out and ran toward the house. Digger raced from the porch, his back and front feet meeting like a greyhound's on the track. Faith accepted his leaping and kissing, then she stopped and waited for Carolee to catch up.

"Thanks, Mom," she said. "I suppose Ivy wanted to make things better, but she made them worse. I didn't know Daddy was on the boat. Why didn't he call me?"

There wasn't a reasonable answer. "I think he's trying to clear his mind. All your life he's been with you." She looked away. "I wish I'd had the sense to figure out I ought to have been there too, and let the music go. But he's been with you and this is the first time he's had to deal with you being away for a while. He's upset."

"You never say anything bad about Daddy. Some people would. But I don't believe that's what's wrong. I'm going to sleep, just for a little while." She went inside with Digger still begging for her to play with him.

Carolee decided to stay out of the house long enough for Faith to fall asleep. For an hour she pottered among her flowers in the perennial garden. The tiny iridescent blooms on the fireweed plants were living up to their name. They glowed like molten embers amid deep green foliage. The afternoon was hot but the ever-present wind stopped the temperature from becoming too much. Carolee kept a wide-brimmed straw hat in a wicker basket on the porch and she had tied this on by a ribbon under the chin.

Bees buzzed in fragrant honeysuckle. The minute flowers of blue woodruff bobbed in groundcover surrounding the stones in a crazy paving path. An Angel Gabriel plant showed off its yellow blooms beneath mossy green leaves veined with white.

The afternoon was so peaceful, but the peace didn't extend to Carolee. She was furious with Ivy. Even giving her some slack

217

for never having had children of her own—evidently because she didn't want any—there was no excuse to discuss painful issues in front of Faith. Why wouldn't a grown woman understand that in Faith's heart there must be a longing for her parents to be together and to live in a "normal" home.

Enough time had passed. Faith and Digger would be curled up together—Faith softly asleep and Digger snoozing and snuffling with each exciting dream.

Carolee went into the house and washed her hands at the kitchen sink. She shook water from her fingers and droplets caught colors from brightness through the window. *Let Ivy's silliness go.*

She turned toward the piano. It should never have been necessary to choose between her family and performing. Balance was the answer, only Kip had made the issue an either-or. Looking at the truth was good, not bad, and the truth was that he had pushed her to become as involved in her career as she'd been. According to Kip, cutting back would have hurt her popularity. And she'd had no idea he was playing games.

Music was, and always would be, her delight and there was no need to let it go completely.

A plate of cookies covered with plastic stood on the table. Each cookie was decorated like a different flower. Linda again. Linda had changed, or was behaving as if she had. And instead of staying only three days, she'd been at Lake Home for ten and showed no sign

218

of leaving. When Carolee had mentioned the big party Linda's friend Albert had arranged for her, she had said, "That isn't going to happen," and clammed up.

Deliberately quiet, Carolee went to the stairs and climbed, trying not to cause any squeaks. She was starting to enjoy having Linda around. The thought made her smile. After a roller-coaster childhood, and the adult years when they'd had their regular spats, she actually thought she might have a sister who liked her. A very good thing.

Carolee carried the warm feeling as far as the open door to Faith's room. Digger was curled up and sleeping deeply on the bed. Faith wasn't there.

The bathroom was also empty.

Giving in to fear would only paralyze her. Carolee retraced her steps quickly and quietly downstairs and outside. Faith could have left without being seen and might well be at Sam's. But if so, why not take Digger? And Sam wasn't home. He and Linda had gone out to buy lumber for another of Sam's projects—a turret, as Linda called it. Sam referred to the structure as a lookout and intended to put his telescope there.

Once more Carolee went upstairs. At the top she stood absolutely still and listened. From somewhere came the sounds of soft crying, and items being moved around. The first thought she had was that Faith was packing to leave.

The girl still wasn't in her bedroom or bathroom and Carolee was bemused. She checked a storage cupboard in the hall, and stairs leading to the attic. At the top of those stairs was a door, but inside, the shadowy shapes of old trunks and half-forgotten treasures stood in silence.

Fear mounted. Carolee's T-shirt stuck to her back. Back in the upper hallway she closed her eyes and concentrated on the continuing muffled sobbing sounds. They came from her own bedroom. She sped in that direction and entered. No Faith, but the sounds were clearer now and came from the bathroom.

The door was shut. Carolee tapped lightly, put her mouth to the paneling, and said, "Faith, may I come in?"

Faith didn't answer and there was much scuffling.

"Sweetheart, please don't do this. Don't close me out. Let me help you."

Faith's sobs turned to heaving sounds but the other noises stopped.

Carolee refused to believe Faith would do something to herself, but she couldn't take any risks. She turned the handle, the door opened, and she saw Faith sitting on the toilet seat cover with the contents of drawers scattered at her feet. She raised a puffy face and said, "I'm sorry. I was hurrying and made a big mess. I'll put everything back."

"It's okay. We'll do it together. I needed to turn out all this junk anyway. What's the matter, Faith? What are you thinking?"

Holding a large, unopened box of tissues on her lap, Faith shook her head. The attitude of her body went beyond unhappy, she was stricken.

"I couldn't find anything," Faith said and her anxiousness sounded like an appeal for help. "Except these. I don't know if they'll work."

That was it. So relieved she didn't want to stand anymore, Carolee sat on the bathroom floor. "Have you started a period?"

Another sniff preceded, "Think so."

"And you really do have a tummy ache?"

"Yes, it hurts."

"That happens with periods sometimes. Why didn't you tell me?"

"I felt silly and I thought I could deal with it on my own."

Carolee remembered something of the sort from her own menarche. "This is the first one?"

"Yes, and I wish it would go away. It's going to be a nuisance. And I feel like anyone who looks at me will know."

Carolee smothered a smile. "It's part of growing up and it doesn't go away. But you get used to it. And no one can tell by looking at you that you're having a period." She was so grateful this had happened while Faith was with her. "Don't worry about a thing. We'll start you out with some of my things, then go down to the drugstore and choose what we think is best for you."

Faith slid to kneel in front of Carolee and hug her. She buried her face in her shoulder. "Thanks, Mom," she said in muffled tones. "I'm glad I'm with you. Dad would have been embarrassed."

Carolee didn't defend Kip this time. She didn't know how he might have reacted anyway. What she thought about was how Max had said a girl needed her mother at this age. And he'd meant for dealing with things just like this. He was right. He was wise and wonderful, and she hated not being with him. And she hated knowing he was trying to stick with the promise they'd made not to meddle in each other's lives when there were other important things going on.

She had to learn to live with seeing Max at a distance without falling apart. Faith must come first.

Nineteen

Late the following afternoon, Kip walked into Carolee's kitchen with a slightly awkward smile on his lips. He hadn't bothered to knock and must have left his car by the road and made his way down on foot because she hadn't heard him coming.

"I'm so mixed up, Carolee. And the only one who could ever make me see straight when I'm like this, is you."

"Thanks for the vote of confidence. I'm sorry you're having a bad time."

"Don't be cold to me, honey. Give me a chance. I know I've been a heel for dropping out on you and Faith the way I just did, but I had to. I had to have time to decide what I needed to do."

What he needed to do? Carolee had showered and towel dried her hair. She was too conscious of wearing a bathrobe with nothing on underneath.

"You're the best thing that ever happened to me."

She groaned inwardly. He needed new lines.

"You're so beautiful. No wonder people want to watch you perform."

"I'd prefer to think they enjoy my music."

"That, too," Kip said. "You're a talent, sweetheart, and I should never have done anything to interfere with that."

"Like divorcing me and making me look like Cruella DeVil to the entire world? By taking away my child and making sure I only got to see her for short periods of time while I died between those visits?"

He looked at his shoes and shook his head.

"You called Leo and suggested I go out on tour again. What was that all about?"

"Hell, I told that man not to let you know I'd called. I did it because I'm worried out of my mind about you. I know you're pining away and unhappy. And it isn't all about Faith, it's about the career you thought you had to give up to impress me."

She hated that he could say with honesty that he'd been able to pull her strings as if she were his puppet. "You never told me any of these things when they would have mattered so much."

Kip moved in close and only through willpower did she hold her ground. "I need you," he said and it would be so simple to be mesmerized by his piercing hazel eyes and a beautiful mouth that moved as if speech were only an exercise before kissing.

"I ought to go and get dressed," she said.

Those eyes darkened. He looked the length of her, and she didn't have to guess if he could tell that only the robe stopped her from being naked. "Go on, if you'll be more comfortable," he said.

Carolee went upstairs as sedately as she could. Grateful that Faith was with her gramps, she closed the bedroom door behind her and found a pair of drawstring terry pants and a waffle weave top, both navy blue, to put on.

First she turned back to a mirror and combed through her heavy hair. She really did have to think. There were too many potentials for disaster.

Her door, opening to admit Kip, startled her to immobility.

He watched her face in the mirror and said, "Please don't be angry with me. It's been too long since we were together. All my fault. But it doesn't have to go on."

Her stomach flipped. He couldn't be suggesting what he seemed to be suggesting.

Kip came to stand behind her. This time they watched each other in the mirror. "Leave my room, please," she told him, as levelly as she could.

He remained where he was, lifted her damp

hair, and kissed the back of her neck. And he murmured unintelligible words against her skin.

Heavy sickness streamed through her.

"Let down, baby. Go with me and we can have what we had before. It was pretty good, wasn't it?"

"I won't deny that. It's over now."

He put his arms beneath hers and slid his hands around to cover her breasts.

She couldn't handle this. "Get away, Kip."

He attempted to part the wraparound robe but she clutched the lapels together. "You don't want me to go. You need this as much as I do." Kip passed his hands over her on top of the robe, rubbing her nipples with his palms, stroking her belly. Finally he tried to push his fingers between her legs. She exclaimed and twisted to face him, pushed at his chest with both of her fists.

"Hush," he said urgently, gripping both of her wrists in one of his hands. "This is going to be so good for us. We don't want to be interrupted."

"There isn't going to be anything to interrupt. Stop it now, Kip." She wrenched her wrists within his hand, but he didn't let her go. Rather, he trapped her hands between them and, with his hands clamped over her bottom, held her against him so hard she could scarcely grab a breath.

His face grew red and he repeatedly looked at her breasts. "They were always beautiful. They were the first thing I noticed about you when we were kids in school. There wasn't a

225

guy who didn't fantasize in the locker room that he was playing with them, but they were mine. Take off the robe so I can see you."

Carolee reeled at his crudeness and struggled to free herself. Kip's response was to force an open-mouthed kiss on her while he pawed at her. She kicked him with her bare feet but he laughed, backed her to a wall, and managed to worm a hand over a bare breast.

She bit his forearm, bit down, and kept driving her teeth in. Kip ripped his hand away, grabbed her hair, and forced her head against the wall. "Stop it." She panted. "Stop it, now. Is this what you want—to drive me away completely? You're pushing me to have sex and I'm not agreeing. Back off."

"Don't be so damned melodramatic." The only reaction in his face was a deepening of color and of the telltale signs of lust. Violence was exciting him, but if she didn't fight, he'd rape her to get what he wanted.

Slowly, never taking his eyes from hers, he unbuttoned his shirt and dropped it on the floor. His physique was as well honed as she remembered, his arms developed from weight lifting. All Carolee wanted was to hide from his inflamed stares.

"I want to talk with you about the custody setup for Faith," she said, and knew she'd never figure out how she'd found the courage to broach the subject at that moment. "She's at a crucial time in a girl's development. She needs her mother as much as she needs her father.

I'm hoping you'll put her first and negotiate a new arrangement with me to split the time. It won't interfere with her schooling or activities because I'm just as capable of getting her anywhere she needs to go as you are." *Or some member of your household staff.*

He undid his belt.

"Damn it, Kip." Her mouth was dry, and her lips. "This is it, the end. Put your shirt back on and get out. Faith should be your focus here. She's the only reason I want to have anything to do with you."

"You like sex as much as I do, baby. Neither of us has forgotten how good we are together." Holding her by the shoulders, he flattened her to the wall and stood so close she looked sideways to avoid seeing any part of him.

"Don't do that," he said, and she heard the anger he barely held back. He rubbed against her, bent to push his face beneath her chin and kiss her, wet, sucking kisses. His body used to be as familiar as her own. Now he seemed like a brutish stranger.

Carolee's heart hammered so hard she took deep breaths to calm it. "This isn't going to happen," she told him. "Damn you, *no!*"

"You need it and so do I. What could be better than to give yourself to your husband."

"You're not my husband." She was afraid and approaching hysteria. "You're my ex-husband because that's what you wanted to be."

"That's what I thought I wanted to be, fool that I am. But I'm back and I'm never letting you go again."

"What about Faith? Will you—"

"Don't talk," he said. "You know what I like."

She struggled, and hit out at him, and squirmed from side to side. And Kip laughed. "Dammit, you drive me over the edge. You're so sexy, and you're mine. Remember that. When other things come along that seem appealing, just remember how dangerous passing infatuations can be and fight them off. They're illusions."

"Don't." Infatuations, he'd said, illusions. He'd heard about Max and was afraid she might get sexually involved with him. Too late, she thought, and tried to concentrate on an image of Max's face.

"Come back to me," Kip murmured.

"It wouldn't work. We both know that."

Footsteps, pounding along the landing, froze Carolee, but didn't stop Kip, who grew more aroused by the second.

"Faith," she told him urgently. "Faith must have been out there."

"She's getting to be a big girl—you said so yourself. She can't always be sheltered from life."

"She may have heard something."

"Then she knows we still love each other. That should make her happy."

He was selfish and uncontrolled—and she should have figured that out years ago.

"God, I want you, Carolee." Kip wrapped her in his arms and pushed a knee between her legs.

She fixed her eyes on the paneling that

covered the walls and ceiling. She fought to quiet her breathing, and to turn herself into an unresponsive stone.

"What the hell is going on here?" Max's voice from behind Kip made Carolee want to die.

"Get out," Kip shouted. "Now. Can't you see we're busy?"

She couldn't let Max think she wanted this. "Help me, Max," she said in a small voice. Faith needed her.

"I intend to," Max said in a frighteningly flat tone. He hauled Kip away from her and shoved him to the floor. "Do you make a habit of forcing yourself on women?"

Kip scrambled to get up. "She wanted it. Tell him you wanted it."

"I didn't want it." She wrapped her robe firmly and tightened the belt. "You pushed your way in here and told me what *you* wanted and what I ought to want. I don't want anything to do with you, ever, except to discuss changing the custody of Faith."

"You can forget that for good, you teasing bitch."

Max's fist, connecting with Kip's jaw, produced a snapping sound. Kip stumbled again but didn't fall this time. He held his jaw with one hand and swung at Max with the other, but missed.

"Then I'll get the best lawyer I can find," Carolee said. "In the meantime, don't come here until it's time for Faith to go back to Bell Town."

"She's coming now."

The room contracted and expanded before Carolee's eyes. "She's not going with you now. If you try to take her, I'll report you for breaking the terms of our agreement."

"And I'll tell them you used sex to try to get what you wanted out of me. How do you think that would help your case?"

"You don't learn," Max said quietly before landing two punches to Kip's belly.

Kip made another futile swing at Max and fell down, drawing each breath with a little shriek.

Max continued, "And I'm a witness, remember. I came to see if Faith wanted a riding lesson and heard Carolee shout. I did what any decent man would do, I came to help her."

"Get out," Kip said. "Ask him to leave, Carolee. We're having a discussion here."

Kip was going to make what little time she had with Faith miserable. Carolee turned from him and would have covered her face if Max hadn't been there.

"Tell him," Kip thundered.

She shook her head and kept her eyes on Max's face. He looked back with a question in his eyes. He wanted her to ask him to stay. Abruptly he swung away and started for the door.

"Don't go," she told him. "Please don't go. I need you."

He stood where he was.

"What are you two to each other?" Kip asked. He was pulling on his shirt.

Max turned around. Kip was tall, but Max

was taller and bigger and looked down on the other man. "Carolee and I are friends," he said.

"Sure," Kip said, buttoning the shirt. "I've got reason to believe you two are screwing each other and I intend to find a way to use the information. I'm leaving."

Carolee said, "You can't be responsible for raising my daughter."

Kip went onto the landing, then put his head back into the room and said, "Friends? Men and women can't be just friends."

Twenty

Faith and Digger had made it to the barn unseen. She'd closed the doors behind them and dragged bails of hay beneath a row of small windows high in the back wall. "I can't go back to Daddy because he doesn't really want me," she told the dog, puffing while she arranged more hay to make steps that would help her climb up and look out the window. "And I can't stay here. They're fighting over me."

Digger studied her face with his head tipped to one side. His teeth made a grinding sound on the rock he chewed.

She loved Digger. Whatever happened, they had to be together. Each breath she took burned her throat. Daddy was trying to make Mom do things she didn't want to do. Faith had heard his voice and the beastly way he shouted and said awful things. And she'd heard Mom cry and ask him to stop—and ask if he'd let Faith spend more time with her.

At last she could climb up to kneel on top of the hay. She took out a handkerchief and wiped a space on a dirty window. She ducked down. Dad was striding toward his car, and the way he held his shoulders meant he was really mad.

She slowly rose up enough to look again. Max's car was there, too, and while Faith watched, Daddy kicked the door of the Cadillac. Then he took something from his pocket and scraped it along the whole side of the car.

Faith wanted to die. Her dad was being like some of the kids at school, really mean because they thought they didn't like someone.

The Porsche's engine roared much louder than usual but Faith didn't watch her dad leave. Instead she dropped into a heap on top of the hay.

She didn't know how long she cried, but when she finally calmed enough to sniff, and wipe at her face, Digger had climbed as close as he could get to her. He whined and all three horses moved restlessly. Her tummy still hurt, but Mom had made her feel better about it all.

Faith clambered down and took one of the apples meant for the horses. She wiped it on her pants and cut it in half with Gramps's knife. The fruit was sour but she was too hungry not to eat it. Once again she felt choked and could scarcely swallow. There wasn't anyone to go to. If she tried to get away, she'd be taken back to her father.

They were going to make everything really horrible again. Mom said she wanted her and Dad said he didn't want to share her. Dad hadn't sounded like himself in Mom's bedroom.

Faith sweated and felt dirty. Dust had ground into the skin on her face. Auntie Linda's husband, Uncle Tom Gordon, loved her. Auntie Linda didn't like him anymore and they were divorced but Uncle Tom had told her a secret she would always keep—he would never be able to stop loving Auntie Linda.

He lived in Chicago and she knew he hadn't got married again, or had any children. She could go to him and ask for help. Maybe he'd let her live with him.

When she'd heard Daddy shouting and Mom crying, she'd known she must escape. Mom already said she didn't want Daddy again, but he was trying to make her say she did. What money Faith had was in her pocket. All she had to do was get to a bus and figure it out from there.

Josh Williams at school had shot himself in the head with his dad's gun. He wrote a note and it said—so everyone was told—that all he wanted was to be quiet. He didn't want to think anymore and he didn't know what to do. He said there wasn't anything he could do but go to sleep. Faith shivered. She'd liked him because he was gentle and nice, and she'd felt sad when he died. They'd put flowers in front of his locker. But he'd got what he wanted: peace.

Digger put his wet nose into her palm and dropped his rock into her fingers. "Thank you for the present," she said, scratching his head. "You want me to be happy."

Did she want to go to sleep? She already did that a lot when she was unhappy, but did she want to go to sleep and not wake up?

The pony watched her, blinking slowly and tossing his head occasionally. She thought Star was pretty.

Buses didn't come down here, but there was a stop a couple of miles away on the main road. Star ate the rest of the apple Faith didn't want and was happy to be saddled up. "You're coming too, Digger. Just stay close." She'd tie the pony up somewhere safe and he'd be found. Her stomach fell again and again. There was nothing for her here so she had to make a change.

She opened the barn doors and checked for Gramps's truck. It was still missing, although Max's car remained where he'd left it. Gramps and Auntie Linda had gone to buy wood but Faith hadn't wanted to go. Star allowed himself to be led quietly outside and Faith used a log to hike herself up and get on his back. Digger started leaping about and barking, but stopped when Faith ordered him to. "You're a good dog," she told him softly. "Let's go."

Max and Carolee set off for Sam's cabin. "She was so upset," Carolee said. "This has been a terrible day for her."

"She'll be at Sam's," Max said confidently. He almost took Carolee's hand but decided she needed a lot more time to sort herself out.

Carolee stopped. "Sam and Linda were going out to buy lumber. Faith must have decided not to go with them," she said.

"Lumber for Sam's lookout." Max nodded. "I'm going to give a hand building. I had plenty of experience growing up."

She gave him a curious look and carried on. They were just about through the trees separating Carolee's place from Sam's when the sound of hoofbeats reached them clearly.

Carolee frowned at Max. He took off, ran to the field in time to see Faith on the pony, riding toward the road as fast as she could make the little animal go. Digger raced along beside them.

"Faith!" Carolee shouted, dashing past Max. She ran uphill waving her arms. "Faith, don't. Where's your helmet?"

Max didn't wait around to tell Carolee that Faith couldn't hear her. He sprinted to the barn and saddled the black in record time. When he galloped past Carolee, he yelled, "Which way did she go?"

"That way." She indicated the right.

The last time he'd forced a horse to run like this had been when he was still on his parents' farm. The feeling of power and vague fear was just as he remembered. The horse's hoofs thundered over dry, hard ground to the road, and Max wheeled the animal right. Standing in the stirrups and leaning over its neck, he loosened up on the reins and used his knees and a whack to the rump to get the horse excited enough to run hard. Faith couldn't have gone far. She didn't have the skill to handle Star at much more than a sedate trot. Max was sweating, but turned cold. Faith was learning but still knew almost nothing about horses.

It was at least another half mile before he saw the pony with his wild-haired little rider. Faith's red sweater showed up brightly—and some sort of vivid scarf on her left arm. Like him, she was bent low over the horse's neck. He felt the moment when she became aware of his presence. "Faith," he called out. "Slow down. We'll ride together."

She didn't slow down. When she looked over her shoulder at him, she slid so markedly in the saddle he thought she'd take a fall. Somehow she righted herself, and veered the pony left across the road, and onto a steep, over-grown track. Digger kept right with them.

"C'mon, Guy," he said to the black. "How long can it take for you to catch that mosquito of a pony?"

The pony in question bolted.

Max cursed and raced after it. Faith was no longer in control. She had lost her grip on the reins and struggled to hold the animal's mane instead. While Max watched helplessly, she lay on Star's back and tried to put her arms around its neck. The creature strained forward, its sides heaving and its head jerking forward with the reckless effort to escape.

Faith's mind felt clear. She had to hold on to Star until he stopped. He would stop, wouldn't he? Little rocks shot free beneath the pony's hoofs and gushed downhill like deafening rivers. Tall grass at the sides of the track blurred. Vaguely she saw Digger running hard, his tongue lolling from his mouth.

The pony stumbled. His front legs started to buckle.

Faith screamed and drove her fingers into his neck. The pony's screech locked her own jaw. She shook and her arms felt lifeless.

Star staggered all the way to a ridge. He caught his footing there and tore downhill. Foam from his mouth flew backward. The ground beneath them was too rough. Fine rocks had given way to clumps of small boulders and Star seemed to dance while he ran faster and faster.

Ahead there were more trees on either side of the track.

"Whoa!" She heard the word inside her own head. Star couldn't hear it in there.

The noises around her were rushing sounds. The trees moved, and the tall weeds and grass. There were no buildings, only wilder and wilder country. Max was somewhere. She'd seen him, heard him call out to her. He wasn't calling to her now.

Star reared his head and tossed it from side to side. Only the whites of his eyes showed.

Faith couldn't stop him.

Without warning, the pony left the track and ran over pocked land and into some trees.

Faith cried, *"Help!"* Her teeth jarred together. Air fled her lungs with each beat of hoofs on the ground.

The trees were behind them now. Star's labored breathing sounded as if the animal must collapse.

A hedge loomed, a ragged, thorny hedge. Faith set her body as firmly as she could and, like a miracle, found the reins. She pulled back hard and raised her voice with soothing words.

Star checked his stride.

"Good boy," Faith said. "It's okay. Good boy." She was going to do it. Somehow she'd learned more than she'd realized. "Whoa, boy."

Star skittered sideways, still tossing his head, but no longer attempting to pull away. Faith stroked his neck and patted him. "Good, good, boy." She would be okay and she'd learn to ride really well.

Digger barked. He ran between the pony's front legs and leaped at him.

"No, Digger!"

Star reared onto his back legs, let out a blowing whinny, and went straight for the hedge. He jumped, and screamed as his belly scraped the woody foliage.

The ground rose before Faith. Foundering at the edge of a shallow pit, the pony didn't regain his balance.

Faith felt herself come out of the saddle and lose the right stirrup. As if a force pulled her, she rose, all but her left leg. Her foot was caught.

She was going to die.

She didn't want to sleep forever.

Max had been frightened in his life. Lying helpless with a pickup pinning his excruciating legs had scared him so badly, he'd passed out. But even then he hadn't been as afraid as he was now.

There was no sign of Faith. And no noise anywhere but for wind in trees and scrub. He'd reached the crest of the first, very steep hill and stood up in the stirrups for the best view he could get. For the third time he made a visual search of the area, this time so slowly his head began to pound.

She couldn't just disappear.

He moved the horse again, almost step by step, downhill, always sweeping the landscape. "Faith!" he called. "Faith, where are you?"

The sounds that came to him were still of the wind, and some small animal noises from the otherwise uninhabited terrain.

This kid hadn't been given a fair shake and it wasn't Carolee's fault, unless it could be through passive acceptance that had lasted too long. He could tell she wasn't about to be passive anymore, but Faith couldn't know that.

Premonition convinced him that something really terrible had happened. Max took off his

Stetson and wiped a forearm over his brow. His legs ached. He'd come a long way since surgery and therapy, but all the training in the world couldn't give him back everything he'd lost under that pickup.

The downhill trail was visible for a long way. He didn't believe Faith could have gone far enough away to be out of sight. That gave him the choice of going to the left, or to the right. How the hell did a man make a decision like that?

Right. He'd go that way as fast as he dared given the mashed-up surface of the ground, then he'd repeat the process in the other direction. He would zigzag back and forth, and he *would* find her.

Minutes after he'd left the trail and while he headed for some alder trees, he heard a dog bark. The dog barked but soon sent up a howl that raised hair on the back of Max's neck.

He'd heard that sound before; it was unforgettable. He rode toward the howl and would have slowed down, so strong was the foreboding that he was listening to a death howl. Crazy. Spurring the black, he passed through the trees. Just because there had been another occasion, another coyote-like howl and a dog standing guard beside a dead man, didn't mean that's what he'd find this time.

This was no place for an expert rider, and Faith was a complete novice. He should have forced the issue of giving her more lessons.

No matter where he searched, he caught no flash of a red sweater, no movement of a blond pony. But the barking and howling continued.

Anger kept him strong. A kid used by a man capable of forcing himself on his ex-wife. He couldn't allow himself to dwell on the scene he'd walked into at Lake Home without wanting to beat the crap out of Burns. Faith had to be found and returned to Carolee, then, as much as she'd try to dissuade him, he'd be having a chat with Kip Burns. Max didn't intend to get physical, but if the man wouldn't play ball with Carolee, there was new evidence to present about an unfit parent and this time the injured party wouldn't be a whining Kip Burns.

Please God let it stand for something that he'd caught and stopped the man from molesting Carolee. If Faith was... If Faith was dead, what would anything matter?

The barking was closer. It was real close. But nothing moved other than a chipmunk that shot through a hedge.

Nickering. A horse was on the other side of that hedge. It had to be Faith's pony. "Faith? Faith, speak to me. It's Max." He dismounted and dashed at the stickery hedge. When he reached it and started to push through, he hissed at the punctures made in his hands and on any piece of bare skin. His clothes didn't hinder any really sharp sticks.

Stinging all over, and bleeding, he broke free and was instantly leaped upon by a wild Digger, who took a mouthful of Max's shirt into his mouth and pulled, ripping the fabric.

"Okay," Max said, grabbing the tossing animal and trying to calm him. "Where's Faith?" A knot filled his throat. The pony stood at a distance, grazing. Sweat shone all over its body.

It must have jumped the hedge. Would Faith have been frightened enough of getting caught and taken back that she'd run away on foot?

The dog would have gone with her.

Immediately in front of him was a wide, shallow pit, rock-filled and overgrown with weeds. Max didn't see any sign of Faith.

Digger somersaulted free and took a sliding dive into the pit. He reappeared almost at once, and the howl went up again.

Max felt the blood leave his face, and every other part of his body.

Digger ran back and out of sight. Clenching his hands, Max followed and looked down. On the side closest to him, the pit was deeper.

The first thing he saw was the red sweater— the colorful scarf tied around Faith's left arm. Weeds all but obscured her head and her legs were turned at unnatural angles.

"Faith," Max whispered, slipping and sliding down beside her. "Oh, sweetheart. It's going to be okay." The child didn't move.

He reached her and knelt at her head to part the weeds. Her face rested straight down on rocks and blood soaked her hair.

Twenty-one

Sam and Linda sat quietly in a family waiting room on the pediatric unit at Olympic Memorial Hospital. Neither of them attempted to smother Carolee with pity. She appreciated her family for understanding she couldn't respond to them now.

Brandy—with Rob helping her—had arrived with plates of fruit and cheese, baskets of crackers, and thermoses of coffee and had left almost at once. None of the food had been touched, but Sam and Linda sat on the edge of a worn orange and pale green striped sofa and drank coffee.

Each time a staff member came into view outside a window in the door, Carolee stopped breathing, only to bow her head once they had passed. She'd been there less than two hours, but it felt like days and days.

Kip threw open the door and stared at her. He walked in and let the door slam behind him. "You two," he said to Sam and Linda. "Out."

"Please stay," Carolee said, as gently as she could. "We're all on the edge, but we need each other."

"I need you," Kip said. "No one else."

And she didn't want to go through this with only Kip at her side. She didn't want him near her at all. "I'm glad the Lesters finally got hold of you," she said. "I couldn't concentrate on telephone numbers anymore."

Kip's eyes slid away, but he settled a heavy hand on her shoulder. Carolee shook him off. She would never forget what he'd tried to do to her.

"You want coffee?" Sam asked gruffly.

"Yeah," Kip said and accepted a mug from Sam. "Where's Wolfe?"

This had to come. "In Emergency. Getting a lot of wounds cleaned out—and some of them stitched."

"To hell with his scratches. He should be thinking about Faith."

"You shouldn't care what he's thinking," Carolee said. "Faith's in surgery and you haven't even asked about her."

He turned from her and paced. "What are they doing to her?"

"Dealing with a ruptured spleen. We don't know the whole story and surgery is going to take a long time. Her face is badly lacerated. There's a plastic surgeon in the operating room, and other specialists. They've got to work on her left leg. They think that when she was thrown, her foot stayed in the stirrup at first and the leg broke in a lot of places."

"Her dancing," he said and there were tears in his eyes. "She loves to dance."

"Living comes first," Sam said and Carolee saw the flash of anger in his eyes. "Making sure she doesn't die, then being able to walk at all."

The mug Kip held slipped through his fingers and landed on the rug, slopping coffee. He stared at it as if he wondered where it had come from.

"It's okay," Linda said. "I'll fix it." And she went to work with paper napkins.

"What d'you mean, die?" Kip said, walking straight at Carolee until she was forced to back away. "Don't tell me my girl could die."

He crowded her and Carolee flinched, but finally managed to hold her ground. "She hit her head on rocks and she fell hard—face first. If Max hadn't ridden after her, she'd probably be dead already."

"He brought her out of those hills on his own? On horseback?"

"He had to," Carolee told him.

"He moved a girl who was badly injured?"

"Everything happened fast. We were lucky to see her leaving Lake Home. He wasn't carrying a cell phone, and when he found her, there was no sign of anyone around. He couldn't risk leaving her there while he went for help."

Kip spun away and punched a green wall. "If she dies, it's going to be his fault. He had to have made her injuries worse by moving her. On horseback, for God's sake. He could have paralyzed her."

"*Shut* your stupid mouth." Linda came out of her chair. "You idiot. You've done enough damage to Carolee and Faith. You don't deserve to be anywhere near them. You don't have any pride. You never did. What kind of man hangs around for years doing nothing while his wife keeps him—and keeps him very well—then uses a bunch of trumped-up garbage to divorce her and make sure she keeps on paying for his nasty little life?"

Carolee sat down suddenly and propped her face in her hands. "Kip's as scared as any of us," she said. "But thanks, Linda." She couldn't stand the wrangling while Faith fought for her life somewhere in this hospital.

Kip dropped to the carpet beside Carolee's legs. He rested his brow on his knees and his shoulders shook. He was crying.

Shifting on the couch caught Carolee's attention and Linda motioned to Sam and herself, then at the door. She held up the fingers on one hand, indicating they'd wait out there for five minutes only. Carolee struggled against a desire to stop them from leaving at all, but nodded.

Once she was alone with Kip, she got up and moved to another chair. "The only thing that matters here," she said, "is Faith. That's where all my energy and emotion will be. *Nothing* else is important to me."

Kip looked up and said, "I'm scared."

"We both are."

"She's all I have. Carolee, I've done a lot of things I regret, but we've got to help each other get through this."

She hated it that she couldn't take what he said seriously. Yes, he was frantic about Faith, but there was something else—the same something else that had led him to attack her in her bedroom.

"She's not going to die," Kip almost shouted. "She isn't. She's young and healthy and she'll recover."

"Yes." But Carolee heard the brave words at a distance. She had been at the hospital when Faith and Max were brought in. No child— no one at all—should be that badly injured.

"I'm not going to make it without you," Kip said.

Creepy was the only word for the sensation Carolee felt.

"Tell me you want to get back together. We'll get married again. You know you've never stopped loving me. Our responsibility is to make a stable home for Faith."

"You were the one who decided to disrupt her stable home," Carolee said quietly. How much longer could five minutes last?

He stared at her. "Okay. I was, but you drove me to it."

"Reconciliation?" She stood up and turned her back on him. "But you'd want to remind me—regularly—of how selfish you think I am, and how much I owe you. I still don't understand why I owed you anything. All I did was give, and you were right there taking."

She heard him get up and her spine tingled. He was coming toward her, she knew it.

"I love you," he said, and took hold of her arms. He pulled her back against him. "You love me. Admit it. There was never anyone else for you and there won't be. Say it, Carolee." For emphasis, he stroked her arms then thudded her against his chest again.

When had he become a predator? He was desperate; she felt his desperation. And he was prepared to do anything to get her back

247

because of some need he had. He did not love her.

"*Say* it," he said.

The door opened behind them. One of the surgeons Carolee had met when Faith was going into the operating room came in. "Mr. and Mrs. Burns?" he said.

"Yes," Kip said quickly. He'd released Carolee. "You are?"

"Dr. Lee. I'm part of the team working with your daughter. We have possibly three hours to go, but I wanted to give you a progress report."

"Why did you leave her?" Kip said. "You don't think you'll save her, do you?"

Dr. Lee indicated for Carolee to sit down and did so himself. Kip remained standing. "We have every confidence that Faith will recover. Barring unforeseen circumstances, she should do quite well. But she has a long and difficult road ahead of her."

"I'm so grateful," Carolee said, gripping the piping on the chair seat. "Whatever she needs, she'll get."

"What do you mean by a long, difficult road?" Kip asked. He sounded more reasonable.

"We believe her head—or her face—hit first but she was lucky, possibly because she must have thrown up her arms to break her fall. She's concussed but not in coma. I already told you there would be a plastic surgeon involved, Mrs. Burns. He called in a maxillofacial surgeon who wired her broken jaw shut. Work on her face will be undertaken in a number of phases. Barring the risk of infection, we're not really concerned about the internal injuries."

Carolee couldn't move or respond. She rocked and watched the doctor's face.

"So she's a mess but she'll live," Kip said.

Dr. Lee looked at him with assessing dark eyes. "Those aren't the words I'd have chosen, but you can make them do if you want to."

"Her leg?" Carolee asked softly.

"There are two orthopedists with her. The fractures are compound and some reduction has been performed. Naturally they're doing as much as they can intrasurgically at this time, but there's too much swelling. The leg will be immobilized until the swelling goes down. Immobilized, and she'll be in traction. Then the leg will be set. After a few days she'll need more surgery. There's also a torn ligament in her right knee. We can't believe she didn't break her arms."

"Or her neck," Carolee muttered.

The doctor patted her hand. "Yes," he said. "That's a miracle. Someone will check back with you when there's something else to report."

She thanked him, but he seemed unaware and left the door open for Sam and Linda to hurry in.

Kip sat beside Carolee and held her hand too tightly for her to pull away without making a scene. "We're in shock," he told Sam and Linda. "She's alive. They expect her to live. She's all broken up though. Carolee and I will come through this together. Sometimes terrible things wake you up and show you what you're missing and what you care about."

"What did the doc say?" Sam asked. He was pale and his white sideburns were darkened with sweat. "I shouldn't have pushed the riding thing."

"There's no blame here," Carolee said.

"Sure there's blame," Kip announced. "A lot of it. When this is all over, we'll figure out the changes that have to be made."

Carolee glanced up and saw Max at the door. She motioned for him to come in and he entered quietly. When she started to react to his battered appearance, he shook his head and perched on the edge of a table.

Linda looked at him with rounded eyes, but said "The doctor" to Carolee and held Sam's elbow while she urged him to the couch. "Please tell us the details."

Kip started to refuse but Carolee cut him off. "He was very nice," she said and told them everything Dr. Lee had said. Kip had stiffened beside her. He moved even closer, switched her hand from his right to his left, and put a possessive arm around her shoulders.

Both of Max's hands were swathed in bandages. More dressings showed through holes in his shirt and jeans. The scratches on his face and neck didn't appear too deep.

He didn't take his eyes from Carolee's. "Faith's a brave little kid," he said. "If she'd had more training, she would never have taken that track. Knowing as little as she does, it's amazing she managed so well."

"No one asked me if my daughter could be riding around unsupervised," Kip said.

"She hasn't ridden unsupervised," Carolee told him. "Faith was upset and running away." She prayed he'd leave the subject alone.

"We're all upset," Kip said, surprising her. "But we'll get past it and things are going to change. Parents have to learn how vulnerable their children are. If a girl can't rely on her parents for security, who can she rely on?"

There were no arguments, but Kip massaged Carolee's shoulder and neck and the blank emptiness in Max's expression overwhelmed her.

"I know I was the one who went for a divorce. I've regretted it ever since."

"So why didn't you try to put things back together then?" Sam said. "Carolee never wanted it. She asked you to change your mind. But you didn't just divorce her, you rubbed her nose in it. You did everything you could to ruin her life. You took and took and you keep on takin'. And you do nothing. My girl supports you and Faith but she's still got to provide for her girl's future because she's afraid if something happened to her, you might not make sure Faith goes to college and has some sort of start in life."

"Shut your goddamn mouth, old man," Kip snapped. "Maybe if you hadn't been hanging around to encourage Carolee, she wouldn't be looking at other..." He stopped and made a disgusted sound. "Faith's got a trust fund because that's the way Carolee wanted it. Parents are like that. They like to provide for their children. They don't hang around like leeches, living on their property because they never made a go of anything."

Carolee yanked away from Kip, and when he still didn't let go, she stamped on his foot and he yelled.

"Don't you talk to my dad like that," Linda said, shooting to her feet.

Max already stood and Kip got up. Jutting his jaw, he advanced on Max.

"Don't," Carolee begged. "Stop it. This isn't the place."

"You has-been," Kip told Max. "The Broncos knew what they were doing when they got rid of you."

Max's chest expanded but he didn't argue with Kip's warped interpretation.

"Carolee isn't your type," Kip said. "You're one more thickheaded ball player who wants a flashy woman on his arm. She isn't flashy, but she's famous and anything is better than nothing when no one's cheering for you any-more."

"Stop it," Carolee said. "You're the failure."

"Let me at him," Sam said and surged toward Kip.

"Please, Sam." Max stepped between Kip and the older man. "He doesn't know what he's saying anymore. Faith's going through hell and he can't help her. That's got to be a bad feeling for a father."

"Don't make excuses for me," Kip yelled. "Smarmy bastard. All you're interested in is looking good for Carolee. What's the matter? Funds getting a bit low? Well, you can forget it. My wife isn't about to be your bank."

When Max didn't say a word, Carolee wanted to cry with gratitude.

"She can't be his bank *and* your bank, can she?" Linda said. "He's a good man and he's successful. He doesn't need a woman to pay his way."

Kip swung at Max, who took the blow on his chin. Blood trickled from an existing scratch and he wiped it away. He smiled ruefully and said, "Whatever they gave me for the pain must be slowing me down."

Kip's next swing missed its target completely, and Max ducked a third.

"This is a hospital," Carolee said, trembling. "Faith's in an operating room here."

"And he's getting out. Now." Kip approached the door as if to open it for Max. "He had a lot to do with my little girl being on that horse in the first place. And he moved her when she should have been moved by professionals. He's probably ruined her leg for good."

"That's it," Max said. Shooting out an arm, he cut off Kip's progress. "I'm not going to hit you for two reasons. One, you want me to so you can cook up some story about me attacking you. Two, I'm afraid I'd kill you."

"Stay away from my family." Pushing Max's

arm away, Kip drew himself up. "My daughter and my wife don't need you around."

The change in Max's stance, his body language, frightened Carolee.

He walked toward Kip, backing the man against a wall, and Kip must have seen and felt what Carolee was noting—Max Wolfe was a potentially dangerous man.

"You drove your daughter to what she did. She ran away because of you."

"The hell she did," Kip blustered. "She was probably trying to get home to me."

"When she knew you were deliberately avoiding her?" Linda said.

Max behaved as if he hadn't heard what she said. With one hand on Kip's neck, he held him against the wall. "Faith overheard what you were trying to do to her mother and she was terrified. The man she was supposed to trust most in the world was behaving like an animal, so she took off. Who would blame her? Now I'm leaving. Carolee, if you need me for anything, call. Same goes for you, Sam."

He withdrew his hand and started walking backward.

"What did he do?" Sam said, his skin turning red. "Max, don't you leave this room without telling us what you're talking about."

Max held eye contact with Kip. "Faith's old enough to figure it out when she hears a man trying to force sex on a woman."

Twenty-two

Convinced he'd be allowed to see Faith eventually, Max hadn't been able to make himself leave the hospital all night. Sitting in the general waiting room for the pediatric unit, he'd known he had to wait until he was sure Faith was really recovering, and he'd accepted that he saw no way to carry on as if he were the man he'd been before meeting Carolee.

He'd never intended to blurt out what he'd seen in her bedroom. Claiming loss of control didn't work—he was too strong a man for that. In that final moment, he'd wanted to hurt Kip Burns badly. He hoped Carolee would forgive him for the shame she must have felt.

She hadn't wanted Burns. She'd been fighting him off. In Max's office Carolee hadn't done any fighting, except to get as close to him as she could. He smiled at the memory and it felt good.

He hurt a lot. He hadn't slept all night—couldn't have imagined trying to do so.

Burns was a first-class heel who didn't want Carolee for any normal reasons, but didn't want anyone else to have her. And he seemed oblivious to the way he used his own child as a weapon, as a pawn. Max couldn't believe that Kip cared a whole lot about Faith.

He knew all about being an unwanted, or more accurately, being a disappointing offspring. His father hadn't been much of a drinker, but when he did take a glass or two, he had the habit of turning even more silent than usual, except on a few occasions when he behaved like a crazy man and knocked Max—and sometimes his mother—down. That was when he would rant about his useless only son and berate his wife for not bearing him a string of boys to help on the farm.

This morning Sam had discovered Max in the waiting room and told him that when it was the older man's turn to see Faith, Max should go instead. Sam reminded Max he should be in bed, but said he figured Max had a right to see Faith before he left since he had been the one to rescue her. Carolee and Kip were with her now.

Max was no stranger to intensive care units: glass-walled rooms open to the corridor, small, high-tech cubicles designed to accommodate emergency after emergency as personnel, many of them obviously tired, moved incessantly from patient to patient.

He pressed the button to open the door into the unit and entered, expecting at any moment to be stopped and told to leave.

"Can I help you, sir?"

Max turned a pleasant smile on one of the nurses watching banks of monitors and said, "I'm to see Faith Burns as soon as one of her parents leaves." He watched her find Faith's chart and made the decision to come clean with his explanation. "I'm Max Wolfe. I was the one who found her and brought her in."

The nurse turned up a plump, pretty face and smiled at him. "We usually have you wait outside the unit but why not go to the end of this corridor? Faith's in the last room on the right. Maybe you can slip in, too."

Slip in with Kip Burns? Max didn't find that a cheerful proposition. Out of respect for those locked in struggles with death, he walked to the opposite end of the corridor without looking from side to side.

He found Faith, not because he saw and recognized her, but because Kip sat on one side of a bed with his face in his hands, and Carolee, her dark hair working free of the clips she'd used to hold it back, was on the other side, staring at the bandaged, sheet-swathed figure of a person much too small to be in such a place.

Max passed the cubicle and drew as far out of obvious sight as he could. The last time he'd seen Faith, she'd been soaked in blood and moaning at the slightest move. He would never forget the horror of riding off that hill with her held against him, knowing that she could have broken vertebrae and in saving her he might be consigning her to life in a wheelchair—or worse. By the time he'd started down the last part of the track and the road came into sight, Sam's old truck was chugging from the direction of Lake Home. Both Carolee and Linda were squeezed in beside their dad. Max had been ordered into the back of the truck where Carolee and Linda quickly spread horse blankets grabbed because Sam, not having passed either Faith or Max on his way home, was prepared for the worst.

With Faith stretched out on her back beside him and Carolee kneeling where she could watch over her, Sam had driven slowly while Linda got 911 on the phone. Max had never been more relieved to hear a siren.

Somewhere a buzzer sounded, followed by an announcement that meant nothing to him, and a team rushed a defibrillator into a room. Max felt sick again, and when he touched his forehead, it was damp.

Kip was looking at Carolee and she shook her head repeatedly. She stood up beside Faith's left leg, which was raised and in traction. Beneath her eyes, dark slashes streaked Carolee's unnaturally white skin. Kip gestured with both hands and also stood. He leaned across the bed, pointing at Carolee.

Max didn't think he could control himself much longer. The guy was blustering at Carolee again and she didn't have anything left to fight him with.

She turned from the bed and sighted Max, and he couldn't miss how glad she was, or the way she took a step toward him. With a plea in her eyes, she held her bottom lip between her teeth.

Kip turned and saw him, and drew himself up straight, and stiff.

Carolee hurried to open the door. "Come in and see her," she said. And he went in, surprised that Kip didn't order him out again.

258

"She's a mess," the man said. "It's been hours and she hasn't come round yet."

"She moved her head," Carolee said and looked from one man to the other. "She did. That must mean she's coming out of it, mustn't it?"

"I should think so," Max said, wishing he could hug her, comfort her.

"When did you become a doctor?" Kip said. "There should only be two visitors in this room. You know what that means."

"Stay," Carolee murmured. She took him by the elbow and urged him to stand beside Faith. "I think she's going in and out of consciousness but she's awake such a little while, she slips away again before she can try to communicate."

"Communicate?" Kip laughed shortly. "That's going to be quite a number with her jaw wired shut."

"Dr. Lee said she'd learn how to speak through her teeth pretty quickly. She's having IV feeding of something now but he thinks she'll be able to take stuff she'll like through a straw."

"You're in luck, Wolfe," Kip said. "There's no sign of paralysis."

"I would have thought we're all lucky in that case," Max said quietly. He bent close to Faith and said, "Hey, buddy," in a very low voice. "This is some hotel but it's not much good if you don't join in the fun. Faith? Are you in there?"

"Of course she's in there." Carolee stood

at his side and touched Faith's head as if she were afraid the girl would break. "She *is* in there."

"I want you to leave, Wolfe," Kip said. "You're upsetting Carolee."

Max ignored him and stroked one of Faith's bruised and cut bare arms. Her fingers curled and she made a sound. "She's coming round," he said and put his mouth to her ear again. "Hi, Faith. You're doing really well. Getting better every second. Your mom and dad are here and this is Max."

Her head rolled to the side but she didn't attempt to open her eyes. Bandages hid much of her face. What skin showed was swollen and bruised, and mottled with speckles of blood that showed through. Both of her eyes were black and puffy and Max wondered if she'd be able to open them if she wanted to. The right leg also appeared to have been immobilized. Max could attest to just how bad torn ligaments could be.

"A mess," Kip said with finality. "You can't argue with that, can you?"

"Faith looks mysterious," Max said, giving the man a hard stare. "I hope she can hear how interesting she looks."

Kip opened his mouth to speak again but Max held up a hand in warning. He knew he was on thin ice, but as long as he could remain, he'd do his best to help Carolee.

Faith moaned and tried to move. "It's okay, sweetheart," Carolee said, sitting down and holding her daughter's hand.

The little girl gurgled and thrashed until she cried out.

"I'll press the call button," Kip said, and did so.

"You're all right," Carolee said. "You took a tumble from Star and hurt yourself, but you're going to be fine."

Faith turned her head from side to side, arched her back, and made noises.

"Tell her about her jaw," Max said. "She can't understand why her mouth doesn't open."

Purple puffs of skin parted a slit to reveal slivers of Faith's gray eyes. What whites were visible were filled with blood. She looked directly at Max.

"Your jaw's been wired shut," Carolee said. "It was broken when you fell. You'll learn to talk and be easy to understand. Not that it'll be wired for long. Think of it, nothing but good-tasting stuff through a straw for a while."

Faith's attention shifted to her mother. Then she turned her head until she saw her father. She closed her eyes.

A nurse came in and went directly to the bed. He held Faith's chart and had an air about him that encouraged confidence.

"She's conscious," Carolee said. "And the wired jaw's upsetting her."

"Of course it is," the nurse said, starting to take Faith's vital signs. "It's a shocker, but you'll get some cool benefits. You'll probably look like a movie star pretty soon. I'm thinking of getting mine wired shut, too. That'll probably be the only way to keep french fries out of my mouth. Not that we want you getting too thin."

Faith rolled her face in the opposite direction again and her eyes opened. Clicks came from her throat, then whispers. Carolee put her ear to Faith's mouth and nodded, nodded again.

"What's she saying?" Kip asked, not looking so hot himself.

Carolee stared at him. "She says this will make you and Mrs. Jolly happy because Faith will stay on her diet."

The nurse finished checking the girl and straightened her bed. He smiled at Faith, but left the room with his mouth in a straight line. Carolee looked at Kip as if she loathed him.

"Good for you," Max said to Faith. The last thing she needed was more harsh words between the people who were supposed to take care of her. "You've still got a sense of humor. Take a look at me. Am I an ugly sight, or what?"

Faith's eyes shut frequently. She was going to sleep again but she did study Max and then she pulled weakly on her mother's sleeve. Carolee leaned close to listen. "Faith wants to know what happened to you. I'll tell her. Do you remember riding away from Lake Home on Star?"

Faith gave a faint shake of the head.

"Well, you did. And Max went after you because we were worried. You rode up a steep track and got thrown when Star jumped a hedge. Max pushed through that hedge to get to you and got all scratched up."

"You're not ever going to be unhappy enough to run away again, Faith," Kip said. "Your mom and I will make sure of that."

Max avoided looking at Kip Burns. If Kip got his way, Max would have to bow out. Maybe that would be a good thing, but he didn't think so, and he felt as if he was battling impossible odds. Kip wasn't any good for Carolee, but he'd use the child to get her back. Question was, why the big change of heart? Was it because he'd found out—and Max wanted to know how—that Max had come into Carolee's life? Was he one of those men who were comfortable making a woman's life hell, and leaving her, but who didn't want to see her happy with someone else?

"Thanks for your help, Wolfe," Burns said, making a move as if to open the door for Max to leave.

Faith became agitated. She plucked at Carolee again and said something short to her.

"She'd like to say something to you, Max," Carolee said, smiling at him. "I think you're her hero."

Max changed places with Carolee and perched on the edge of the chair. He winked at Faith, lifted her hand, and gave it a kiss. "You're my hero," he told her. "Most people would have come right off that pony, but you hung on."

Her mouth moved and he got close enough

to hear hoarse murmurs. "Where's Digger?" she said, sucking to swallow saliva. "And the horses?"

Max grinned at her. "Nothing wrong with that mind," he said. "Clicking over very nicely, I'd say. Your mom's friend, Brandy—she's my friend, too, and another friend of mine and Brandy's called Rob Mead—they came over and got Digger from your gramps's truck. They're looking after him. We had to tie up Guy and Star, but someone picked them up for us."

"Who's Digger?" Kip asked on cue.

"Our dog," Max told him brusquely. "He'll be great," he told Faith.

She was staring at her father and darting little looks in Carolee's direction. The slack hand Faith raised to Max's collar was cold and small. Her weak tug on him transmitted urgency. She wanted to talk to him again.

"Tell me a story," he said lightly, crossing his arms on the mattress and positioning his head to listen.

"Max," she whispered. "Please keep my mom safe."

Twenty-three

Max buzzed Rob Mead past the security gate and into the condominium complex where he lived. Rob's timing stank, but Max wasn't about to brush off a man who sounded lost.

The walk from the outside gates to Max's place took only moments. He opened the front door before Rob rang the bell and took hold of his hand as he came inside. Promptly, Rob put his arms around Max and thumped his back.

Hissing inward through his teeth, Max managed to say, "Come on in. I was going to open a beer and watch some baseball." He'd been trying to sleep on the couch, having been unable to stay in bed.

"Geez." Rob stared at him, at his face and bare chest. Max had taken off his shirt because any pressure on his skin made it more uncomfortable. "Brandy said you'd gotten scratched up. Did she see you?"

"No. The two of you came when I wasn't around. She hasn't tried to intrude anymore. Brandy's a good girl."

Rob's finely cut face became ever more serious. He glanced toward the windows and the terrace—and Lake Washington visible beyond the roofs of buildings on the opposite side of the street.

"Did I say something wrong?" Max asked.

"Brandy's more than a good girl. I knew I was falling for her before, but now I don't think of much else. I just don't know if I have a right to try making her more than a friend."

Max said, "Sit down. You want that beer?"

"Sure. Are you into a game right now?"

"Nope," Max said. "Haven't even turned the box on and don't need to. Come through and sit down." He led the way to the sitting room, where a panel television hung on one wall and the brain of a sound system considered a piece of wizardry was kept. Rob settled in a green bucket chair and swung it toward the windows.

The kitchen was open to the sitting room. Finished with black granite and stainless steel, more than one or two people had begged to cook in that kitchen, but Max liked the simple life here. If God had intended him to get stoves and ovens dirty, He wouldn't have allowed the invention of microwaves—or microwavable meals.

Two beers poured into frosty glasses and a can of nuts...he was the perfect host.

But he would cook for Carolee. Max stopped where he was and watched Rob looking out of the window without seeing him clearly. He wanted to see her face, to hear her voice, to feel her touch. And he wanted Faith to recover a whole lot more than he cared about what happened to him.

"Beer coming up." His voice felt unused. "Put your feet on an ottoman and quit dwelling on whatever's turned you into such a miserable son of a gun."

Rob accepted the beer and took a handful of nuts. "Are there any other condos for sale here?"

"I don't know," Max said, and he didn't. What was it with Rob and his sudden need to be as close to Max as he could get?

A tossed pecan landed in Rob's mouth and he chewed. "I'll find out. I like it here and I know Brandy likes the place."

Max sank into a purple couch, kicked off his thongs, and put his feet on a jungle print ottoman. "Okay, I'm as comfortable as I'm going to get anytime soon. Let's have it. What's going on with you? You want to quit the Broncos. You want to work with me. You want to live here. You don't know if you have the right to go after Brandy. What the hell is all that?"

"You think I'm a pest and you wish I'd get lost."

Pity parties had never been Rob's thing—until now. "I'm not arguing with you," Max said. "But think about what you just said and you'll know what an ass you're making of yourself."

"Thanks." Rob drank beer, and tossed more nuts. He got up and went close to the windows. "I can almost see Brandy's from here."

"Sure you can."

"I think she's still got a thing for you, Max."

"Brandy likes the idea of having *things*

about men. She likes me so I'm the one she's supposedly mad about. We were together for a few weeks. It didn't work—or at least, it didn't work for me."

Rob turned abruptly, and knocked a freestanding globe hard enough to have to stop it from falling. "She's not good enough for you, is that it?"

"You've chosen the wrong day for this. Not that there's ever going to be a right day. In a certain way, I love Brandy, but not in the way I'd need to love her if we were going to get together for good."

"Sorry," Rob said. "It's just that I want her badly and I've taken way too long to do anything about it."

"Tell her that," Max said. "I know she thinks a lot of you."

"Maybe I will." Rob's broad chest expanded. Even Max recognized what a good-looking guy he was. His skin was coffee tan and he had eyes that were a hazel-green color and startling. And Rob had a mind.

"Do it," Max told him. "Don't mess around and put it off. You'll have to get back to camp or face the music. Speak to Brandy before you go and give her a little time to sort out her feelings."

"I've told you I'm not going back."

"I'll be your best man," Max said, trying to lighten things up. "And I'll pray Faith's up to being a bridesmaid."

"Thanks. I'm not going back—ever."

"Okay," Max said slowly, crossing and

recrossing his ankles on the ottoman. A cloud of swallows so large and so thick it darkened the sky dipped and swirled over Kirkland like waving black silk. Max looked away from them. "Okay, back to my original question. What's going on with you?"

The phone rang and he picked it up.

"Max? This is Carolee."

"I know. How are you?" Dumb words, but the best he had. "How's Faith?"

"This is something I have no right to say, but I wish I could be with you."

He was certain his heart quit beating. "Anytime." He got up and went into the kitchen. "Just say the word and I'll come get you."

"We still haven't been home. I can't make myself leave."

We. "Has something happened?"

"She's stopped waking up." Carolee's voice broke. "The doctors keep saying everything's okay, but I can tell they're puzzled. They did a test on her brain and said there were no abnormal signs. But they can't tell me she isn't in a coma now."

Max worked his jaw.

"Are you still there?"

"Yes, yes, of course I am," he told her. "Where are you—exactly?"

"At a pay phone in the waiting room. Ivy's in there with Kip now. Linda's asleep in the family waiting room—so is Sam. I worry about him, he's not strong enough for all this stress."

"Don't try to baby him, sweetheart. He

would hate that. He needs to be right where he is—close to the granddaughter he loves."

"Yes," she said. "You're very wise. And I shouldn't be selfish enough to involve you. That's a burden you don't deserve. I worry I'm like my... I worry about not being strong enough."

She'd stopped herself in mid-sentence but he wouldn't press her on that now. He turned his back on Rob. "I want you and need you. If that makes me selfish—tough. It also makes me a frightened man because I never felt this way before. My challenge is to stop myself from beating your ex-husband to a pulp and running away with you and Faith."

Her small laugh didn't do much for the tension. "Too bad you can't do it. You know how to make a woman feel wonderful."

"I can't do it, *yet*," he told her.

"Not ever if Kip has his way. He not only keeps suggesting reconciliation, he talks as if it were inevitable. And he looks at me so strangely if I argue. He still won't discuss joint custody."

Max thought of Faith's request and brought a fist down on a countertop. "You don't have to be alone with him," he said. "Don't get taken in by anything he says. You mustn't be alone with that man."

"I don't want to be." Her voice shrank.

"Then you won't." Anger and panic were a bad mix. "Say you won't."

"I may have to, but I'll be very careful. He wants to go somewhere with me and talk about—about us."

"There isn't any 'us' for him."

"No, there isn't, but you know what I'm saying. And he keeps hinting without actually saying anything directly. I mention custody and he says we need to be alone to talk."

"He's with Ivy in Faith's room now?"

"Yes," Carolee said. "Ivy's being so good, and Brandy and Linda."

"I don't want to pile on more worries," Max said, "but did the bit about Mrs. Jolly and eating mean they've had her on a diet to lose weight?"

"Oh, Max, I think it does. What a disaster this is. Yes, I believe that's what it means."

"Damn them."

Carolee sniffed, and coughed. "That's all coming to an end. I'm jotting notes. It's my turn now and Kip isn't making himself look great."

"That's the way the game has to be played this time," he said. "But you have to sleep, sweetheart. Right now would be good."

"You keep calling me, sweetheart."

He looked at his bare feet on a red Turkish carpet. "Do I? That's because I like calling you sweetheart. Let me come and get you. We'll make sure you can be reached easily and you'll only be minutes away."

"Where will I be only minutes away?"

Max screwed up his eyes. "Here. From my place to the hospital is no distance at all. I'll get you and tuck you into a soft bed."

"What about Kip?"

"There isn't room for him."

271

Carolee laughed. "Only you would say something like that when everything's so serious. I meant—"

"I know what you meant. It's none of his business where you go, remember? He's poison and it's my job to take care of you." He wouldn't tell her about Faith's request unless he had to. "I'm coming for you."

"No! No, Max, not yet. And it isn't your job to take care of me. That's not what I need. Most of all I wanted to hear your voice and let you know Faith's condition. When I can come to you, I'll let you know. If you aren't at home, may I call you at the office?"

"I won't be going to the office until I've seen you again."

"Max—"

"Call me the minute you can." He hung up before she could protest anymore and returned to the sitting room with his beer.

"There's a name for that kind of grin," Rob said. "You've decided you like trouble, is that it?"

Max wiped the unconscious smile off his lips. "I hate trouble. We both know that. Faith Burns is coming up to twelve and one of her legs is too smashed and swollen to set yet. Her face is pulp, her spleen had to be repaired. Her jaw is broken and wired shut. And the mildest head injury she's got is a severe concussion, but now she's not waking up at all, so there may be something worse going on."

"Sorry," Rob said, looking into his glass and frowning. "I know how I felt when... I felt like

272

hell when that pickup slipped on top of you and I couldn't stop it. You must be going through some of the same stuff, not that you could have done anything about what happened."

"And you couldn't do a damn thing about what happened to me, other than join me in the hospital because you ended up getting injured, too. You're tied up in reef knots because you really think you should have been able to save me. Forget it, will you?"

Rob ran a hand over close-cropped hair. "I guess I'll have to." He didn't meet Max's eyes. "But you were grinning when you hung up the phone just now. It's all about Carolee for you, isn't it? You've got a real case on her."

"I don't have much experience to go on," he said, resting his neck on the back of the couch and looking at a mural of an evening sky painted on the coved ceiling. "I'm not sure I know what to do about it, but I think I love her."

Twenty-four

"I don't want to leave her," Carolee said Kip held her hand firmly and continued toward the hospital lobby and swinging front doors. "Faith's in very good hands. You need a break and so do I. Ivy and Linda will take good care of her and we'll be called if we're needed before I intend for us to get back."

She shouldn't be leaving with him. He'd managed to convince her because he said they needed to be alone to talk about the future. But Max had begged her not to do this and she didn't want to. Please let her be able to keep Kip reasonable, and avoid anger or anything physical.

He had never shown a tendency to violence before he'd tried to force sex on her at Lake Home.

One of the nurses from ICU passed and said, "Time you two got some decent sleep."

"She's right," Kip said to Carolee. "I called the Widmark in Kirkland. You'll like it. Great hotel. And it's really close to the hospital."

Her breathing grew shallow. A hotel room with Kip? How much more obvious could he be? She believed he intended to get her into bed, and to push for a reconciliation on the grounds that they should put their family back together. What she didn't know was why he'd made this sudden and total change of heart toward her. She didn't care what his reason was, there would never be intimacy between them again.

"I know what you're thinking," he said. "And you're wrong. What I want more than anything right now is to see you sleeping and not thinking. You think I don't care what happens to you. That's wrong, too. I care a great deal and I always will."

Every word he spoke had a phony ring. She could be overly suspicious, but she felt it nevertheless. "That's nice," she said. "But I won't be doing any sleeping. Is this one room or is there a sitting room?"

"It's a suite," he said and the anger was already there.

"Good. I'll make sure Sam's got the number in case they need to reach me."

The first flash went off the instant they pushed through the doors and Kip had to shelve any comebacks he had in mind. People with cameras ran forward and took shots so rapidly, the lights caused Carolee to squint and try to refocus. Questions were flying at them, but she couldn't concentrate. It was all so familiar. Years of dealing with the paparazzi because of what she did for a living had been one thing, the prying publicity hounds during the divorce had been another.

"Smile, honey," Kip said, pulling her arm beneath his elbow and pausing on the top step outside the doors. "Don't give them any ammunition this time. Smile and nod and leave the talking to me."

How had these people found out Carolee and Kip were together at the hospital, and how could they be so obviously prepared for them to leave now?

"You look like the happy couple again," a reporter shouted. "Are you getting back together?"

"Damn him," Carolee muttered. "Doesn't even have the decency to ask how Faith is."

"He's a reporter," Kip said. "He's looking for the juicy bits."

Carolee had a desire to scream. "Don't talk to them, please."

They started down the steps. "You've been missed, Carolee," a woman reporter yelled. "Does this mean we're going to see you on the stage and screen again soon?"

She didn't answer.

"Come on. Don't be coy. Your husband divorced you and you quit performing. You look cozy again now. Are you going to make a comeback?"

"My wife isn't ready to answer any questions," Kip said, but he grinned in all directions.

"You'll do, Kip. Give us a hint."

"Children need two parents," he said. "Carolee and I know our daughter has suffered because we haven't been together. That's all I can tell you."

"Uh-huh," the woman said, walking backward and jotting on a pad as she went. "So you're going to get married again? After all the things you said about Ms. Burns when you were divorced?"

"If we're lucky, we never stop growing up," Kip said.

More flashes.

"How's the kid?" a woman reporter shouted. "She going to make it?"

"Sure she is," Kip said quickly, and held Carolee's arm more tightly against his side.

"I've got to get away from these horrible people," Carolee said.

"What did you mean about growing up?" a man called.

Kip stroked Carolee's forearm and squeezed her hand. "It means people can change. They can learn to forgive."

Carolee tried not to hear anymore. Kip was telling these people he was a generous man who'd decided to forgive her. She let her eyes rove. Sooner or later this nightmare would be over. She'd *make* it over.

Max stood by a tree on the nearest lawn. With one leg nonchalantly crossed in front of the other, he leaned, but his stance was the only nonchalant thing about him. He stared into Carolee's face. Max was angrier than she'd ever seen him get before. And there was something other than anger in his eyes, but she couldn't keep looking at him.

"Kip." They'd reached the sidewalk and she turned to him. "Please carry on without me. I know where to find you now but I've got to go back and check on Faith."

"You just left her," he whispered.

"I don't care. Let go of my arm or I'll have to make a scene."

He released her at once. "If I do leave, will you come?"

She took a deep breath and said, "I have to be alone with Faith. I need that. Can you understand?"

"I asked you if you'll still come to me?"

If she didn't agree to do as he asked, he wouldn't leave. "Yes."

"Okay, I'll trust you." Before she could

react, he kissed her mouth and hurried to hop into the Porsche at the curb.

Without waiting to see him drive away, Carolee hurried back the way she'd come. Max had left. There was no sign of him, and she entered the hospital with a heavy heart. She'd wanted to be with Faith—and have Max see her turn her back on Kip. But how could she blame him for deciding she wasn't worth hanging around for?

When she entered the ICU, no one seemed surprised to see her again so quickly. Maybe Faith would be awake. She reached the door to the room and saw that Ivy was still there, but Linda had left.

Carolee went in. "Hi, Ivy." She walked softly to Faith's side and bent over her.

"Nothing," Ivy said. "Sometimes she's restless and squirrelly, but she never opens her eyes—or tries to open them. I don't see how she can."

Carolee ignored the comment. "Where's Linda?"

"She left a few minutes ago. Said she was goin' to take Sam home because he needs to be in his own bed. So I'm on duty till she gets back."

"I'm here now and I'm staying. But thank you." She wanted to talk to her daughter and rub her arms and hands and rearrange her pillows. She wanted to kiss her face, and try to smooth her tangled hair. "Faith," she said. "Faith, it's Mommy. Can you hear me?"

Faith lay completely still.

"I told you," Ivy said, sounding choked. "Poor darlin' girl. But don't you worry. She'll come around. She isn't going to die."

The flip in Carolee's belly meant she hadn't needed as much as a suggestion that Faith could die. She'd barely stopped herself from crying at the reporter's callous questions. "You mean well," she told Ivy, "but there's no right thing to say to me now. I'd like to be alone with Faith, okay? I'll call you later."

"Yes, I'm saying all the wrong things." Ivy reached for her purse but dropped her hand. "I...I haven't been a true friend to you," she said, and for the first time Carolee noticed the other woman's eyes were red. "I've tried to be impartial and it's made me unfair. Oh, Carolee, I feel just so awful."

The tightness in Ivy's voice, her pink face, and the way she held her hands as if pleading for understanding turned Carolee cold.

"You shouldn't go back to Kip. Not ever. If you do, you'll regret it. Bill warned me a long time ago not to interfere between you two but you know how I am—headstrong."

"That's enough." Carolee glanced at Faith. "You told me all this at Brandy's. We're *not* talking about this here. We can't be sure Faith isn't hearing and I won't have that."

"She's not conscious. And I've got to talk now, or I'll lose my nerve. At Brandy's I couldn't say everything."

"Outside," Carolee said. She went to the door and held it open for Ivy. "Outside, *now.*"

Ivy rushed into the corridor and turned on

Carolee. "He was never what you thought he was, and I don't know if he's changed at all, or if he's just learned to hide the kind of man he is even better."

"What kind of man is that?" Carolee had to be calm.

Ivy held Carolee's wrists. "I'm afraid to say. If he finds out I talked about him, he could get nasty. I've seen him angry with people before. He's ruthless."

Carolee told her, "I've known Kip since we were in high school and he's gentle." She defended him, but he wasn't anything like the boy he'd once been.

"Was he gentle when he got mad at you after the senior prom?"

Carolee opened her mouth, but couldn't find the words to answer.

"When he thought you looked at someone else and he pushed you against the wall?"

"Keep your voice down or someone will come and tell us to leave," she told Ivy. "I shouldn't have told you that. It was a kid with too much testosterone behaving that way."

"It wasn't you who told Bill that Kip liked having the girl with the biggest boobs in the school."

Carolee shuddered and shook her head. "Boys talk like that."

"Bill wasn't there at the time. You and Kip were twenty-one when we met and Kip didn't say it to Bill until you two were getting a divorce. Sick, that's what I call saying a thing like that."

"Sick and foolish," Carolee said. "He made a fool of himself. It doesn't mean anything to me."

Ivy shrugged but showed no sign of backing off.

"There's nothing new about men bragging about their women." Carolee looked through the glass at Faith.

When Faith had turned two, Kip started railing at Carolee because they couldn't have more babies. He'd gone for a sperm count without being asked, and when the report came in, he'd backed her into a corner and told her the problem was hers, she wasn't a whole woman. Later he'd apologized, but he'd often avoided touching her, or speaking to her, and only relented when she begged him to forgive her. But he'd stopped being angry after a few months.

She'd apologized for nothing, darn it. That kind of stupidity was in the past.

"He isn't good to Faith," Ivy said. She crossed her arms and turned away. "I think he could kill me if he knew I'd said these things."

"He's not going to know," Carolee said. A clear head was important because this was a time to gather evidence against Kip if possible. "Just say what you know."

"She's a dear little girl and she loves him to pieces, but Mrs. Jolly and the staff in Bell Town bring her up."

This was an opportunity to find out about Faith's diet. "Does Kip talk about Faith's weight?"

Ivy nodded. "He tells her she's fat but he

281

still loves her. She has to eat only what's made for her."

"Oh, dear Lord." Carolee simmered, and felt sick at the same time.

"She makes herself throw up," Ivy said.

Ivy had held back information that proved Faith's life was in danger? "Bulimia. And you didn't think you owed it to her and to me to let me know as soon as you found out?"

"I told you I'm afraid of Kip's temper. I've told you about it now, though. That ought to count for something."

It counted for very little. A friend didn't cover for someone's ex-husband while he victimized a child. Even if Kip argued that he was doing the right thing by making Faith be careful what she ate, he had to know she was making herself throw up and he couldn't think that was less than very dangerous. "My poor baby. I didn't know what I was doing to her, but I never meant her to suffer at all. What I was trying to do through her early years was to provide a good life for all of us."

"And you did," Ivy said. "Look, Kip was wrong and you deserve to spend as much time with Faith as he does. Fight him for it."

Carolee didn't want Ivy's advice but said, "I'm going to." And she really doubted she'd win without a legal battle.

"If you spend time alone with him, you'll weaken your case."

She frowned. "I'd like to deal with this out of court."

Ivy faced her and came close. "He doesn't

want to be alone with you to discuss Faith. He wants to have an affair with you and keep you dangling about Faith. He's never going to give you what you want because if he did he'd lose his bargaining tool."

Carolee's heart thumped harder and harder. "Why does he need a bargaining tool with me?"

"I don't really know." Ivy passed her tongue over her lips. "Don't ask me how, but he seems to know everything about you and Max. I've always known he didn't want you to be with someone else. But maybe he's just sick and wants to have you and his other woman. Or maybe he's going to get more money out of you. He's got expensive tastes and he still hasn't gone so far with his painting."

"What other woman?" Carolee asked. "From everything I've learned, there isn't another woman."

"I've seen them," Ivy said, her eyes downcast. "They're together on his boat all the time while Faith's alone at the condo. Be grateful. At least he doesn't bring a woman home and sleep with her."

The ridiculousness of a divorced man sneaking around with a woman almost had Carolee laughing. She smiled. But good old Kip still wanted to hang on to a double standard where she was concerned.

"Faith does know about it," Ivy said. "Damn, I'll just have to finish this now. He told Faith if she ever talked about seeing her father in bed with a woman, he'd do what her mother did, and leave her."

Twenty-five

As he approached Faith's room, Max passed Ivy Lester. She behaved as if she didn't recognize him and went on her way, her face expressionless. When he glanced over his shoulder, it was in time to catch her looking back at him and there was plenty of expression now. The lady wasn't happy—big time.

He wasn't happy either. The kind of fury and disappointment he'd felt watching Kip Burns with Carolee in front of the hospital wasn't healthy. It lingered.

Inside Faith's cubicle, Carolee smoothed the girl's hair, gradually tamed the riot of curls into a tail on top of her head. She searched around, probably looking for something to hold the hair in place, and her eyes met Max's through the window. He held up a finger and went to the nursing station.

With a rubber band in his hand, he joined Carolee and Faith. "One rubber band," he said, producing the item. "She has great hair. Curls are the thing now but most girls have to do all kinds of stuff to get them."

"I think Faith's finally beginning to appreciate hers," Carolee said.

He heard how troubled she was but didn't have anything useful to say. He wanted to ask what the scene outside had been all about, but made himself wait. It had taken time and coffee in the hospital cafeteria to control his anger enough to come up here and be reasonable.

"What about these," he said, remembering the braided chiffon scarves he'd been carrying around. "When I found her, she had them on her arm like colors. I took them off and kept meaning to give them to you. They'd look cute in her hair."

Carolee said, "You put them on, then. She can blame you for making her look ridiculous."

She spoke to him as if he were part of her family, or at least as if he belonged here with her.

"Don't think I can do it, do you?" Max said. He slipped the scarves around Faith's geyser of curls and tied a big, floppy bow. "There, she looks great. Don't tell me you could tie a better bow than that."

"I could not," Carolee said. "Beautiful. She looks like Cindy Lou Who."

"Take another look at Cindy Lou. Unless you're talking about in the movie version, she's a baby with two hairs on her head. Now if you said Pebbles Flintstone, I'd have to agree. Only Faith's even cuter."

He ran out of prattle. Carolee sat on Faith's bed and chafed her hands and arms. Max wasn't good at doing nothing, and he went to the girl's other side to rub one of her shoulders gently.

After several minutes, he and Carolee changed sides, and he massaged the other shoulder and Faith's neck. He and Carolee worked quietly together. She spoke to Faith incessantly. In a low, soothing voice she told her daughter she had to get better fast so she could continue her riding lessons with Max. She said that Max thought she was a natural on horseback and so did she. Digger, Carolee said, ran out every time someone went to Lake Home, but once he saw Faith wasn't there, he plodded away again. Everyone was waiting for her to be back where she belonged.

Carolee talked and talked, frequently kissing Faith's forehead. She was willing the girl to open her eyes.

"She is going to wake up, isn't she?"

It took a moment for Max to realize Carolee had asked the question of him. "Yes. *Yes,* of course she is. I'm no expert but the brain is so complex. You hear about people being unconscious because their brains are taking time out to heal."

"You think she's got a brain injury? You think they missed it earlier?"

He silently cursed his slip and met her frantic stare. "I don't think that. How would I know about such a thing?"

"I'm scared, Max."

Being strong was the pits sometimes, especially if you'd like to quit thinking at all, then check back in when someone came to give you good news. "I know you are," he said, and wrapped a hand around both Carolee's and Faith's. He squeezed gently and Carolee kept looking at him while their three joined hands rested on Faith's tummy. "I'm here for you." He bent to touch his mouth to Faith's fingers, then kissed the back of Carolee's hand. He closed his eyes and wished this were his wife and child.

Remaining where he was, where Carolee couldn't see his face, was the safest course. Letting her see the emotion he felt would puzzle her at best, and shake her if he got really unlucky.

He didn't imagine that she ran the fingers of her free hand through his hair and stroked the back of his head. Tenderness had played no part in his life until now. It couldn't have when all the time—without knowing—he'd been waiting for this woman and her gentle touch.

"Max," she said, and he reluctantly sat up. "You've helped me be strong again. I'll never go back where I was before."

"You were healing," he told her. "It takes time."

Without knocking, two doctors entered with a small entourage of medical students in their wake.

A nurse popped in after them and beckoned to Max. "Phone, Mr. Wolfe."

He checked his cell phone. There were no messages waiting. "I'll be right back," he told Carolee, and followed the nurse.

"This is Dr. Lamont." Dr. Lee indicated the tall, austere man at his side. "He's a neurologist we decided to call in for a second opinion on Faith."

The blond-haired Dr. Lamont gave Carolee

a smile that didn't appear to come easily. "Mrs. Burns," he said and went directly to Faith's side. "Were you here the last time she was conscious?"

"Yes. I don't know why—"

"Tell me what you saw."

Carolee swallowed. "Her father and I were here—and a good friend, Ivy—"

"Yes, yes, but the patient?"

Dr. Lee stepped forward. "Explain how Faith was when you last saw her apparently awake, and if there was any warning that something different was happening."

"She wasn't talking at the time," Carolee said, gaining composure. "Just watching us. Then she closed her eyes and didn't open them again."

"One moment she was awake and aware— she was aware?"

"I'm sure she was."

"And the next she was like this? Unresponsive?"

"Well...yes."

Dr. Lamont parted one of Faith's eyelids and flashed a small light into the eye several time. He said, "Hm," and moved to the other eye. "We're going to run some more tests, Mrs. Burns. It might be easier if you went and found some coffee. We could be as long as an hour. If you come back after we've left, have us paged, please."

He gave all his attention back to Faith while issuing orders to Dr. Lee.

Dismissed, Carolee slipped out and wandered

down the corridor. A staff member wheeled a piece of equipment rapidly to Faith's room.

"Mr. Wolfe's in one of the family waiting rooms," a male nurse told her from the monitoring station.

She thanked him and left the unit. Max's voice was indistinct but came from the first waiting room. Carolee hesitated on the threshold. Kip was still waiting at the hotel. To make sure he didn't come here, she'd called and said she'd be there as soon as she could, and he'd spread a warm blanket of understanding over her. He'd be there as long as he had to be.

"Is that everything, Mrs. Fossie?" Max said. "Okay, you're having to deal with a lot of calls for me. You're so efficient and tactful I have every confidence that you'll do very well without me. If I know you, we'll have more clients when this emergency is over than we did when I was last there."

Carolee put a hand over her mouth and swallowed a laugh.

"No," he said, his patience obviously wearing very thin. "No, I don't want to talk to Steve. I know he's my company lawyer."

He was needed at the office. Her problems were interfering with his professional life.

"Geez, Steve—I just told Fossie I didn't want to talk to you. Yeah, okay. So you forced her to hand over the phone. I'd like to see you or anyone else manage that." Max remained quiet for a few moments before saying, "I'm not leaving this hospital, or my friends, until I can. I can't yet."

Through a space between the open door and the jamb, she caught glimpses of Max pacing.

"Yes, yes, and yes," he said, then, "Steve, listen to me. Are we filing bankruptcy? No? Then I'll call you. Later."

This had to be stopped. Carolee walked in and shut the door behind her.

Her sweet, sad expression overwhelmed Max. "What did they say?" he asked her.

"Nothing yet. They're doing some tests. That tall man is a neurologist they brought in to give a second opinion. He isn't optimistic."

To stop himself from pulling her into his arms, Max slid the cell phone into a pocket and put his hands behind his back. "You just told me they hadn't said anything yet."

"I could tell. It was the questions he asked, and the way he looked at her eyes then asked me to leave."

"Sweetheart, you're buying trouble."

She sat on a chair and rubbed her thighs. "You may be right. This isn't fair to you. You don't have to be here for us. You've got your own life to live and you need to go to work."

Not a word she spoke rang true. She was struggling not to cry and losing.

Max pulled a chair close to hers and sat down. "Listen to me carefully, please. Don't say anything until I've finished." And he'd hope they were left alone for as long as it took.

Carolee straightened the skirt of her simple green cotton dress and wouldn't meet his eyes.

He traced the fine bones in one of her wrists

and waited for her to withdraw her arm. She didn't.

"My life has changed in these past few weeks," he told her. "What you heard me say to Steve is true. I'm not leaving this place until I know the people I care about are okay. You come first, you and Faith."

She stared at him and tears slid from her unblinking eyes. The moisture shone on her cheeks but she didn't make a sound.

"You've made me different," he said. "I feel things I never felt, or even knew about before. I'm making a hash of this, but I am trying. I never thought too much about all the things they say—how women talk, and want to talk about feelings, but men don't like to get too close to any of that. Could be right on because I keep looking around and wondering if this is really me. Talking about feelings, I mean. But I'll keep stumbling on." He smiled at her, and felt vaguely foolish, but going back was for cowards. "I want to be with you and Faith from now on. We can make a family, Carolee. We can. I'm going to help you get what you deserve—a fair share in Faith's life. And we'll be happy."

"Max—" She shifted forward and put fingers to his lips. "You don't know what you're saying."

"I'm saying I'm in love with you," he said, removing her hand.

"Do you think you really know me?"

"Hell, yes." He laughed. "I think I know you very well."

She held on to his thigh and bowed her head. "Because I behaved like someone even I don't know? And because it was good between us?"

"That must be it." The thumping of his heart was unpleasant. "Let's get real. If you used me, I wanted to be used. But what happened wasn't all we could, or can, be to each other. Sure it was a wonderful start, and it made sure I understood there's a whole lot I want from you. But what's making you think the way you are?"

"I'm a human being. I don't know if I'll ever forget what a fool I made of myself."

"Don't forget what happened, but don't feel foolish about it either. And don't give in to fear. That's it, isn't it, you're afraid of being hurt again and you don't even want to rub shoulders with that scenario. You want to be safe and you don't ever want to flirt with danger, even for a moment."

There was no stopping himself from easing up her chin and kissing her, not only with sexual ardor, although there was some of that, but with the sensation that if he kissed her like this forever, he wouldn't need anything else.

They drew away slowly and her parted lips shone. "I'm not in this hospital to do what makes me feel good," she said.

He kissed her again, quickly, before she could evade him. "But kissing me does make you feel good. I'll take that as a good sign. I can't even try to forget you. If you told me I had to get out of your life, I'd be lost."

"Max, please don't."

"You don't want me to say you've shown me how wonderful life could be? Do you want me to pretend we never met, or touched, or started to know each other better than I've ever known a woman? No, I don't believe in chance. I believe we were meant to be here together, today, and every day. I want you to marry me."

Max's face was unnaturally clear to Carolee. How could timing be so cruel? She didn't want to consider being without him, but she'd never actually thought they had a chance for a future together.

A brief tap on the door, and it opened to admit Dr. Lamont and Dr. Lee.

"We'd like to talk with you, Carolee," Dr. Lee said. He hadn't addressed her informally before. He glanced at Max.

"Max is almost a member of the family," she said. "I'd like his company, please."

Both doctors nodded. "Who did you say was with Faith when she became unresponsive?" Dr. Lamont asked.

"Her father, a friend of ours, and myself."

"And nothing unusual happened? She just seemed to go to sleep?"

Carolee swallowed repeatedly. "Yes. Well, not really. Kip and I weren't happy with each other."

"And you were shouting, perhaps?"

"I don't shout," she told him, feeling as if she were being stripped naked.

"Does your husband?"

She breathed through her nose. "Yes."

Telling tales on Kip wouldn't change anything. "We've been under a lot of strain and it just happened."

"Were threats made, accusations, anything that might make your daughter unhappy enough to want to close it all out?"

"Look," Max said. "What's the point of an obscure fishing expedition?"

"Did things get nasty, Mrs. Burns?" Dr. Lamont asked.

"I suppose they did. Mr. Burns and I are divorced. A lot of cruel things have been said. It got a bit out-of-hand this morning but we'll be more careful in future."

"Children are sensitive creatures," Lamont said. "Add insecurity to the severe injuries Faith suffered and who knows what could happen to her mind. The tests we've run give no indication of brain damage. In fact, although it's unlikely, it's possible she isn't unconscious at all—just refusing to respond. You've got a lot on your hands and so do we. But you can't do anything else to upset her and she may be listening to whatever you say."

"I don't believe it," Max said.

Carolee couldn't grasp that Faith might be pretending to be unconscious. "You really think she could do this?"

"She'd have to be quite an actress," Dr. Lee said. "But she wouldn't be the first patient to pull something similar. For now I think she needs to be very quiet and to have a chance to fall asleep. In my opinion she's extremely tired. However, with your permission, we'd like to have a psychiatrist spend some time with her."

"Why?" Carolee met Max's eyes and he smiled reassuringly.

Dr. Lee also smiled and said, "Just to make sure we're not missing anything."

"Quite," Lamont said. "In the meantime, let's allow her to be alone with her thoughts. And we'll hope she falls asleep naturally."

"But you're absolutely sure she isn't asleep now?" Carolee said.

Lamont shook his head. "No, we aren't. But there's a chance. She should be heading out of ICU—her physical therapy should have begun—but that isn't going to happen as long as we don't know if she's really conscious— or unconscious. Stay in the area, Mrs. Burns. We'll talk later."

He swept out with Dr. Lee scurrying behind like a bridesmaid.

"I'm going to wait in this room," Carolee told Max. "You need to get to your office. Please don't worry about us. If Dr. Lamont is right, all we need is time. Faith needs a lot of peace and confidence."

"You're right about everything but where I should be. I've already made up my mind that I can't work. I'm here for the long run."

She got up and Max joined her. "You don't understand."

"What I understand is that you're trying to run away from your feelings—and mine."

Carolee looked into his face. "I don't like Kip Burns. I stopped liking him a long time

295

ago, and now I don't respect him either. He makes me sick, and he makes me nervous because he's turned into someone I don't know. So I'm stuck trying to appease a man I'm not sure isn't dangerous to my health because I can't pretend he isn't my daughter's father, or that she needs him."

Max's eyes narrowed. "I don't argue with that. In an ideal world, all children would have two parents. What difference does that make to us? I'm not Kip. I don't have any motives that aren't written all over me. No strings. I mean every word I say, and I'm saying I want you, just you. And I'll do the best job I can with Faith."

"I know you mean what you say," Carolee said, her face beginning to crumple. "I want to take what you're offering, and I hope I'll be able to. No matter what Kip says or tries, I'm never going back to him."

"No kidding." Even as he recoiled from the aggression in his own voice, he had to go on. "You'd have to walk over my dead body to get to him."

Twenty-six

"This had better be good, Sam," Max said. Sam had been calling since the previous evening which, by Max's figuring, was probably when he found out what had happened between Carolee and himself.

"Gimme a chance to get my act together, will ya?" Sam said. He'd just arrived and sounded short of breath.

They sat at a table in Nellie and Fritz Archer's diner. Outside, the light grew dim and a strong wind whipped the tops of trees planted in sidewalk beds. Even the Archer's old Irish terrier, Darby, had retreated indoors where he violated health regulations by curling up where he could sniff and watch every plate that left or returned to the kitchen.

"Consider yourself together," Max said, pointing with the fork he swung between his fingers. "I was asleep when you called."

"Every time I called?"

"Don't grill me. I was asleep the last time you called." He hadn't wanted to be awake at all since he'd left Carolee at the hospital the day before—not until she figured out how to cut Kip Burns out of her life for good.

Sam snuffled and said, "At seven in the evening you were asleep?"

"Drop it, will you? You're having some bad days but mine aren't so good, either."

"Because my daughter's mixed up and you're not doing whatever it takes to make her see straight? We're not allowing her to get back with the...with the loser she married."

"She'll never be with him again." Max didn't remember feeling this tired. "And I'm not getting any argument from her about that. Nellie," he said loudly. "Could Sam and I have some fresh coffee, please?"

"Coming up," Nellie said. "You ready to order dinner?"

"No, thank you. I'm not hungry."

"You're starting to sound like a broken record," she said. "Sam, you'll eat, won't you?"

He frowned and sniffed. "I'll have a French dip. No one can ruin that."

Max shook his head, but Nellie was already on her way to the kitchen and didn't appear to have heard Sam's snide remark.

What few customers remained were seated where they could watch a muted television behind the counter. From time to time they grumbled, or cheered at baseball action. Max couldn't remember who the Mariners were playing.

"I've got things to say about Kip Burns," Sam said. He didn't, Max thought, look so hot. "He's poison. I've known him a long time—too long—and I've always thought he was sly. If you saw the way he lives, without earning a thing toward it, you'd know what a lowlife grabber he is. I can't draw water, but if I was an artist, I'd damn well have turned into the new Liberace in the studios he's had. The one he's got now has been in magazines. More than I can say about anything he ever painted."

Max listened, but his attention wandered. "Liberace?"

"Er—" Sam wetted his lips. "Slip of the tongue, I meant—*Picasso*. Hell, I don't know who I mean. A famous artist."

"This is a fresh pot," Nellie Archer said. She never allowed customer conversation to interfere with a mission. "Say the word, Max, and I'll make sure you get something in yours to really warm you up."

With an innocent stare, Max said, "You wouldn't serve cold coffee?"

"Wouldn't say no to a little something in mine," Sam said.

"You can both drink what you've got," Nellie said, her ropes of Niihau shells rising and falling dramatically. "I'm glad you've still got a joke in you, Max Wolfe. And as for you, Sam, you're already throwing us all off, being here this late. Now this. You know you aren't allowed to have—"

"I was kidding," Sam said quickly. "How's the French dip coming?"

Nellie flounced away without answering.

"No sense of humor," Sam muttered.

"How long d'you think someone can go through the motions of being okay?" Max said. "I'm not okay anymore, Sam."

"Yeah, I know, and it's killing me because Carolee isn't okay either. And Faith's not okay. And Linda, too, if you ask me. She's just making it through the days and I think being involved with Faith is what's giving her an excuse not to deal with her own problems."

"Maybe." Max could concentrate only on Carolee and Faith. "Could Kip Burns be... could he be unkind to his daughter?"

"Not physically. Not in an obvious way. But she's not happy and it isn't only because he's

299

convinced her Carolee didn't love her enough to put her ahead of the music. A father who cares—" He stopped suddenly and took a long time to get several swallows of coffee down. "A good father would never let a kid think he'd taken off the minute she went away for a few weeks, then make sure she couldn't reach him. He started cutting Carolee down a long time ago and I think he's manipulating both of them now.

"Burns has got an angle. First he behaves as if he can't get rid of Faith fast enough—he'd already made it clear he'd never want Carolee back. Then he shows up after Faith's accident and talks about not wanting to live without the wife he divorced. Carolee insists all he did on the day of Faith's accident was come on a bit strong. I believe your story, not hers.

"He's blackmailing her now," Sam continued. His lips had a faint blue tinge and he wasn't successful in hiding difficulty holding his mug. "That's my take on it. She asked to change the visiting stuff and he said they should get back together. Doesn't take Einstein to figure out he's saying she only gets what she wants if he gets what he wants. But I don't know why he's changed his tune. In my gut I'm sure he's up to something we can't even guess at."

"Carolee has to come to her own conclusions," Max said, but believed Sam had figured out the way things really were. He turned sideways in his chair and hooked an elbow over the back. "I can't force her to change her mind. I've told her how I feel. Now it's up to her."

"What did you tell her?"

"That's personal."

"Did you say you love her?" Sam's chin jutted. "There's no shame in admitting it if it's true."

"I'm not ashamed to be in love with Carolee. I just wish it wasn't making me feel someone's got their big hands around my neck and they're squeezing real hard."

Sam opened his mouth, but shut it again when Fritz Archer arrived with two plates.

"Are you the head waitress now, Fritz?" Max asked.

"Smart mouth." Fritz slid a giant French dip sandwich in front of Sam and a plate of eggs Benedict with a heap of fresh fruit on Max's side of the table. There were three eggs. "Put the toast here," he told a boy who worked evenings.

Thick slices of hot, buttered wheat toast and some corn muffins filled a basket.

"I didn't order anything," Max said.

Fritz crossed his arms and said, "And I've been told to get some food into you whenever there's a chance. I remember you saying you liked eggs Benedict."

"I didn't say I—" Max gave up. "Thanks. Mind telling me who the mole is?"

"My son-in-law is no mole," Fritz told him. "He's a good boy and don't you forget it."

Steve would hear about this later, but for the moment, Max nodded and put a piece of pineapple in his mouth.

"You really over the football career?" Sam asked.

Non sequiturs never failed to catch Max off guard. "Not completely. Football gave me opportunities I never would have had otherwise. I still think about the accident. The freakishness of it—and another thing or two, and I don't believe I've found quite all the missing or mangled parts of what's inside me."

"That's what I thought," Sam said. "Know what I reckon?"

The eggs had begun to taste good. "What?"

"If you had Carolee, you wouldn't be missing anything at all."

The hands Max had imagined around his neck tightened some more and he put down his fork. Auburn hair and green warm-ups caught his attention. Brandy stood on the sidewalk, waiting to cross the street. Rob Mead jogged to join her and said something. Brandy turned on him and poked his chest. Max doubted her finger made much impression.

They were fighting. Or rather Brandy was waving her arms, pushing her head forward, and her face wasn't nearly as gorgeous as usual. Rob shook his head, spoke the odd word when Brandy paused for breath, and looked miserable. They both stopped speaking and stared into each other's eyes. Then Rob took Brandy into his arms and they clung to each other.

"See that?" Sam said. He watched the scene Max was engrossed in. "Brandy cares about the guy, and he cares about her. You can tell. I never saw Brandy look like that before. Know who he is?"

"Rob Mead."

"Speak of the devil." Sam quit looking out the window. "Right here in Kirkland?"

"He says he's here to stay and I can't speak for Brandy—not for sure—but Rob's crazy about her."

"I kinda thought she might be crazy about you."

"Maybe you need a nice lady to occupy your imagination," Max said to Sam. Brandy and Rob had crossed the street and were holding hands.

Sam dipped his sandwich and said, "Only one nice lady to a customer. I had mine. You don't have to do anything about this. It's just information I'm going to pass along. Okay?"

"Depends on the information."

"Carolee's worn out. She's talked to Faith until her voice is packing it in, but our girl is still out of it. Kip was there again last night and then most of today. Carolee doesn't tell me what he's saying to her, but she looks terrible. Then there's the docs. Questions, questions. She's had enough."

Max looked at a lonely painting of the Eiffel Tower near the front door. The artist would never be famous. "She told me not to make things tougher for her by interfering, Sam. What do you think I can do about any of this— except wait and keep letting her know I'm here for her?"

"That's up to you, but Dr. Lee persuaded her to go home until the morning. She's there alone."

Bill Lester was ten years older than Ivy, but it wasn't hard to understand why Ivy had picked him out from the crowds of admirers she'd been known to mention. A young Redford look-alike, he was a cords and plaid shirt kind of guy who looked at the world with fine and intelligent blue eyes. Gold wire-framed glasses suited him.

He stood in front of the empty fireplace and managed to smile while Carolee felt his discomfort at being in her house. Ivy and Bill had shown up at Lake Home without calling, to find Carolee in a nightgown and robe making herbal tea to take to bed. She wasn't amused, or grateful, and didn't want them here.

Ivy—who had taken over as usual—finished making the tea and poured glasses of wine for herself and Bill. "We came on a whim," she said, carrying the drinks into the living room. "Or sort of. We tried to get you at the hospital and they said you'd come here. You mustn't be alone at a time like this."

Carolee longed for only three things: Faith's recovery, Max, and a chance to be alone and asleep. "I'm good at being on my own," she said. She wasn't up for polite lies.

Ivy sat so close beside Carolee that it was difficult not to move away. "We've got to talk," Ivy said. "And no being coy this time.

You're having a thing with the football player."

Several beats passed before Carolee said. "Ex–football player. End of subject."

"This isn't our business, Ivy," Bill said, still smiling indulgently.

"Hush," Ivy said. "Women know about these things. Men don't. You're having a thing with an *ex*–football player then. You really like him?"

"I like Max a lot. We're not having a thing." But she was hoping. "Didn't you hear me tell you I don't want to talk about this? If you keep it up, I'll have to ask you and Bill to leave."

"You're not yourself," Ivy said. "If you were, you'd never speak to the best friends you ever had that way. The point is that you and Kip are all muddled up because of what's happened to poor little Faith. He's worried out of his mind and thinks if the two of you get back together, everything will be okay again. You're almost ready to go along with him because you'll do anything to be with Faith all the time. You don't love Kip—I'm not sure you ever did."

"Ivy," Bill said, but the rebuke was mild.

Carolee wasn't too tired to be furious. "You are so way out of line, Ivy," she said. "I'm embarrassed for you."

Ivy ignored both her husband, and Carolee. "Sometimes people pretend to be in love because it's easier than making waves," she said.

"I loved Kip very much once," Carolee

told her. "He made a mistake by not letting me know he didn't want to go on with our marriage because he thought I didn't care about him or Faith. *Before* asking for a divorce. Not picking up on his unhappiness was my mistake."

"But you don't love him now," Ivy insisted. "You could never make a life together again."

"We don't know what Carolee can do," Bill said. "If she wants to go back with Kip for the sake of Faith, she should do that. Couples have always made the decision to stay together for the sake of children."

"*Hush,*" Ivy said. "We aren't experts because we've got a great marriage—and we never had children because we didn't want to. I just know that if Carolee gives this a chance to cool down, she'll be able to get what she wants from Kip without throwing her life away. She can't be happy with him."

Carolee's eyelids were heavy. She thought of Faith—and of Max. He was dangerous because he had the power to divert her. She did want him—too much.

"Stretch out on the sofa and take a nap," Ivy told her. "I'll run upstairs for a blanket, and Bill and I will be here when you wake up. You don't have to worry about a thing."

"I don't want a blanket," Carolee said. "And I don't want you here. I don't want you playing guessing games with my life. You're butting in, not helping me."

Bill said, "Listen," and held up a hand. "Car coming."

Carolee did listen and she heard the engine

of Kip's Porsche. She forced a smile and said, "That's Kip. It would be better if you left."

"Well." Ivy's eyes filled with tears. "I can't believe you're treating us like this."

"Carolee's right," Bill said. "Kip's here to talk to Carolee, not us. *Don't* interfere, Ivy. We'll say hi to him on our way out."

The engine drew close and cut out. A car door slammed. Kip's running feet sounded before he entered without knocking. "There you are," he said, looking only at Carolee. "I kept waiting for you to come back to Faith's room. Why wouldn't that lamebrain sister of yours have told me where you were as soon as I arrived?"

"Why would Linda think you were there for any reason other than to be with Faith?" Ivy said promptly.

Amazingly, Kip held his tongue, but his annoyance showed. "You and I need to talk," he told Carolee.

She stopped herself from saying they'd already talked—and talked and talked—too many times and she couldn't think about anything but sleep now.

"Okay, Ivy," Bill Lester said. "Kip's here to be with Carolee. Time we moved on."

"No such thing." Ivy got up and slipped an arm under one of Kip's. "Forgive me for what I said. It's no excuse, but I've been frantic. Let me get you some wine."

"No, thanks."

Bill took his glass to the kitchen and said, "Come on, Ivy."

"Have you even thought that Carolee and Kip might like our company at a time like this?"

"They wouldn't," he said and glanced at Carolee. "Would you?"

Kip said, "It would be better if we could kick back on our own. Faith's just the same, honey."

"I don't understand why she seemed okay, then this happened." Carolee refused to consider that Faith might be deliberately unresponsive.

"Kip," Ivy said. "It isn't my place to say so, but don't push Carolee to make big decisions when you're both under such stress. Neither of you knows what you want right now."

Bill took a firm hold on her arm, said, "We're thinking about you two, and about Faith. We'll be in touch tomorrow. Take care of yourselves," and took Ivy out of the house.

Kip stood, expressionless and silent, until the Lesters' BMW fired up and scrunched away. "I'll have that wine now," he said. "You, too?"

"I've got tea, thanks."

Instead of wine, Kip searched through cupboards until he found a bottle of bourbon. He filled a highball glass and didn't even flinch at the first, neat, mouthful.

They were alone. The day before, she'd been about to go to a hotel with him, but she'd found excuses to stay away. She was afraid of him and had a right to be.

"You gave permission for a shrink to see Faith," he said. "I still wouldn't know about it if your sister hadn't blabbed."

Carolee had difficulty focusing her eyes. "That was when Dr. Lamont first saw her. I haven't thought much about it since, but I'd do the same thing again."

"It wasn't your decision to make." Kip said. "There's nothing wrong with my daughter's mind. She's strong-willed and maybe she could pretend she's unconscious, but I don't believe any of that crap about the psyche or whatever."

"They're not sure either, are they? I never really heard anything else about it—except the suggestion she might be faking it. Drop this, please."

"I'll drop it," he said, a shadow passing over his features. "Linda asked me about my boat. She never did like me and she'd do anything to make me look bad to you."

Carolee didn't answer him. She sniffed the tea instead.

"You knew I'd bought a boat. It was used— I'm the fifth owner—but it's in great shape."

"I didn't know you had it," she told him.

"I can't believe that. Faith would have told you."

"She didn't. Forget it—I have."

"I can't," Kip said. "Linda talked as if you were suspicious about how I could afford to buy something expensive like that. She was suggesting I must be using money you provided for Faith's upkeep. And that's wrong. Couldn't be more wrong. My paintings are selling very well and I'm making a lot of money."

That wasn't, Carolee recalled, what Ivy

had said about Kip's level of success. And so far she'd never heard anyone talk about going to a Burns show, or having any of his pieces.

"Between us," Kip said, "we can have a great life with our little girl."

"Why doesn't she wake up?"

"You know I can't answer that." He went to her piano and absently rubbed the burnished old finish. "But they keep saying they can't find any evidence of brain damage."

Carolee moved to a chair—just in case he decided to join her on the couch. "What if it *is* emotional? She could be too scared to deal with what's going on so she's decided not to wake up."

"I don't buy it," Kip said. He'd already passed the halfway mark with his bourbon. "What's she got to be scared about?"

"You're burying your head," she told him. "She's at a difficult stage anyway. Growing up and dealing with changes in herself. And she's lived through her parents' divorce and being encouraged to believe I don't want her—"

"I resent that. She believes what she knows. And she's a little kid who isn't going through any changes except she's facing a lot of surgery on her face, and who knows how her legs will be after all this."

Carolee was already on her feet. "She *believes* what you've told her. I made mistakes, but so did you. And she is changing. She started her periods, Kip. That's a big deal to an eleven-year-old girl. She's mixed up and it's our job to make her life calm. If she was convinced I've always loved her and wanted to be with her, and you hadn't deliberately dropped her off here for her visit and left without giving her a hug or a kiss—" She was shaking and couldn't stop her teeth from chattering. "You didn't even look back when she called after you. Then you told your housekeeper— the latest of a number of housekeepers and nannies and other staff you always had while you were being *Mr. Carolee Burns*—you told her to tell your own child you were away and that no one knew where you were."

"I don't give a shit about the stories you make up. This is now and it's all that matters. Faith needs to come home to both of us."

Anger had already overcome fear. Carolee looked into the face of a stranger and knew the worst was still ahead.

"Oh, honey." He dropped his voice and smiled at her. His eyes were damp. "We're going through hell and the pressure is too much. I don't mean half of what I say. Maybe I didn't behave so well after I left Faith with you."

She wasn't accepting any olive branches. "You didn't. And it was deliberate—and selfish. You wanted to unsettle her. The sleeping bag thing, to remind her of *home*— that was to remind her that her home wasn't with me anymore. But you'd already given her the idea you might be getting ready to take off somewhere and do your thing. She's afraid of being left with Mrs. Jolly and never seeing either of us. And you've had her on a diet, Kip.

She's eleven and she had a bit of baby fat hanging around. But she was already trimming down. Are you aware that she's been making herself throw up?"

He smacked his empty glass down on top of the piano and came closer. "How would you know that? The diet, as you call it, was only to make sure she ate healthy food."

"Oh, yeah? And that's why almost the last thing you said to her before leaving was that she had to watch what she ate so she didn't ruin all of Mrs. Jolly's efforts."

"That's not what this is all about," he shouted.

Carolee flinched, but didn't retreat. "It's part of everything. She needs her ego built, not smashed. And that's apart from the health implications. You've been making her *ill*. I can't let that go on. I won't."

Kip closed his eyes and took several deep breaths. When he looked at her again, he seemed more reasonable. "I'm sorry. If I've made some wrong decisions about bringing up Faith, it's because I needed you there to help me do it." He held out his arms. "Come here, you. I want to hold you. We've got a lot of lost time to make up for."

She didn't move, couldn't move. "I haven't been there because you forced me away." This was a nightmare.

"Please," he said. "I love you, Carolee."

"You don't love me." Her own anger had only cranked higher. "Stop this."

"I can't. There's too much at stake. I don't

expect to rush anything, but we can make it again. I want to take you back. That's the way to make Faith happy. You and me together and making a home for her. It's the only way."

If she held her temper and tried reason one more time, he might actually hear and understand her. "That would be the ideal, but you're right, we can't rush a thing. If you agree to working out a change in the custody arrangements—now—it'll stop me from thinking you don't trust me. Give me a reason to believe that you're sincere about only wanting what's best for all of us."

Kip made fists and there was little doubt what he'd like to do with them. "Give in to you? Just like that? No. It would stop you from giving me what I want. I want to marry you again."

"Why?"

His mouth opened, but he didn't say anything.

"You obviously can't stand me. Why would you want to marry me—again?"

"Because it's right for Faith," he snapped. "It wouldn't be right for Faith to spend a lot of time with you as long as you're hanging out with that has-been."

"But it's all right for her to be with you while you're sleeping around? She walked in on you, Kip. How right was that?"

"Who..." Swinging away, he went to sit at the keyboard and slammed his fingers down to make meaningless crashing sounds.

"Not Faith," Carolee yelled over the noise. "It wasn't Faith who told me. She's too loyal to you. But you aren't denying it."

Someone hammered loudly on the door.

Sweating and red-faced, Kip wiped his hands on his jeans. "We don't want company."

Keeping her pace as even as she could, Carolee walked to the door and opened it wide.

"My God," Max said, pulling her into his arms. "I can't stand seeing you like this. Sweetheart, Faith's going to be okay. I know she is."

"Kip's here," she murmured.

Max already knew. He kept her in his arms and used a foot to slam the door. Burns stood a few feet away and Max was glad the man wasn't holding a gun.

"It's all right, Carolee." This was new territory for Max. "Why don't you—"

"Why don't you take your hands off what doesn't belong to you?" Burns said. "Then get out. You saw the Porsche and you know it's mine. Why would you keep on coming?"

"Until I saw the Porsche, I wasn't sure I would come in," Max told the man. "It was the car that made up my mind. Have you keyed any Cadillacs lately?"

"Not since yours."

Max wanted Carolee out of the way. "Why don't you get dressed and go for a drive?" he asked her. "Go see Brandy. She'll make sure you're taken care of."

"We don't need this guy." Burns dropped to a couch and let his hands hang between his knees. "Carolee, tell him to get the hell out of here."

She eased herself away from Max. "Max was the one who brought Faith off that hill, remember?" she said quietly. "Please let's be civil—for her sake."

"You're like your mother." Burns glared at Carolee. "She had the morals of a bitch dog. She couldn't be without a man. And she preferred one in reserve, just in case."

Max hauled Kip Burns from the couch and let him land body punches while he threw him out.

Ashen, Carolee stood mute.

From outside, Burns screamed obscenities at her until his voice broke.

Scuffling followed and Max said, "Get down, *now,*" to Carolee, at the same time as a rock smashed one of the kitchen windows.

Out of concern for her, Max didn't go after the jerk. Seeing Burns beaten to a pulp wouldn't make her happy.

Stumbling footsteps on gravel were music to Max's ears, but he gritted his teeth when he heard an unmistakable noise. The Cadillac was wearing a second stripe.

Twenty-seven

Carolee grabbed the phone before the first ring ended and prayed Max was in a deep sleep and would stay that way. "Hello."

"Don't hang up on me."

She peered at the clock. Kip had taken three hours to give up the furious silence and call.

"Carolee? Please say something. I'm sorry. How could I behave that way at a time like this."

She scooted to sit up in bed.

"Don't punish me. Is he there? He is, isn't he? He's there with you."

"I'm in bed, Kip. Max isn't in bed with me."

"Damn it, don't talk like that. I'm sorry. I don't know what else to say. I'm an ass, an idiot. But I want us to be together while we go through this—and afterward."

"I called the hospital," Carolee said. "Sam's there now. There's no change."

"I know. I called, too."

She felt no connection to him, as if she didn't know, or want to know, him at all. "Get some sleep," she said.

"He is there," Kip said. "I'm coming over."

"No, you're not. If you aren't tired, I am."

"You're angry about the window."

"Grow up." He'd managed to make her simmer again. "You behaved like a spoiled kid, but I don't care about the window. I do hope

Max sends you a bill for what you did to his car. I'll see you at the hospital in the morning, and we'll play nice for Faith's sake. Good night."

The phone was removed from her hand and hung up while she could still hear Kip talking.

"That's enough," Max said. He'd arrived from Faith's room silently and without putting on any lights.

"Did you hear everything?"

"Probably. Get to sleep."

"Okay. I'm glad you're here." Even if she did wish "here" meant lying beside her.

He left with as little sound as he'd arrived. Carolee listened and soon heard the creak of bed springs.

Max had offered to take her to stay with Brandy. Carolee hadn't wanted to be alone, but she'd wanted to stay at Lake Home. She turned over and pushed down until she could bury her face in a pillow. What she'd wanted, she'd got. She and Max were spending the night in the same house and he was close enough to reach if she needed him.

She did need him—now.

The possibility that Max might turn her away left as quickly as it occurred to her. Carolee went to him, and he gathered her beneath the covers.

"Good morning, Carolee," Dr. Lee said. He and Kip stood outside the doors leading to the

317

Intensive Care Unit. "I was just explaining to your husband that we've moved Faith to another room. She's on this floor but we needed her bed in ICU."

"Dr. Lee and Dr. Lamont and all the same people will still be looking after her," Kip said, smiling while his eyes held hope. "I know where she is. I'll take you there."

"Is there any change?" Carolee asked Dr. Lee.

The man took his stethoscope from his neck and pushed it into a pocket in his white coat. "I think she's improving. The swelling in her leg has reduced and we'll probably be setting it today. The plastic surgeon took another look at her and he's pleased with what he sees. Of course, that doesn't mean there is not a lot of work to be done. We do want you both to think about taking her to Texas, to Houston, when she's ready. There's a man there we'd like to take over some of the work on her jaw. Don't worry too much about it right now. Dr. Lamont will be along to see you later."

Kip held Carolee's elbow and steered her to a nearby corridor. As soon as she was certain the doctor couldn't be watching, she shook off Kip's hand.

"I don't blame you," he said. "But one day we'll laugh at all this nonsense. It's good news about them moving Faith."

"Is it?" Since he'd stopped moving, Carolee had little choice but to stand still beside him. "Couldn't it be a sign that they don't see any point in wasting an ICU bed?"

"No. You heard how well she's doing."

"She needs some fancy surgeon in Texas, and she's unconscious."

"We don't know that for sure," Kip said. He carried on past several patient rooms until they reached one where Carolee saw Faith through an open door.

"Make up your mind," she said, careful to keep her voice down. "You said you didn't believe what the doctors suggested. Now you say you do."

Kip ignored her and went into the room to kiss the top of Faith's head. Her ponytail had become a sorry thing but someone had retied the chiffon bow. The glaring colors only caused her to look pale enough to be almost gray.

"Hey, sweet thing," Carolee said. "It's your mom and dad. Back to keep their favorite girl company." She did the only thing she knew to do and rubbed whatever parts of Faith she could reach. To ward off bedsores, an inflatable blue mattress pad moved in waves beneath her body.

"How is she?"

Max had entered the room from behind Carolee and she watched Kip's reaction. He didn't smother his intense dislike quite soon enough, but he was quick to return his attention to Faith.

"The doctors say she's improving physically," Carolee said. "They think they may set her leg today."

"That's good news," Max said.

Kip's "How would you know?" was on cue.

"I've been there," Max told him. "It can take a lot longer for the swelling to go down enough so the leg can be set."

"A truck slipped on top of him, and—"

"I'm not interested in your friend," Kip told Carolee. "I don't know why he's here, and if he doesn't leave, I'll have him thrown out. It's his turn."

"*Kip.*" Carolee massaged Faith's hip and thought she felt the merest tensing there. "Not now." Not ever if she could help it. She didn't dare look at Max because Kip was intuitive and he'd see what she didn't want him to see yet: how much she wanted another man.

"You owe me," Kip told her.

She felt Max standing behind her. "You're tired, Kip," he said. "Why not let me sit with Faith awhile?"

"You'd like that." Kip knew how to sneer. "You and my wife alone with my daughter."

Carolee waited for the flood of angry exchanges, but Max said, "I was thinking the two of you could go to the cafeteria together while I stay here. You may not like me, but I like Faith a lot and I won't be disappearing—the way you want me to—until she's a lot better."

She could have kissed him. She *wanted* to kiss him. The thought caused Carolee to smile. "That sounds like a great idea," she told Kip. "Coffee. I'm buying. Can we bring some back for you, Max?" He intended to cool things off and she would help him.

"Please. Black and leaded."

At first, Kip didn't budge, but when Carolee arrived at the door and looked at him questioningly, he joined her.

Once he could be certain he and Faith were alone, Max stationed himself close to the bed and where he'd see if someone approached. "Here we are again, Faith. Just the two of us. What would you like to do?" Carolee spoke incessantly when she was with her daughter. Max figured that was because she thought she could call her back from this long sleep. He didn't know anything different or better to do, so he'd follow suit.

"I could read to you." The child seemed to shrink even as he watched her. Helplessness was something he'd never done well—not since he'd been able to stand up for himself. "I don't see any books. What is that about? I've seen all the books you've got so you must love reading. We'd better fix it so you've got plenty of good stuff waiting when you're ready."

He'd done more than see the books in her room, he'd spent hours watching them become clearly visible as night faded and dawn approached. And Carolee had slept, curled into his body with her head on his shoulder. He wanted a lot of nights just like that—with minor adjustments.

"I'll tell you a story. Make one up. How about that?" He'd never read to a child, much less dreamed up a story to tell. "This is about a beautiful girl with the kind of curly hair that made her the envy of all the land. She had so many people who loved her but she didn't seem to know this."

He studied her face. Nothing moved.

It wasn't weak to admit you were out of your depth. Max lifted Faith's childish hand and another feeling came to him for the first time: intense protective tenderness. Perhaps this was why fathers would fight lions for their children, this urge to keep them safe mixed with the notion that a man ought to be able to take any suffering away from their lives.

"This girl had a father and mother who loved her so much. And a grandfather. Her Aunt Linda and Brandy and Ivy and Bill and so many people who thought she was the best."

He lifted her arm and checked for irritated skin. There wasn't any redness. Holding her hand between both of his, he braced his elbows on the mattress. Her eyes moved beneath her eyelids and there was a flicker of lashes.

"Faith?" he said, leaning close. "Say something, Faith. Help me to help you. The doctors say they're very pleased with you. Today they'll set your leg which means it's getting much better. I know because I had an accident once and hurt my legs. I had to wait longer than you have to get them properly set." He wouldn't mention how many surgeries he'd had. "You're doing well, which takes me back to the beautiful girl. She had a tumble from a pony and Star, that's the pony, feels so guilty. The girl's gramps is going to buy the pony for the girl so he'll always be there whenever the girl wants to ride."

Her eyes moved again and he thought there was the slightest moisture on her lashes. Max's heart speeded up. Should he call for a nurse?

He answered his own question. If magic was happening, it was in this quiet place and while they were alone.

"Then there's Digger. He's Faith's dog, a leaping, digging type of dog. Black, with shiny eyes and a tail that talks, and a tongue that reaches a long way to lick. They've loved each other from the day the girl's gramps gave Digger to her. I think she misses him a lot now. But she's going to get well and go home to him. She has to because he's lonely and doesn't eat much."

A nurse's shoes squeaked on the tile in the corridor but the woman passed with only a smiling glance into the room.

"Then there's a friend called Max. He's never had a child of his own and for the first time he wishes he did because of Faith. She makes him see what he's been missing and he hopes he'll get to be her friend forever. He could be a kind of uncle and she could talk to him whenever she needed someone to listen— and he'd do his best to help. Maybe Faith and Max could ride together again when she's better." Talking to children should be a required subject that had to be aced before graduation. Placing his brow on their hands, he searched for something else to say.

"I'm not very happy, Faith. Things will work out the way they're meant to, but I'm not sure I'll be good at not having someone I love anymore. I've never loved anyone this way before. I know that because of the way I feel. And I think she loves me, too." That hadn't been anything he should have said. "When you were hurt—right after—I was looking for you. I was on a big black called Guy. You know him. He looks scary but he's easygoing. We followed you, and when we got to the top of a ridge and looked down, I couldn't see you anywhere so I figured you'd left the trail.

"Then I heard a dog howl. That was Digger trying to get some help for you. But I was scared because I heard a dog howl like that before—a long time ago. When I got to him, my dad was there. He'd... Dad had an accident with a horse, too. Like I told you before, I grew up on a farm and my dad and I rode quite a bit. Anyway, he was hurt real bad, much worse than you, and I thought you were going to be like him."

Stop. Warm, fuzzy "story" had taken him to a place no man or woman should want to revisit.

Between his palms, trapped fingers moved.

Max stopped breathing and looked at Faith without moving his head.

Her face was turned toward him and she looked into his eyes. Her lips moved.

"Hi, buddy," Max said softly and shifted

closer. She curled her fingers. "Tell me what you're thinking," he said and put his face close to hers.

"Mouth hurts." Her words came in an indistinct whisper. "I'm tired."

"I know you are. Your body's trying to heal." He couldn't reach the taped-up call button without releasing her hand and tried to will someone to come.

"Listen," she said, gulping as if having difficulty dealing with saliva. "Promise you won't tell anyone I spoke to you."

"Faith..." How could he keep this from Carolee? "I've got to tell your mom."

"I won't—" This time she moaned when she swallowed. "I won't speak again and they won't believe you. Promise me."

This was a no-win. "Okay, I promise. Why did you pretend you couldn't wake up all this time?"

"Sometimes can't," she said. "Then don't want to. Everything's wrong."

"No." He lowered his voice again. "That's not true. Your family is living through every hour praying for you to come through this quickly. They love you."

Her eyes closed and he was afraid she'd slipped asleep once more.

"Do you love me, too, Max?" Tears slid from the closed corners of her eyes.

Did he love Carolee's daughter? Was that something he knew how to do? "Yes," he told her. "I understand you and that means I have to love you."

She frowned.

"I mean...I just mean I love you a lot."

"Okay," she whispered and opened her eyes again. "Max, when I can go home, will you help me? Will you take me away before they can—and hide me?"

Twenty-eight

"Mr. Wolfe, you have visitors," Mrs. Fossie's well-modulated voice announced on Max's intercom. "Miss Brandy Snopes and Mr. Rob Mead. I've already told them you've been out of the office more often than you've been—"

"Thank you," Max said, irritably shoving a pile of papers aside and glancing at the list of e-mail he was dealing with a few posts at a time. What hours he'd started spending at the office each day weren't productive enough. "Please send them in."

He hoped he wasn't about to be asked to play Cupid—or referee.

Brandy entered first and Max barely stopped his mouth from falling open. A long, gray cotton dress and matching cardigan were completely out of character. Equally out of character was smooth hair swept away from her face and wound into an elegant knot at her nape.

And pretty, but *flat*, black suede shoes.

And almost no makeup.

And discreet pearl studs.

"Are you all right?" she said, frowning at him.

Max remembered to smile, at Brandy and at Rob, who had followed her in and closed the door. "I'm doing as well as I can," he said with honesty. "You look wonderful."

"Doesn't she?" Rob said. "She never stops amazing me." No man looked at a woman the way Rob looked at Brandy if he *didn't* find her amazing.

Rob's perfectly tailored dark suit didn't slip past Max, either. These two made a show-stopper couple.

"I'm going to run over to Opus for a fitting. Gorgeous clothes. I shouldn't be too long."

As she left, she didn't even glance in Max's direction.

He and Rob didn't speak for longer than was comfortable. Rob dragged a chair in front of the desk and sat down. He laced his fingers and circled his thumbs.

"We could always sing a cappella," Max said. "How about a verse or two of Taps—just to get the right mood."

"What's that supposed to mean?"

"I just wanted to see if you'd laugh. You didn't. You are one miserable SOB."

Rob loosened his dark red tie.

"You came to me," Max said. "I didn't ask for your company—"

"I'll go—"

"Hell, no. Okay, I'll behave if you will."

"You don't need my issues. You've already

got more than enough of your own to cope with," Rob said. He put his feet on Max's desk. "Brandy offered to take me to see Faith. Would that be okay?"

"I'm not her father—unfortunately—but I think you should go. You'll like her. And she loves company."

Rob inclined his head and lifted his perfectly arched eyebrows.

"What?" Max said. "Why are you looking at me like that?"

"*Unfortunately* you're not her father?"

Damn his careless mouth. "I meant almost anyone would make a better father than the one she's got—including me."

"Ah, I see. Poor kid."

Max looked at his hands. "Yes. She's got a wonderful mother and family, but Burns holds the winning cards in what happens to her and Faith's afraid of him."

"How do you know?"

"She told me."

"When was that?"

"What's with the third degree, Rob?" Max was on his feet. "What does it matter how I know, or when Faith told me? Why are you trying to rile me?"

Rob stayed where he was and the only move he made was to uncross and recross his ankles.

"Answer me," Max said, but he'd already begun to feel foolish. He'd given himself away.

"Nothing to answer," Rob said. "I asked, you answered. I think you're in love with Carolee and falling for the little girl is part of the package. But since she's unconscious, I wondered when she'd told you how she feels, that's all."

"Drop it. For my sake, okay?"

"Sure. But be careful, Max. Make sure you don't get hurt. Women can do that to you, sometimes without meaning to. If Carolee decides to go back to Burns, I don't want you joining the walking wounded."

Max's attention shifted at once to when he'd see her again. This evening she was coming to his place for the first time and he had a decision to make. It had been around two weeks since Faith had first spoken to him in secrecy and he wasn't sure he could watch Carolee grow more distraught with each day. It didn't help that in theory Faith's stay at Lake Home was almost over and Carolee refused to face the possibility of her leaving the hospital to return home with Kip.

But tonight Carolee was coming to his place, to be peaceful and relax. "I'm not going to be hurt," he said. Relaxing wasn't what he'd prefer to do with her, but it was better than nothing. "She'll never go back to him. Let's change the subject. You and Brandy. It's serious, isn't it?"

"Yes."

Max sat again and puffed up his cheeks.

Rob chuckled. "Sorry if I've disappointed you, but there's nothing to argue about on that subject."

"Back as far as when I introduced you to Brandy, I thought you two could be good together. You took so long doing something about it, I just about gave up. Congratulations."

"Thanks. I came to talk about something else, something about you and me, Max." This time his feet hit the floor again and he sat up, leaned forward.

"Are you going to tell me how you should have been able to move the pickup—again?" Max asked.

"No."

Max looked up sharply.

Rob met his eyes. "I want to talk about that day, and the days that came after."

"It's over. There's nothing to be gained by raking it up again." He didn't want to talk about any of it. Dealing with the nightmares was more than enough.

"This is about me, not you," Rob said. He got up and paced, looked briefly from the windows, and returned to stand in front of Max. "I owe you and I want to make it right so there's a chance I can move on. I told you I'd like to work with you. What I should have said was that I want to put money into this place and have you teach me to be useful."

This was where he ought to say he didn't need more capital and he wasn't sure he would ever want Rob hanging around.

"If you don't want me here, all you have to do is say so. I won't be leaving the area and I've got to get started on something worthwhile, but it doesn't have to be with you."

"What I don't get is why you want to work with the kind of thing we do."

Rob smiled, showing the teeth women had been known to gape at. "Say it. Say you think I'm a mental midget. Have you forgotten we went through most of the same classes together—and that my degree's in computer science, too? Sure, I don't have the practical experience you do, but you didn't have any when you began this company either."

Well, hell, Max thought, he had forgotten that stage of their lives. "Let me think about it," he said. "But you're turning your back on one hell of a career, Rob."

"I'm going out while I'm on top. I've got that choice. You didn't."

"D'you get a charge out of reminding me?"

"No. My momma and daddy didn't have a whole lot of polish. I've had to make my own—with the help of that scholarship and the people it exposed me to—but I still mess up with the social skills from time to time."

All he wanted, Max thought, was to see Carolee walk through the door and into his home. She was always tired now and would probably fall asleep but that was dandy as long as he could be with her.

"Max? You listening?"

"You're a social mess. Sure I'm listening. Is there a point?"

"Brandy and I are going away for a few days. I didn't want to leave without asking you to think about me going in with you. By the way, I think we'd make a great team. And I need to get everything else off my chest. Let me talk. If you feel like punching me out—go right ahead.

331

"The day you came close to being killed was the worst day of my life. It was also the best one for a long time after."

Max's head snapped up. He gripped the arms of his chair. "What the hell does that mean?"

With his knuckles on top of Max's desk, Rob supported his weight. "You were the best friend I'd ever had. You were the brother I'd *never* had. I tried to tear that truck off you, kept waiting for the rush of adrenalin they talk about at times like that, but it didn't come and all I could do was call for help and wait what seemed forever for them to come."

"All I remember is the pain—and the fear." Max bowed his head.

"You went through the months when you knew you'd never play again and people pitied you. You sat on the bench and did your time— and you cheered for me whenever I went on the field, when it should have been you running out there."

If Max didn't figure Rob needed to explain some real bad feelings, he didn't think he could listen anymore.

Rob brought a fist down on the desktop. "I was glad." He raised his voice. "*Glad.* Hear me? Even before they took you to the hospital, I was thinking about what it would all mean to me. You were great but I was second string. I always thought I was as good as you—that's human, isn't it?"

Max couldn't speak.

"I prayed for you to get well, but I didn't pray for you to play ball again."

What did the tears he wanted to cry mean? Max wondered. Did he want to cry for himself or for Rob?

"Say something," Rob said.

Max shook his head.

"The ironic thing is that I did play well. I really was good and I got better. I'd become the hero instead of you, and I liked it. It's the truth, all of it, only I started to make myself sick. You were so good to me when I was out of my depth with all the rich kids and didn't have a clue how to deal with them."

"What you didn't know," Max said, "was that I was playing a role all the time. I'd learned to watch how other people behaved. Then I did what they did. I already had my disguise in place so all I did for you was pass it on."

Rob nodded. "And after all that, I couldn't even have the decency to root for you to come all the way back, because I was jealous. I wanted what you had."

If he were like his father, Max would never be able to reach out to Rob Mead, but Max had nothing in common with Art Wolfe. However, Rob had spent his ration of self-pity. "For God's sake, put it behind you, will you?" Max said. He'd have chosen a more civil approach, but he was past being polite. "So you were glad you were getting a chance to be a star. You're human. Big deal. Did you want me to die?"

Rob pinched the bridge of his nose and shook his head. "Hell, no."

"Did you want me to be a cripple forever?"

"No, Max. I swear I never wanted you hurt at all."

Max stood up and put his hands in his pockets. "If you weren't so damn decent, you wouldn't be beating yourself up over this. You aren't a saint. You're a rotten son of a bitch, in fact, but you've got possibilities." He didn't feel as flip as he hoped he sounded.

One of his lines buzzed. Max stabbed the conference speaker on and said, "Wolfe here."

"You don't really know me but I'm Ivy Lester's husband, Bill—an old friend of Kip and Carolee Burns."

Max brought his back teeth together. He didn't know Bill at all, but Carolee was nice enough about the guy and she had great taste. What he didn't like was hearing Lester talk about Carolee as if she were still Kip's wife. "Hi, Bill," he said and felt Rob's curious eyes upon him as they both listened.

"I have no right to make this call, Mr. Wolfe."

"Max, please."

"Thank you, Max. My wife is an emotional woman who wears her heart on her sleeve, but she loves Carolee—she's very fond of Kip, but not in the same way—she loves Carolee and she's scared. She's scared Carolee will make a bad decision that'll put her in a worse mess than she's in already. I think I know Kip better than Ivy does. We've talked about what's happening and he's convinced me he's sincere in wanting to get back with Carolee.

He wants them together to take Faith home. He wants them to build a new life together."

"*He* wants these things," Max said. "You're not talking about what Carolee wants. Don't you know I've been with them and seen Kip attack her—*threaten* her."

"Kip leads with his mouth," Bill Lester said. "I can't tell you I don't believe he's been an ass. But you weren't around when Carolee was taking off all the time and leaving Kip behind to look after a little girl. I can forgive him for doing the craziest thing he could do—divorce the woman he adored, and still adores. I don't want to keep you on the phone. Calling you wasn't easy, but I did it for two good people. All I'm asking you to do is get out of the middle and give them a chance to work things through."

Max pressed his temples. "Thank you for sharing your opinion with me."

"If you stayed away, Carolee would come around."

Max said. "She's the one you ought to ask about this. Goodbye, Bill." He clicked off.

"Kip Burns put him up to that," Rob said.

Max shook his head. "I think Lester's a good man doing what he thinks is right. But who knows?"

"You're going to give Carolee up?" Rob spread his big hands. "You're going to step out and let that crazy bastard have his way?"

"Nope."

"Kip gives Brandy the creeps, she thinks he could be... No? You're not giving her up?"

"I don't actually have her," he said. "But I will if I get my way. I figure I've got a fighting chance. I'm never going to get that Super Bowl ring but I won't miss it if I get Carolee. No contest."

Rob smiled, then grew serious again. "That's the guy I know and love. I think she wants you, too.

"On what we were talking about before, Max. How is it going to be between us? It's not a decision I get to make. You don't have to do it now if you want to think about it. But tell me when you can."

"I can tell you now," Max said. "You've cleared the air. I needed that, too. Is it okay if we don't talk about it anymore right now?"

Rob spread his hands and a faint flush showed under his dark skin. "Okay. I'll take that and be grateful for it."

"How long did Brandy say she'd be?" Max didn't pretend he wasn't in a hurry to get rid of Rob.

"She's probably out in your Mrs. Fossie's room. She said she'd come back and wait for me to call her in."

"Brandy knew what you were going to tell me?"

"She knew," Rob said, scrubbing at his face. "She said she thought I had to lay out what was on my mind. Brandy knows you pretty well. She warned me you might have a hard time when I told you."

Max said, "Listen to her. She knows people and she doesn't make many mistakes about them." Evidently Brandy had decided Rob was good people. "You two are more than close, aren't you?"

Rob gave a wry grin. "Yes. In fact, we got engaged at breakfast this morning."

Max pressed a button on his phone and asked Mrs. Fossie to send Brandy in if she was back. He hadn't finished speaking when Brandy entered the office, sounding as if she'd been running.

"Hey," Rob said. "Settle down, sweetheart, you shouldn't hurry so much."

"I wasn't hurrying. I was sitting out there chewing my fingernails and forgetting to breathe."

"Max knows we're getting married," Rob said.

"Congratulations," Max said and actually felt jealous of their happiness. "Rob will always make sure you're happy."

"That's going to be a two-way street. We've got to keep each other happy. Rob?" She looked at him, and he nodded. Her expression glowed.

"Max and I have a lot of good stuff going for us," Rob told her. "But he's a busy man and we'd better get out of his hair."

"I wish you the best of everything," Max said.

"Thank you." Brandy put an arm around Rob's waist. "Max, I can't go without saying some things that are on my mind."

Rob looked down at her and said, "Maybe this isn't a good time."

"I'm not sure there'll ever be a better time,"

she told him. "I don't know how much Carolee has shared with you about Kip Burns. Or what Sam says—or maybe Linda. Sam's the most likely to tell it like it is, or like he thinks it is."

When she stopped to assess his reaction, Max said, "There have been lots of vague suggestions, but nothing I could hang a hat on."

He gave Rob a sideways glance, warning him not to mention Bill Lester's call. Rob nodded almost imperceptibly.

"Kip is just too desperate about wanting to reconcile," Brandy said. "And it happened fast, Max. That scares me."

"Sam alluded to something similar." But Max was confident of his ability to keep Burns at bay if necessary.

"I don't think the reason Kip wants Carolee to marry him again has anything to do with Faith, and I don't believe he's just discovered he loves Carolee after all. I've known him a long time—even in school—and I never liked him much. But now he's weird. He behaves like someone desperate.

"And he's involved with another woman." Brandy blushed. For all her flamboyance, she didn't gossip. "That's not rumor. It's fact and it only makes me more frightened about what he might do once he's got what he wants with Carolee."

"And you've decided he wants Carolee back and completely under his thumb?"

Brandy leaned against Rob. "That, yes. But I don't believe he intends to stay with Carolee for long."

"She won't be going back to him anyway." Finally the words didn't sound hollow to him.

"I hope you're right," Brandy said. "But I think he will keep on trying to force her to remarry."

"There are a couple of possibilities I can think of to explain his behavior," Max said. "Kip could just be spiteful enough to hate the idea of seeing her happy with someone else. Or he may be afraid for her to have someone who will free her from his control, and maybe even manage to take away his instant line of credit."

Brandy said, "He's always gone straight to Carolee for money. And she always gives it to him."

"Exactly my point," Max said. "He must hate that idea enough to do anything he can to stop it. He won't get his way."

"There's a frightening possibility." Brandy rubbed her left hand up and down Rob's arm and an impressive emerald ring shone on her finger. "If Carolee died, he'd be in control of the estate until Faith is twenty-five. A new man in Carolee's life could change that because she'd probably rewrite her will. But I'm going to put my immediate concerns right out there."

Max longed to tell her to drop the subject. He watched Brandy's face. She blinked rapidly and drew in her lips. Then she said, "We all think Kip's lost his sense of reality. He's gotten away with everything so far. Why wouldn't he think he could get away with harming Carolee?"

Twenty-nine

He hadn't bought roses. Roses were too ordinary for a woman like Carolee Burns, who had probably been given thousands of them during her career. Max sniffed the fragrant gardenias floating in a crystal bowl at the center of the dining table.

She was two hours late.

Probably meant she wasn't coming.

He moved a box of matches around on the granite-topped pass-through to the kitchen. The moment she called in to say she'd arrived, he'd light white tapers flanking the gardenias.

His jaw tightened. Carolee wasn't coming.

Continuing to keep the exchange with Faith secret was unbearable to him. Not an hour passed when he didn't try to pick up the phone and tell Carolee. Then he remembered Faith's threat. And he told himself he was using a child's rash warnings as an excuse not to face the music. Carolee was going to be furious with him. She had a right.

If she'd decided to stand him up, she'd at least have called. There was too much between them for her to deliberately brush him off.

Salmon, marinating in the refrigerator, would taste wonderful fresh from the barbecue. Nellie and Fritz had provided vegetables that could be warmed in the microwave, a spinach salad, and a bean salad. There was fresh bread from the market on Lake Street, a bowl of berries, and one filled with star fruit, kiwi, and Asian pears. A liqueur sauce, whipped cream, and ice cream were topping choices. White wine was chilling. Red wine was breathing. Coffee was made and mineral water stood ready.

Fritz had offered to put on an apron and wait on them, but even if Max hadn't instantly figured out how badly Fritz wanted to snoop, this was a night when all he could think of was having Carolee to himself.

He could try to call her.

No, he couldn't.

He should call and tell her about Faith. She definitely wouldn't come then. Darn it, she was a big girl and she'd get over it.

A low sun still shone on petunias overflowing from planters on the terrace. Many-colored petunias, geraniums in the most shocking red, marigolds, and daylilies crowded together. Deep blue lobelia draped from pots of hostas. Max slid open a door and walked outside. Fragrance hung heavy and bees leapfrogged from flower to flower. He crossed his arms on top of the railings and watched Central Avenue and the intersection with Lake Street below. There was always a chance Carolee would drive past on the lake side of the building, and that he'd see her.

Brandy had talked about Kip doing harm to Carolee. Growing tense, searching in all directions, Max drew away from the railings. He smiled a little at himself. What did he expect, a shooter on a roof with a good view of the terrace? Anything that happened to Carolee would trace straight back to Kip. The man wasn't that stupid.

Suggestible he might me, but Max's scalp felt too small and the skin on his arms and legs prickled. He wanted her where he could see her.

Bill Lester was a likable guy and seemed to think Kip was sincere in his sentiments toward Carolee. He and Ivy had known both of them for a long time. It might be worth having another chat with Bill.

A group of Harleys revved their engines and drew away from parking spots that stretched from JJJ's Café to the Lake Shore Gallery. The bikers roared to the T-junction with Central Avenue, waited for the light to change, and turned right in a cloud of leather fringe and shiny black brain buckets that allowed long hair to blow free.

Inside the condo again, Max peered through the peephole in the front door. He didn't want Carolee to know how anxious he was, did he? Sure he did. In fact, it was just fine with him if she knew.

Paolo, the red Abyssinian cat left behind as a bonus by the previous owners, slunk from the direction of the bedrooms and leaped on the dining room table.

"Down," Max hissed. "Pig-headed, ornery, arrogant feline—get *down*."

Paolo slowly blinked his upslanted golden eyes at Max and delicately drank water from the gardenia bowl.

Hands outstretched in grabbing mode, Max rose to his toes and worked his way behind the cat. That was when the phone rang.

Max didn't bother to answer. He flung open the front door, flicked off the lock, and hurried to the security gates with the cell phone in his hand—just in case Carolee hadn't just buzzed in.

She stood on the other side of an etched glass door staring at the intercom keypad he'd ignored.

"Hi, there," he said, unable to tone down his grin. "You hungry?"

When he opened the door, she came in. "How did you know I was out here? Are there cameras or something?"

"There are, but I don't use them." He drew her with him and into the condo. "I felt you arrive, how's that? No, I'm a lousy liar. I've been waiting for you to come, like a kid waits for his birthday. The phone rang and I figured you were out here so I came to bring you in. You look fabulous."

"I feel as if I've had an encounter with The Terminator, but thanks. What a cat. You never mentioned her before."

"Him. Paolo the squatter." Paolo, who could frown like no cat Max had ever seen, frowned at Carolee now. "This is his condo and he lives to remind me I'm still on probation around here. Get off the table. Shoot, I forgot to light the candles. That's your fault, cat." He took a match to the white tapers and was pleased with the sparkle of light on water in the gardenia bowl. Hey, there was nothing to this interior design thing.

"How pretty," Carolee said. She hadn't moved from the blue Persian rug inside the front door. "Nothing's what I expected, but it's all exactly right for you."

A few compliments shouldn't make a guy feel so self-satisfied, but he hadn't been getting many lately. He waved her forward. "Come on. Join me. You make me feel as if you'll suddenly run away."

"I'm not running away from you anymore."

Paolo jumped into Max's arms and rubbed his face along his boss's jaw. And Max was grateful to feel something moving, because Carolee's words had frozen them both into a still frame.

"You didn't even ask why I'm hours late," she said. "Or say a word about the way I look."

He stroked the cat and wished it were the woman in his embrace. "You're late because you had to be. My only bad times were when I doubted you'd come at all, but reason hung on and I knew you wouldn't do that to me. And I said you look wonderful, which you do. I've never seen you in red before." If they'd been golden brown rather than green, her eyes would have reminded him of Paolo's. He liked her rich, dark hair however she chose to wear it. Tonight it was loose and fell below her shoulders, a frame for her heart-shaped face. "Oh, yeah, sweetheart, I really like you in red." She wore a boat-necked cotton sweater and cropped silk pants. A lady who wouldn't

344

make it as a model because she was the kind of armful meant to be held as well as looked at.

She placed a fingertip beneath each eye. "Look at these. You could carry groceries in them."

"You're nuts," he said. "Your eyes are beautiful and so is everything else about you." He gave her a deliberately wicked grin. *"Mama mia,* what that red does for you."

Carolee was smiling. "The Terminator didn't think much of me in red. Too obvious, he thinks. And it didn't help much when I said I was going out and couldn't sit with him to listen to more of his latest blackmail efforts."

"Kip?" Max said, knowing he shouldn't feel so good. "He doesn't know you're going to be with me, though?"

"I think he might just have figured it out. Actually I said I had a date and he told me what kind of a woman I am for leaving my sick daughter to run around with you. I won't give you the exact gory details." She put her purse on a writing table by the door and slid off strappy red sandals. "You'd have been proud of me. I didn't argue with him, just left when I was already almost two hours late. Max, I was so scared you'd be mad and would either have gone out or wouldn't open the door. But you even came out to meet me, and I could see how glad you were to see me."

"You've got that right." So right he didn't care if dinner ever got eaten. "How hungry are you?"

She shook her head and approached him to stroke Paolo. The cat honored Carolee with a sniff to the chin followed by a lick so rough the scraping sound was audible. "I'm not hungry," she said and looked up into his eyes.

"Neither am I. Where did you and Kip have this latest discussion?"

"Outside Faith's room some of the time. But he wouldn't stop whenever we went back in. He doesn't seem to care if she hears or not. If she would only wake up, she could come home." Her eyes filled with tears and she turned away. "Go *home*. Kip keeps pointing out that the summer visit is about over."

The question of dealing with Burns on that matter would come, but not tonight. Before him stood the evidence that keeping a certain confidence had definitely been wrong. He couldn't allow Carolee to continue suffering over the uncertainty about Faith's supposed unconsciousness. Neither could he have Faith hearing the things her father was saying to her mother. No child should hear a so-called man insulting his wife. Max understood all about the fear that came with that.

Max put the cat down and held a hand out to Carolee. She took it without hesitation and raised it to her lips. Her mouth moving on the backs of his fingers did things to him that he doubted she could guess at. Max ran the fingers of his other hand through her hair and guided her face against his chest.

Who knew how long they stood there, and

who cared? He'd say staying just like that all night would be great, but it would be a lie.

"Leo Getz called again today," she said, both arms wrapped around his waist. "I don't know if I told you he's my manager. Leo is a friend before he's a businessman—with me. For the second time Kip has called him to suggest Leo find a juicy tour for me. That's Kip's term. A comeback tour to celebrate my reconciliation with Kip and Faith. This is supposed to be sweet and poignant and really pull in the crowds. We wouldn't leave until Faith could be transported easily enough. When I told Kip what I thought about that, he did what he did last time—blamed Leo for saying who had initiated the idea. He wants me away from here."

"He wants you away from me," Max said.

"Kip would want me away from any man who threatened the control he's enjoyed. I really think he does want to marry me again and I think it's because in his head I belong to him."

"Wine?" Max asked.

"Uh-huh. White, please."

Max left her, and when he returned with two glasses, she'd settled into a magenta chaise and was staring up at the sky mural. "Love the sky," she said. "But I clash with this chaise."

Just seeing her there, in his home, made him insanely happy. But the margin for withholding information grew narrow. "Makes for a daring color scheme," he told her. "I like it."

She settled on her side with one elbow over a cushion, and accepted the glass. Her first sip was small, her lip barely touching the pale wine, and leaving a red lipstick shape behind on the glass.

He swallowed.

From his aspect, each time she moved her lips, he caught a glimpse of straight, white lower teeth and the push of her tongue when she'd swallowed.

Telling her that everything about her was killing him would be self-indulgent.

"It's good," she said, but didn't look at him. She drank again, shifted on the cushion, and a fleeting impression caught him. The sleeveless sweater was cut high on her shoulders, and the neck was low. Carolee moved inside that sweater and he didn't think a bra allowed that kind of natural sway.

Abruptly, he set his glass on a Chinese chest and sat on the floor in front of the couch. He leaned back and closed his eyes. She was only inches away, but at least he wasn't looking at her.

The way he shrugged his big shoulders, the firm but gentle mannerisms displayed by hands with broad palms and long, blunt-tipped fingers; each detail mesmerized Carolee. She didn't have to touch him to feel him, but she didn't think she'd part from him tonight without really feeling him.

She had a giant case on Max Wolfe and ought to be ashamed of having lost all ability to control her feelings for him. But she had lost it. What happened when you no longer had much influence over your feelings and seemed to enjoy your own weakness more each day?

With a forefinger, she followed the line of one sharply delineated cheekbone, and made a fleeting pass over his ear.

He seemed unable to concentrate. Her fault and she was proud of it. Spurred on by this forward imp who seemed to have taken her over, she put a finger in her wineglass, rubbed it across her lips, and leaned down to kiss him.

For a little while Max kept his hands on the floor, a very little while before he rose over her, pushing her down on the pillows. He drew away to look at her. His lips were parted and he studied her mouth. With his hands loosely around her neck, he kissed her repeatedly, looking into her eyes each time he raised his head. One of his hands slipped beneath her sweater to rest on her ribs, and she felt warm at the knowledge that she'd deliberately decided not to wear a bra. Where his hand lay, it touched the underside of a breast and he spread his thumb to frame her sensitive flesh.

Carolee planted her hands on his chest and squirmed from beneath him. She bent to kiss him, a long, long kiss, until he grabbed for her. Dodging him, she took off for the dining room to snuff out the candles on the table. When she turned around, he waited for her in the hall and pulled one of her arms beneath his when she reached him. He urged her toward parts of the condo she hadn't seen.

Urgency made Carolee shake. He held her

arm too tightly, but let go when he swung her to face him. They kissed. Max held her in hard, yet trembling hands and she knew that in his need he'd forgotten his size and strength. She thumped against a wall but didn't care. She was beyond caring. Once more his fingers were beneath her sweater, this time on her back, smoothing up and down her spine. His breath came in bursts. Tension built in her swelling breasts and in her belly and thighs. Finally, staggering against each other, they arrived in what had to be the master suite.

"You've got a fireplace in your bedroom," she said and felt inane.

Max turned a switch and the fire leaped to life.

"I find fires sensual," Carolee said. "They make me feel like stretching, and rolling around, maybe."

He swallowed. She read desire in his eyes and felt both nervous and excited.

"What a bed. It's huge, but then, you're a big man." Carolee looked him over. "A very big man."

She smoothed the down comforter in its dark purple cover and held one of the four bedposts while she swung around. When she did that, her sweater didn't meet her pants and her waist was revealed.

"You are one curvy, curvy woman," Max said. "But I think you know that."

He clammed up and sat on an ottoman near the fire. His hands curled into fists on his knees.

"You're quiet suddenly," she told him. "Never mind, I'm going to talk for both of us." Had she always been something approaching a sex addict with a man who excited her? She didn't think so, but then, she'd never felt this kind of excitement before.

"I'm not so quiet," Max said. "I'm planning strategy. That's tough when you can't think straight."

Carolee leaned against the bedpost. She rested her forehead there and settled the gleaming mahogany into her cleavage. Max stood and studied her. There was sweat on his temples and upper lip. He tried to maintain eye contact but frequently failed and looked at her breasts.

"Are you tired?" she asked him.

He laughed. "What do you think?"

"Would it be okay if I got into your lovely big, soft bed? I'd have to have you with me. I'm tired of being lonely. I thought I was used to that. Then I met you."

He half closed his eyes and muttered something unintelligible.

"Is that yes or no?"

"I'll be glad to keep you company."

Too jumpy to stand still, she let down ceiling-to-floor blinds and busied herself throwing back the comforter.

Max took off his shirt and let it fall.

Carolee undid the buckle on the narrow, beaded belt at her waist and pulled it from the loops. This landed on a padded bench and was followed by the silk pants.

With narrowed eyes, Max approached her slowly, undoing the belt from his navy blue chinos and opening his zipper as he came. Muscle and sinew moved beneath tanned skin on his chest and arms.

The beat of Carolee's heart became overwhelming. She wore no hose and her red panties were cut to the waist on either side.

She glanced at Max and found him staring at her legs. He realized she'd caught him, and muscles in his jaw flickered. "Your legs are a total turn-on, sweetheart. I hope you don't think I can't see through the panties."

Rather than respond, she rested her weight on one leg, splayed a hand over her stomach, and looked pointedly at his pants. He sighed and slid them off.

"*You,*" she said, "have great legs. You ought to wear shorts— a lot."

"Not anymore," he said and she realized she'd never seen his legs before.

Promptly she walked around the bed and bent over to examine some fierce-looking scars. She could see where there was permanent loss of muscle in places, but none of it mattered. Long, muscular, and covered with light brown hair, Max Wolfe had the kind of legs a woman would be stupid not to want to feel snaking around hers.

She kissed his right thigh, knelt, and stroked his legs slowly, from beneath his shorts to his ankles and along his finely boned feet.

"Oh, Carolee." He groaned. "You don't have to do that."

Kissing the inner side of his leg in a spot where his erection was solid against her temple, she shuddered and felt her own flesh swell, harden, tingle. Immediately she slid her hands up the backs of his thighs and inside his shorts. His solid tush didn't even dent beneath her fingernails. She squeezed the flesh and traced the line between his buttocks.

Max reached down and swept her sweater over her head. He stood there, breathing through his mouth, repeatedly raking his fingers through her hair.

Sitting on her heels, wearing nothing but the scanty red panties, Carolee looked up into his darkening face. She pressed her breasts to his knees and rose slowly, passed her aching flesh over his legs, the bulging evidence of how easily he could lose control, his belly and waist, and finally came to rest against his chest. There she rubbed slowly from side to side, gasping at how his hair stimulated her nipples until she burned between her legs.

Max grasped her by the shoulders and held her off. He gave her a small shake. "I want you too much," he said. "I don't think that's ever going to change."

Desire burned her skin. "I want to be with you. I'm not going to lie and say this is a spur-of-the-moment thing. I've done nothing but think about it from the...since your office. And I wanted you at Lake Home, but I could tell you thought the best thing to do was comfort me and keep things simple."

He frowned. "I'm sorry. Making love didn't seem the right thing."

"It wasn't. And I loved being held by you. I slept better than I've slept in months. I'm the one who should be sorry. I don't know what it is that makes me come on to you the way I do. You're the only man who ever made me feel—*sexy*. You make me feel I can't keep my hands off you." She turned from him and crawled rapidly under the covers, which she pulled up to her chin.

Max left the fire on and slid between the sheets. He was tired, but not *that* tired.

Carolee lay on the side of the bed closest to the windows. Right on the edge, and very still with her eyes flickering beneath closed lids. By design or otherwise, the lady tended toward cat and mouse games. Since he was obviously the cat, he found the chase irresistible.

Max settled down on his back, in the middle of his side of the bed, with his face turned toward her and his eyes wide open. How long, he wondered, would they have before either a call came from the hospital or Carolee couldn't stay away from Faith another minute.

The deep green sheet had settled across Carolee's collarbones and the tips of her shoulders. He raised his head and propped it on a hand. What she wore, or rather didn't wear, beneath that sheet wasn't a mystery. He raised a hand and let it hover inches from her face. If he touched her, she might jump. He'd kiss her instead and figured she might still jump but she'd soon sort things out.

Max kissed a naked shoulder first. He closed his eyes and felt weak, the kind of weak that was nothing but good. He kissed her again and again from her shoulder, along her collarbone, and up the side of her neck to her jaw.

She didn't stir. In fact, she held her breath while her eyes moved more rapidly.

Max touched his lips to hers and used his tongue to open her mouth. Beneath the sheet, he filled a hand with one of her breasts and kneaded gently. The soft flesh overflowed his fingers and the nipple budded tight against his palm. Her chest rose and fell rapidly and she covered his hand on her skin.

Their mouths slid from side to side. He touched the inside of hers and couldn't be gentle. He slid a knee between her legs while he darted his tongue in and out of her mouth. She arched from the bed, and the covers slid down before she pressed herself against him. Max held her bottom, rubbed the curve of her hip. Their bodies were damp and urgent, and shifted constantly to find new places to touch.

All the words had fled.

Max threw the covers all the way off and sat astride her hips. She opened her eyes into glittering slits. Her hair was a tangled mass. He raised her hands over her head and clasped the fingers of each one around polished slats in the bedhead. "Hold on," he whispered against her neck.

She didn't answer him, but she followed his instruction.

Minutes stretched. He had no idea how

long he stroked and kissed her, ran his thumbs over her erect nipples while he pressed her heavy breasts together. He liked the red panties where they were and kept his hands on her breasts while he changed positions and knelt between her thighs. His mouth and tongue he ran down her center line to her navel. When he nipped her there, she wiggled and he moved his attention to a hip. A single silver line, almost invisible, showed there. He didn't think he'd ever made love to a woman who was a mother, but he was sure this was a stretch mark and he liked it, rubbed his cheek against it, and had only one thought: that he wished he had caused that mark.

He eased out of his shorts and considered her panties again. There was time to make decisions. There was no difficulty moving the silk aside to get his mouth fastened on her, between her, and to nip at tender flesh with his teeth, suck firmly, flick his tongue over that place that already had her rocking and crying out.

"As you were," he said when she lowered her arms.

She ignored him and pulled his hair.

Max drew his lips back from his teeth and returned to the sweet task that made her helpless and had her thrashing. She grabbed the sheet beneath her and thrust her hips against his mouth.

It was over too quickly, and her body was slick. She stared up at him, her eyes questioning.

"What do *I* want?" he said. "Why don't I

show you, and if you have a different idea, speak up."

She nodded. With ridiculous ease he flipped her onto her stomach, pulled her up onto her knees and drew down her panties. His blood turned to water and his limbs, although strong, shook somewhere deep inside.

He guided himself into her, heard her gasp as he filled her. Moving carefully, he leaned over her back and rested his hands where he could feel her breasts sway against his palms.

Carolee's breathing came in sobs and she met him, slapped against him each time he entered her. Their panting filled the silence.

Max slammed his fists into the mattress and rested his forehead on her back—and emptied himself into her.

They were spent. Carolee fell flat on her stomach and Max lay half over her with a possessive leg hooked across her bottom and his face pressed against the back of her neck.

Thirty

Rain drummed on the terrace and hissed beneath the wheels of the occasional car on Kirkland's dark streets. Max had been awake a long time, watching Carolee's sleeping face by the muted light in his bedroom. She stirred and murmured, and turned toward him. The sheet was around her waist and he brought his lips softly to her breasts. He closed his eyes but stopped moving when he felt her hand in his hair.

"Max," she said sleepily. "Make love to me again."

He smiled, slyly sucked a nipple, and rolled onto his back.

"What is it?" she said.

He clamped his hands behind his head. "I've got something to tell you," he said in a rush. "You're going to be mad at me."

"Nothing you could do would make me mad at you." She smiled. "Not for long, anyway. I should have told you I've given your number here to the hospital, just in case something changes and they want to get in touch with me."

Max worked his jaw. "Good idea," he said. She might think she couldn't get mad at him but he'd give that about a minute to change.

Carolee decided she'd never seen Max more awkward, or more appealing. The latter was hard to imagine. "Promise me one thing," he said. Grace in such a large man was going to continue turning her on. "Think about my position before you do anything rash."

She thought his position was just perfect.

"You're not answering me," he said. "Give me a chance, will you?"

"You get all the chances there are, Max. Now, let's get this over. You're starting to scare me."

"You'll like what I've got to say, but that won't stop you from wanting to push me in the lake."

She remained quiet for so long he thought she'd fallen asleep again. "Sweetheart," he whispered. "You asleep?"

"Uh-uh. Just waiting for you to do something about the way I ache all over. You have the cure."

"I want to," he said, nipping her at her ear. "But I'm just going to hope we get to pick up where we're leaving off."

Carolee leaned her chest on his and played with the slightly curly ends of his hair, then felt him shudder.

"You've got to find a way not to have any discussions with Kip—or anyone else who's in the mood for an argument—in Faith's room."

She rested her hand on his shoulder. "I'm trying. Each time Kip starts getting angry—I walk out so he has to follow me if he wants to talk. What makes you mention this? Now?"

"They say hearing is the first thing to come back when someone's been in coma or whatever." Stalling wouldn't make anything easier.

"I've heard that," Carolee said. Her fingers had tightened on his shoulder. "You think she can hear, don't you? Max, that doesn't make me angry, it makes me so excited I can hardly stay still."

"She can hear."

Carolee was silent before saying. "You sound sure."

"I am sure, because she can."

"Max." Her voice rose. "Look at me. What are you saying?"

He did look at her, but not averting his eyes took effort. "About two weeks ago Faith spoke to me."

She rose onto her elbows, and shocked didn't come close to describing the expression on her face when she looked at him.

"Remember a morning when I got to Faith's room and found you and Kip there? It was after the night when he'd shown up at Lake Home and turned nasty. You were arguing and I got the two of you to go for coffee while I sat with Faith."

"I remember."

"I didn't know what to do, so I copied you and kept on talking. I said I was making up a story, but Faith was the main character and I talked about all the people who love her." He paused and put a hand on her back as if he expected her to shrug it off. She didn't, never would. "I mentioned I was her friend, too, and her fingers moved in mine. I looked at her and her eyes were wide open. Her jaw hurt badly but she talked."

"Dear Lord," Carolee said. She leaned toward Max, hung on his every word. "What did she say? Did you ask why she hasn't been talking?"

"She said she gets tired and doesn't want to talk. She's been listening to a lot of conversations and they make her unhappy. Especially Kip's. She says he's not kind to you. I think it's too much for her so she goes away."

"My poor baby," Carolee said. "She must have heard some things she should never have to listen to. There won't be any more of it. Why didn't you tell me before?"

"I knew it wouldn't be long before you asked that," he said, making to shift away from her. She clasped his upper arm and held him where he was. "I didn't know what to do. And I'm not sure I should be breaking that girl's confidence even now. If Kip finds out the whole truth, I'll know I made a mistake because he's likely to insist on taking her home at once and hiring a slew of nurses to look after her. I don't know much, but I'm pretty sure that's not what she needs. She needs the people she loves around her. Carolee, she told me she couldn't live with you or Kip because the fighting over her would never stop."

She rested her face on the pillow beside his head. "This has to have been so hard on you. I understand why you didn't tell me before."

"Faith asked me if I loved her, too."

In a muffled voice, Carolee asked, "What did you say?"

"That's obvious, isn't it? I told her I do. Maybe if I'd ever really gotten to know any children before—or had my own—I'd have learned what wonderful things they are, but I didn't. Faith's managed to steal my heart."

"And you've stolen hers." Carolee pressed her cheek to his. "But I still say I'm way too much trouble to you. It's time you got on with the rest of your life. You need someone different from me. You need someone you can have that family with."

"I'll never need anyone but you."

He could still say something like that when she had enough baggage for several women? "Did Faith say anything else?"

His sigh was long. "Yes. When she's well enough, she wants me to take her away and hide her."

Carolee cried, she couldn't stop herself. She struggled from the bed and rushed to lock herself inside the bathroom. She and Kip had alienated their child to a point where she was asking other people to take her in. The only bright spot was that she trusted Max enough to make him her confidant.

He tapped on the door. "Please come out. I may actually have a good idea—not that Kip will think it is."

She sniffed and gulped.

"But he can't afford to be shown up as a father who doesn't care enough for his daughter to put her happiness ahead of his own."

Carolee peered at herself in the mirror. She poured cold water and splashed it on her face. Her body, bare but for her panties, didn't embarrass her even though a sexy rosiness still blossomed on her skin.

One deep breath, another, and she slid open the door. Max confronted her. "Look, I should have told you what happened at once. I wanted to because you were so worried. But Faith warned me that if I gave her away, she'd behave as if she'd never opened her mouth."

"You did the right thing. She needed the time

to think. Now I've got to find a way to get her out of the hospital. Everything's healing so well and she can really get going on rehab." Deep sadness clouded her eyes. "Kip's changed. He loved Faith to pieces and I think he still does, but he's really rattled and I think that's my fault. Max, he'd make gingerbread houses with her, and he led a Bluebirds group. *Bluebirds*, Max. That's strictly Mom territory. A man who hates being around his child doesn't do those things."

Max didn't want to pin medals for fatherhood on Kip Burns but said, "I'm sure you're right. Would you like to go to the hospital right now. Just talking to her and knowing she hears you will be good for you."

"The first thing I want to do is figure out what to do about getting her out of that place. You said you've got an idea we're going to discuss?"

"Yeah." He had to think before every word. "Have you noticed anything about this condo?"

She looked blank.

"Nobody does, that's why I kept it after I got over the accident. It's wheelchair ready. All the doors are wider than normal, so's the hall. The showers have doors that swing either way and the floors slope down inside. There are benches built in."

"I didn't notice a thing," Carolee said. "Don't worry. Not a soul would look at this place and think it was for an invalid... Oh, you mean... Max, I couldn't let you take on such a task."

"Yes, you could." He slipped an arm around her and felt a possessive charge. "There's a sleigh bed in one guest room and I know she'd probably love it in there. She could be surrounded with books and have a TV and her own music. Digger would be a happy condo dog. There are parks all around. I'd get a couple of first-rate nurses to be available 'round the clock and this is more suitable for her than either Kip's place or yours. She can go right out onto the terrace in the sunshine, or out through the front for a ride around as many blocks as she feels like going." He led her back into the bedroom.

Carolee leaned against him. "You already admitted you don't know a thing about having kids around but you came up with this."

"I'm not going to lie. I'm very fond of Faith, but I'd do anything to have you near me."

With her head on his shoulder, Carolee pushed an arm beneath his and closed her eyes. "Kip has the final say and it'll be no."

"I say we try. Hell, I'll play Mr. Nice Guy and invite him to stay here whenever he wants to. I just hope I can get that out without gagging. If he tries to use the offer against you, he'll look like an ass for making a sick child's life so difficult. She'd be close to all her family members and primarily looked after by them rather than by strangers."

"Max, I just want her to get well and I think that could happen more quickly here. I'm going to fight for it. I'll get Sam and Linda to fight with me."

He sat on the bed and pulled her down beside him. "Brandy will, too. And Rob. Did you know they got engaged?"

She blinked and screwed up her face. "Brandy and Rob are engaged? What... Is that what you meant to say?"

"Yep. They stopped by my office when I was there and looked sickeningly happy. They were going away for a few days."

Carolee looked cross. "She never said a word to her best friend."

"They just wanted to do it quietly and be on their own."

"They told *you*," she said, sitting very straight. "Well, there will have to be a party when they get back."

Max nodded emphatically, although he didn't think a party was necessary until Brandy and Rob wanted one. "We'll look into it when they get home." He'd needed to talk about what Rob had revealed of his feelings, but tonight it didn't seem so important. "Should we go to see Faith now?"

"I'm not ready," she said. "Linda's staying with her for a few hours. And Ted Gordon, Linda's ex-husband. Now there's a guy some smart woman ought to grab. Sam will be taking over from them much later and Kip said he couldn't come again until tomorrow afternoon.

"Maybe you don't understand, but now I know she's not unconscious, only hiding out—which is a bit Faith-like—I'm so excited and happy I could pop. I can't rush to her and insist she speak to me. I have to wait for that. So I'm taking a few hours off." She climbed into bed and lay on her stomach.

"What are you thinking about?" Max asked when he couldn't be quiet any longer.

She twisted onto her back and urged him into her arms. "All the things you don't know about me, and whether you'll want to be with me like this if you do know."

"Terrible stuff, huh?" He was out of smiles, but he landed a kiss on the tip of her nose.

"You didn't even mention birth control this time."

Caught. He finger-combed her hair and decided he could never look at her for too long. Carefully, he slid beneath the covers and eased her to stretch out on top of him. He played his fingertips over the sides of her breasts.

"Max?"

"The other time you told me it wasn't an issue," he said. "So I assume you're taking the pill. But can I tell you something?"

She nodded while she pinched one of his nipples. The sensation jolted him.

"Okay," he said. "It wouldn't hurt my feelings if you got pregnant. We aren't teenagers with no idea about responsibility. Being responsible for you, Faith, and our baby is about the best thing—next to making love—that I can think of."

The abrupt closing of her expression, her quick move to put space between them, might as well have been cold water hitting him.

Carolee scrunched herself up in the bed

and pulled the covers tight around her. "I don't take the pill. I don't have to. I can't get pregnant again, Max. I'm not the woman who'll have your children."

Thirty-one

Faith wished Aunt Linda and Uncle Ted would come back. They'd left to have coffee and to allow Mr. and Mrs. Lester some time with her. She didn't understand why they were visiting at all unless they thought they ought to be.

Her body hurt in lots of places. When she was sure she was alone, she moved a little, but she had to be so careful and the nurses were very nice about rubbing lotion on her. She wanted her mom. She wanted Dad, too—and Max. And Gramps. And she wanted Mom rubbing cream into all the dry places that itched.

When she'd started her period, Mom made her feel special and not afraid or embarrassed. Dad never really told Faith nasty things about Mom, but he said them to Mom herself when he thought Faith couldn't hear, and he wasn't truthful all the time. When they were at the condo, Dad wasn't usually there. Mostly Mrs. Jolly looked after her.

"She's so thin," Ivy Lester said and Faith's

mind stopped turning and turning. "She was always, well, a bit unusual looking. All that hair. But now she's just skin and bones, she isn't a pretty sight. I don't suppose the mess on her face will improve a thing."

"Ivy," Bill Lester said. "Faith isn't the cute child model type but she's the most interesting kid I ever saw. Plastic surgery's wonderful these days. Once Faith's finished with hers, I'll be expecting you to beg for tucks and lifts."

"Tucks and lifts? Why, Bill Lester, I do believe you're deliberately insulting me. I don't need a single tuck or lift anywhere."

"Of course not, dear."

Ivy puffed. "You don't say it like you mean it."

"Be a grown-up," Bill said. "I do worry about Faith still looking so ill. She should be well on the mend by now."

Faith's nose itched. She'd never liked Ivy. Now she liked her less.

"It's Carolee who could use a few tucks. Maybe some liposuction. There's a point when pleasingly curvaceous starts to sag and that's about where she's arrived. Must be her diet. She probably eats to feel better."

If only she could yell at the woman to get out of her room, Faith thought. And this was someone Mom thought was her friend. She'd like to tell Mrs. Ivy Lester that she was jealous of Mom being really beautiful and clever.

"Carolee's a lovely woman," Bill said. "She's natural and that's rare today."

"Are you sayin' I'm not natural?"

"I'm saying Carolee looks good to me. Since we're on the topic of Carolee, let's deal with something important. I want you to stay out of her business and Kip's. When he says he wants his family together, he really means it. I believe that. The floating gallery is starting to show promise, and Kip is getting himself together. He needs Carolee."

"Why do you keep sayin' that? It was fine with you when they split. You thought she was neglectin' him and takin' away all of his ambition. And you were right, baby."

"No," Bill said, "I was wrong."

"I don't think she's good for him," Ivy said. "She can't give him what he needs—support in whatever he wants to do. For his sake, and for hers, they should never be together."

"Will you stop and think? Kip's over so many things. He isn't trying to prove himself anymore because all he wants is for the gallery to work. And his paintings, of course. Sure he did the number about wanting more kids—we both know what that was about. He had other irons in the fire and wanted an excuse to stay away from his wife. But he's not about to bring any of that baby stuff up to Carolee again."

"Bill." Ivy dragged her husband's name out. "You've got a convenient memory. Sure he got distracted, but you know why there weren't more kids and it wasn't anything to do with Carolee."

Faith felt shaky and nervous. She grew hot and the hospital gown stuck to her. What did they mean? Daddy had told her he and Mom only wanted one child. He used to joke and say they got the first baby so right, they didn't want to risk being disappointed. But the Lesters were saying he had wanted more children. And it sounded like he'd said it was Mom's fault they didn't have more babies when it wasn't at all. She didn't understand what all those things meant.

"Damn it all," Bill said suddenly, and Faith heard a chair move. He must have stood up. "That does it. You piss me off, you stupid bitch. Don't ever bring the subject up again, Ivy. We both promised Kip we'd keep his confidence. That means we will not run the risk of making things more difficult for him."

"I don't think it's wise for you to threaten me," Ivy said, then, "Think about that, baby. Hush, Linda's coming in."

"We'll go," Bill told her. "Hi again, Linda, Ted. Your timing is perfect. We've got to run along. We'd hoped to see Kip and Carolee. I expect they'll be coming later."

"Of course they will," Ivy said, her voice all different and soft. "Will you tell them we dropped by and we're pleased to see Faith looking so much better."

Aunt Linda said, "I'll tell them you came," and Faith heard mumbled good-byes.

"I thought Carolee would be back by now, Ted," Linda said. "Maybe she fell asleep, which would be a good thing. Let me check at the desk to see if she's called in."

Aunt Linda opened the door and let it swing shut.

Uncle Ted picked up one of Faith's hands and just held it. "You'll be joining us again soon," he said. "I don't blame you for ducking out. What you're going through isn't much fun. I've felt like hiding out myself on more than one occasion."

Faith wanted to share what had been happening with him. She didn't think he would give her away if she spoke to him. But Max made her feel so safe and she did love him. He would make everything right again and she shouldn't take more risks.

"No calls," Aunt Linda said, walking back in. "I asked about how long they can keep someone in a hospital room like this. The nurse said that depended on insurance and she didn't know. I'd think they'd want to put Faith somewhere else before long. One of those long-term nursing facilities or something. Ted, I couldn't bear it."

"Come here," he said, and footsteps crossed the floor slowly. "You used to be able to believe I knew a thing or two. Faith will not go into one of those places. None of us would allow it, would we?"

"She needs special care."

"And she'll get it at home—wherever that's going to be. Trust me, darling, Faith will be with her own people and she'll get better."

Aunt Linda sniffed. "Okay. You sound so sure. I think that's why I used to feel like... It can be hard to keep up with really smart people who see things clearly and don't fall apart if times get hard."

"Look at Faith," Uncle Ted said. "She's much too thin, but she'll get over that. I think she'll be a lovely woman once the surgeons have finished."

"So do I. Ted—"

"If I was too full of myself to give you a chance to feel important when we were together, I'm sorry. I wish you'd explained that but you never did. For the record, you're very important and you're very smart. I miss you, Linda."

Faith held her breath. It was like being at the movies, or listening to stories on the radio.

"Do we have any chance at all?" Uncle Ted asked.

Aunt Linda sighed. "Maybe it's too late. That's my fault."

"Only maybe?" He laughed. "That's the most positive thing you've said to me in years."

"I won't hurt you again," Aunt Linda said. "I care too much about you for that."

"Would you at least open your mind to the possibilities?"

A long time passed before Aunt Linda said, "We'll see."

"I'll accept that," he said. "Do you think music would be a good idea for Faith?"

"She grew up with it. Could well be."

"Hey, you two." It was Mom's voice and Faith felt a smile inside. "Ted, it's so great to have you here. Thanks for coming. This is my friend, Max Wolfe."

"Hi, Ted," Max said.

"Is it okay to say I'm sorry about what happened to you?" Uncle Ted said. "You were one hell of a player."

"Thank you," Max said. "Sometimes it's nice to be reminded."

"Any sign of movement from Faith?" Mom asked.

"No," Aunt Linda said. "I just want to hold her in my arms and cuddle her. She needs contact with people who love her and all this paraphernalia's in the way."

"I know how you feel," Mom said.

"We'll all be hugging her again soon," Uncle Ted said. "It's time I took your sister somewhere relaxing. She puts on a good front, but she's not doing as well as she'd like you to believe."

"I guessed that," Mom said.

"I'll take her home, then," Uncle Ted said.

As soon as Aunt Linda and Uncle Ted were gone, Mom said, "I wonder what that means? Take her home? Take her somewhere relaxing? He's never stopped loving her, y'know."

"You surprise me," Max said with a chuckle. "I'm going to tell Faith about my idea. You never know, she might have started hearing something."

Faith barely stopped herself from frowning. Max was inviting her to stop pretending she was unconscious—at least to Mom.

"My condo would be a perfect place for you to recover, Faith. It's close to the hospital and we'd never have to worry about stairs. Your Mom agrees. And I'd love to have you."

A lump formed in Faith's throat. He was going to try to keep her safe.

"You're going to have to leave here soon, sweetie," Mom said. "And of course I'm going to look after you—and your dad will, too—and everyone who loves you. We just have to persuade your dad that Max's place makes the most sense."

And that, Faith thought, fighting back tears, would never happen.

"She's crying," Mom said.

"That's because she's a smart girl and somehow she knows it's going to be hard to talk Kip into this."

"Sam!" Mom sounded shocked. The door had opened and there was a lot of scuffling and some funny sounds. "Shut the door, Max. He's going to get us thrown out of here before we're ready."

"Baloney," Gramps said. "Nothing to do with you. It's all my fault. I don't know the rules. I'm old and senile and I gotta be forgiven."

"I've heard everything now," Max said. "You can't do this."

"Watch me."

A grinding noise puzzled Faith, then Gramps said, "How's my favorite girl? You're looking wonderful and I've brought someone else who thinks so."

"No, Sam," Mom said, sounding frantic.

The sheet was raised and a gangly, softly hairy body landed beside Faith with a plop. She wanted to laugh and shout.

"You go watch the door, Max," Gramps

said. "Let me know if you see someone coming."

"Don't you be an accomplice," Mom said.

"I already am," Max told her. "I haven't turned him in and neither have you. What could be better for Faith than Digger?"

One cold, wet nose poked at Faith's neck and a long tongue began to soak her. Somewhere in the greetings, rocks tumbled into the bed. Finally, Digger put his head on her shoulder and snuffled contentedly.

"Will ya look at that," Gramps said. "Two kids asleep together. It'll help Faith."

"It might at that," Max said. "Now, since I'm a tired man, I'm going to put a chair against the door and sit in it. You two make sure Digger doesn't make any moves that would hurt Faith."

Thirty-two

Sam was asleep on a chair with his head propped sideways against the wall. Since Max appeared to be dozing, Carolee spent her time watching Faith and Digger—Digger who continued to sleep with what could be taken as a smile on his face.

Within half an hour, someone would come in to check on Faith. The dog must be gone by then. Carolee rubbed her eyes and looked at Sam's haggard face. All of this had taken too much out of him. She smiled. Trust him to think of smuggling a dog into a hospital because he'd decided it would help his granddaughter.

With her heart turning, Carolee studied Max. His chin fell on his chest, then he jerked his head up, only to have it slip downward again. She could look at him forever, and if she thought she'd never again sleep with him, she wasn't sure how she'd cope.

A sharp slam woke Sam, startled Carolee to full attention, and all but knocked Max from his chair, which he righted and moved aside.

Rather than a nurse, it was Kip who came in, frowning deeply in all directions. "Why were you blocking the door?" he asked Max. "What the fuck are you doing barring the way to my daughter's room—with my wife?"

"Let's take this up somewhere else," Max said, glancing at Faith, then Carolee.

"I'm not going anywhere with you. You're a violent son of a bitch and I've got the bruises to prove it."

"Outside," Sam said, on his feet and bristling. "No unpleasantness in here with Faith. And no talk like that with Carolee listening."

"Oh, I'm sorry," Kip said. "I didn't realize she was too sensitive for normal conversation."

He curled his lip when he looked at Sam. "Past your bedtime, isn't it, old man?"

Digger whined.

Kip strode to the bed and looked down on Faith and her buddy. "That dog? What's the dog doing here? In Faith's bed? In a hospital? Are you all fucking crazy?" He turned on Sam. "It was around Lake Home. You said it was your dog."

"He said Digger was our dog, Kip," Carolee said. "Settle down. He's about to leave."

Kip narrowed his eyes and advanced on Sam. "He's yours, isn't he? Or something to do with you. What did you do? Get the thing for Faith? You knew it couldn't be at my place, so you planned to have it at Lake Home just so Faith would want to go there all the time. No go. As far as I'm concerned, the mutt can be thrown outside, now."

"Don't be an ass," Max said. "Sam? Sam, what is it?"

Sam's face was putty gray and he swayed on his feet. Carolee rushed to him and pushed him gently into a chair. From an inside pocket in the vest he wore, she took out a bottle of small white pills and put one under his tongue.

"I'm okay," Sam said. He was already breathing more easily.

"He needs to see someone," Carolee said to Max.

"Gotcha," Max said, and rang for help. "And I'm going to call for someone to come and take Digger until we can bail him out."

"Use the window," Kip said. "It'll be quicker."

"Stop it." Carolee took hold of her ex-husband's collar and yanked. "This isn't about a dog. It's about you not getting what you want when you want it."

Max had left the room and Kip's expression turned remote. He withdrew to a corner and stood there silently.

"Sam," Carolee said. "You need to be checked over."

"I will be. See that Digger gets safely out of here. And you leave this hospital with Max Wolfe, understand? No one else."

"Don't worry about me."

"Understand?"

"I understand."

"Your wife ran around on you," Kip said, "so it's okay for my wife to run around on me. Is that it, Davis?"

Sam gawked at Kip.

"Linda told me years ago. She told me how it was and how you kept coming back each time—after you'd made the break and gone away."

Carolee marched to Kip and smacked his face with all the force she could muster. He raised his hand to hit her back, but stared into her eyes and gradually let his arm drop.

"You don't know anything," she said. "And you won't ever talk about private matters concerning our family again."

"I don't take instructions from women."

He sickened her. "Instructions are just about all you don't take from women. If you want to stay, be quiet. My father is ill."

Max returned with the duty nurse, who went directly to Sam.

"My father isn't feeling well," Carolee said. "He's got angina and he's been under a lot of strain. Is there somewhere he could lie down? He ought to lie down."

"I can still talk," Sam snapped. "I'm Sam Davis. Dr. Brothers is my GP."

"I know him," the nurse said. "I'll get a gurney."

Sam got up and made for the door. "I can walk. Just take me where I need to go."

"I'll come with you," Carolee said.

"You stay with Faith. I don't need no nurse-maid," Sam said, and the nurse led him away.

"Honesty wins out again," Max said when the door had closed. "I told the duty nurse we broke all the rules by bringing in a dog. He says as long as we get Digger out of here fast and with as little trouble as possible, he'll look the other way."

After twenty minutes of trying to avoid Kip's glowering presence, the longest twenty minutes in Carolee's life, Fritz Archer from the diner in Kirkland arrived. He came in smiling, but after seeing the company he'd entered, he plastered a somber expression on his face. His black hair was mussed and his shirt wrongly buttoned. He carried two gift bags and went on his tiptoes to the bed. From one bag he took a very large box of chocolates. "Kids like candy," he said and Carolee hid a smile. Evidently he wasn't thinking about wired jaws.

Max said, "Thanks, Fritz," and didn't even try not to grin.

"Nel made this for our first grandchild," Fritz said, and tugged out an ugly doll with a face made from a stuffed sheer stocking, and black yarn hair parted in the center and pulled back into a bun. She wore some sort of cape with pockets all over it.

"We can't let you do that," Carolee said. "That's too special."

Max, ever the diplomat, said, "You don't have any grandchildren."

Fritz shrugged. "Nellie likes to be prepared." And he put the doll on the other side of Faith from Digger. "It's an old lady doll."

"I wondered if it was," Max said.

Carolee wouldn't allow herself to check for Kip's reaction.

"The old lady who swallowed a spider. You know the one. It wriggled and squiggled and—well, it did something else inside her." He took a yarn spider out of one of the pockets and pushed it into the doll's mouth.

Carolee said "Yuck" under her breath.

Max laughed aloud and Fritz looked injured. "What's with you?"

"It's just—so—sweet," Max said. "I know Faith will want to thank Nellie herself."

She'd thank Nellie, Carolee thought, barely holding back the chuckles, but she'd wonder why someone would give her a little kid toy.

"Get the dog out," Kip snapped

Fritz tilted his head to see him better. "Evening," he said. "You Faith's dad?"

"Yeah." Kip snapped his fingers. "Deal with the dog."

Fritz shot out a hand. "I'm Fritz Archer. I'm a friend of Sam, Max, Carolee, and Faith." He got a halfhearted shake for his efforts. "Pleased to meet you, Mr. Burns. You sure you should be in here? Your color ain't so good, like you're real sick or something."

Kip looked alarmed and touched his face.

"Out you come, Digger," Carolee said, glad to hide her smirk. She put her arms around the big puppy and all but lifted him from the bed. He promptly lay down. "I don't think Sam brought a leash."

"Got it covered," Fritz said and took one from his pocket.

Keeping a wary eye on Kip, Fritz said his good-byes and led Digger away.

"Who's that clown?" Kip said. "Faith's leaving this place the minute she can and going where she can be around the type of people she's used to."

"In the corridor, Kip," Carolee said and led the way. Max followed, paying no attention to Kip's narrowed eyes. Once the three of them were alone, she tried the reasonable approach. "We're both uptight, Kip. We've got decisions to make about our daughter's immediate future."

"*I've* got them to make."

Carolee felt Max move, but shook her head at him. "I'm not folding this time. Whatever I need to do to have a say in my daughter's future, you can consider done. Before you get any nastier, there's a proposition I didn't expect to be offered and it's a good one for all of us."

She told him without emotion, explaining

381

the benefits of Max's condo and how Digger could be there and it would be easy for Faith to be on the terrace in the sun and to get to therapy.

Kip didn't say a word.

Carolee waited. Max stood with his arms crossed and his eyes fixed on Kip.

"You've done a lot of things," Kip said to her. "Taking me for a fool hasn't been one of them till now."

"The condo in Bell Town would be difficult and I'm honest enough to say Lake Home would present problems. Max's is perfect. It was designed for handicapped use."

"Forget it," Kip said. "My daughter will be going home with me. If you want to be with her, you'll come too, Carolee."

Max put his hands in his pockets. "I don't completely blame you, Burns. And I don't know what I'd do in your position—probably fight just the way you are. But consider doing this for your daughter. Everyone will be welcome there. It'll be a way for her family to care for her."

"Give it up," Kip said.

Carolee stood close to him. The corner of her right eye twitched uncontrollably. "That's it," she said. "I'm seeking legal counsel, Kip. Do what you like—you can't hurt me anymore. A court's going to find out how you've damaged Faith and victimized me. You'll lose primary custody all by yourself."

Kip pummeled the wall with a fist. He bared his teeth and put his face near Carolee's. "Dream on. It'll never work. I've got too much on you." He looked at Max. "On both of you." He slammed back into Faith's room.

"You're right and he's wrong," Max said softly. "You're doing the right thing. You'll win."

He was behind her when she entered Faith's room.

Kip's smile turned Carolee's stomach. "Okay," he said. "Why not have Faith go to your place, Wolfe? Since Carolee's obviously already accepted, it's up to me to support her decision. When she's there with Faith, I'll be visiting, too. Should be cozy."

"No!" Faith's distorted voice shocked them all to silence. "You don't want me. None of you want me. And I don't want you."

Thirty-three

She shouldn't have made everyone madder than they were before. Even though she'd closed her eyes again—tightly—they'd kept on talking to her because they knew what she was doing. Well, Mom hadn't got mad, only real quiet, and Max kept asking Daddy to put Faith first, but he and Daddy shouted at each other. They'd gone outside again, but she could still hear their voices.

When they came back in, they got quiet

again. Daddy had told Mom and Max that he wanted to stay with her on his own and they'd finally left. They didn't want to, Faith could hear how sad they were to go, but Mom said it was best for now.

It had been a long time since then and Daddy hadn't said anything. Sometimes he wouldn't speak when he was mad.

He whistled and she jumped.

He hummed and his shoes clipped on the floor. Her bed moved like he'd leaned on it and her leg in traction hurt, then he walked away again.

Faith made fists inside the bed. She held Digger's rocks in her left hand.

Someone came in. "Hi, Mr. Burns. You pressed the call button?"

"Yes," Daddy said. "Faith could probably have pressed it herself, but she's playing games with us, aren't you, Faith?"

"Are you all right, Mr. Burns?" the nurse asked. It was Sara, the really nice one. "You look tired. Why not stretch—"

"I'm not tired, I'm angry. Kindly don't tell me what to do."

"I didn't, sir." Some of the gentleness was gone. "I started to make a suggestion."

"Say something, Faith," Daddy said. His voice scared her. It was the loud one that shook a bit. "I told you to say something."

"I'll have to call someone else, sir. We can't have you—"

"Faith. You heard what I said. Look at the nurse. *Now.*"

She felt dizzy, but she opened her eyes.

Sara smiled at her—a bit sadly, Faith thought.

"There," Daddy said. "All this time she's been pretending she was out of it, just to make us all suffer. She can start rehab now, can't she? We could get going right here for a few days—before she leaves the hospital. Money's no problem."

"That's something you'll have to discuss with the business office. I'm sure she can start therapy. If she hadn't been... If she hadn't been so confused, she would already have started."

Faith squirmed. Daddy liked to tell people he had lots of money. This time he wanted to use it to make sure she didn't go to Max's.

"Hello, Faith," Sara said. "It's okay, honey. Please don't be worried. You must be so tired. You probably need some good sleep. We were pretty sure you needed quiet time to think about what's been going on for you. Dr. Reilly said you'd join in again when you were ready. The doctors know you were running away when you had your accident."

"She wasn't running away."

"I'm only repeating what's in your daughter's chart. I'm going to have a doctor look at her now. I expect he'll want to talk to you—and Mrs. Burns. I'll call her."

"You *won't* call Mrs. Burns. Faith is *my*—" He looked really funny again. "Of course, you're right. Forgive me. This has been a terrible ordeal."

Sara went away. She'd be calling Mom and asking her to come.

"How long has your mother been seeing Max Wolfe?"

"I don't know."

"Maybe a long time?"

"I don't know."

"You've got to know something. Wise up, Faith. Are they tight? You know what I mean—close?"

What should she say? "I think they like each other a lot. Max is nice and he makes Mom laugh sometimes. She didn't used to laugh—not for ages. And she plays the piano more, and sings. That's because he likes to listen to her, I think."

Daddy crossed his arms and his knuckles were white. "That's nice," he said at last. "I want to see your mom happy. I thought that could be with me, but maybe I was wrong. Wouldn't you like your mom and dad back together again?"

The room was too cold. Faith shivered. What did Daddy want her to say?

"You don't need to answer that," he told her. "I guess it would probably be a good thing if your mom married Wolfe. How about you? Have they talked about it?"

She relaxed a little. "I think they're, you know—they're in love. So does Gramps. He said not to say anything to Mom until she shared it first, but he's sure they'll get married."

Dad stood up and turned his back on her. He raised his shoulders.

She'd said the wrong thing. Why couldn't she ever get anything right?

Faith looked at the telephone beside her bed and wondered if it worked. If she could call Max, he'd know what to do. *Please, if Mom comes, don't let them argue anymore.*

Thirty-four

Ignoring Sam's complaints, Carolee tucked a blanket around his legs. The evenings weren't so warm anymore, and anyway, she wanted to coddle him.

"I had a talk with Linda this afternoon," he said. "She came over while you were with Faith."

Almost a week had passed since Faith gave herself away. She'd started therapy the next day but wasn't doing well. Kip was with her almost every moment. He urged her on, he lost his temper, he apologized and hugged her. And he was so nice to Carolee that he made her nervous. He even went so far as to tell her he realized she'd been right to allow Dr. Reilly, the psychiatrist, to see Faith.

"Don't let me forget to tell you about Kip and Digger."

"What about 'em?"

"You first."

Sam wagged an arthritic finger at her. "I've

got to be humored, remember. What about Kip and Digger?"

"Kip came over and got him this morning. He had permission to take him into the physical therapy department at the hospital because he thought he would help Faith, improve her mood. Shocked me. And Faith asked me to take Digger home with me when I left. I'm sure she doesn't trust Kip with him."

"That's my girl. No flies on that one."

"She's not improving the way she should, Sam. Today they said she eats almost nothing and won't read or watch TV. Just lies there and stares—and falls asleep."

Sam spread his hands on thin thighs. "We gotta do something. I know what she wants and she doesn't think there's a way to get it. So she's punishing herself."

"Why would she punish herself?"

"You're the newfangled generation, daughter. You're supposed to know about these things. She thinks it's all her fault."

Carolee sat down hard beside Sam. "I know that with my head but my heart doesn't want to admit it."

"We'll work it all out. One good wedding would work wonders."

She shook her head and looked into the woodstove.

"We'll leave it for now," Sam told her. "But I believe in intuition, and intuition tells me Faith's gonna get what she wants."

Sam was a dreamer. That wasn't news.

This time Carolee wanted the dream as much as he did but wasn't sure it would be fair to go after it.

"Like I said, I talked to Linda."

Carolee shifted gears. "Where did she go? I haven't seen her here in days?"

"With Ted," Sam said, and their eyes met. There was no need to say that was an off-limits topic. "I thought she might get angry but she did pretty well."

Carolee raised her brows inquiringly.

"Did you think I'd forget what Kip Burns said about your mother the other night? You slapped the man's face when I've never seen any violence in you before. You hit him because he insulted your mother.

"I'm gonna tell you what I told Linda. And I know what you went through as a kid. I'm sorry for that, Carolee. I wish I'd known at the time.

"This is damn dashed hard. Linda's mother, my first wife, had an illness. It was mental and there wasn't the help we've got around now. She had to be in a sanitarium because she was dangerous to herself. They gave her so much of that electric treatment, and drugs to keep her quiet, she didn't recognize me at all in the end."

"Sam," Carolee said, putting an arm around her shoulders. "You don't have to get into all this again."

"Yes, I do. I married Ella while I was still married to my first wife."

At first Carolee didn't get the impact of what he'd told her. Then she said, "So, you were never really married to my mother?"

"Yes, I was—just not legally until Ava died. But she'd get really bad and I'd go to her. I couldn't do anything, but I thought I had to give her that much. It wasn't her fault she was ill.

"Ella and I—well, we decided it was best if I didn't constantly run in and out of your lives—you and Linda. So rather than a couple of days at home, then leave again for a week, and a couple more days here, I stayed away till each crisis passed."

"I understand," Carolee told him, not really understanding at all.

"I doubt you do. We did the best we could with what we knew about raising kids. But your mom and I couldn't bear being separated." He turned so red, Carolee felt his forehead.

"Nothing wrong with me but embarrassment. How do you tell a daughter you were so crazy in love with her mother you sneaked back to...well, to be with her, then left again before your kids could know about it. Lookin' back now, we must have been mad, but we just didn't put our minds inside our girls' heads."

Carolee was in danger of laughing and crying at the same time. She hugged Sam. "You devil. And Mom. You couldn't leave each other alone."

Sam started to chuckle, but cleared his throat and sniffed. "That's no way to talk about your parents. A little respect would be nice."

"So Linda was serious and respectful?"

"She didn't take it as well as you are. But she had to find out the truth about her mother and the way she died. Stored up pills in a bag under the mattress and when she thought she had enough—well, she took the lot. Didn't die right then, but they lost her after a few days. Poor Ava. She was full of life when I met her. And she was beautiful. That's where Linda's looks come from."

The striped bathrobe, the nightgown, her mother's laughter by the light of a fire wove their way through Carolee's mind. She looked around and thought how ironic it was that Sam was telling her his story in this very room.

"Sam, I'm so glad you told me all that. I'm sad for Ava, too, but I'm glad there was a happy ending for you and Mom."

He sniffed again. "I wouldn't call it exactly happy. We loved a lot, but we fought a lot, too. It's a good thing the lovin' made up for the fightin'. I think I'd like some water."

Carolee got up. "I talked to a lawyer," she said.

Sam sat forward.

"I've retained him. It's time to fight."

"Hot damn," Sam said, grinning. "Finally. That's my girl. We're all behind you."

She brought him the water and said, "I know."

"That phone of yours," Sam said, as if she couldn't hear it ringing in her pocket. "Could be the hospital," he added, which was always the first thing she thought of.

She answered and a muffled male voice said. "Mrs. Burns?"

"Yes."

"Are you alone?"

Carolee felt a sickening thud in her chest. She wetted her lips. "No. Who—"

"*Don't* ask any questions. You're with Sam?"

He used her father's first name. "That's right."

The caller cleared his throat. "This is very serious, Carolee. How serious it gets for Faith depends on you. Her future is in your hands. I've got her with me, and I'm watching you. Start being an actress. I'm just a friend and you're glad to hear from me. Got it?"

"K—" She barely stopped herself from saying his name.

"Good catch," Kip said. He didn't sound mad, just flat and intense. "Hi, Kathleen will do fine. Say it for Faith. *Now.*"

She jumped, glanced at Sam, who was frowning, and said, "Hi, Kathleen." Smiling wasn't easy, but she managed it and saw Sam relax.

"Very nice," Kip said. "You need to go to your place. Tell Sam I'm a friend from your touring days. I'm looking for a piece of music I remember you playing but I don't remember the title. Maybe if you look through the pieces you played in Chicago two years ago, you'll find it for me."

She could scarcely breathe, not at all if she closed her mouth. "Oh, no trouble. I'll go take a look."

"Take your phone with you. Don't turn it off."

"Of course it's no bother," she said. "I'll run over right now."

Sliding the phone into her pocket, being careful not to switch it off, she said to Sam, "That was a friend of mine. Or I should say an acquaintance I really like. Kathleen. I'm going over to my place to look for a piece of music she hasn't been able to locate anywhere, mostly because she can't remember the title. I think I can find it."

"Right now?" Sam frowned. "We got stuff to talk about."

"We'll talk, but you know how musicians are." She chuckled. "They get a tune on their minds and can't rest until they get to play around with it. I want you to keep on taking it easy, Sam. I'll be back later."

She ignored his disgruntled expression and left the cabin. Digger waited on the step, his body in the droopy mode that didn't leave him much anymore. The light had faded and her depth perception didn't immediately adjust. She stumbled several times on her way to the trees and knew it was because she was frightened. The motives for Kip's behavior were a mystery, but he wasn't planning anything she expected to enjoy.

With Digger loping at her side, she reached the trees and became aware of sounds coming from her pocket. Kip was talking. It amazed her that she'd all but forgotten he was communicating with her—and that she'd just about managed to convince herself there really was a Kathleen.

The instant she put the phone to her ear, Kip must have heard her breathing. "Stand still," he snapped. "You're panting. Get your act together or you'll do something we'll all be sorry about."

"Kip." She backed against a fir tree with rough bark that plucked at her sweater.

"I couldn't hear what you said to the old man."

"What you told me to say," she whispered.

"Did he buy it?"

"He didn't like it, but he accepted it."

"Start walking again," Kip said. She heard him cover the mouthpiece at his end. He must be talking to someone and he didn't want Carolee to overhear.

He'd said Faith was with him, but she couldn't be. She was at the hospital.

"You there." He didn't wait for her to answer. "I checked Faith out of the hospital a few hours ago. I told them it was time for her to go home where she could start getting back to normal."

"And they just let you do that?" She was so angry and scared that blood pounded at her temples. "I don't believe you. I'm calling them now. Good-bye, Kip."

"You want to talk to her?"

With sweaty hands she pressed the phone against her ear. "Yes."

"Faith," Kip called on his end. "Tell your mother hi."

When Faith said, "Hi, Mommy," her voice was high and uneven.

"Satisfied?" Kip said. "Are you at your place yet?"

"No," she muttered, straightening away from the tree and starting to walk. "What are you doing? Faith wasn't ready to leave the hospital. They wanted to stabilize her food intake and get her rehab going better."

"I convinced them I'd make sure she kept regular appointments. This is all your fault!" His shouting shook Carolee to her toes. "You threatened me and you wouldn't do what I told you to do, so I had to take steps to make sure you started obeying me. Wives are supposed to obey their husbands."

"You're not my husband," Carolee said. Each footfall jarred her voice.

"That's for me to decide. It's over when I say so."

Desperation, that's what she heard now—and agitation. "You already said so," Carolee told him. "You divorced me."

"And I changed my mind, you stupid bitch," he yelled.

Faith was hearing all this, just as she'd heard so much that wasn't suitable for a little girl. Digger took the lead and Carolee ran, smacking into branches, stumbling on rocks, dragging in breaths that made her throat raw, she ran. The phone hung at her side and she held her other arm before her face. When twigs snagged her hair, she ducked her head and rushed on—and didn't stop until she'd staggered onto the porch at Lake Home and burst into the kitchen.

Sobbing, her legs leaden, she made it to the table and sank into a chair.

"Carolee? Carolee?" Kip's voice came to her from a great distance. "Carolee?"

She looked at her watch. Almost ten. She set the phone on the table and stared at it.

Kip had stopped calling her name.

Carolee panicked and snatched up the phone. "I hate you, Kip Burns. I don't want any part of you. I'm going to call the police and tell them what you've done."

"What have I done?" The softness was worse than his shouting.

"You took a sick girl out of the hospital and now you're threatening to hurt her."

"Oh, no, I'm not," he told her. "I removed my daughter from the hospital—with permission. You're hysterical and making things up. Your mind is going—again. You were always slightly unbalanced. Look at the state you're in. Look at yourself. You look disgusting. Wipe your face."

She pulled Kleenex from a box and rubbed them across her eyes—and screamed, *"Where are you?"* On her feet again, she stared at the windows. The house was silent. If he'd been inside, she'd have heard something, or felt something—which meant he was outside, watching from some hiding place.

"You should have kept to yourself," Kip said. "Women don't have the same needs as men, not nice women. You should have stayed alone."

"Just stayed alone," she said, "just kept myself available for you to torture." He wasn't out there. Even in the dark that would be too much of a risk.

"If you know what's good for you, you'll stop baiting me." A dreaminess entered his words and that was the most frightening thing she'd heard yet. "He's never going to have you, Carolee. Not Max Wolfe, not any man who would interfere with us. He's a gold digger. If you didn't have money, and if he didn't want control over that money, he'd never look at you."

"If you say so." She would outwit him. "I want to see Faith."

"You will. When I'm ready. Call Sam and tell him you're tired. You're going to bed early and you'll see him tomorrow. Only you won't see him because there are things you have to do before you meet me—and Faith."

"I can't do that to Sam. He'd worry."

"Do it. He won't worry, he'll sulk because he's not getting his own way. Then he'll get over it and go to bed."

She wanted Max.

On the brass hooks near the door hung two Stetsons, one black and one brown. She had joked with him once that she'd soon have to install more hooks for the hats he forgot.

Max.

This was something—the most important something she'd ever confronted—that she'd have to do alone.

"Be reasonable," Kip said. "You used to love

me. You'll love me again. I want you away from this place—it's no good for you. Too many distractions. You're being misled. You're not yourself anymore. Don't worry about another thing, sweetheart. Everything will be taken care of and we'll put this bad time behind us. Trust me and I'll take care of you."

Kip would never harm Faith.

Carolee took a calming breath. "Faith needs to be where she can have professional care at a moment's notice. Please take her back to the hospital. I'll meet you there."

He was quiet for too long.

"Kip?"

"I'm trying to be patient with you. Faith's going to be great now she's back with family. She already looks better. Now, go and pack all of her things. And your own. Call Sam and say you're tired. You're going to bed. Tomorrow there'll be another call to make to him."

"He needs me," she said, panic mounting. She blinked and sweat burned her eyes.

"Shut up and listen. You're going to write a note saying you and Faith are going away for a rest and you'll be in touch. Say you want everyone to respect your need for peace."

How did she know if she should call the police? If she did, and Kip did something dreadful, she'd know the decision had been wrong. Oh, God, let her know what to do.

"Go pack now. Leave the phone on and let me know—"

"Give me your number and I'll call you when I'm finished." She held her breath.

"You'd like that, wouldn't you?" His snort turned her stomach. "I don't suppose you'd call the cops and give them that number, huh? Don't make a move like that. Don't ever do it. I'm not wasting time spelling it all out. You know what would happen, and it would be all your fault. Pack and tell me when you're done. I'll help with the note. Then we wait for morning. I'm not sure of the exact time."

"Please don't do this."

He didn't respond.

"Kip?"

"You don't have any wriggle room, baby. Get packed. Take anything you're ever likely to want again. You won't be going back. Bring the dog." He hesitated. "Faith misses it."

She climbed the stairs, and went into Faith's room. Digger had beaten her there and stretched himself out on the bed. Carolee began pushing things into a suitcase, but had to stop. She sat down and buried her head in her hands.

Half an hour later she was downstairs again. Reluctantly she put the phone to her ear and said, "Kip?"

"All packed?"

"Yes. Why can't I just come and see Faith now?"

"I know you'll feel better if you get some rest. Call Sam."

As if she could rest.

"No. I'm not upsetting Sam."

"Don't argue with me, dammit. Be quick."

Sam would be best kept out of all this. His health wouldn't take another shake-up. She picked up the kitchen phone and dialed. Sounding cranky, Sam answered at once. "Taking your sweet time, aren't you. You said you'd be right back."

Gently, she told him she was very tired and had decided to go to bed. He didn't argue or complain and she hung up before returning to the cell phone.

"Good," Kip said. "Now the note."

"I can write my own note, thanks."

"Don't write a word I don't tell you to write."

Why argue?

"This is going to be real short and sweet. Got a paper and pen?"

"Yes," she muttered, pulling out a pad and a ballpoint from a drawer in the table.

"Dear Sam," he began. "I'm having a really hard time with everything and I need a break to get my head together. Don't try to find me. I won't thank you if you do."

Carolee wrote, and with each word her mouth grew drier and she felt more terrified for Faith. She'd bet everything she had that this was a setup, but she would have to go along with it.

"Got that?" Kip said and continued immediately. "Faith and I need to get away. I've spoken with Kip and he doesn't like it, but he's agreed because then we may all have a chance together. Please, for Max's sake and mine, keep him out of it. Sam, I'll never forgive you if you contact him—or anyone else. I'll call you soon."

Thirty-five

Max made it inside from the terrace in time to snatch up the phone on its fourth ring. "Yeah?" He'd been sitting out there in the dark, thinking about what he always thought about these days: Carolee.

A gruff voice said, "Getz here."

Max drew a blank. "If this is the latest in solicitation calls, it's a dud."

"You Max Wolfe?"

He prepared to hang up.

"A friend of Carolee Burns?"

Max was listening. "Yes."

"This is Leo Getz. I'm her manager. She's told me about you."

He felt insanely happy and foolish at the same time. "She's mentioned you, too. How did you get my number?"

"You're listed."

This time Max only felt foolish. "Oh, yeah."

"She with you?"

Mr. Getz wouldn't win any charm contests. "No, she's not," Max told him. He hadn't seen her since they'd had coffee at Nellie and Fritz's on Saturday. Last night she'd planned to be with Sam, and when Max

401

had called her this morning, she'd been in a hurry and told him she'd be busy all day.

Getz's breathing was loud and slow.

"Something on your mind?" Max asked.

"You know where she is?"

It was getting late. This call was starting to unnerve him. "I talked to her this morning. She said she had a busy day planned. I was going to call her at home shortly. I'll tell her you're trying to get in touch with her if you like."

"She's not there. I spoke to Sam. He said she called this morning and reckoned she was going away for a couple of days. He thought she'd be with you."

Max stared at his own reflection in the sliding doors to the terrace. Carolee had said she was going away for a couple of days? He felt very cold. "Did Sam sound worried?"

"Nah. Whatever she said, he bought it."

This guy was a stranger. What proof was there that he was Leo Getz?

"I'm not sure how much I should say to you," the man said. "I'm worried about her and she talks about you as if you're close. Are you?"

Carolee had said Getz was a New Yorker. The voice fitted, and he'd used Sam's name as well. "I hope so." He'd have to take a chance. "What are you thinking?"

"That ex-husband of hers called early this afternoon. What he said didn't sit right all day. I decided to check things out with Carolee." He made a sound as if he were whistling through his teeth. "Her kid's sick in the hospital and she's taken off—and the people who should know where she is, don't? Shee-it, I bet Burns pushed her on the old contracts and she can't take it anymore."

"I don't know about old contracts," Max said.

"Kip Burns has been trying to persuade me to get Carolee's career back on track. I made the mistake of calling her a couple of times, then I got the message she wished I wouldn't, so I stopped. But he's pushing again. You know there's a trust for Faith?"

"It's been mentioned."

"Burns reckons Carolee isn't adding to it like she used to. Inflation has to be considered, blah, blah."

Max's chest was too tight. "What did he want you to do?"

"There are some old contracts that are up for renewal. The residuals from them are earmarked for Faith. Burns wants me to make sure Carolee gets 'em signed quickly. I'm supposed to stay on the recording companies for the money and make sure Carolee understands how urgent it is to get it deposited. Burns reckons he's really worried that Faith's trust isn't keeping up with the times."

"But you haven't been able to talk to her about this?"

"No," Getz said. "Kip said he'd have her call me tomorrow. The guy doesn't get it that some things take time."

"I guess not. Look, Leo, would you do me a favor and call if you talk to Carolee?"

Leo assured him he would but gave the

impression he really didn't expect to hear from her. The conversation ended with Leo saying, "I don't think it would be such a good idea for her to know I've been calling around—checking up on her," and Max agreeing.

Kip was going to have Carolee call Leo tomorrow? Or so he said. Did that mean she was with him? She couldn't be, not willingly.

Okay, he couldn't stand around and do nothing.

There was nothing he could say to the police—yet.

A key turned in Max's front door and someone with a light step walked onto the wooden floors. Other than himself, only one person had a key to the condo and she had tried to refuse it since, in her own words, "I'd never use it."

"Carolee?" Max called and strode into the hall. Showing he'd been close to panic wouldn't be a good idea, but he felt euphoric with relief.

"Max," she said, slipping off her shoes and walking into his arms.

His heart made the kind of turn he didn't remember even from his teenage years. "I was just going to try calling you." He'd never make an actor.

If Carolee noticed the hoarseness in his voice, she didn't mention it. She held him tightly and didn't feel too steady. He kissed the top of her head and she stepped away from him. A black suit and white silk blouse looked great on her, great and businesslike.

Carolee herself didn't look so great.

"Come and sit down," he told her. "It's late, you look tired. When did you eat? Did you have dinner? Can I make you some coffee—or would you like a drink?"

She didn't look at him, but took off her suit jacket and draped it over her folded arms. "Nothing, thanks."

Max felt fear, deep, formless fear. Carolee was different. "I'm glad you're here," he said quietly. He must not hover, must not push. Everything about her warned him to wait and let her make the moves—or no moves.

"This has been a hell of a day, Max." She shook her head and, with her eyes still downcast, offered a phony little smile.

"I wish I could have been with you." And he would have if she hadn't put him off when he'd phoned her first thing in the morning. "I was at the office all day but now I can't remember what I did."

"You wouldn't believe how many times I thought about you today."

Certainty swept through him with the force of an electric shock: He would never give up on having Carolee in his life—forever. But close on the heels of the good feeling rolled another premonition; she was distracted and she was saying much less than she was thinking. He pulled one of her hands free and took her into the sitting room. She dropped her jacket and purse and sat down with her head bowed.

Paolo arrived, jumped on the couch, and stretched his long, red body. He put his paws on Carolee's shoulder and stared at her until she looked back. Slowly, he withdrew to sit on the arm of the couch. Along his spine, his fur stood on end. Max sat on an ottoman. He was out of his depth.

"I can't stay," she said, and looked at her watch.

"Wherever you're going, I want to come with you."

She sighed and rested her head back.

Max got up and sat beside her on the couch. "There's nothing wrong with Faith, is there?"

Carolee looked at him and the sadness in her eyes took his breath away. "Faith will be okay. I'm going to make sure of that."

"I love that child." How easily the words came.

Sliding sideways, Carolee closed her eyes and nestled against Max's shoulder. "Faith's fallen for you, too. I've seen the way she looks at you. You're her knight in shining armor."

"Suits me," he said, resting a hand on her cheek. "She's my hero, too."

"Today I went to examine Faith's trust fund."

He looked at her until she opened her eyes. "How come you did that?" he asked. There might be no choice but to mention Leo Getz's call.

"Because I had some thoughts about the way Kip's behaved. I've known he didn't really want me back so there had to be a reason for him to keep pushing me to marry him again. I thought it was probably jealousy—hate even. He didn't want me, but he didn't want anyone else to have me.

"This isn't what I came to say to you, to ask you." She touched his jaw lightly and there was no missing the welling tears. "I've tried to convince myself I shouldn't involve you anymore."

That was it. "Something's really gone wrong." He pulled her into his arms. "You're shaking. My God, Carolee, don't do this to either of us. Tell me what's going on so I can do something about it."

She shook her head and settled her face against his chest at the open neck of his shirt. "I want you to know what I've found out." She raised her wrist until she could check her watch again. "And I need your help."

Max held her tightly. "I'll do whatever you want me to do. I will not sit back and watch you suffer, though. If there's something I need to be doing, don't shut me out."

"It's corny, but I love you for loving me. It still amazes me."

He kissed her forehead.

"Kip's been afraid I'll marry again," she said. "It panicked him. That's the way it's looked to me. Then there was the way he was after Faith's accident. Of course he was shattered, but there was something else, a kind of desperation that didn't quite fit with anything normal. He seemed angry with her all the time. So I had to try to find out if my hunch about him was right."

"It's all about money, isn't it?" Max said. She sat up. "What makes you say that?"

"A lot of things. The stuff you're talking about, but also I took at look at the boat you said had been through five owners and wasn't that big. Well, I may not know what *that* big is, but his is a huge hummer. I know people who are into art and I asked questions. Kip is hosting big gallery parties on the boat. It's all rigged out inside for just that purpose, and aimed at getting people comfortable enough to spend money like water. It hasn't caught on so far. There have been comments about not liking to feel trapped. I've heard more than a few good comments about Kip's own work, but his paintings aren't selling because he's been around for some time without catching on, and his prices are out of sight. There's also talk about his stuff being too much like a number of other people."

"He started out with a lot of talent," Carolee said. "Discipline was what he lacked. Max, there have been large withdrawals from Faith's trust fund. Max has the right to take out money for Faith's needs, but these are so large. He's run through a big chunk of it."

No wonder the guy was pushing Getz to channel more money into the fund, and fast. Max held one of Carolee's hands on her thigh. "Didn't he know you could find this out?"

She bowed and shook her head. "He knew, but he never thought I would. I think he's afraid of getting caught now. At the beginning I told him the fund was all in his control but that

I'd add to it regularly. If I had another man in my life, that might change, mightn't it?"

"I guess."

"Of course it would. Another man would want to make sure all my finances were in order."

"I wouldn't unless you asked my opinion. It wouldn't be my business."

Carolee threaded their fingers tightly together. "But Kip wouldn't even be able to imagine a man being like that, so he's assumed you'd be the same as him."

Max noted how "a man" had become him specifically. "This isn't pleasant, sweetheart, but if Faith died, the trust would be over too, wouldn't it?"

She whispered, "Yes."

"So he's been hovering over her and getting angry because she hasn't improved fast enough." He shouldn't have said that. "Or that could be a possibility."

"I wish I wasn't sure that's exactly what was going on. Not that it makes much difference."

"The hell it doesn't." Max stood up and pulled her to her feet. "You can't let him rob your daughter."

"He could be prosecuted, couldn't he?" she said, absently rubbing his arm.

Max nodded. "I assume so."

"Once I'd made up my mind I'd be a fool to go on without you, I came here as if I were coming home."

"Wherever I am is your home—if you'll take it."

She held his hand and took another look at her watch.

"You're watching the clock, sweetheart. Tell me what's going on."

A cell phone rang in her purse and she sat down to answer it. She emptied her bag with a kind of frantic anxiety that turned Max's stomach. He could see her hands tremble.

She grabbed up her phone and answered, "Yes."

While he watched, her face grew paler. Frequently, she passed her tongue over her lips. "Yes," she said again. "I've got everything you wanted. I told him nothing. His heart's too bad to take the shock. No, I've written it all down. I'll write it again. Yes." Scrambling, she pulled out a pen and a thin pad of yellow sticky notes and flipped up the top page. "I'm listening. Yes, yes, I've got it. I'll be on time." She continued to hold the phone to her ear, then slowly took it away and switched it off.

Max stood in front of her. "Who was that?"

She started. "Kip."

"He terrified you."

"Would you help me no matter how dangerous it might be?"

"My God, yes."

She turned her head away, then looked sideways at him. "It has to be done my way, Max."

"What the hell does that mean?" He stood close to her.

"That if you can't agree to my rules, I'll have to do this alone. I think my chances of dealing with Kip and not getting myself into big trouble are shaky—if I try to do it without you. But Faith's in the middle, Max. He's discharged her from the hospital. He more or less threatened that she'd suffer if I don't do exactly what he tells me. When I show up at the airport to meet him, you can't be with me. Not where he can see you."

Max moved his mouth but the words wouldn't come. Instead he sat on the arm of the couch. He couldn't do what she asked. Thinking of letting her go to Kip Burns alone when the man was threatening her and using their daughter as bait started the kind of rage Max knew could be dangerous.

"I don't have any more time," she told him. "I have to get to SeaTac."

"I'll drive."

"He's going to be out there with Faith, and waiting for me to go away with them. That's what he says, but he wanted things done that made me think... He doesn't want me, Max."

"Come on." He pulled her up. "My car's in the garage."

"We'll drive separately."

"*No.*"

"Don't argue. I can't be with you. Do you understand? I'll be there and you'll be there, but not together. And if I don't call your name, you'll know I don't want your help."

He didn't know how he said, "If that's what you want, of course."

"Max." She studied his face. "You won't do anything unless I call you, will you?"

He folded his hands into fists. He needed to hold her. "I love you," he told her. "The police should—"

"No! Not until Faith's safe."

"Are you armed?"

"I'm not good with guns. I won't risk hurting the wrong person."

Or having Kip use the gun on her. He had to agree to her terms. "Okay, we'll do it your way," he told her.

Drawing his face down to hers, she kissed him hard and fast, and broke away. "I've got to go. Main Terminal. This is the information." She tore off one of the yellow notes and crammed it into his hand. "Park on the fourth floor. Give me five minutes start, then follow. Please, Max, keep out of sight when you get there. I don't think you'll have any difficulty keeping up with whatever goes on. He chose a public place. It's probably going to be fine, but in the end I couldn't risk going alone."

With her coat and purse bundled in her arms, she hurried to put on her shoes and open the door.

"Wait, I can't let you go," he said. But he looked at her and knew he wasn't helping. "Okay, okay. Five minutes and I'm behind you."

Thirty-six

Even at 11:15 P.M., traffic on I-405 South was heavy. Fine rain fell steadily onto oil-slicked roads and looming trucks sprayed filthy water behind them, turning taillights into hazy orange and pink globes.

Max's windshield wipers were on full. He drove too fast and would have driven faster if there'd been fewer vehicles in his way.

He looked repeatedly at the clock. He was more than five minutes behind Carolee.

Kip Burns was insane. Insane people were unpredictable. After briefly considering asking Rob Mead to come as back up, Max had decided Rob was too easily spotted, not that hiding would be easy for Max.

A 11:52 P.M. flight from Gate A6.

Burns was drawing Carolee and Faith into a net. Once he got them away from any support, he could decide to do anything. Max had started praying Carolee wouldn't do anything heroic. "Do what the man says, sweetheart. Leave the rest to me." *Just stay alive and safe, my love.*

Carolee drove rapidly up the ramps in SeaTac's multistory car park. She knew what she had to do. With Max backing her up, she felt a hope that hadn't been there since last night.

She reached the fourth level and took the Mercedes up one line and down the next, looking for a parking spot. "Somewhere anonymous," Kip had said. "At least where the lights aren't too bright. We don't want someone finding your car too quickly." They were flying out at 11:52. She didn't even know where he was taking them.

She was to park, then walk to the far end of the floor, to a construction area, and keep out of sight until she saw Kip arrive.

The airport was quiet. Usually was at this time of night. Max knew he looked wild. He drew stares from what reservation clerks were on duty. "To hell with you," he muttered, striding toward the "A" concourse and cursing when he went through Security and set off alarms. Back and forth through sensors they sent him while he emptied pockets, took off his watch and belt, and checked for metal caps on his heels. With his heart jammering in his throat, he stood still for the wand to be passed over him, and wasn't interested in making any of the jokes signs warned him not to make.

At Gate A6 a bored-looking group of passengers waited in the departure area. A look at the board over the desk announced a flight leaving for Minneapolis at 11:48. Nothing showed for 11:52. So Carolee had got the time a bit off—it was close enough. He scanned the area but saw no sign of her, or of Faith or

Kip. Minneapolis didn't mean a thing. They could go anywhere in the world from there.

The announcement came that general boarding would begin shortly. That meant first-class, frequent flyers, and people who needed assistance were already aboard.

Max paced until he remembered he shouldn't be in the open. He was some PI in the making. While he waited behind a bank of telephones, boarding continued.

Five more minutes and the plane was due to leave.

Under bright lights, passengers shuffled toward the jetway. Tired faces assumed resigned patience.

People who needed assistance! Damn it all, what was with him?

"Sir," he said, racing up to an agent who was holding his temper with a guy who wanted an upgrade to first class. "Sir," Max repeated. "I'm looking for someone."

The agent glanced at him and smiled. Max admired his patience.

"My wife and daughter—and my brother—are on this flight. My daughter left her passport behind and she's going to need it later."

"Just a moment, please, sir," the agent said and returned to explaining that there were no seats open in first class.

"My daughter's been ill," Max said. "She walks with crutches but was probably in a wheelchair when she boarded."

"A moment, sir."

Departure time had arrived.

"What's the frigging point of all these frequent flyer miles if I can't upgrade when I want to?" the passenger beside Max said. "I was told I'd get into first class."

"There aren't any seats."

"Maybe you could sit on someone's lap," Max suggested, showing teeth to the passenger. "Or maybe you could get another passenger to..." He stopped himself and mumbled an apology.

The guy walked away to the boarding gate, sending hard stares back in Max's direction.

"That worked," the agent said. "Thanks. Now, you were asking about your daughter."

Max patted his pants pocket. "I've got to get her passport to her."

"Crutches or wheelchair?" the agent said.

Time hung suspended within Max, but moved like dust in a wind tunnel all around him. "Yes. Faith. Faith Burns. With Carolee Burns and Kip Burns—he's my brother."

"So you said."

Max would happily throw up, or pass out, or do anything that would get some attention.

"No Burns on the list," the agent said, checking his computer, and a hard copy on the counter. "And no one needing any assistance."

"You missed them," Max said, sidestepping away. "Let me check the plane."

"That's not possible."

Of course it wasn't. "Okay, *you* check the plane. Have *someone* check the plane. Please. I'm begging you."

That earned him a speculative glance, but the man called to a woman and sent her to the plane with instructions to check for the passengers Max insisted were there.

If Kip's Porsche was anywhere around, Carolee didn't see it. Where was he—and Faith? A few cars wound up and down the spiraling ramps. Some got off on the fourth floor, others carried on. The flight must be boarding by now. One of the cars that had come onto the floor must have been Max's. He would have gone directly into the airport.

Her heart pounded. She'd done as she was told and parked as out of the way as possible. The construction area Kip told her about was walled off from the rest of the floor with concrete dividers. In the dim light wires and ropes trailed from the ceiling and snaked over the floor. Muddy water dripped steadily down the inside of tarpaulins draped from overhead beams.

The headlights of a car bounced over a speed bump and came toward her.

Carolee backed up, turning her head to shade her eyes from the glare. The vehicle came to a stop and the lights went out.

A silver Porsche.

The driver's door opened, a man got out, and the door slammed shut. The thunk reverberating amid concrete pillars.

Kip's tall body approached, his heels clicking distinctly. He did something with his right hand

and Carolee flinched. There was a click. He'd locked the Porsche.

Stepping through a gap between two concrete retaining blocks, he reached Carolee and said, "Did you keep your head? You didn't call the cops?"

She shook her head.

"Smart girl. Don't look so scared. This is a no-brainer and we all come out of it smelling like roses."

"Where's Faith?"

His hand, landing on her shoulder, startled Carolee. "Faith's in my car—asleep," he said. "She's in great shape and looking forward to having us all together again."

She caught at the neck of her blouse. "Asleep? With all this going on?"

"A couple of pills aren't going to hurt her. You don't want her awake and frightened, do you?"

"The flight," Carolee said. "We're missing it. Fetch Faith." She wanted to see her, to make sure she was all right.

"We're not taking a flight," Kip told her. "I couldn't risk telling you everything just in case you did something stupid with the information. We're driving. In your car. You packed everything?"

Her body felt unnaturally still. "Yes." She lied. Nothing had been packed.

Max was watching the gate inside the terminal and wondering where she was. He'd have no reason to come back out here looking for her.

"Got the money from the bank? Everything I told you to get?"

She patted the shoulder bag she'd carried from her car. Rather than all but emptying her accounts as he'd instructed, she'd only made sure she had enough money for any emergency she might encounter.

"And the dog's in your car?"

"No." If he picked out her car and didn't see Digger, he'd get suspicious.

"I told you to bring the dog," he said through gritted teeth, and shook her by the shoulder. "It was important."

"Why?"

"Because I said so. Everything has to be exactly the way I planned it. You'd bring her dog because..."

He turned his face away sharply and she could see his throat moving as he swallowed, and the way the corner of his mouth turned down.

"It doesn't matter," he said. "You should never have tried to do this, Carolee. If you really loved Faith, you wouldn't even consider doing anything to me."

She gaped at him. "What are you talking about?"

"You're going to kill me and pretend it was in self-defense."

She backed away, unable to close her mouth or make her voice work. Not searching around for Max took almost more restraint than she had.

Kip followed her. "You set the whole thing up."

An engine roared onto the floor and cut out almost at once. Kip held a hand before her face and hissed, "Not a sound."

Running footsteps quickly faded.

"Kip, please listen to me," Carolee said. "I don't know what you intend to do, but we can work things out for the best. It's because of the money, isn't it? The fund? You're afraid I'll raise a fuss about you spending Faith's money. I won't. We'll deal with—"

"Shut up."

He laughed. "I knew you were figuring it out. Not that it matters anymore. You had your chances, now I've only got one left. Let's get this over with. If I didn't follow your orders tonight, you threatened to accuse me of taking Faith's money and make sure I was out of her life for good. You forced me to get her discharged from the hospital and set up this meeting. You told me we would go away together and I thought it was going to be by plane, but that was only a story. What you really intend to do is get me in your car, drive me somewhere, and kill me. You'll go sobbing to the cops that it was all an accident. Then you'll have everything you want."

"I wouldn't do any of those things. You're crazy."

"Shut your mouth." He raised a hand as if to strike her, but stopped himself.

"I couldn't kill anyone if I tried."

"Who says you're going to kill anyone?"

She cast about. If she ran, he'd still have

Faith. "You said it. I don't know what you're talking about."

"I told you a little story. It's the story I'll be telling the police about the way you set me up. Too bad I'm so much bigger and stronger than you."

"Stop it!"

"Keep your voice down. I'm only doing what you've made me do. This isn't what I want, Carolee. I love you, but you don't want me. You want to destroy me and be with another man. He probably helped you work all this out."

"Max would never—"

"That's his name, Max. Poor Max. He's not going to get what he wants after all. He's not going to get what's mine."

"Listen to me." She steeled herself and stepped closer to him. "Nothing's happened. We can go home and pretend we were never here."

"Liar," he said. "You always made the mistake of taking me for a fool. You ruined my life so I taught you a lesson, or I thought I did. You still haven't learned that I've always been smarter than you."

"Kip, I swear I mean it."

"So do I, baby. Push me. Kick me. Just don't scream till I hit you."

"Mr. Burns?" The counter agent hurried to Max. "You've made a mistake, sir. There are no groups matching your description on the

421

plane. No one's using crutches or needs wheelchair assistance."

The doors to the jetway closed and a clerk checked the combination lock.

"You're sure," Max said. He held Carolee's note in his hand. "Yes, you are, aren't you? Thank you." He turned away but couldn't decide where to go.

When he arrived at the down escalator to the garage sky bridge, he stopped and looked at the scribbled note again. Something had changed. And he had failed Carolee. Burns had pulled it off. He had her and Faith and there was no way of knowing what he intended to do next.

The parking meter didn't want the crumpled bills he took from his pocket and he resorted to a credit card. Inside he was a hollow man. He would go directly to Lake Home—to Sam, who couldn't be kept in the dark anymore, and decide how best to approach the police. And he'd pray.

He found his car, dropped into the driver's seat, and started the engine. Heading for the ramps, he rolled down his window and was aware again of how quiet it could be at the airport late at night.

"I can't hit you," Carolee told Kip.

"You managed it when I called your mother a whore."

She clutched the lapels of his leather jacket and tried to shake him. "That's a lie."

"Who cares if your mother was a whore? From what I can gather from Linda, your father was a lecher and a bigamist."

His attempt to rile her wasn't even subtle. Carolee removed her hands. "Let me go. Let me take Faith and leave. If you do, you can walk away and live a normal life. I know what you intend to do. You want to get into a struggle with me, and..." She couldn't finish.

Without warning, he gripped her by the waist and hoisted her to sit on a wall above a sheer drop. Tarpaulins flapped at her back, smattering muddy water over her hair and down her neck. Wind whined in ropes threaded through iron rings.

Carolee tried to hold on to Kip but he gripped her wrists and pushed her backward until she hung at his mercy, four stories up. She peered down and faintly made out construction vehicles parked below.

Kip released one of her wrists and she screamed.

He shook her, and she yelled, "I didn't do any of it. I didn't pack Faith's things, or mine. I didn't take the money out of the bank. I didn't write your note to my sick father. *I didn't set things up for you!*"

Kip opened his mouth wide and made a sound that was more animal than human. And he bent her farther over the void.

As Max turned down the first ramp, the headlights of his car passed along the side of a silver Porsche, a familiar silver Porsche. At the same time he picked up lights in his rearview mirror. A vehicle approached from above him.

He flipped on his emergency lights and put the heel of his hand on the horn. Not drawing attention would be his choice, but whatever it took to get him back on the fourth floor would be worth it.

Brakes screeched.

Max didn't wait to find out if the other car would stop in time. He backed up until he could swing into the garage again and immediately drove away—just in case an irate driver decided to follow him.

He stopped between two parked cars and switched off his headlights. A man's voice yelled but was quickly drowned by another engine. Within seconds the commotion was over and he sat, peering through the poor light to locate the Porsche again.

He could have imagined seeing the thing.

Turning off the interior lights, he got out of the Cadillac and left the door ajar rather than slam it. A pillar to his right afforded cover while he tried to search for the Porsche.

What he saw was Carolee's car. He ducked down and walked softly to look inside. It was empty.

Then he did see the Porsche—at a distance, alone, and close to a construction area—and set off again, swiftly and quietly, still doubled over.

A slight movement inside the car stopped him.

Step by step he drew close until he could peer into it. In the reclined passenger seat, her eyes closed, sat Faith.

The wrist Kip still held burned where his hard fingers ground into bone. A car had left the garage and there'd been some sort of altercation on the ramps. Kip had clamped a hand over Carolee's mouth until they were completely alone again.

He yanked her from the wall and she fell to the ground with his weight on top of her.

"Struggle," he ordered, his lips drawn back. "It'll still work. You still lured me out here."

Carolee struggled, and she pushed at him, drove her fingers into his face, and slapped him openhandedly.

"I always knew the cool reserve was an act," he told her. He rolled over until she was on top of him, and wrapped his legs around her to clamp her close.

She hit him. Acid flooded her mouth. Her vision blurred, and she used both of her fists on his face.

Kip grappled with her. Her knees scraped concrete, and the heels of her hands. Her hair stuck to her face and neck.

A hard object wrapped in cloth was pushed into her right hand. She shook her hair back to look, although she could already feel the shape of a gun. Kip covered her fingers with his and slid a piece of thin flannel away from the weapon before he made sure hers was the hand that held it.

He was going to shoot her. In self-defense.

"It's the gun I bought you when you started touring," he told her, each word a hoarse, spitting bark of triumph. "Shoot me, baby. Go on, shoot me."

While he goaded her, he pointed her hand and the gun away from him.

Carolee fought him with everything she had. He rotated them again, coming down on top of her so hard he winded her.

She bucked, and he sniggered. And he turned the gun too easily toward her neck.

Her own scream jarred her brain. Adrenalin pumped and she managed to skew the angle of the gun away.

Kip squeezed her finger on the trigger and a shot racked every nerve in her body. The noise rang in her ears.

He grinned, and raised their hands until she could see the barrel pointed at her head.

And Carolee brought up her right knee. She slammed Kip between his legs, drove him inches higher so that her face was crushed beneath his chest.

Sudden wailing terrified her. Faith? No, not Faith. The man squirming on her wailed and groaned and writhed until he fell off her.

She saw the gun on the ground and grabbed for it—and realized Kip hadn't fallen away from her. Max had lifted him by his hair and was twisting it while Kip's screams rose.

Max had a gun and he rammed the butt into

Kip's belly, and held him away when he retched.

Voices made loud, senseless sounds. The night buzzed and chattered.

Running footsteps became men in uniform, guns drawn and pointing upward, and Kip was on his knees holding his gut and crotch while Max, still tearing at the man's hair, smashed at any body part he could reach.

Thirty-seven

Tucked inside a fluffy blue bathrobe and with a towel wrapped around her hair, Faith came from her bathroom at Lake Home. She remained far too thin, but was more adept on her crutches. They'd been together at Lake Home for three weeks while the case against Kip continued to come together.

"It's starting to be winter," Carolee said, standing by the window seat and watching rusty red leaves fly out of the darkness and down past the illuminated porch. "I don't know if I've just had the longest or the shortest summer and fall in my life."

"What time's Max coming?" Faith said, sounding breathless as she did after exertion. The wires had been removed but she continued to move her jaw cautiously. Within days they would leave for Houston.

"You tell me," Carolee said, but not without an extra bump of her heart. "You're the one who went behind my back to invite him over—for dinner, no less."

"I told you I was seeing to dinner."

Carolee smiled at her defiant daughter. "You're headstrong. You know you can't cook at the moment. Even if you'd had a lot of practice throwing dinner parties, you're not strong enough to stand up for more than a few minutes at a time. Sit down now, please."

"Mom"—Faith swung herself to the window seat and pulled Carolee to sit beside her—"I need you so much and you're here for me, but I haven't been nice to you. Everything's a muddle. I get angry, then sad. Sometimes when I'm alone, I'm afraid I'll go looking and everyone will have left."

"You've been through too much, but I won't be leaving," Carolee said, with a lump in her throat. She smoothed a long, red scar on Faith's forehead. "And your Gramps would be camped out in this house if I'd let him. You have a family that loves you very much, and that includes your father."

Faith looked out at the swirling leaves caught in lighted funnels through the darkness. "I don't think Daddy can love anyone. In the paper they said he planned to kill you. I only kept quiet when he took me from the hospital because he said something awful would happen if I didn't." Her mouth quivered and she blinked rapidly. "And it was because of me. Because you worried about my future and put money for me where Dad could get into trouble for taking it for the boat. I think Daddy will go to jail—maybe for a long time."

"And we'll hope he gets treatment and becomes well again while he's there," Carolee said. "I asked you not to read any papers. There aren't any in the house. Where did you get them?"

"I'm not saying."

Carolee didn't press the question, but she had a good idea of the answer.

"You haven't seen Max for ages, Mom." Digger jumped off the bed and plopped at Faith's feet. "I miss him and I know you do, too. Whenever he comes to visit Gramps, you go out. He looks for you. I see him. And his face is so sad."

"I have seen him. Just not the way I'd like to. There's been so much to do and he's got his own life."

Faith made a growling sound and held Carolee's forearm so tightly, it pinched. "Do you know what a martyr is?"

"Ah, yes." Surely she hadn't ever asked her mother such questions.

"Well, you sound like one. I don't think you've got the guts to get married again—just in case something goes wrong. I think you're avoiding him."

"I think that's about enough, Faith," Carolee said. "You really like Max—"

"So do you."

"Don't interrupt me again. You can't make me have the feelings you have for him."

Faith unwound the towel from her hair and curls bounced in all directions. "That's pretty silly, Mom. We *don't* have the same feelings at all." Digger dropped a pebble on the floor, scrabbled until he'd turned back a corner of the rug, and stuffed his treasure underneath. "Are you saying you don't like Max?" Faith asked.

"Of course I'm not."

Using the tip of a crutch, Faith hooked a pair of panties from the bed and pulled them on. "But you don't love him?"

"Oh, Faith." Interrogated and outwitted by a twelve-year-old.

"Well, do you?"

"I—yes, yes I do. I love him so much. I really hope it's all going to work out for us. If that's going to happen, you mustn't push, honey. Okay?"

Faith got up and made it to the bed, where she finished dressing in a long, deep blue fleece dress. "Okay," she said at last. "Max will be here in about an hour."

Carolee nodded and said, "I'll go and see what we've got to eat."

"It's already ordered. Pizza. It'll be delivered at the right time. That nice Mrs. Archer brought over a salad and a pie while you were out."

"You *asked* Nellie for salad and pie?"

"I wanted to pay for them but she wouldn't let me. I thanked her for my granny doll and told her she sits on my bed. And I said I've never been a doll person but I love this one."

"That's great," Carolee said, glancing at stocking-faced Granny, who seemed to have emptied every pocket in her clothes. "Where are the critters?"

"She ate 'em," Faith said and laughed. "I'm working on becoming eccentric. I want to be more interesting."

"I love you," Carolee said. "You are already the most interesting child I've ever known."

"Thanks. But I'm hardly a child. Ooh, this hair." She balanced before the mirror over her dresser and raked away with a wide-toothed comb.

Within ten minutes Faith announced, "I'm beautiful. Wait until the doctor in Texas finishes with my jaw. If I get more beautiful, everyone else will feel inadequate. That's what Max tells me. Let's go down." Sometimes she cried when she looked at her face, but each day brought small improvements.

Faith never missed an opportunity to mention Max, and she always said something that reminded Carolee of the reasons why she loved him.

She went ahead of Faith, who insisted she could manage alone—and she did, if slowly.

"Mom, could you help me with the table," Faith said, and Carolee waited for orders. She fetched maple leaves, carefully brushed off, and dried on a sheet of paper towel, from a counter. Faith produced a silver toast rack and slotted the leaves in at various angles. "This is for the middle of the table."

Obediently, Carolee did as she was told

and went on to set the table, including the placing of leaf-patterned napkins at each place. "When did you do all this?"

"Well, it's a secret. I promised."

"Sam," Carolee said under her breath.

"It's too early to get the salad out, isn't it?" Faith asked and Carolee agreed that it was.

"We have cider and milk, and wine—for you and Max, of course. Now, Mom, promise me you'll smile a lot. You're so pretty when you smile."

"I'll do my best."

"And you'll play for Max. He looks absolutely happy when you play."

He *used* to look happy when she played. Now she was torn each time she sat at the keyboard. She couldn't bear to be separated from her music, but it reminded her of Max sitting close, listening, touching her. "No. I don't think that's a good idea until things are settled."

"I do."

"Don't whine, Faith. Some things are best left to others to decide."

Faith made a prissy face that Carolee assumed was intended to show what she looked like when she chastised her daughter.

A car engine approached and tires scrunched like big spoons in sugar.

"It's too early," Carolee said, suddenly agitated. "The pizza isn't here."

"That isn't Max's car," Faith told her, frowning. "What if Daddy—"

"It isn't Daddy's car, either," Carolee told

her. "And he wouldn't run the risk of being picked up for ignoring a restraining order. He's also on bail, and he was warned he's absolutely not allowed to come near us. He can't afford to make any mistakes."

Without knocking, Ivy Lester came into the house. Her blond hair was loose and the wind had made it unkempt looking. She wore a long orange and pink mohair coat over a high-necked sweater and skirt, also made from mohair and in the same colors.

"Hi, you two," she said, running her fingers through her hair. "It's just wild out there. I had to come to you, Carolee. I'd be real grateful if you'd give us some privacy, Faith."

"I can stand in the kitchen," Faith said promptly. "Or sit on the stairs and work my way up. Which would you prefer, Mrs. Lester?"

"Faith isn't going anywhere," Carolee told Ivy. "Please make this very quick."

Ivy ran her eyes over the table and said, "Expectin' company, are we?"

"Say what you came to say and leave." They were both aware that Ivy was no friend of either Carolee or Faith.

Moisture stood in Ivy's blue eyes. "I can say this now because you don't want Kip. We're everything to each other. If I lose him, I've lost the only man who ever meant anythin' to me. Do you think there's a need to be mean to me?"

Faith made her way to the couch and sat down.

"I'll make it very brief," Ivy said. "Please withdraw the charges against Kip. Say it all got out of hand and everything was as much your fault as Kip's—that you'd threatened to take Faith away. You could tell the police things got out of hand."

Carolee felt behind her for the back of a dining room chair and managed to sit down. "Kip's guilty—he's already incriminated himself," she said. "I couldn't reverse anything if I wanted to."

"Yes, you could." Ivy's voice rose. "Tell them you made the whole thing up. You lured Kip to the airport. He's Faith's daddy. What kind of mother takes part in putting her girl's daddy in prison?"

"You're concerned about Kip. How does Bill feel about that?"

Ivy took another chair at the table. "Can I have a drink?"

"No. You're driving."

"You always had the makings of a first-class bitch. Bill's been a convenience for years. He's nothing to me. Sure, I want him to have a decent time of it, but a girl has to stand up for what matters to her most. That's Kip. And it's not his fault or mine that other things were more important to you than he was. He's a man with a man's needs and I was there at the right time. If you go to the courts and tell them the whole thing was a joke that went wrong, I'll make sure he leaves Seattle and never comes back."

"That's about the third suggestion you've made and not one of them is going to happen." Carolee couldn't feel any pity for Ivy. "What makes you think there won't be more questions about why Kip threatened to push me off an upper ramp at SeaTac? Or why he held a gun to my head?"

Footsteps approached on gravel, then hopped up the porch steps. Carolee left the chair and opened the door to Max. From the expectant expression in his eyes, she could tell he'd planned to kiss her. She stood back so that he could see Ivy, and said, "Come in, please."

He entered, never taking his attention from her, and stood there with his boots apart and a tan Stetson held by the brim.

"Hi, Max," Faith said. "We're having pizza. It'll arrive soon."

"Sounds great," Max said. He rotated the hat brim through his fingers. Carolee felt as if he could see inside her mind and knew how upset she was. "And Ivy's joining us, I see."

"No, she's not," Faith said promptly. "She came to ask Mom some questions. Now she has to go."

Under other circumstances Carolee might have reprimanded Faith for rudeness, but not tonight.

"Max," Ivy said, turning into the coquette. "Will you please ask Carolee to forgive Kip and help him not have to go through all this unpleasantness?"

He hung his hat beside the other two on brass hooks near the door. "You don't have any pride. You also aren't very smart. Forget using Carolee for your own ends again. You were the one who told Kip about me, weren't you?

You let him know each time you knew Carolee was with me. What was that about? You tattled—maybe he'd been dragging his feet over encouraging you to divorce Bill and marry him—and you thought if he found out she was seeing someone else, he'd get mad enough to forget about her? Strange logic. But then he started giving her too much attention again and not enough to you? You ought to have understood he'd probably try to wheedle his way back into her good graces because he was afraid she'd find out he was stealing from Faith."

"It's time for you to go, Ivy," Faith said. "Our pizza's going to be here."

Carolee put a finger to her lips and stared hard at Faith.

"Okay then," Ivy said. "I came and tried to be friendly, but I know when I'm not wanted."

"You're no friend," Carolee told her. "You're two-faced and manipulative. You hung around me, looking for things to use against me that would ingratiate you with Kip."

"She was always around the condo a lot," Faith said. "She came to visit and Daddy said she was his friend."

"I *am* his friend. I'm the best friend he's had and the only lover he ever wanted."

"That's enough," Max said sharply.

"How long?" Carolee asked.

Ivy raised her chin but didn't quite manage to look triumphant. "Nine years. The best nine years of our lives. Max, I'd appreciate it if you'd see me to my car."

Max showed no inclination to comply, but Carolee said, "Please take her," and he opened the door for Ivy to go outside.

From the doorway, Ivy said, "He doesn't love you, he loves me."

"That's fine," Carolee told her. "I've stopped loving him, too."

"I hate you," Ivy said. "Kip hates you, too. Controlling him with your money. He doesn't need you. We'll manage. It was for me that he had the vasectomy. He didn't want me to worry about any problems at all."

What Ivy had blurted out would change everything. It couldn't help but boost Carolee's confidence. She wouldn't meet his eyes, but the faint smile on her lips gave him a good feeling.

The pizza arrived and the three of them, with Digger at Max's feet, sat at the table.

"Put her out of your mind," he told Carolee while she served pizza. "You don't know what's true or false when that woman talks."

"You mean"—she looked at Faith and sighed—"you mean it may not be true that she and Kip have had a relationship for years so I shouldn't feel badly about what she said? A lot of things fit now. But he was with her for so long. That's painful. I thought he was as in love with me as I was with him. They deserve each other."

"Have some more salad, Mom," Faith said, holding up the bowl.

Carolee took it, kissed Faith's forehead,

and set the bowl down. "Thank you." She didn't touch the salad and had a full serving still on her plate anyway. "You've eaten fairly well, sweetie. Are you full?"

"Yes, thank you." Faith looked not at Carolee but at Max. The girl was begging him to get rid of the uncertainty in this room, to make everything all right.

"You're tired, Faith," Carolee said. "You've done too much today and dinner was beautiful, but I'd like you to go upstairs now. Don't try to get changed for bed until you've taken a little rest. By then I'll be up to help you."

When Faith got up immediately, took her crutches, and went to the stairs, Max was surprised. He'd expected her to argue.

"I'll probably take quite a long rest before I'm ready to go to bed, Mom," Faith said. "I think I'll read. Come on, Digger."

He might occasionally be slow picking up on the workings of the feminine mind but this was obvious. Faith was leaving them alone so they could talk—and, she hoped, come to the agreement she wanted: to try being together.

Max ached from wanting to make Faith happy and confident—and he ached from wanting Carolee for himself.

Finally Faith made it up the stairs, and once she was on her feet in the upper hallway, she closed the door to the stairs.

"Fortunately," Carolee said, "I don't think she fully understands what was discussed here tonight."

Max didn't argue, but he was pretty certain Faith had a good grasp of the subject.

"We haven't had much chance to talk," Carolee said. "How have you been?"

"Good." Lying had its place. "It is really getting nippy out there. They're forecasting a snowy winter."

"Do you ski?"

"I used to ski a lot and I expect to go back to it this winter," he said rapidly before she could regret the question. "How about you?"

"Not since I was a kid."

"Then you'll have to go up again. You'll find you haven't forgotten everything you learned."

"Maybe I'll give it another try if I have any time."

"Sweetheart, I really love you."

She averted her face. "Not as much as I love you. It wouldn't be possible."

"It sure is possible. I definitely love you... Let's just say there's no contest and make up our own minds what that means. I don't want to wait any longer to be with you."

She got up and took dishes to the kitchen. When she returned, she said, "If we get together, it has to be forever. I'm not prepared to fail again."

"We won't fail." He stood up and reached for her. "We can have each other and make a family with Faith."

She skirted him and stood at a distance. "I hope so. You're a man who will make a great father, but that shouldn't only be to another man's child."

"You heard what Ivy said."

Carolee squeezed her eyes shut and crossed her arms tightly. She nodded. "Faith and I have to leave for Houston in a couple of days—for the surgery she's having down there. We may be gone several weeks."

He almost asked to go with them, but knew he'd be making a mistake. "Will we talk while you're there?"

"We'll have to talk," she said. "I couldn't stand it if we didn't."

Thirty-eight

Snow in November.

Carolee's heart beat too fast. She walked away from Max's condo with her red parka zipped to the neck and her gloved hands shoved into her pockets. Hard-pack covered the roads and downy snow mounds heaped bushes and outlined dark tree limbs. All softly dramatic but unseasonably early.

She started uphill, her low black boots squidging with each step. This was an area she didn't really know. City Hall with its high windows was at the center of a grass-edged property to her left. A Kirkland police car passed in front of her and she saw the station in the lowest floor of the building. She doubted she'd ever see another police vehicle without

440

getting goosebumps and thinking about Kip and how he'd messed up his life.

The snow deadened sound. An intrepid runner passed and startled her. He turned left on the street Carolee would take. She glanced up and small flakes brushed her face. A pale gray morning sky pillowed rooftops.

She made the left turn just in time to see the runner reach the far end of the street and cross another road. But she wasn't interested in runners now, or snow. Her pulse thundered. Outside the main entrance to City Hall was a stone bench. A bronze statue of a man, his hair, shoulders, forearms, the book he held, his thighs, and the toes of his boots wearing liberal white trim, sat at the middle of the bench.

But it was the flesh and blood man beside the statue that made each breath Carolee took shorter and shakier.

Max hadn't seen her and she stood at a distance, observing him. He walked this way every day—he'd told her as much on the phone during the hours they'd spent talking while she'd been in Houston. He must wonder why he'd been unable to reach her last night. She and Faith had arrived back in Seattle yesterday, but Max didn't know they were coming. It seemed important to see the expression on his face when he first saw her, the raw expression with no chance to prepare.

Faith had been up early this morning and beseeching Carolee to go to Max, so here she was. Recently he'd stopped pressing her for a commitment. Maybe he'd changed his mind.

Cold struck through the black fleece pants she wore. If he no longer cared about her in the same way he had, she'd be left dealing with a worse loss than ever.

Carolee's eyes stung. She'd rather wonder than be sure he'd stopped loving her.

Max looked up from the bronzed sheet of poetry on Robert Frost's writing stand and saw a woman in a red parka and black pants. He was cold, but blood ran in a hot wash through his body.

She'd paused, but looked toward him. If he had to guess, he'd say she was feeling shy.

He opened his mouth to yell, then remembered how she detested exhibitions.

Carolee broke into a run. Her elbows pumped and she slithered, but caught her balance. "Max!" she cried. "Max!"

So engrossed was he in watching her, that he forgot to stand until she reached him. He swept her up and swung her around, and said, "Hi, you stinker. When I couldn't get you last night, I was worried to death. Why didn't you say you were coming? I'd have been at the airport."

They stood like that, with him holding her tight against him and her feet swinging off the ground.

"I wanted to surprise you," she said, clamping a hand on either side of his head and looking into his eyes. "And I didn't want to put you out by having to go to the airport in such awful weather."

He let his head fall back and shouted, "Aaaaah," while she laughed, and shushed him. "Put me out, Carolee? Kiss me or I'll say something I'll regret."

Her lips were soft and cold. The tip of her nose made icy contact with his. Slowly, he lowered her to stand, but they didn't stop kissing. He'd been chilled, but parts of him were warming up rapidly.

At last their mouths parted and he said, "I think you were looking for me. Am I right?"

She laughed and punched him softly. "Yes. It wasn't hard to find you. You told me you walk this way a lot, and Brandy and Rob told me they'd seen you leave."

Rob and Brandy had done as Rob threatened and bought a unit in the same building as Max. The wedding would take place in a few weeks. So far he and Rob were making progress together. "I walk a lot. And think a lot. How's Faith?"

"She's okay. Getting stronger every day. Still no sign of aftereffects from what Kip put her through, thank goodness. Not that I don't expect some in time. I left her with Rob and Brandy."

He frowned at her. "Faith's with Rob and Brandy?"

"I didn't want her walking with me in case I had to go a long way to find you. She misses you, Max."

The happiness he felt filled him up. "She's a special girl."

"Who's that guy?" She pointed to the statue on the stone bench.

"Robert Frost."

"Oh. Reading on a bench. Might be nice in summer but it looks cold now."

"He's writing," Max told her. " 'The Road Not Taken.' "

The subtle change in her expression, the distance in her eyes, showed she knew the poem and found it ironic for this moment—it also brought a forcible reminder of how he'd come to want her more than he'd ever wanted anyone or anything.

"Two roads," she said, "and he wrote that he took the one less traveled."

"And that made all the difference," Max finished for her. "Life's like that. We get choices when we least expect them. They come along and we have to make decisions. If we don't pick one thing or the other, we never know what we've missed at all. We could pick one and be so fulfilled we might wonder about the other one, the one we didn't pick, but not care about it."

"Or we could pick one and become very certain we'd made a mistake, Max."

He waved her closer until he could look down into her face. "I don't believe it's smart *not* to take chances sometimes, do you?"

"I don't know." She pulled the neck of her parka high enough to cover her chin and he wrapped an arm around her shoulders.

"Why didn't you tell me you were coming home?" he asked her.

Her gaze shifted away. "Maybe I was a

little bit scared of your reaction." She flung her arms wide and her face crumpled. "I've missed you so much. And I've been so lonely because I longed for you. I thought if I just showed up... I thought I'd be able to tell if you still really want me."

"May I hold you?" He was so damned afraid of doing the wrong thing and sending this little miracle up in smoke. "I'd like to hold you for the rest of our lives."

Her nose was red from the cold, and tears coursed down her face. "Why would you want to?" she asked and covered her mouth with one hand. "I look terrible. Max, I never want to hurt you."

He slid an arm around her waist and stood pressed against her. "You wouldn't hurt me, my friend. Not willingly."

Her breath made clouds of steam. "Are you sure I haven't already hurt you?"

"Yes," he laughed, but sobered instantly. "Hell no, I'm not sure, lady. You've made me hurt like hell. You cut a hole around my feet and I dropped through the bottom of my world just when I thought it was coming together. I wouldn't say those things, but you asked. How about you? Have I hurt you?"

Her smile turned the tears to a sheen on her green eyes. "You bet you have. I was coping, then you came along and reminded me of how it felt to want a man, then to fall in love with him."

"And to want to make love to him until you almost killed us both," he said very softly.

Carolee didn't feel like laughing. She pushed lightly on his chest and bowed her head.

Max's hand behind her neck planted her face against his black down vest.

"So what are we going to do about us?" he asked. "You'll have to be the one to make the decision."

"That's not fair," she mumbled. "We talked about your needs and whether or not I'd be able to meet them. I think we've got as good a chance as most people of having a baby, but I couldn't bear to watch you become bitter. You'd never be direct about it, but I'd know you were disappointed and why."

"Hey," Max said, spreading his hand over the back of her head and holding it still. "This is hard to imagine, but we're being watched."

She tried to turn around, but he held her where she was. "Not Faith," she said. "She knows she mustn't take risks."

"Our helpful friends drove her up here," Max said. "Now they've let her out of the car and they're waiting with their heads resting back as if they weren't even aware of us. Very subtle."

"Faith could fall," Carolee said anxiously.

"I don't agree, but stand right where you are and I'll go and walk with her."

Daring to hope they were about to begin again, Max jogged to Faith and planted his fists on his hips. "I understand you weren't supposed to come out and walk on all this stuff."

The scars on her face were fading. Her lower jaw had been made to look as if there'd been no accident. She looked pretty—and impish. "It's really hard when the people you care about most can't be trusted to do the right thing," she said. He noted that she continued to speak through barely parted lips. "Brandy and Rob are hungry and so am I. They're taking me to Carillon Point to eat, then we're going to shop in Bellevue Square."

Carolee arrived beside them and said, "You aren't up to walking around Bellevue Square."

"I know. I'll use a wheelchair. We did that before, remember?"

"Mm."

"Before we left, I thought I'd better come find you and make sure you weren't messing things up again." She took a deep breath. The anxiety she felt wasn't completely hidden by the lighthearted delivery. "You two wanted to be together. Mom still wants to be with you, Max."

"Faith."

"You know it's true," Faith said. "She cries a lot when she thinks I'm asleep. Last night she took one of your hats to bed."

Max didn't regret feeling so pumped. He touched Carolee's burning red cheek. "If men cried, I'd have cried too," he said.

Faith snorted and drew her mouth into a thin line.

"Well, I guess I've cried anyway," he said, looking at Carolee. "I've been scared you'd come back without the answers I wanted to hear. Could we go back to my place and talk?"

Faith pulled on Max's vest and he bent to

receive her kiss on his cheek. "I'm off now. Take care of Mom. Mom, you take care of Max. I'll call before I come back."

Away she went, and into Rob Mead's car. At the wheel, Rob gave a salute without turning his head toward Max and Carolee.

"She'll call before she comes back?" Carolee said, sounding unsure if she should be amused.

"Kids grow up fast," he said. "I'm cold, how about you?"

"Freezing."

Lying beside Max in front of the fire, their heads on cushions from the couch, Carolee had grown comfortable with their saying little or nothing at all. Max held her hand and frequently carried it to his lips and rested it there. They hadn't even kissed since they came inside.

"Fear was what got in our way, wasn't it?" Max said, his voice unsteady. "From the start. In our different ways we let fear call the shots. We were afraid to let go and just allow love to carry us along, because we didn't trust that we could hold on to it. And we couldn't face losing it."

"That's the simple version, but yes, that's why I was so hesitant. That and the fact that I fell so hard for you I couldn't seem to control my feelings for you." She didn't want to rehash events that would bring a wave of heat for as long as she lived.

"I love you, Carolee."

The shades had been lowered, darkening the room. She stared at leaping firelight reflected on the ceiling.

He couldn't keep quiet. "I... Listen, you asked me if I'd like to have my own children and I said I guessed I would. I'd never even thought about it. I mentioned my dad to Faith once. I told her he'd been injured in a riding accident, just like she was. That was a stretch. My dad was a bitter man who hated the world and everyone in it—especially my mother and me."

"Oh, no—"

"Yes. Please let me say this now or I never will. I haven't talked about this to anyone before. People who lived around where I grew up knew some of it, but not all by a long straw. Dad wanted lots of kids—sons to help him run the place. Farming's hard and you don't make enough to afford much labor. That's the way it was for us. But I was the only child and Dad blamed my mom for that. He'd curse her and break what few things she had that mattered to her. And he blamed me for..." This was even harder than he'd expected. "He blamed me because I was the only son he got."

Carolee put an arm over him and settled her face on his chest.

"He started drinking. Hell, it sounds like one big cliché. The more he drank, the meaner he got. Eventually he hit my mother. She's a little woman and she... He hurt her for nothing that was her fault. But for his sake, he'd

449

waited too long to do that. I was bigger than he was by then, and a tough kid. I smacked him down and told him what I'd do if he ever put a hand on her again.

"When he got up, I could see it in his eyes. Empty. He was empty. He hadn't had much to hang on to before, but now he couldn't even pretend to be the man in his own house."

He could feel Carolee crying.

"Right then, he left. Took off with our old dog and one of the horses. My mom kept begging me to go after him, to make sure he was all right. I didn't want to go near the bastard, but Mom wore me down and eventually I went.

"I heard the dog bay. She howled and it was worse than hearing coyotes under the moon on a cold night. It's a noise that slices your insides like a scalpel in shaky hands."

Tighter and tighter Carolee held him. She murmured, "I wish I'd been there for you."

He stroked her hair. "Dad rode out under some big old trees. He tied a rope to a strong branch and made a noose for his neck. Then he must have whupped that horse and sent him running. And my dad hung there. He died with his feet not more than six inches from the ground."

Then Max didn't want to talk anymore. Telling the story had exhausted him as badly as running all day in the sun would.

"No child should have to suffer," Carolee said. "Right now I'd like to turn the clock back and tell Max the boy that he'd be okay. And

I'd be right, because you are. But it's there inside you. Things like that don't go away."

Max gathered his composure as best he could. "I only told you to explain why I came to the idea of having a family so late. If we were to have a child together, it would be great, but we've already got Faith. And if we can't get pregnant but decide we want another kid, we'll adopt one. Or however many you want. I happen to think I'll make a great father. Faith thinks so, too."

She smiled.

"Will you say something, please?" Max asked her. "Anything. Almost anything. No, will you say you love me and you'll think about us getting together?"

"I'm not going to think about it," she told him. "I'm taking a road with you and I'll plan on it being the right one. Okay?"

"Does that mean you'll—"

"Yes, probably, but for now could we just let the idea sink in?"

Max brought his teeth together to hold in a whoop. "Don't move a muscle," he said. "I've got something for you. It's been waiting here forever."

Bouncing off a wall on the way to his bedroom, Max still didn't put on any lights. They spoiled a good mood. He hurried back to Carolee and sat cross-legged beside her. "What do you think?"

She pushed up onto her elbows. "A keyboard?"

"You don't like it. I knew you wouldn't.

You'd only play a piano, but I didn't think I could pick one of those out on my own. Darn it, I bet it's too late to take this back."

"I expect so," she said, and giggled. She leaned toward him and pecked his cheek. "What a complete surprise. It's wonderful. What made you get it?"

"I got it for you."

"I realize that. But why?"

"Well." He rubbed his face. "Oh, I thought we were going to have a long, sexy courtship and hoped you'd be here all the time and I could get you to play for me. Satisfied?"

"Oh, yes, Mr. Wolfe. Very satisfied. With the keyboard, and with your ideas."

"Will you play just one piece before I take you to bed?"

She looked closely at the keyboard.

"Are you going to marry me or not?" Max asked.

She ran her fingers across the keys. "I think there's a good chance I will."

"Good. I want to make love to you. Seems appropriate, huh?"

"Could be." If she appeared cool to him, she'd become good at hiding intense excitement.

"So you'll play for me first?"

"What do you want to hear? Hurry up, I'm feeling tired."

Max laughed. "You can be a wicked woman. The night we met you performed a piece that didn't have any lyrics. It was the most arousing thing I'd ever heard, but only because you played it and you seemed to be looking at me."

"I was. You'd been there before."

He let out a slow breath.

Carolee stroked out a few bars and Max closed his eyes. The passage of light across his features was an image she would never forget. She kissed his mouth and he kissed her back, a long, possessive kiss.

Slowly she withdrew from him and continued the piece. Perhaps now she'd be able to find the words for a song that had wrapped her in a sense of intimacy. She'd tried before but nothing had come but the title.

It was Max who said, "I know you in the dark. And you know me."

Carolee settled her hands on her thighs, then got to her feet. "Come on," she said and he held the hand she offered him. "It's dark enough to test that out."